I0583178

FATE'S DANGEROUS FORTUNE

MIRRORS OF FATE BOOK 1

NICOLA VICTORY

For Emily
I'm proud of us.

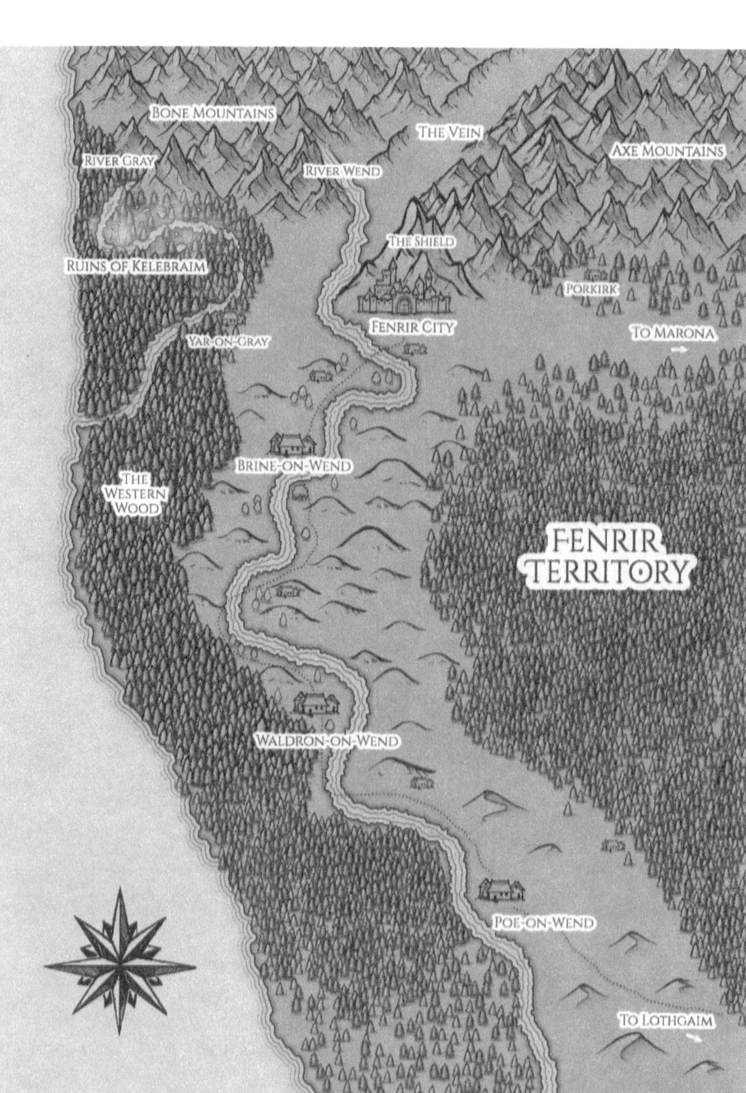

BONE MOUNTAINS
THE VEIN
AXE MOUNTAINS
RIVER GRAY
RIVER WEND
THE SHIELD
RUINS OF KELEBRAIM
PORKIRK
FENRIR CITY
TO MARONA
YAR-ON-GRAY
BRINE-ON-WEND
THE WESTERN WOOD
FENRIR TERRITORY
WALDRON-ON-WEND
POE-ON-WEND
TO LOTHGAIM

1

ECHO OF CHANGE

ANYA

The sound came from the Western Wood, a distant and eerie whine.

I barely noticed it over the din inside the Pretty Possum Inn & Pub, but my hearing magic didn't lie. Threaded through the braided strands of merry music, laughter, and raucous conversation was something *other*.

"Will you excuse me?" I asked Hugh, who was seated at the counter among a row of regulars, gesticulating enthusiastically as he relayed a long-winded story about a candle wax debacle at his chandlery.

He and the others barely seemed to notice as I circled out from behind the bar, but Hattie—my best friend and barkeep, in the midst of delivering stew to a nearby table—arched a brow at me as I hurried past her through the crowded dining room.

I flung the front door open and stepped out onto the porch, listening intently. A frigid wind ruffled the loose strands of hair that had escaped my braid, tickling my temples. The strange, distant call hadn't been the howl of a hound, nor the screech of an owl. Not livestock nor evening travelers or even the foxes that lived along the forest's edge.

No—it had been entirely foreign. Something I'd never heard before. Like an animal in peril, but...more sinister.

A comforting presence brushed against my hip. My ancient wolfhound, Wicker, seated himself beside me at the threshold of my inn. I wondered if he'd heard the unnatural sound, too. I stroked his ears as I stared into the darkness, seeing nothing past the orb of light cast by the lantern that hung on a hook by the door.

Holding my breath, I lifted my sensory magic down the cobblestones that led through our quaint town of Waldron, along the burbling waters of the River Wend that paralleled our main road, to the sheep bleating on the surrounding hills, but—*nothing*.

The weird whine didn't occur again.

Vaguely disturbed, I sank my fingers into the wiry gray fur at Wicker's shoulder, which was almost level with my waist. When he stared up at me with his soulful brown eyes, his feather duster tail *thwapping* against the hardwood, I smiled.

The shattering *crack* of a glass breaking set me in motion again.

With one last glance into the darkness beyond my porch, I closed the door and made my way back through the busy common room, Wicker returning to his pile of blankets by the hearth—but not without a few head pats and morsels from guests along the way.

The pub was brimming with familiar faces. Every table was taken, and folks were elbow-to-elbow at the bar, sipping hot cider and dark ale. Sharp laughter, celebratory drunken cheers, a bard crooning in the corner—these were the sounds that made my heart sing. The Pretty Possum Inn & Pub was Waldron-on-Wend's hub for all travelers, town gossip, and general merriment—but it was *my* everything. Childhood home, sole inheritance, pride and joy.

Back behind the bar, I lifted the broom from Hattie's hands and finished cleaning up the shattered glass, freeing her to pour drinks.

"Expecting someone?" Hattie teased, inclining her head toward the door. "A *man*, perhaps?"

I shot her a warning glance. "No. I just thought I heard..." I trailed off, frowning.

"Hoofbeats? The squeak of wagon wheels?" Her eyebrows bounced.

I widened my eyes, willing her to keep the teasing to a minimum lest she capture the curiosity of the busybodies seated at the counter, but—

Too late.

Martha, the town baker, swiveled toward us. She had a round, matronly face that distracted from her shrewd personality. "What's this about a man?"

"*Nothing,*" I said, glaring at Hattie.

Hattie's dirty blonde curls were heaped atop her head, and she puffed out her bottom lip to blow a rebellious ringlet out of her face, entirely unbothered by my withering stare. She slid a fresh cider across the bar in Hugh's direction.

Abandoning his candle story mid-sentence, Hugh joined in. "Anya has a man?"

"There's no man," I insisted.

"There never is," Vera, the florist, piped in.

"Wow." I rested my hands on my generous hips. "This conversation has gotten out of hand."

Hattie's chuckle was ebullient.

I pointed toward the door. "I thought I heard something, is all—an animal, maybe," I explained to my audience, "—but it was nothing."

Vera tucked a wavy strand of silver-streaked black hair behind her ear, her brown cheeks scrunching. "That's it?"

"That's not very interesting, now, is it?" Martha complained.

"*Exactly,*" I said.

Hattie smirked. "Don't be so testy. We all know who you're expecting."

My face blazed with a blush. "I'm not expecting anyone," I insisted, begging Hattie with my eyes not to spill my secret.

Of course there was a man. Remy rolled through Waldron-on-Wend with his merchant caravan once every two months to make deliveries and warm my sheets. He was due tonight, and *maybe* I'd worn a nicer dress than usual. But even the keenest gossips in town—Martha, Hugh, and Vera at the top of that list—didn't know about Remy. They'd never understand or approve of our casual arrangement.

"Of course you're expecting someone—we all are," Hattie said. "I'm obviously talking about the impending arrival of the Fate Mirrors. The reason the whole town has been in a frenzy for the past week?"

"The Mirrors, right," I said with relief.

The tour of the Fate Mirrors was an annual occurrence. All notable townships in the territory of Fenrir hosted the Mirrors of Fortune and Death for one night, so citizens could glimpse their futures in the massive magical relics. Following the Fate Ceremony, the people of Waldron did what we did best: a full night of dancing, eating too much, and drinking ourselves into pleasant stupors.

This morning, I'd awoken before dawn to finish preparations for tomorrow's Mirror Festival, starting at the bakery to help Martha make an obscene number of sweet buns. In the early hours of morning, we'd sung old folk tunes to the rhythm of our kneading and whispered about the cobbler's daughter, Illian, who Martha had seen kissing the jeweler's apprentice. After that, I'd helped Vera dress the town in cedar garlands, then stopped by Hugh's shop to retrieve a crate of orb candles to set along the path up Stone Hill, where the festivities took place. It was there among the old standing stones that I noticed Farmer Quinn's escaped flock; while Wicker and the farmer's collie, Annie, romped in the grass, I'd fixed Quinn's broken gate so that his sheep didn't wander through the party grounds.

By the time I'd returned to the Pretty Possum to prepare rooms for tomorrow's influx of Mirror Knights, the day was mostly over.

"Don't tell us you're interested in finding yourself a Mirror Knight?" Vera asked, still stuck on the topic of my love life.

"*Fates*," Hugh swore, wiping his gray mustache with his sleeve. "Anya knows better than that, doesn't she?"

Martha was quick to pile on. "Tempting as they might be, all knights are bad news," she lectured. "Selfish sell-swords more interested in roaming than settling down."

Vera took a bite of her stew, then aimed her spoon at me. "Lone wolves, the lot of them."

I didn't bother pointing out that most knights were not *lone wolves*, but, in fact, were part of large militaristic regiments. When this trio sat on a high horse together, there was no winning.

"Selfish lone wolves," Hattie mused from beside me. "Sounds like someone, doesn't it?" It was an obvious dig at Remy, who *wasn't* a knight, but also wasn't the settling-down type.

Two could play this game. "You know Noble is a retired knight," I pointed out.

Now it was her turn to blush. She'd had an eye for Noble, the reclusive metalworker, ever since he arrived in Waldron this past spring and took up work with the town blacksmith.

"Noble just proves my point," Vera said, oblivious to Hattie's discomfort.

"Odd duck, isn't he?" Martha added.

Hattie cleared Martha's empty plate, clearly not coming to her crush's defense for fear of drawing more attention to the topic.

"I'm not looking for a knight," I assured everyone.

"What *are* you looking for, then?" Vera asked.

Some damned peace from this conversation, I wanted to say.

"Definitely *not* true love," Hattie said.

There was a wash rag looped through the belt of my apron. I yanked it free and snapped it in Hattie's direction. She jumped back, giggling.

"Why seek a man when I have Wicker, Hattie, and the Possum?" I said grandly.

"Sexual satisfaction?" Hattie supplied.

Hugh choked on a sip of cider, Fates bless him. Martha and Vera merely smirked.

"Trust me, I'm just fine," I said. Remy was satisfying enough, and—even better—he didn't stick around long enough to hurt me.

"Francis will be so disappointed," Martha tutted.

I held a shushing finger up to my lips, glancing around the room for Farmer Quinn, whose son, Francis, had taken an interest in me as of late.

"Wait," Hattie said, "is that why you won't take Francis up on his offer to sweep our chimneys?"

"You know his offer is more about wanting to sweep *my* chimney, not the inns'," I said.

Poor Hugh coughed again.

"If I accept," I went on, "I'll give the wrong impression."

"What's so wrong with that?" Martha asked. "Francis is sweet."

"He's too timid for her," Vera said.

Timid was an understatement, but I didn't want to bad-mouth him. Francis was nice enough, he just wasn't for me. I preferred men like Remy—storied and a little complicated. As someone whose life revolved around socializing with strangers, I liked men who could keep me on my toes.

"Timid, or simply kind?" Martha argued.

While Vera, Martha, and Hugh launched into a debate about Francis, a hand went up in the dining room, hailing me over.

As I brushed past Hattie, I leaned in close and whispered, "I'd break that poor boy in half."

Hattie snorted a laugh. "That's probably true."

2

FAMILIAR THREAT

IDRIS

Idris thrust his dagger into the abomination's neck with a wet crunch, black blood spurting onto the muddy grass. The creature let out a low whine and slumped at his feet, defeated. *Thank the Fates.*

What had once been a wolverine had become grotesque with disease: gnarled black horns pushed through the top of its head, sharp bony claws protruded from its paws, and a sick red glow was fading from its eyes. This hadn't been Idris's most challenging kill—not by a long shot—but the creature had been vicious and stubborn, and he was glad the fight was over.

The Oath tattoo that ringed the base of Idris's throat tingled faintly as his kill was reported to Lord Haron's magical Oath Ledgers in Fenrir City. Fifteen years of hunting monsters, and the sensation still grated on his nerves.

Track, kill. Track, kill. His duty wore on him lately. Weariness was a sign of weakness, he knew—yet still, he chafed.

With a sigh, Idris wiped the flat of his blade on the cursed animal's matted fur, sheathed the dagger, then rose out of his crouch, his knee joints creaking. He took in his surroundings. Broken branches and bent saplings evidenced the struggle, but otherwise, the moonlit forest was peaceful. He scented livestock in the distance, woodsmoke. The heady aroma of stew, so tantalizing he could almost taste it. What he wouldn't give for a hot supper and an ale right about now.

Months had passed since he'd last ventured out of the wilds. As a Knight of the Order of the Valiant, he was tasked to keep the rest of the realm blissfully unaware of the existence of monsters like this one. It's why his current proximity to civilization wasn't a comfort, but a concern. Year by year, monsters encroached on the quaint towns of Fenrir Territory from their spawning grounds deep within the Western Wood. This cursed wolverine had been the closest yet, and that troubled Idris.

This was no time for dwelling, though.

Idris tromped across the clearing to retrieve Halgren, his greatsword, which had been wrenched out of his hand during the fight. As he slid the sword back into place at his hip, his clavicle twinged. The old scar—running from his right pectoral, over his shoulder, and across his back like a baldric—tended to ache when the weather got cold, hindering his range of motion. At thirty-five, Idris was by no means an old man, but his body was nonetheless worn.

And bleeding, he realized, staring down at his hand. The wolverine had bitten him; slimy black saliva slicked his knuckles, mingling with the ooze of blood from the puncture wound. The slobber emitted a rotten-carcass scent, mixed with a familiar cloying sweetness that turned his stomach. *Curse the Fates* for giving him the gift of scent magic—the reek made him want to wretch.

Careful not to get the black sludge on any clothing or gear, he wiped it on the beast's fur as he had his dagger, then got to work on cleanup: building a fire, burning the diseased body, cauterizing his hand to keep the venom from spreading, and waiting until the only trace left of the abomination was ash. Then he dragged a few felled branches over to cover the evidence of the fire, hiked a mile south to escape the stench of burnt hair, and made camp.

After a scant supper of foraged mushrooms, Idris spread out his bedroll and laid down on his back with Halgren at his side. A lengthy sigh gusted out of him, curling into the starry night sky. The first freezes of autumn had come to these hills, hardening the ground and Idris's tired muscles. Normally, he fell swiftly into slumber; while he'd wake at the slightest sound of movement in the underbrush, his body knew the benefit of rest. It was a skill he'd honed after years spent roaming the wilderness—but tonight, sleep evaded him.

It was the damned wound: aching as if it'd already festered. Idris sat up, peeled back the crude bandage, and inspected his skin in the pale glow of the gibbous moon. In spite of his efforts, the veins in the back of his hand had already turned black.

"Fuck," he grumbled, and swiftly packed up his bedroll.

While it was unfortunate that the monster had ventured so close to civilization, tonight, Idris was glad. He hoped the nearby town was big enough to have a proper apothecary—one who wouldn't mind being woken in the middle of the night for some antiseptic and a healing tincture.

One who wouldn't ask too many questions.

3

FIXED FATE

ANYA

I kept my ears alert for the strange sound all evening—as Hattie and I dished up stew, made small-talk, delivered the final round of drinks, supplied tonight's lone guest with an extra blanket, and wished the last of the regulars a good night as they stumbled out into the night—but I didn't hear it again. Nor did I hear Remy's wagon rumbling down the cobblestones.

After locking the front door, I joined Hattie in the back kitchen, where she was prepping dough for tomorrow's breakfast hand-pies. I took up a knife from the block, ran it quickly over a steel to sharpen the blade, then started chopping potatoes.

Everyone had a bit of sensory magic, usually no more than a proclivity for a single sense. Hattie's gift was taste, and she'd honed it expertly, able to concoct not only delicious drinks and meals for my pub, but also medicinal tinctures and the occasional potion (though she was not a licensed apothecary). The Possum might've been my establishment, but in the kitchen, Hattie was boss.

Silence spread between us, but it wasn't amiable tonight. I could tell by the way Hattie worked the dough with rough, frustrated hands.

"You're mad about the chimney thing," I said.

"Martha said she saw you up on Stone Hill fixing Farmer Quinn's gate today, and yet you won't let his son help us?" Hattie shook her head, not bothering to look up from her task. "You *really* ought to say 'no' more often."

This was not a new argument between us. Hattie was always going on about my need to slow down, give less, and accept help every once in a while—but *helping* was in my nature. It was how I'd been raised. My mother had come to Waldron as a pregnant teenager, newly cast out by her parents, and the town had welcomed her with open arms. She'd spent her life here showing her appreciation through acts of service, and even now, long after her death, I continued to live by her example, always lending a hand, always eager to demonstrate my gratitude for what this community did for her—for us.

"You can't possibly be chiding me for being helpful."

"You and I and the Fates themselves know you could do with a good chiding every once in a while, *especially* when it comes to helping," Hattie said, swinging the dough onto the table with a smack. "You never stop. It's a wonder you haven't keeled over from sheer exhaustion."

"Are you saying you'd prefer to make the hand-pies by yourself tonight?"

She arched a brow, unamused. "I'm *saying*," Hattie emphasized, "that you can't pour from an empty cup."

"Who says my cup is empty?"

"*I* do."

"It's not that bad," I protested. "So, the inn needs a few repairs—that's *normal*."

Hattie halted abruptly and faced me, her pretty face pinched. "They're piling up! There's the roof leak in room five, the mold problem in the storeroom, and that iffy-looking pine out back that really ought to be felled before it crushes the garden shed." She rubbed the back of her wrist across her forehead, as if even the *thought* of the chores I'd let slide in favor of town-related tasks fatigued her. "You're so busy helping folks with *their* chores that you've let ours worsen into problems you can no longer fix on your own. There's no shame in taking care of your own needs *first*."

My mother never refused anyone, though. It's why the town loved her so much. "I think you're forgetting all the work I *have* done around here as of late. Reupholstering the dining chairs, building new bar shelves, and the tables—"

"Yes, yes, you're very *handy* and capable," Hattie said with a dismissive wave of her flour-coated hand.

"And you, my dear friend, are *not*," I pointed out.

She scowled but didn't deny it as she started rolling out the dough. Her skills in the kitchen were well balanced by my skills with everything else. It's how we worked so well together.

"All I'm saying is, there's no shame in asking for assistance every once in a while, and it doesn't have to be mine," Hattie said. "Need I remind you of the *last* time you tried to repair the roof by yourself?"

I rubbed my wrist reflexively. "It was only a sprain."

Hattie narrowed her eyes.

"I'm not saying I disagree about the repairs," I relented. "But with the Mirrors arriving, and no one else to manage preparations...I've just had a lot on my plate. You know how important the town festivals are to me."

Hattie sighed, her voice softening as she relented, "Yes, I do."

My mother had loved festivals. Especially Astrophel, Waldron-on-Wend's six-day festival leading up to winter solstice (which also happened to be my birthday). I'd been vying for the town's trust to take the lead on organizing Astrophel this year, and the Fate Ceremony was the perfect trial run.

"Are you nervous about the Mirrors this year?" Hattie asked, letting up on our argument—for now.

"I suppose I'm a bit nervous about the food being finished in time," I mused. "Martha's apprentice seemed quite frazzled this afternoon, and—"

"No," Hattie cut me off. "I mean: are you nervous about what you'll *see*?"

In all the hubbub, I'd lost sight of the actual point of tomorrow's ceremony: to glimpse my Fate. Though the Mirrors of Fortune and Death visited every year, what folks saw in them rarely changed. It was widely known that, after the age of thirty, one's Fate became "fixed"—unchanging—and seeing as I would turn thirty in two months' time, I didn't expect my Fate to change now.

"I'll see what I always see," I told Hattie with a shrug. "Not much of anything."

Ever since I was a girl, the Mirror of Fortune showed me peaceful fog drifting over rippling water: the surface of the River Wend, confirmation that my greatest fortune was living here in Waldron-on-Wend. And, to my relief, the Mirror of Death showed me the most coveted killer: old age (specifically, the wrinkled backs of my hands resting upon a flowery bedspread, gently fading from my vision).

"You aren't thirty yet, though," Hattie pointed out, cutting the dough into neat rectangles. "Your Fate could change."

"I am happy with my Fate," I insisted. "And seeing as I have no big adventures planned, I don't see it changing now—or ever." Slicing the last of the potatoes, I moved on to the onions. "What about you? You still have two years to change yours. Fancy a man to appear in your Fortune?"

Eight years ago, Hattie had come to the Pretty Possum as a bruised, shaking twenty-year-old newlywed, seeking shelter from a cruel husband. Her parents had married her off to the mayor of Poe-on-Wend, the town to the south, and Hattie had escaped by the skin of her teeth, trekking through mud and snow for six days to arrive at Waldron-on-Wend. I'd given her shelter, but more importantly, I'd scared off her husband's henchman with a bit of cheeky echo magic and a well-placed Wicker in the woods. A letter of divorce had arrived by messenger two weeks later.

Yet, of the two of us, *Hattie* was the head-over-heels romantic. Given her history, I found that quality both miraculous and inspiring.

"I must admit, seeing a nice man in my future wouldn't be an unwelcome occurrence," she said bashfully.

"A nice man, meaning…Noble?" I teased.

Mauve colored her cheeks, obscuring her freckles.

"Haven't you only met him, like, twice?"

"I see him around plenty," Hattie said with a huff.

"*Where?*"

"At the market. On the street. Sometimes I glimpse him through the shop door of the smithy."

"How romantic," I deadpanned. "How do you know he's…interesting?"

I couldn't imagine being with someone who didn't know how to hold a conversation.

"Affection can grow from afar," Hattie said. "You of all people would know."

"I don't hold any particular affection for Remy," I lied. "And affection from afar isn't necessarily accurate. What if you built Noble up in your head as a man completely unlike who he actually is?"

Hattie blinked rapidly, cheeks flushing. On a sigh, she said, "It's for the Fates to decide."

It was a common saying. A comfort to most. But I found the implication of my limited autonomy rather disconcerting—even though, paradoxically, I *did* look forward to the peaceful certainty of a fixed Fate.

Not wanting to spoil Hattie's hopefulness, I merely said, "We'll find out soon enough."

On the inside, however, a sickly-sweet sense of dread was forming in my gut, like an apple rotting in the pit of my stomach. The feeling took me back to when I was thirteen, peering past my mother as she gazed into the Mirror of Death and—for the first time—saw not old age as she had before, but the illness that would take her just three months later. She had been twenty-nine, the same age as I was now, and her Fate had indeed changed.

For all the many ways I wished to honor my mother's legacy, a changing Fate was certainly not one of them. I loved my life in Waldron-on-Wend. I thrived here. My most coveted outcome for tomorrow's Fate Ceremony was for everything to remain exactly the same.

4

KNIGHT'S SECRETS

IDRIS

Idris's hand throbbed with worrying intensity as he hiked east from his abandoned camp. At least the movement warmed his muscles, banishing the cold-induced aches and pains. In spite of the circumstances, the night was serene: his path through the trees was lit by the moon, the fallen leaves of mid-autumn were soft with decay underfoot, and the serene call of an owl echoed over the hills.

He broke from the forest on a slight rise, the small pines and birches giving way to tall grasses mounded under the weight of frost. A herd of sheep were huddled at the base of the hill, the gamey scent of muddy fleece and manure filling his nostrils. Their white watchdog huffed warningly as Idris emerged and headed in their direction.

A boy was out with them, and Idris offered a friendly wave to dispel whatever fear his unexpected appearance might induce. At six-foot-two, with a breastplate and greatsword, Idris was well aware of his intimidating effect.

"Good evening," he called out cheerfully.

The angle of the boy's shoulders softened slightly at the pleasantry, but his voice quavered when he returned with a questioning, "Good eve?"

"Apologies for disturbing your sheep," Idris said. "If only they could tell the difference between a wolf and a ranger."

The boy's shoulders lowered another inch, and he let out a little huff of acknowledgement at Idris's joke.

Idris halted five paces away, hoping the respectable distance would also set the boy at ease. The sheep had formed a tight crowd in the corner of the pasture, a few bleating nervously. At the boy's back, a gate led to a dirt road that ran parallel to the fence; southward, a cluster of shops and small homes marked the edge of town.

"I've just arrived from the north, and I've had a bit of a mishap," Idris said, lifting his bandaged hand. The dog, who'd come to sit beside the boy, let out a soft growl. "Is there an apothecary in your fine town of…?"

The boy patted the fluffy white head of his canine, eyeing Idris's hand. "Waldron-on-Wend."

"…in your fine town of Waldron-on-Wend?" Idris finished.

"A ranger, say?" the boy asked. "Where's your bow?"

"It broke," Idris replied stiffly.

"Your armor is fancy for a ranger."

The boy was astute.

Idris's black metal breastplate had once belonged to his brother, Grinnick, who'd had the edges tooled with a delicate flower motif. Paired with the silver vambraces on his wrists and his indigo cloak, Idris appeared far more heroic than he truly was. The disparity between his inner flaws and his gallant exterior was a constant reminder of why he lived the life he did, one of danger and repentance.

"Are you a Mirror Knight?" the boy asked.

Idris frowned. He'd forgotten the Fate Mirrors were making their tour across Fenrir this month; he didn't know the exact schedule, but the boy's question implied that the Mirrors would arrive in this town soon enough.

All the more reason for Idris to get his hand healed swiftly and make himself scarce again.

Idris took a tentative step closer. "The truth is that I *am* a knight, but not the sort you think." He tugged at the cloak around his neck, revealing his Oath tattoo as proof.

The boy's eyes went wide with wonder. "What sort of knight, then?"

"The secret kind." The magic of Idris's Oath tasted bitter in the back of his throat—a warning not to divulge more.

To bear an Oath tattoo wasn't unique. Lord Haron of Fenrir Territory—who stewarded the western bulge of the continental kingdom of Marona—employed legions of Oath-bound knights. But not all Orders were known to the public, and not all knights could speak of their duty. Idris's Order of the Valiant was one such secret.

"I was wounded in an altercation," Idris went on, "and unfortunately the gash has become infected. It's important that I get medicine for it." Idris rested his uninjured palm on Halgren's hilt—not intimidatingly, just to draw the boy's attention, which had turned rather excited. "Tell me, can you help a noble knight on his quest?"

The boy was ensnared, now; he nodded enthusiastically. "There's no apothecary here, but Hattie at the Pretty Possum could help you."

Idris nodded gratefully. "Can you take me there?"

The boy grinned and turned toward the gate, leading Idris through. The dog watched Idris with wariness, protective not just of the sheep but the boy. Idris admired such principle and duty; they were qualities he, too, aspired to. He reached into his pocket and offered the dog a small scrap of jerky as a peace offering. When the beast nosed Idris's wounded hand, she raised her lip in a snarl, scenting the monster, before she delicately took the meat.

Remember that scent, Idris thought, glancing over his shoulder at the dark slash of the forest. *There are threats greater than I in those woods.*

5

NEWCOMERS

ANYA

"**I**t is good to be back in Waldron-on-Wend," Remy said, rolling off me and folding his lean arms behind his head.

As my heartbeat calmed, I turned my head on the pillow, staring at his mess of blond hair and the strong angle of his nose. "You know I take pride in being a welcoming host."

"Your hospitality is unmatched."

I'd heard the rumbling arrival of Remy's wagon just as Hattie was pulling the hand-pies from the oven. Now, just past midnight, my body was pleasantly heavy from both the long workday and Remy's attentions.

"Are you staying through Mirror Fest?" I asked, feigning casualness. "Eager to see your future?"

Remy shrugged noncommittally, then tugged me closer. "You know how I feel about the Mirrors."

I might've downplayed my affection for Remy around Hattie, but in truth, I *did* care for him. He was charming, interesting, and funny. We'd met years ago, when he stayed here on his first trek as a newly minted merchant under the Lord Haron's banner; he'd plopped down at the bar and proceeded to entertain me all night with tall-tales from the road.

The next time he came through Waldron, I'd taken him to bed, and thus began our covert pattern. I'd been the one to insist on secrecy, as I was not interested in responding to the town's inevitable prying questions: *Is there relationship potential? How can you stand his absence? Why give your time to a man who doesn't find you worth staying in one place for?*

The truth was, they were questions that plagued me, too, and I wanted to avoid the painful reminder of my lack of satisfying answers. His long absences could be hard, but what we had was also comfortingly predictable. His life was on the road; my life was here. Though it hurt sometimes, I'd long ago stopped wishing he'd surprise me by settling in Waldron. Coasting along was preferable to asking for what I truly wanted and learning that Remy didn't find me worthy of the sacrifice.

After a long beat of silence, Remy added, "But I'll stay for the festival if you want me to."

"Really? I thought festivals were too 'silly and quaint' for you?" I said, repeating his words from the last time he'd passed through. I hadn't had the heart to tell him that festivals were my most favorite thing—silly and quaint at times, sure, but also filled with meaning, celebration, connection.

"Why not? I could use a break from the road," he replied, but didn't elaborate.

"Well, I'd love for you to stay for Mirror Fest," I said. "As the person planning the festivities, I guarantee it'll be a good time."

He slid his palm along my naked torso, cupping a breast. "Good times are always guaranteed when you're around."

"Then it's settled," I said, heart fluttering stupidly.

"Hopefully I'll be able to find lodging," Remy joked, "what with all the knights and out-of-towners soon to descend."

"I think I can spare a room for you," I said, playing along, "if you can spare a dance for me."

"A *dance*?" he said, drawing out his surprise. "Won't your beloved, nosy neighbors start all sorts of nasty rumors if they see you dancing with a handsome fellow?"

"Handsome strangers abound during Mirror Fest," I assured him. "It's not a rare occurrence for me to dance with a few of them."

Remy frowned. "Suddenly I'm regretting avoiding Waldron during festivals. Who else have you been dancing with?"

"Are you jealous?"

"Deeply," Remy said, but his tone was good-humored.

It smarted like citrus in a scratch. Trying to shove down my desire for him to feel jealous for *real*, I slipped out of bed, wrapped myself in a long dressing gown, and poured us each a glass of fermented cider from the bottle on my vanity.

The room was dark and downright frigid. I'd left the hearth cold on purpose; my chimney had become clogged with debris during the first autumn storm, and filled my room with smoke every time I started a fire. Hattie was right: with or without Francis, I really needed to make time for repairs around here, before winter set in.

After tomorrow's Fate Ceremony, of course.

Handing Remy a glass, I settled back under the covers, gown still wrapped tightly around my body.

"Tell me again why you've never looked in the Mirrors?" I asked, sipping my cold cider with a shiver.

Gazing into the Fate Mirrors wasn't mandatory, but most folks—myself included—were too curious about the future not to. Remy's abstention puzzled me, but I also found it admirable. Mysterious, even.

"Because I take comfort in not knowing my Fate," Remy said. "What if I see something awful? I'd live the rest of my life in fear."

"You could see something nice, though," I pointed out. "Something to look forward to."

"Seeing something nice wouldn't make my life better."

"I disagree," I said, thinking of what I'd seen in the Mirror of Death, proof of a long life and peaceful end—the very thing my mother had been robbed of. "The Mirrors can provide hopefulness, even gratitude."

"*If* you see a favorable Fate," Remy argued. "To me, it's not worth the gamble." He finished his cider and set the glass aside. "Will you look?"

"Of course," I said. "Especially this time, what with it being the last year my Fate could change."

"I heard about a man of ninety whose Fate changed," Remy said. "Last year, over in Brine-on-Wend."

"No way," I said. "That must be rumor."

"Apparently, the Mirror of Fortune showed him the path to a buried cache on his farm," Remy said. "He found the crate of gold in the exact place the Mirror promised, and he gifted it to his granddaughter so she could travel to Fenrir City for an apprenticeship."

"At the age of ninety, it sounds like he merely *forgot* his fortune and mistook the Mirror's image for something new," I said. "Did anyone else witness this change?"

Remy nodded. "A few folks from town confirmed it. I'm surprised word hasn't spread more widely."

Doubt and wonder swirled together in my chest. "Disbelief, probably. I'm having trouble believing it, myself. But, for the sake of argument—"

"It's still not enough to convince me to look," Remy interrupted, catching my meaning. "Especially now that my Fate is, supposedly, fixed. The last thing I need is to know is that I die a grizzly death and can't do anything to stop it."

Now it was my turn to entertain the story from Brine. "I don't know," I said at length. "If an old man's Fate truly can change at ninety, perhaps Fate isn't as fixed as they say. Wouldn't you want to know about your death, to try and prevent it?"

He gave me a wry smirk. "I reckon everyone in Waldron over the age of thirty is having this exact conversation tonight."

I smiled, about to argue a little more, when a sound outside caught my attention—not the whine from before, but a new note interrupting the predictable chords of wind, tree branches, and skittering nocturnal creatures. I lifted my head off Remy's shoulder, focusing on the disturbance with my magic.

"What is it?" Remy whispered.

"Someone's here."

6

POTIONS AT THE POSSUM

IDRIS

The door to the Pretty Possum Inn & Pub swung open before Idris had the chance to knock. A woman stood in the doorway, arms folded, a wiry wolfhound planted at her feet. She wore a floor-length dressing gown, wrapped tightly around her shapely figure. Her hair was the color of fall foliage, her eyes the bright amber of autumn sunlight.

For an inexplicable moment, Idris found himself tongue-tied. He chalked it up to his solitary existence, which rarely required him to speak to beautiful women—or anyone, for that matter. It didn't help that the warm, welcoming smile on her mauve lips faltered as she appraised his appearance.

Idris cleared his throat. "Are you, uh, Hattie?"

Her remaining congeniality morphed into something sharper, and she gripped the edge of the door a little tighter. "State your business."

Idris unceremoniously held up his hand, showing off the spidery black streaks emanating from underneath his bandage. Then he gestured north, to where the boy had already disappeared back up the road. "I need an apothecary," he said. "A shepherd boy pointed me here."

The woman's eyes narrowed, fixating on his hand, then his face, then the yard beyond the inn's front porch. Idris was well aware of his threatening appearance; he chose not to take offense at her suspicion, and instead forced a lopsided grin. When she took him in again—staring up through long lashes to meet his gaze—her cheeks flushed.

Was it unease that made her blush? With his magic, he picked up the pleas-ant scent of lemon and rose, along with the indescribable musk of her skin. Pheromones of fear and something heady—*desire?*—clouded the air around her, confusing him.

His heart kicked up nervously, and he glanced down at his bandage, frowning at the dark seepage that mottled the dressing. "I'm afraid it's infected," he went on.

Her shoulders relaxed an inch. "Clearly," she quipped, and opened the door wider to allow him inside.

As he passed her, Idris breathed deeper, relishing the fresh natural fragrance of her skin, even as his magic sorted through the underlying pheromones. His nose wrinkled as he caught the distinct whiff of sex. The scent made more sense when Idris spotted a lanky man leaning against the bar counter, his green eyes a little too cunning for his pretty face.

The woman latched the door behind Idris. "Sit at the bar. I'll go get Hattie."

"You aren't Hattie?" Idris asked.

"I'm Anya, the innkeeper."

She was young for an innkeeper, but Idris kept that thought to himself.

"And you are...?" Anya prompted, pausing at the base of the stairs.

"Idris," he grunted.

A nod. "Remy, get Idris a pint, would you?"

Forty minutes later, Idris was seated at the bar, wincing as Hattie—with wrin-kled brow and pursed lips—finished tending to the back of his hand. He'd drunk his first ale while she painstakingly cleaned the wound, chased the pint with a bitter-tasting healing tincture, and was now onto his second ale as she lathered on a sweet-smelling salve.

Hattie had initially raised a brow at his request for both a tincture *and* a salve containing dried Hylder flowers, but—*thank the Fates*—she hadn't bothered to question him. Hylder was a common botanical in medicine, hardly worth noting, but in matters such as this, Idris knew it was essential.

Not that he could've explained *why* he required Hylder, even if she'd asked.

Idris took another long pull of his ale, trying to ignore Anya's persistent stare as Hattie prepared a fresh bandage. The innkeeper was perched at the bar with one stool separating them, watching Idris with excruciating attention. Remy had wandered back upstairs almost as soon as Hattie had appeared, but the innkeeper seemed intent on witnessing Idris's every flinch and fortifying sip. She didn't seem nervous—rather, she seemed protective of her friend and suspicious of his wound.

He respected that. Hers was an attitude that he, too, would've taken if their roles had been reversed.

Nonetheless, Idris had done his best to appear as unassuming as possible (disadvantaged as he was with Halgren still strapped menacingly at his hip). It was hard to make small talk through the pain, so he'd mostly kept his gaze on his ale and gritted his teeth to keep from grunting as Hattie poked, picked, and prodded.

"There," Hattie said, knotting the bandage tightly against his palm. "All done."

"Will I live?" Idris asked her.

In his periphery, he saw the left corner of Anya's mouth quirk up—but her show of amusement was quickly smothered.

Hattie was more generous with her smile. "Probably," she said, collecting her medical supplies and wiping the counter with a rag. "Unless you get into another tangle with whatever bit you."

"A wolverine," Idris said, immediately tasting the bitter warning of his Oath urging him not to elaborate. "Must've been diseased."

"I'll say," Hattie remarked. "That was a nasty infection, not helped by your crude cauterization. I'm going to get you some extra salve and another tincture for the road." She disappeared into the kitchen, leaving Idris with the innkeeper.

Anya's bright brown eyes traced his bandaged hand, her attention almost tactile.

"Your friend is quite skilled for a novice apothecary," he remarked, hoping to put her at ease with his reverence toward her friend's work. The compliment was true: Hattie had been deft in her ministrations.

Those observant eyes flicked to his. "Where did you say you were from again?"

"I didn't," he said, and when she cocked her head, he elaborated, "Fenrir City."

She jerked her chin, gesturing at his armor. "Explains the fancy getup. Are you a mercenary?"

"Something like that." He dragged the neck of his cloak aside, revealing his tattoo.

Her surprise was evident only in the slight tremor in her lips, which Idris noticed were slightly wet with the moisture of her own pint. The pleasant scent of her was diminished by the potent atmosphere of her inn—worn wood, washed linen, malted barley, and hound. He found himself appreciating the homey aromas too much.

Idris cleared his throat and rested his elbow on the counter, facing her more fully. "I appreciate your hospitality, in spite of the late hour."

"Are you...apologizing?"

"I'm sorry for the late-night intrusion," Idris added.

Now she did smile—an unexpectedly full one, spreading those mauve lips and crinkling the corners of her eyes. Her chest quaked with a soft laugh; apparently, she was amused by his discomfort.

"What?" Idris asked.

"This is an inn."

"I'm not sure what you mean."

"I *mean*, you can't *intrude* at an inn."

"Then what's with the cold reception?"

The words came of their own volition, not exactly flirtatious. Had he *meant* to sound flirtatious? If he *was* flirting, he was bad at it, but—no. Idris was just trying to lighten her mood, ease the awkwardness.

Her head tipped as she regarded him with those keen, fire-bright eyes. "First you compliment my hospitality, then you call it cold?"

Idris pressed his lips together, befuddled. He felt oddly squirmy under her attention. He might've spent most of his time in the woods, but he did not think himself unskilled at socializing. As a boy growing up on the streets of Fenrir City—with only his older brother Grinnick to look after him—all interactions had been a matter of life and death.

Was Idris out of practice, or was Anya just strangely hard to read? He couldn't seem to put his finger on *what* she was feeling. Suspicion? Annoyance? Even his magic didn't offer clarification. The scent of her fear had diminished, but the desire remained, lingering even after Remy had left. He didn't know what to think about that.

He didn't particularly *want* to think about it.

The moment stretched, and he waited.

Then she *laughed*, the sound melodic and fulsome. Her old wolfhound lifted his head from his blanket by the hearth, his tail thudding in response.

"What's so funny?" Hattie asked, returning from the back room.

Idris lifted his big palms in a bemused shrug.

Anya beamed at her friend. "Just making the newcomer uncomfortable with some gentle teasing," she said cheerily.

Idris huffed a reluctant chuckle.

"Your teasing is rarely gentle." Hattie arched a brow at Anya, then gave Idris a sympathetic look.

"Perhaps I'm a little squirrelly after the long day—and the late night," the innkeeper said, pinning him with those dazzling eyes again. "I'm assuming you need a room?"

He was tempted. It wasn't technically against his Oath to take the occasional room, but the expectation was that he spent most of his days outside, monitoring the border between the fertile belt of civilization and the unknown threats within the Western Wood. He didn't like how much he wanted to stay.

Seeing his hesitant expression, Anya added, "I promise no harm will befall you."

Idris stared at her. "Can't say I fully believe you."

Anya laughed again, and he took too much joy in knowing he'd caused it.

"I think I'll take my leave." Idris rose from his stool. "What do I owe you?" he asked Hattie as she handed over the tincture and extra salve.

"Nothing," she said. "I'm happy to help."

He reached for his pack, tucking the medicinal gifts into a safe pocket before rifling around for his coin purse. "I insist on paying."

"She's unlicensed, remember? She can't accept payment," Anya said.

"Allowing me to experiment on you is plenty," Hattie added cheerfully. "Just take that tincture twenty-four hours from now and remember to reapply the salve for the next five days. That should stave off the spread of infection."

Idris nodded. "My sincerest thanks for the care, Hattie."

Anya slid off her stool and stepped toward him. "You sure you don't want a room?" she asked. "We're about to fill up for Mirror Fest."

All the more reason to go. "I prefer the outdoors."

She rested her fists on her fulsome hips. "You might think my countenance is cold, but I assure you, it's far chillier out there."

Idris forced a smile. "Thank you, again, for your...*warm* hospitality, Anya."

Before she could object, he walked out into the night, back to where he belonged.

7

THE ARRIVAL OF FATE

ANYA

At dawn the next morning, a chorus of horns echoed through the valley, announcing the arrival of the Mirrors of Fate to Waldron-on-Wend.

A crowd had already collected, filling Swan's Row—the main road that cut through town—with an excitable chatter. The cobblestones were bordered by the River Wend to our right and a line of thatch-roofed shops to our left, creating a chute for sound to collect. Shrieking children darted amongst the throng, twirling streamers; dogs barked; Martha's apprentice hawked sweetbreads—but all noises were secondary to the horns' blare. The notes were low and earthy, with a metallic undertone that bounced off the buildings and zinged along the Wend's calm surface, causing the ducks to scatter.

Hattie and I held hands as we pressed amongst our neighbors, standing on tiptoes to watch as the Mirror Knights crested the northern hill. There were sixteen of them in total: twelve on horses and four stationed on the ornate carriage that held the Mirrors.

As always, the knights appeared noble and grand. They were dressed in the rich orange and crimson of Fenrir, their rose-gold helmets glinting. Some bore crossbows, others swords, and the two directly in front of the carriage carried the flags of the Lordship of Fenrir and our Kingdom of Marona. The pair at the front of the procession were blowing the horns.

As the Mirror Knights approached the edge of town, Mayor Tomilson pushed his way to the front of the crowd and spread his arms in welcome. Townsfolk waved to familiar faces among the knights, calling out to those they knew by name. Then the procession was directed across the stone bridge and up Stone Hill to start the final preparations.

The rest of the morning unfolded smoothly yet swiftly. Hattie showed the off-duty knights to their rooms at the Possum, while I managed the setup on Stone Hill: directing vendors to their designated festival tents, introducing myself to the fresh faces amongst the knights, and organizing a couple of young shepherd boys to whisk our guests' horses off to the town's stables.

The Mirrors themselves were unloaded efficiently and without fanfare. Moving the heavy seven foot tall relics and setting them upon their gilt stands was quite the ordeal—but the knights were practiced. Locals eyed the process with a mix of wariness, awe, and excitement, but with the Mirrors wrapped in burgundy velvet, no one could glimpse their visions prematurely.

Once the Mirrors were settled in the center of the Standing Stones, I wandered over to one of my favorite Mirror Knights, Hammond, to say hello. He was a big bear of a man and infectiously jolly—when he wasn't on duty.

When he saw me, he pulled me into a bone-crunching hug, lifting me clean off the ground before releasing me, unsteadily, back on my own two feet.

"Fates bless this day," Hammond said. "It's a pleasure seeing you, Anya Alvara."

"Likewise, Hammond," I said. "Tell me, how's fatherhood treating you?"

His cheeks, ever-pink, deepened in color with pride. "I'll be twice the father come spring!"

"Ellie is pregnant again?" I exclaimed.

"Indeed, indeed!"

I beamed. "Oh, Hammond, I'm so happy for you—the both of you."

I hadn't met his wife or son, but I'd heard all about them over the past few years. Ellie had a bit of trouble conceiving, and Hattie had given Hammond a tonic two years prior that he still claimed had done the trick—even though they had far more trained apothecaries at the capital.

"Say, where's Hattie?" Hammond asked.

"At the Possum," I told him. "Along with pasties and fresh sheets."

"Fates bless you both. We've had six nights on the road now and I'm desperate for a proper bed," Hammond said, already walking backwards down the hill. "Coming?"

"In a bit," I told him. "Lots to tend to!"

I didn't make it back to the Possum until sundown, and even then, I stayed only long enough to change into my party dress and retrieve Wicker, who loved a festival as much as I did, what with all the dropped food, generous ear scratches, and his collie-girlfriend Annie in attendance.

I'd commissioned a new dress from Kara, the town's seamstress, for tonight's occasion. It was a pale, cool-toned green, with teal and cream-colored floral embroidery on the bodice and elegant matching stitching around the sleeves and hem. The cut was practical and modest, with only a sliver of cleavage poking out of the curved neckline, but the waist hugged close, and the skirts were luxuriously—and warmly—full.

For my hair, I'd plaited twin sections against my scalp, which combined into one thick braid down my back. Around my shoulders, I'd secured my nicer gray cloak with my mother's heart-shaped pin. I'd even gone so far as to wear the labradorite necklace Hattie had gifted me last Astrophel, one of my most treasured possessions.

"What do we think?" I asked Hattie when I emerged, doing a little twirl at the base of the stairs.

"Fabulous," Hattie exclaimed. She, too, had dressed up, donning a stunning shade of cobalt velvet that complemented her fair complexion.

Remy, who'd been lounging by the fire in his black finery, stalked over to pinch my waist. "Sensuous," he purred, bending down to kiss my cheek.

Hattie let out a little *eep*.

The Possum was empty, what with the entirety of town and all the knights congregating up on Stone Hill. But Remy's public affection—even just in front of Hattie—was unusual.

"You're in a cheeky mood, aren't you?" I asked.

"Hard not to be when you're wearing that." He offered his arm, and I took it, allowing him to lead me out the door.

Outside, the sun had set, but its light still illuminated the sky in a soft palette of peach and periwinkle. The plateau to the south of the Standing Stones was already bustling: people mingling amongst the food and craft tents, grills sizzling and steaming, dancers twirling to the first band's up-tempo beat, and bonfires roaring on the fringes. The Mirrors would be unveiled at midnight, so for now, the town was focused on drinking, eating, and enjoying the festivities.

Still, a tension swirled in the air, anticipatory and reluctant. I heard it in the faint worried whispers of folks in line for hand-pies, baked apples, and madrone berry necklaces. I recognized the bated breath as something I felt, too, awaiting my last chance to gaze into a Fate capable of changing. Once the majority of the town had gazed into the Mirrors, the festival would take on a lighter, freer mood, but for now, we were all antsy (save for the dogs and children under ten, who need not concern themselves with the Mirrors at all).

While Remy wandered off in search of hot cider, Hattie and I distracted ourselves by standing in line for slices of pumpkin cake. We tapped our feet to the beat of the band, giggled at the children racing by, and clapped when the fire-breathing performer blew a hot blaze past our faces. Wicker was off wrestling with Annie under the cheerful attention of Farmer Quinn, and with everything running smoothly, I felt finally free to let my mind wander farther from tonight's logistics.

Unfortunately, it went straight to last night's unexpected visitor.

I found it hard not to dwell on the mystery of Idris, wondering what sort of business he had in *Waldron*, of all places. Even during a festival that drew plenty of newcomers, his armor, fine cloak, and massive sword weren't common for these parts—and he hadn't even stayed for the Mirrors' arrival. Plenty of intimidating folks had passed through my inn over the years, but never someone like *him*. A knight of an unknown Order. Clearly dangerous. Strangely disarming. Almost charming.

And his wound, I thought with a shudder. It had been alarmingly festered, completely at odds with his calm demeanor and that alluring, reluctant half-smile. When I first heard the frantic racing of his heart with my magic, I'd thought it was due to the wound, the pain. But his heart had only raced when he looked in my direction, rhythmic as festival drums.

Remy's heart never beat that quickly around me.

"You and Remy seem extra cozy tonight," Hattie remarked, speaking low enough for only my ears. "Do you think he's coming around?"

I blinked, clearing thoughts of Idris from my mind. "Doubtful," I said. "Remy has made his intentions clear."

"Intentions can change." She elbowed my side. "Maybe that'll be your new Fate."

"As I said yesterday, I'm happy with my lot in life."

Hattie's brow arched, just as it had last night when she caught me flirting with Idris. "Unless last night's sexy stranger caught your—"

"Not every man is the star of a romance novel, Hattie," I said, perhaps a bit too harshly.

But my harshness only egged her on. "I *knew* you fancied him. You could barely take your eyes off him! And you two had a vibe."

"A vibe?" I repeated.

Hattie nodded, waggling her eyebrows. "An intense vibe."

"He was a wounded stranger with a greatsword," I said dryly, "the vibe was suspicion."

"He seemed plenty nice," Hattie argued. "And handsome. You *have* to admit he was handsome."

He was. Hulking stature, dark wavy hair, with a rugged yet humbly capable countenance that few men—their egos too fragile—possessed. I'd been dismayed to note that his eyes were the blue-green color of my beloved Wend. And—frightening wound aside—he had the most beautiful hands I'd ever seen: strong, graceful, huge. He hadn't been particularly charismatic, but he'd made up for that with reluctant wit.

I shook off the memory, disinterested in the curious longing it stirred up like sediment in my chest.

"Wasn't he handsome?" Hattie pressed.

"*Yes*," I relented. "And what of it?"

She smirked. "Just wanted you to admit it."

We'd reached the front of the line, where Martha insisted we take our cake slices for free, given all the work we'd put into the festival. With gratitude, we carried our treats off to one of the communal tables set up in the grass.

To my left, the Standing Stones rose from the ground, resolute; with the moon spilling silver across the field, their silhouettes were sharpened in stark relief against the starry backdrop of the night sky. Without the insulation of clouds, the air was frigid, the stars bare and crystalline. Cold stung my cheeks, and I thought of Idris's comment: *Thank you, again, for your…*warm *hospitality, Anya.* The joke made me smile to myself even now, but it was the raspy resonance with which he'd spoken my name that left a residue in my magic's memory.

When Hattie and I had finished our cakes, we rose from our seats to find Remy. We located him sipping cider over by one of the bonfires, standing on the fringes of a crowd of couples flying over the muddy ground in a fast-paced dance. When I came up to his side, he smiled affectionately down at me.

"Fancy a dance, m'lady?" Remy asked, passing his cider to Hattie and offering me his hand.

His formality made me laugh. "Only if you promise not to call me 'm'lady' again," I said, allowing him to spin me into the fray.

Hattie laughed and cheered from her spot on the sidelines.

I was not a particularly talented dancer, but since I'd been practicing the steps of Waldron's most popular dances since birth, I could keep up with the crowd. Remy's hold, however—with one hand gripping mine and the other splayed on my low back—made me rather light-headed as he took me through the familiar turns. I had the sinking feeling that I was one ale away from admitting to myself that I *did* hope he was changing his mind about settling down in Waldron. That I *did* wish this particular part of my life would change.

We were still dancing when the horns cut through the merriment, announcing the beginning of the Fate Ceremony. Tucked against Remy's chest, I lifted my chin to stare up at the pleasant planes of his face. "Look into the Mirrors, won't you?" I begged, suddenly deeply invested in what he might see—hoping it would be me. "Please?"

His mouth pressed into a line, and he swallowed thickly. "All right, maybe I will."

"Really?"

"I'm afraid I can't bring myself to say no to you," he said, gripping my hand as he led me toward the back of the queue, my heart fluttering in that stupid way it always did around him.

Hattie and the rest of town were congregating on the orb-lit path. When we reached her, I snaked my arm through hers, not wanting to appear too chummy with Remy around watching eyes.

"*Remy*," Hattie intoned, "are you going to gaze into the Mirrors tonight?"

His gaze slanted toward me. "I've been convinced."

"It was surprisingly easy," I told her. "Have you run into"—I dropped my voice to a nearly inaudible whisper—"Noble?"

Hattie stiffened, then jerked her head toward the front of the line. "He's up there. I ran into him amongst the craft tables, said hello, and he turned and walked the other way."

"Maybe he's just shy?" Remy offered.

Hattie groaned. "I'm beginning to think he hates me."

"Only a monster could hate you, Hattie, and even then, I have my doubts," I told her. "But if he's not keen, it's his loss—truly."

Hattie rested her head on my shoulder, her curly hair tickling my nose. "I love you."

"I love you, too," I said, squeezing her arm a little tighter.

The line moved quickly, the sounds from up ahead a mix of cheers, gasps, and loud sighs of relief. Word traveled back through the line about fortunes changing to show babies, weddings, and large harvests. Farmer Timmons' eldest son saw a new and rather disturbing death by a toppled haystack, but as he was yet twenty-one, there was hope in avoiding such a frightening demise.

Mostly, Fates remained the same, with the majority of the town enjoying the security of small fortunes and peaceful deaths by old age. The more I heard about the visions happening up ahead, the less I believed the rumor Remy had relayed from Brine. Everyone knew that even an *unfixed* Fate was difficult to alter—especially the closer to thirty I got.

Eventually, our little trio made it to the front of the line. The Mirrors were as they had been earlier, arranged beside the center stone in the circle, facing south. Their velvet covers were gone, revealing ornate metal frames and odd, swirling surfaces. Knights guarded either side of them, stone-still, with hands resting on hilts. Only one citizen was allowed in the stone circle at a time, so as not to crowd the Mirrors and distort the visions.

Hugh was standing before the Mirrors now, and given my place in line—my vantage somewhat parallel to the Mirrors' faces—I could only see a partial image. But Hugh finished his turn quickly, smiling at those of us in wait. At sixty-one, his Fate was long-since fixed, and I knew from previous years that it was favorable. Still, it was nice to see his relief. Encouraging, even.

But now, it was our turn.

With my heart suddenly in my throat, adrenaline lacing my blood, memories of my mother's death edging into my thoughts, I whispered to Hattie, "I need a moment. Can you go first?"

She nodded, gave my arm one last squeeze, then let go, stepping into the circle.

I shuffled sideways a little so I could see what the Mirrors showed her.

She faced the Mirror of Fortune first, her shoulders trembling. The fog in the Mirror's silvery surface cleared, revealing a spread of potions on a table. The image was from her vantage, her own fingertips brushing over multicolored bottles. It might not have been a man, but her same old fortune was, indeed, favorable, as it showed her working with potions, an activity she loved.

She moved, next, to the Mirror of Death. I held my breath as the image of a ceiling appeared, her upheld hand wrinkled and spotted with age, so similar to the death I, too, had been shown in previous years. Her hand lowered to her side, and her vision swiveled toward the window, where sunlight streamed in through the branches of a great oak. It was the same death she'd seen before, and when the Mirror cleared, she looked at me and visibly sighed.

Then she walked to the opposite side of the circle, congregating on the sidelines with the other revelers who'd already had their turn. One of the Mirror Knights managing the line beckoned me forward.

"Good luck," Remy murmured.

Heart pounding, I walked across the grass to observe my Fate.

8

CHANGING FATE

ANYA

Sixteen years had passed since my mother gazed into the Mirrors and my world fell apart. Sixteen Fate Ceremonies, and anxiety still gripped me with each passing year. The night her Fate changed for the worse had been a waypoint in my life—a sharp pivot from what I'd known—and tonight felt like another waypoint: my final unfixed Fate before my future solidified forever.

According to legend, the Mirrors were forged in the Well of Fate, where magical waters filled the frames and bestowed in them the eyes of the Fates. The Fates themselves were not gods nor deities, but innate currents in the cosmic turning of time; they governed our lives like the tides governed the sea. The story of the Mirrors had been passed down through generations, the telling a little different depending on the speaker, but one thing remained the same: the Mirrors' visions—though malleable in one's younger years—were not to be questioned.

The Mirrors provided a sacred glimpse into the unknowable ether of life itself.

I thought of all this as I picked my way across the flattened grass. My limbs felt heavy, shaky, beyond my control. My heart thudded erratically, racing too fast only to seem to skip a beat.

The Fate Mirrors were as large as doorways, and I remembered from past experience that their images would appear clear enough to step through, as if I could enter the reality they revealed. The effect could be disconcerting, and paired with tonight's unique context, I felt altogether panicked as I stepped up to my first vision.

The Mirror of Fortune's ornate frame was made of solid gold, carved intricately into vines, leaves, and flowers. The apex of the arched top was adorned with a sun-shaped carving, an *F* in its center. In the torchlight surrounding the stone circle, the metal flickered with fire and shadow. Unlike a regular mirror, I did not see my reflection in the Mirror's silvery surface; it started out blank, foggy.

I froze with anticipation, unable to breathe. A few seconds passed, then the Mirror's surface shifted, like storm clouds parting. It revealed the image I'd seen before: the surface of blue-green water, glasslike and edged by fog. The Wend. Peaceful, constant, and representative of home.

My Fortune had not changed.

I heaved a shaky breath; relief and hope coursed through me as I moved on.

The Mirror of Death was Fortune's dark twin: its silver-black frame had been forged with the pattern of woven twigs and bones, and the *D* at the top was encased not in a sun, but a crescent moon. I thought of the old age I'd seen in previous glimpses, willing the Fates to show me the same image now. Desperate to have my future affirmed with a favorable end.

The Mirror of Death's clouds began to shift, swirling and turbulent and ominous.

Something new and unexpected took shape. In the foreground, I saw a man. Dark, wavy hair tangled and wet. Stubbled jaw clenched, his soft mouth grim. Huge, exquisite hands balled into fists. Eyes the color of the Wend. A purple twilit sky above.

I watched in horror as Idris gripped my waist and lowered me into…water? My head thrashed as I choked, airless, pushed deeper by his unrelenting palms. Bubbles fizzed in my vision as I screamed, blinded by my desperation, my terror.

I was drowning.

I was…*drowned.*

Behind me, the crowd gasped. I looked over my shoulder, finding Hattie; her face was ghostly pale, eyes wide. When I turned back toward the Mirror of Death, its surface was again blank.

Then everyone was moving: Hattie was grasping my wrists, Remy was rushing toward me, Hugh was wrapping a huge steadying arm around my middle—which was good, because otherwise, I might've collapsed.

Hugh lowered me off to the side in the grass, pressing his kind hands to my face. "Do you know who he is?" he asked.

I looked around wildly for Hattie, but I'd lost her among the press of concerned neighbors. "I—" I stuttered, then shook my head disbelievingly. Shock had rendered my tongue leaden.

Somehow, last night's chance encounter with Idris had changed my Fate. I pushed the image of his solemn face away, pushed it down, denial building rapidly.

"It can still be prevented," I heard someone say.

"This close to her thirtieth year? I wouldn't bet on it."

"Has anyone seen the man?"

"Didn't recognize him, myself."

The voices were suddenly too loud, and I fumbled for my magic, muffling them.

"Hattie?" I croaked, pushing off the damp ground and onto my feet.

Within the stone circle, the Mirror Knights were rushing to control the mayhem. They guided Remy toward the Mirror of Fortune, keeping things moving. I caught only a glimpse of his vision, but it was enough to break my heart all over again. A woman—not me—cradling a baby.

I stumbled again, landing hard on my knees in the mud. Pain lanced through me, both physical and emotional. The knights were directing Remy to the Mirror of Death, now, determined to maintain order despite the stir caused by my new vision.

From my place behind him in the mud, I watched as the fog in the Mirror of Death cleared to reveal...

No. It couldn't be.

A dim forest. A flash of steel. His hand lifting, as if he could block the blow, fingernails long and grimy with dirt. And *me*. My face pale, filthy, crusted with blood, pulled into a snarl. A blade slashing across his vision.

Cutting him down.

For a moment, nothing happened. Then I heard Hattie's voice cry out my name, and the crowd erupted into chaos. People rushed toward me, toward Remy. Hands grabbed at my forearms, my bodice. Shouts of protest and anger confused the scene, filling my head with panic.

One of the Mirror Knights—Hammond, *thank the Fates*—came to my side, gripping my arm. To steady me? Or to restrain me?

"Come," he said firmly, yanking me up to my feet. Other knights arrived, protecting the Mirrors and redirecting the crowd, allowing Hammond to guide me away.

"Hattie!" I screamed, even as I trailed Hammond, my biceps aching in his iron grip.

"We'll let her see you later," Hammond said.

"And Remy?" I pleaded. I needed to tell him I wouldn't do it, wouldn't *dare* hurt him—or anyone, for that matter. "I am not a killer," I told Hammond, my voice strained with fear and conviction. "I am not a killer! I am not a killer!"

But Hammond didn't respond. He only bent down, grunting as he hoisted me over his shoulder, carrying me away toward an uncertain Fate.

9

CRIMINAL

ANYA

The village lockup was located on the southern end of town. Aside from the occasional drunkard needing to cool off, the small jail was rarely used, and therefore was quite dusty when Hammond deposited me there.

"What's going to happen to me?" I'd asked as he locked the barred door, my face snotty and tear slicked.

"You'll be sent to the capital to appeal your case," he'd said, softly adding, "I'm so sorry, Anya," before leaving me to my misery.

That had been a few hours ago.

Weak morning light now spilled through the narrow window on the back wall of my cell. The tiny building butted right up against the Wend, and through the slit, the river sighed the scent of decay on an icy breath, making me shiver. Its relentless trickle had been my lullaby throughout girlhood, a tune to frolic to as a teen, and in adulthood, its voice had become that of an old friend.

But now, it taunted me.

My body ached from a night spent on the cold stone floor. My head ached with the horrifying visions I'd seen in the Mirror of Death, replayed on a constant, disbelieving loop.

The capital. A trial. I'd heard of would-be criminals caravanned to the city to appeal to the Lord of Fenrir, but never in my wildest nightmares had I ever expected to take such a journey myself. The last time someone from Waldron had been implicated in a Mirror crime was before I was born. I'd only seen a criminal caravan once, at the juncture of the High Road and the path into Waldron. It'd been a grim sight: barred wagons filled to the brim with grimy bodies and frightened faces.

I was sure I fit the picture, now, filthy and terrified as I was.

How many of those prisoners had been innocent? At the time, I'd assumed they were all guilty, the Mirrors proving their nefarious future deeds. Now, I wondered how many of their Fates had, indeed, been malleable enough to change course. And of those who *had* followed through with the Mirrors' predictions, had they always known their capacity for wrongdoing? Or had they imagined themselves incapable of their own crimes, only to find a deeper darkness in themselves later on?

Even considering the betrayal I felt when I saw the woman and child in Remy's Mirror of Fortune, the mere *thought* of harming him made me feel sick to my stomach. I would never. Could never. There was not enough heartbreak in the world to make me *violent*.

But then there was the matter of my own Mirror of Death.

My new Fated end was now eerily similar to my Fortune. I'd always thought of the river as a natural friend, but it seemed the Wend was destined to become my grave, instead.

And Idris...why in the Fates would he find reason to drown me? An act of justice for Remy, perhaps? Idris hadn't seemed like a Knight of the Order of the Lawful—they usually made their charge quite obvious—but if not that, then what?

I couldn't reconcile his deed with the man I'd lightly flirted with last night. He'd seemed quiet, sure, but not nefarious. Perhaps I wasn't as good a judge of character as I imagined myself, though. When he'd walked out the door of the Possum, I'd assumed it was for good—but now, his visit seemed more calculated.

Given my potential crime, maybe I deserved a watery end.

After all, Remy's Fate was supposedly fixed. Was the malleability of my own future enough to change his, too? I squeezed my eyes shut. It was all too frightening to consider. Now more than ever, I needed to muster up my courage. Believe in myself. Prove my innocence.

I was still on the floor, clutching my knees to my chest, when hinges shrieked, announcing the arrival of a visitor.

When Hattie saw me, she sunk to her knees in the narrow hall outside my cell, gripping the iron bars with her delicate hands. She was still wearing her party dress, just like me, but hers was clean, whereas mine was wrecked with mud.

"Fates above, Anya, what have they done to you?" Hattie cried.

"Mercifully, nothing, except the discomfort of a night spent in a cell." I exhaled a little laugh. "Suddenly I feel sorry for sending drunkards here on occasion. Though I can see how an excess of ale would make a night's stay here far less uncomfortable."

"How do you manage humor at a time like this?" Hattie asked, her blue eyes searching mine. "It's *criminal* for them to lock you up when you've done nothing wrong!"

"The Mirrors don't lie, Hattie," I whispered, voice quavering as I spoke my fear aloud. "My Fate isn't fixed, but the Mirrors still revealed the most likely path forward." And somehow, my most likely future was murder—as both perpetrator and victim.

Perhaps Idris would be the *hero* in this story.

"Don't talk like that. You aren't thirty yet. You still have time to change your Fate," Hattie insisted.

I clutched the labradorite necklace she'd given me, holding it against my chest. I couldn't bring myself to point out that Remy was thirty-two, his Fate already fixed.

"I spoke to Hammond this morning," Hattie continued. "He said he'd write down some suggestions for your trial."

"That's kind of him," I said, crawling forward until I knelt across from her. "What of the rest of town? What do they think of me?"

"They're concerned, of course! Nobody believes you'd actually—" she broke off, unwilling to say the words. "Hardly anyone even knows Remy, aside from in passing; not that we wish death upon him, but we're all on your side, Anya, truly. His Fate might be fixed, but yours isn't. We know you wouldn't do such a thing unless provoked."

"He wouldn't provoke *that*," I said with certainty. Remy was mercurial, but never unkind or threatening.

Hattie nodded. "Hugh has been organizing character statements from everyone in town, for you to take with you. He'll deliver them later."

The thought of the town rallying behind me shook loose my resolve, and tears quickly filled my eyes.

"Oh, love," Hattie said, grasping my hands through the bars. "I'm so sorry this is happening to you. I remember when I escaped Poe-on-Wend, how frightened I felt. I'm not sure this helps, but I found it steadying to simply focus on the next step, one at a time. Your next step is making it to the capital. Then your trial. Then, once you're home, we can worry about preventing what you saw."

"That's a lot of steps."

"You have two months before your birthday," Hattie said encouragingly. "That's plenty of time to sort this all out."

I'd never heard her sound so decisive; normally, I was the self-assured one. The older sister. The reversal of our roles had the opposite effect Hattie intended. I sobbed even harder, her strength allowing me to be weak.

"Oh, oh, oh," Hattie cooed, drawing me into an awkward hug, cold iron between us. "It'll be all right."

"Sorry, sorry," I said, pulling back. "I'm determined to rectify this, Hattie, don't you worry. It's just...*scary*." I laughed again, wiping at my eyes. "What an understatement."

Her lips pursed.

"What?" I prompted.

"It's just..." Her eyes lifted to the ceiling. "I don't mean to upset you, but I've been thinking about it all night, and I'll regret it if I don't say something, so I'm just going to say it: did you notice anything...*strange* about Remy's vision?"

My lip wobbled as I remembered his fortune. "You mean his child?"

Hattie shook her head. "In the vision with...you in it," she said delicately. "Did you notice his hands?"

I had, vaguely. His fingernails had been long and grimy. But the clearest part in my memory was my own snarling face, streaked with dirt and blood as if we'd been rolling around on the forest floor.

"His hands were dirty," I told Hattie. "So was I. Like we'd been...struggling."

"Not just dirty," Hattie said. "His nails were *elongated* and black. Like claws."

"Hattie…" I began doubtfully.

"I'm telling you, Anya, they were grotesque. Almost…inhuman."

I frowned. "What are you saying?"

"I don't know, really," she said. "There was something disturbing about them. They reminded me of Idris's wound."

"Don't invent stories for my sake, Hattie."

"I'm not," she insisted. "I saw Idris's hand up close. He'd made it sound like an old wound that'd festered, but there was no evidence of scabbing or rot. The puncture was *new*; the infection had spread rapidly. And it was *black*, Anya. You saw it yourself, spiderwebbing up his wrist."

"So?"

"He asked for *Hylder*," Hattie said, as if I should know what that meant.

I stared at her blankly.

"Hylder is a powerful botanical for healing, but also protection," she elaborated. She glanced over her shoulder, then dropped her voice to a whisper, even though no one else was here. "Ancient apothecaries used to use it for purification from *evil*."

Goosebumps rose on my arms. "I'm not sure I'm following, Hattie," I said slowly.

"What if Remy becomes afflicted with the same ailment that plagued Idris? What if it makes him aggressive? There are plenty of diseases that change one's personality."

"I'm not interested in finding out," I stated firmly. "I'll go to the capital, get myself absolved of this hypothetical crime, and stay far away from Remy—and Idris." I straightened my back, telling her what I needed to hear. "It'll all be fine. I'll fix it before my Fate is set, and everything will go back to normal."

Hattie nodded, eyes welling. Then she reached for the rucksack she'd brought with her, which I hadn't really noticed when she came in. Now, I realized it was the same pack she'd traveled with to Waldron-on-Wend eight years ago.

When she spoke again, her voice was breathy. "I brought you some provisions," she said, wedging the bag and its weighty contents through the bars of my cell, the clatter of glass bottles plinking against the iron. "Extra clothes, a bit of food, and some medicinal items in case you get into trouble."

I took the bag, hugging it to my chest.

"I'll look after Wicker and the Possum," she said. "Just...have faith in yourself and remember, your Fate is not yet fixed."

10

UNCERTAIN DEPARTURE

ANYA

As I was escorted to the barred wagon, I studied the guards' uniforms, which consisted of the same red and orange garb as the Mirror Knights, but with silver armor instead of rose-gold. It was a bland thing to focus on, but as I was paraded down Swan's Row with shackled wrists and ankles—my friends and neighbors lined up to watch—it was easier to ponder an innocuous detail than my harsh reality.

That is, until Wicker wrenched himself free of Hattie's hold and raced toward me across the cobblestones. Then, I was only in the present moment.

With a cry, I bent down, looping my arms around his lanky body in a makeshift hug. The two guards at my side kindly allowed me a moment with my beloved wolfhound. I held on tightly, desperately, as Wicker lapped up my tears. He woofed and whined, and I implored myself to remember the exact notes of his voice; Wicker would be one of many bolstering memories to call upon as I made my way north.

"That's enough," one of the guards by the wagon grunted.

"Wicker, dear," Hattie called.

Then the moment was slipping away, and I reluctantly let him go, waving awkwardly in my chains at my two dearest loves.

Too embarrassed by the horrid spectacle of my new Fate, I tried not to make eye contact with anyone else—though I did hear Martha crying on the sidelines. When the guards deposited me inside the awaiting wagon, I didn't look at any of my fellow prisoners, either—but I did count the boots of five other would-be criminals. *They're just as innocent as you*, I told myself, in an effort not to fear them.

After a thorough search for weapons, my rucksack—weighed down with tinctures from Hattie and countless letters from my neighbors to Lord Haron about my upstanding character—was dropped at my feet. Apparently, my status as a hypothetical prisoner still allowed me my gear.

A sharp whistle announced my departure, and then the wagon lurched forward. Six mounted guards encircled us, angling into place. Their horses' shoes clattered on the stones; the wagon's wheels rumbled with increasing speed.

"We love you, Anya!" Hattie called.

"Take care, dear!" Martha said.

"We'll see you again soon!" Vera added.

"Hear, hear!" Hugh agreed.

Then the whole crowd was shouting my name, wishing me luck.

Finally, I dared a glance at what I was leaving behind, knowing it would break me but needing to see it all the same: quaint cottages, calm river, and the entire community of Waldron-on-Wend gathered in the street. Waving, jumping, yelling encouragement. For *me*.

Soon, one voice cut through all the rest—Kara, the seamstress, beginning a song. "*O hollow night, when will the light arrive? / Hear my song, so shadows know my might.*"

It had been my mother's favorite tune, a slow song sang during Astrophel.

The crowd joined in, their harmonious voices filling Waldron-on-Wend, following me in my moving cell. "*O blessed morn, come before all is lost. / My voice does call, forlorn into the dark.*"

Then, in the highest registers: "*I shall live on, into the breaking dawn / I shall prevail, if only to sing my song. / Oh stars shine true, my dazzling hope is you.*"

I wiped my nose, watching and listening as my community serenaded my departure with the most meaningful songs. My magic clung to the tune as Waldron-on-Wend shrunk and disappeared behind the hill.

At the juncture that led out of town, my wagon joined two others, completing the caravan that would travel north along the High Road to the capital city.

Though it had been many decades since a citizen of Waldron had been implicated in a murder during the Fate Ceremony, the caravan's organization—its very presence on the outskirts of town—proved that many across Fenrir had indeed found themselves with similar futures as mine.

I wondered how many of us would return home after this heartrending adventure.

Wracked with uncertainty, I clung to the strands of distant sound still rising from Waldron-on-Wend, holding onto my community's encouragement for as long as I could.

For the first long stretch of road, none of us inside the wagon spoke. We did share glances, however, our eyes narrowed warily. The six of us were seated on two benches, facing one another in trios. As I'd been picked up last, I was perched in the back left corner of the wagon—it was bumpy in back, but I preferred the wagon's jostling over being wedged between my fellow would-be criminals farther forward.

Of the five other prisoners, four were men. Next to me sat a young man of barely twenty; he stared off at the countryside with a clenched jaw. On his other side sat the eldest man, who had a gnarly scar across his cheek, but appeared frail. The only other woman sat across from me in the rear of the wagon, her fingers interlocked with the man beside her—a couple. On the other side of them, farthest from me, was a middle-aged man with cracked lips, which he licked on occasion—usually when his beady eyes swung in my direction. The starvation in his gaze was enough to set me on edge, the vague danger banishing any exhaustion that tried to creep into my limbs.

By the time we pulled off the road for the night, my muscles ached from bracing against the constant jerking of the wagon. Disconcerted by the persistent stare of Beady Eyes, I had swiveled my body to face the road behind us, and my twisted position had no doubt contributed to the soreness in my back and shoulders. Thankfully, my fellow prisoners were all slumped and quiet now, too, seemingly lost in their own grim thoughts.

The guards parked the caravan in a half-moon along the edge of the Western Wood, tucked into a low grassy depression just out of sight of the High Road. A bitter wind whipped through the small valley, mussing my tattered festival braids. I nestled into the folds of my cloak, smelling Hattie and Wicker in its fibers, and tried to imagine myself at the Possum instead of chilled down to my bones and imprisoned.

Camp was made, and we were eventually tossed rolls of bread through the bars, which we all snatched up hungrily, gnawing on the tough stale crusts. For once, I wished I possessed touch magic, to draw the sensation of the guards' cooking fires closer. Instead, all I could do was listen to their asinine conversations: about tonight's watch shifts, the women they'd bedded in the towns they'd passed through, and petty arguments about sleeping arrangements and camp chores.

Our wagon was located in the back of the line of three. As night fell, someone in the middle wagon began to wail. The sound wore at my frayed nerves, disturbing me. It persisted for a while, then a shout pierced the air, and a ruckus ensued. I couldn't see the details in the darkness, but the fight was clamorous, with people screaming, chains clattering, and the thudding of fists on flesh. The guards were shockingly slow to intervene; eventually, I lifted the echoes of the fight in their direction, the racket finally rousing them enough to take action with verbal threats and proffered swords.

As the commotion died down, I rested against the bars in my corner again. My body cried out for sleep, but I feared letting my guard down. I waited long into the night, until our escorts' fires had died and everyone—including my threatening cellmate—nodded off.

Finally, for the first time in nearly twenty-four hours, I reached for sleep. I nodded in and out, uncomfortable both physically and in my heart. I resettled my head against the hard iron, trying not to become too lost in fearful thoughts. With the trees at my back, I could hear the rustling of possums, raccoons, owls. I let their presence comfort me. Sleep edged closer once more—

Until a twig cracked.

I lifted my head, pulling at the thread of sound. Boots across the understory—unmistakable.

More steps neared, and I swiveled on my wooden bench, chains clinking. I stared out into the depthless dark inside the trees, wondering who it might be.

"Anya?" a male voice whispered.

"*Remy*?" I breathed.

He materialized by my corner of the wagon, crouching beside the rear left wheel with his back to the forest. I glanced over my shoulder at the clearing; no guards had roused. It was late, the moon tucked behind clouds. I mustered my magic, swaddling us in a blanket of silence; it wasn't foolproof, but hopefully we'd be able to speak without anyone waking.

"What are you doing here?" I whispered, a part of me hoping he'd written his own character reference, a letter for me to take to Lord Haron.

He grasped my hands through the bars; his palms were so warm compared to my frozen, gloveless fingers. "I rode out late this afternoon and followed your path. I had to talk to you. To—apologize."

"What?" I shook my head. "No. Remy, I should be the one—"

"My fortune...my fortune is real," he interrupted. "It's real and it's coming soon."

"I don't understand."

"Listen, Anya. I have to clear this up," he said, his green eyes catching the silver light of the stars. "I have a wife."

I yanked my fingers from his, curling my hands against my chest. "What are you talking about?"

"I have a wife," he repeated, as if that would make it any more conceivable. "In Fenrir City. It happened quickly, this summer. She—she became pregnant and I—I felt I had to—" He broke off, his words strangled with emotion.

To his credit, we had never agreed to be monogamously faithful to one another, but I had hoped...

Fates above, I had *hoped*. Stupidly. *Foolishly*.

"I meant to tell you about her when I arrived in Waldron, but—well, you were just so irresistible. You always have been. And I thought, 'One more time. One more night. Then I'll tell her.'" He ran his fingers through his blond hair, causing it to stand up messily; I despised how visceral my urge to smooth it was. "Then you asked me to look into the Mirrors, and I thought, 'Maybe they'll tell me what to do. How to handle this situation.'"

My anger flared. "How to *handle* this situation?" I repeated. "Was it not evident?"

"It is now," he said emphatically. "My Fortune is my family."

"You *slept* with me," I exclaimed. "You are *married*, and you slept with me."

"She already knows I came to Waldron to tell you," he promised. "And now, so do you. Once I return to her, I'll be starting fresh."

"You rode all the way out here to dump me?" I asked incredulously.

"I rode out here to be honest with you," he said. "You deserve my honesty."

"I don't deserve any of this," I said, remembering where I was, chained up because of *him*. "I'm the victim here!"

Remy winced. "I do care about you, Anya," he said, his tone oddly...careful. "I thought if I could just explain, and apologize—"

"You're afraid I'll actually do it." The realization was a slap, a bucket of cold water. Of course he wasn't bringing me a character reference, he was here to protect his own Fate. "You're afraid that I would see your Fortune and—and—kill you? Out of jealousy?" It sounded absurd.

But Remy had backed away a step.

I gripped the bars, becoming more shrill in my fury. "Do you really think so highly of yourself?" I snarled. "Do you really think so harshly of me? That I'd take a father from a child out of anger? Fates above, Remy, you truly are an imbecile—"

The clanking of chains cut off my tirade. "You have quite the mouth on you, don't you, love?" Beady Eyes said, rising from his seat.

Apparently, my outburst had reached beyond my feeble magical buffer. The other prisoners were awake now, too, watching him creep toward me.

"What else can it do?" he cooed, grinning.

I stole a glance over my shoulder, but Remy had disappeared—*the fucking coward*.

I stood, too, ready to do what I must to defend myself.

But then an eerie, piercing whine cut through the dark, drawing our attention northward.

11

FAMILIAR FACE

ANYA

Seconds after the fearsome wail, a grotesque creature leapt out of the woods, landing on top of the first wagon. Prisoners awoke, screaming in terror. Their cage shook violently, the wooden roof cracking under the creature's thrashing weight.

From my vantage at the back of our caravan of three, all I could see was the beast's vague silhouette in the nighttime darkness: a bear, but with spindly antlers and too many legs. It screeched as it reached through the splintered roof, swiping with unnaturally long claws.

The sound of *wet* hit my ears like an axe. Blood splattered the grass.

Guards rose from their bedrolls, shouting out to one another as they searched for their armor and weapons. A few simply ran off toward the road. The horses—tethered to nearby trees—whinnied and grunted, some tearing free of their headstalls to make their escape.

In mere moments, the first wagon became carnage. The second wagon took longer, diverted as the creature was by the efforts of the guards trying to hack it back. But one by one, all fell.

Then the beast swung its glowing red eyes on us.

"What the fuck?" the young man beside me moaned. "What the *fuck*."

Beady Eyes cowered behind the elder fellow. The woman across from me curled into a ball on the floor and began chanting a prayer to the Fates while her partner—logically, incredulously—cried out, "This isn't how I'm supposed to die!"

I had the same thought, but any predictable Fate seemed moot in the face of such a creature. I'd never heard a myth, legend, or tall tale involving something so terrifying, twisted, evil. Monsters were supposed to be fiction, and even then, the ones from folklore paled in comparison to *this*.

The bear-like abomination crept toward our wagon across the blood-slicked grass, its maw dripping crimson. A low, growling hiss emanated from its throat. Claws scraped the front bars of our iron prison, its overgrown paws too wide to reach through.

Among my fellow prisoners, prayers turned to whimpers. Whimpers turned to silence. Bodies pressed into the back of the wagon, all of us united in our terror. I smelled urine. I kept as still as possible.

The axels of our wheeled cage groaned as the monster climbed up, disappearing from our view onto the wooden roof. Its shadow blotted out the starlight streaming through the slats. I braced for the moment the beams split; I would try to escape through any gap I could, I decided. I couldn't run fast in shackles, but I could hide. I would not die this day.

I drew a steadying breath, even as I quaked in my chains.

Then the wood groaned, cracked. The beast fell through in a great crash, snapping its teeth. It crushed the elder and caught Beady Eyes in its teeth, and I turned my head before I could witness the rest.

Behind me, the bars of our cage had bent, creating a gap. I lunged for it, forcing my shoulders and torso through—but the iron was too narrow and unyielding for my wide hips.

With Beady Eyes shredded apart at the monster's feet, it swung its attention on the couple. The woman shrieked; her partner stood gallantly between her and the beast. We were powerless in here—completely and utterly powerless.

I wiggled frantically against the bars, desperate to escape. My chains rattled against the iron, announcing my struggle—but they were no longer the only metallic sound to reach my ears. Distantly, I heard the unmistakable *shing* of metal freed from leather.

A figure appeared from the northern stretch of woods, his arrival announced by the ringing of his steel. His black armor rendered him nearly invisible, but his sword—it *glowed* with blue flame, casting odd light on the wreckage. He ran full force toward us, his primal roar piercing the night. Without hesitation, he jumped up onto the driver's bench of our wagon and thrust his sword into the creature's haunches.

The monster *wailed*.

I recognized that wail, but there was no time to contemplate.

The beast swiped out with one of its many claw-tipped legs and knocked the couple sideways as it rounded on the newcomer, our savior. Black blood leaked from the gaping wound by its flank. All the other prisoners in my wagon were either unrecognizable or unmoving, but I forced that observation out of my mind before it could immobilize me with fear. With the creature distracted, I had to *move*.

I dislodged myself from my attempted escape through the bars and climbed onto the bench, hoisting myself through the caved-in roof. My dress caught on the splintered wood, but with a few tugs, I cleared the jagged beams and dropped down onto the ground with a thud. A stabbing pain shot up through my right shin, like a thousand hot needles, and I buckled, rolling under the wagon and out of view.

I panted, testing the range of motion in my ankle as a battle was fought above. The ground felt cold and wet beneath me, and some of the beast's black blood had dripped down, slicking my hands. It was sticky as pitch and stung like hot oil, and I whimpered as I wiped it on a clean patch of grass, careful not to get any on my clothes. Then I shimmied backwards on my bum, out from underneath the wagon and away from the growing pool of sludge; from the new angle, I caught sight of the man with the flaming greatsword.

In his expert hands, the weapon arced in elegant flashes. He made it look like a dance, dazzling and graceful as he circled the fearsome monster, heaving his sword in precise but powerful blows. In the onslaught, the beast became agitated, snarling and snapping at him—but his footwork was surprisingly quick.

His self-assured bravery awed me.

Then it frightened me.

With a guttural cry, he ran straight for the beast, blade outstretched, black armor reflecting the blue fire so that he himself appeared aflame.

My heart lodged itself in my throat, strangling my warning: "Watch out!"

The creature swung at him with a huge paw, but at the last moment he dropped onto his hip, sliding under the beast's would-be blow, and lodged his blade deep into its chest.

It whined the same sound I'd heard two days prior, eerie and strange. Then it stumbled backward on its haunches, allowing the man to slide his sword free of its chest as it slumped onto its side, defeated.

The night around us paused, as if all the animals of the wood were holding their breath. The loudest sound became my own blood in my ears, my heart pounding furiously.

On shaky legs, I stood, pain lancing through my right ankle. All around me was wreckage. Blood, bodies, destroyed wagons—and a rotting, cloying reek on the wind. If it weren't for the shock that paralyzed me, I might've wept, or ran, or crumpled onto the flattened grass of this clearing—but my knees locked, keeping me rooted in place.

The monster slayer rose from the ground slowly, the dark waves of his hair obscuring his face. He raked it back with his fingers, assessing the scene as I had—only to pause when he noticed me. "You, there! Are you harmed?" he called out, circling round the beast to get to me—only to halt again when our eyes met.

His were blue-green—the color of the Wend.

Idris, my future killer, had just saved my life.

12

SONGBIRD

IDRIS

Two years ago, while Idris was tracking an abomination through the snowy wilds of the Bone Mountains, he happened upon a brown-speckled thrush. Idris hadn't recognized the small songbird at first, two months past time for its southern migration. It had seemed so out of place in the barren, icy peaks.

Anya was similarly out of place among the wreckage of the prisoner caravan, her pretty green dress streaked with mud and gore. Like the bird, she did not appear particularly delicate—just lost, as if she'd found herself in the wrong place at the wrong time. And like with the bird, Idris felt an odd twist of protectiveness in his sternum.

How in the Fates did she end up here?

She'd seen too much. *Far* too much. But he'd address that later.

Idris sheathed Halgren—flameless—at his hip and went to Anya, heart racing anew, questions on the tip of his tongue. But as he neared, she backed away from his advance, as if they were in some sort of anxious waltz, matching each other step for step.

Halting, he asked again, "Are you harmed?"

Wide-eyed, Anya merely stared at him, as if she were trying to come to some sort of conclusion but didn't have all the facts.

Perhaps she was in shock. It was a natural civilian response. While it was startling for Idris to see the monsters encroaching on civilization like this—despite the efforts of his Order to track and kill them without witnesses—he sometimes forgot how commonplace their existence was to him. How hardened he was to them.

"You're safe now," Idris said, but she didn't seem comforted. Idris glanced behind him, wondering if another abomination lurked—but, no, just the dead heap of the one he'd already slain. "You're safe," he repeated. He gestured back at the monster. "I assure you, it's dead."

Anya hobbled backward further—only to stumble and fall on her rump. "Don't come near me."

"You fear...*me*?" Idris realized aloud. Perhaps it was Halgren; after fifteen years with the Order of the Valiant, he'd grown accustomed to the sword's magic, powered by his Oath—but to the average townsperson, his flaming sword *was* quite threatening. "I promise I won't harm you. I'm here to help."

She crab-walked backward on the ground—dragging her right leg, Idris noted. "Please—just leave me alone."

The ferocity in her tone didn't sound like that of a woman overcome with shock—to Idris, she sounded fierce.

"What are you doing here?" he asked, gesturing at the wrecked wagons. "How did you end up in a *prisoner caravan*?"

She narrowed suspicious eyes on him—fierce, even from her place on the ground.

Two nights ago, she'd been running an inn in Waldron-on-Wend. What had changed in that time? Idris wracked his brain for clues, recalling their conversation and her offer for him to stay.

"The Mirrors," he stated.

She flinched.

Ah, so he'd guessed correctly. Which meant: "You were implicated in a crime."

"It's none of your concern," she bit out.

He huffed a silent laugh. He might've spent most of his time in the woods, but human nature remained consistent: it tended to face the exact thing it wanted to avoid.

"Seems like it *is* my concern," Idris replied. "Why else would you be wary of my mere presence, after a perfectly amicable interaction at your inn?" Those light brown eyes widened again, and he stalked forward, solving the mystery aloud. "You saw me in a Mirror," he said. "Was I the victim of your crime, and that's why they imprisoned you?"

"Would you fear me if I said yes?"

"Not necessarily," he answered honestly—not because he doubted her viciousness, but because his duty warped Fate in ways that could make it unpredictable.

"Do you not think me a formidable foe?" She almost sounded insulted.

He raised a brow. "Is that a warning not to underestimate you?"

"You should *never* underestimate me."

He rested a palm on Halgren's hilt, amused. "And where do I fall in your estimation?"

Their stares entered a standoff. Anya's was the first to run, her pretty brown irises darting off in the direction of the dark underbrush of the looming wood. *She's afraid of me*, he reminded himself, turning that nugget of truth over in his mind like a stone.

Realization cracked through his veins like breaking ice; for a moment, his blood turned cold. "You fear me because you saw me in your Mirror of Death," he whispered.

Though the work of his Oath rendered his Mirror visions unreliable, Idris gazed upon his Fortune and Death every year. It was a compulsion, an obsession, a fascination with the strange lies they told, of many deaths and one terrible Fortune. As long as he bore his Oath tattoo, he need not fear the Mirrors' visions, only take a disturbed sort of curiosity in them.

And disturbed, he was.

But even so, Idris could reliably guarantee: he killed monsters, not innocent women.

Her eyes cut to his again, blazing with inner fire. "Impressive deduction skills," Anya said bitterly. "I'm glad to know my killer isn't stupid."

He thought of the bird again. He'd kept it in his pocket for three months, feeding it small bugs and frozen berries until spring broke and its flock returned.

"I would never harm you," he swore.

"The Mirror said otherwise."

"Seems like it said otherwise about you, too," Idris retorted. "What sort of crime were *you* implicated in? One of Fortune? Or one of Death?"

Abruptly, her fire extinguished; she hung her head, shoulders trembling with a sob.

Death, then.

Affection twisted in his chest again—sweet and painful and perplexing. In the brief interactions he'd had with the innkeeper, he'd deduced that she was strong-willed and kind—two qualities he admired. *If* the Mirror of Death was right about her crime, he couldn't imagine it done in wickedness; she would have a good reason.

And if she had a good reason...

Idris balled his fists. It wasn't his job to judge her deeds; she needed to appeal to Lord Haron.

Idris glanced around at the gruesome mess in the clearing, feeling a bit like he'd stumbled into a diversion. He was a monster hunter, yet now he had this songbird to look after. But she was more than that, wasn't she? Not just a lost woman, but a prisoner of his Lord. Which meant her prospects weren't just a matter of Idris's morality, but his Oath. By all measures, it was his *duty* as a knight to escort her to the capital.

Shit.

He turned, making his way toward the abandoned camp. He rifled through saddlebags, packs, and bedrolls, eventually finding the items he sought: a canteen, the prisoner records—which he tucked into his pocket—and a set of keys.

Ignoring Anya's earlier attempts at evasion, Idris returned to where she sat and sank to his knees on the ground beside her. "Hold still," he said gruffly, gripping her wrist shackles and trying keys until he found the right fit for the lock. The cuffs squeaked open, falling to the grass with a clatter. She rubbed the reddened skin of her wrists, grimacing.

"Rinse your hands with this," Idris ordered, handing her the canteen and gesturing at the black abomination blood staining her palms.

She did as she was told, dribbling water onto her hands and rubbing off the grime with her thumbs.

Without delay, Idris got to work on her ankle chains, freeing her of those, too.

"Thank you," she managed softly.

He grunted, focusing next on her injured leg. He quickly palpated her calf, ankle, and foot, relieved when he found no obvious break. But now that they were face to face, he noticed her scent again: lemon and rose. Like a fresh breeze, it cut through the whiffs of sweat and dirt and the reek of the abomination at his back, clearing his head. The scent made him feel unburdened, in a wistful sort of way.

"Can you stand?" he asked, rising to his feet and offering a hand.

He was surprised when she took it, fitting her clean fingers in his calloused palm. He pulled her up easily, steadying her with his hand on her waist as she found her balance. She felt...soft in his grip—not just the silky texture of her bodice but the give of her body underneath. In a life of armor and steel and hard ground, his hands were unaccustomed to softness.

He let go.

Anya tested her weight on her ankle, wincing. "It hurts, but not terribly."

Idris stared down at her, imagining the past day through her eyes. A merry festival, worrying visions in the Mirrors, imprisonment, and the abomination's attack. The grime on her extravagant dress mapped her fraught endeavors. Her braids were in tatters, stray strands poking out of the plaits. But even with dirt smudged on her face, her features were pleasing, from her pert nose to her square jaw to her lips, of which the top was slightly, captivatingly fuller than the bottom—

"Idris?"

He cleared his throat, tearing his gaze away from her mouth and out toward the mess around them, frustrated by his own distractedness. He felt off-balance in her presence—and not just because of the uncommon interruption of company. He thought of the bird again, how it had been essential that he not become too attached.

"I need to tend to this," he said, his voice as splintered as the wooden beams of the wagons. "Why don't you get some rest while I clear the wreckage?"

"Don't we need to…?" She glanced around, giving up on her thought.

He recognized the crumpled posture of someone coming down from adrenaline. "You need not do anything tonight except sleep."

She stiffened, but before she could object, he walked over to the camp, collected an armful of unused logs scattered around one of the ash circles, and started a fire for her. While he worked, Anya pulled a modest rucksack from the wreckage, then hobbled slowly toward the heat. Gratitude, hesitation, and distrust shifted across her face like clouds across the moon.

"Knights don't murder innocent women in their sleep," Idris said, brushing off his hands. "I promise you'll know it if I'm trying to kill you." He hoped the joke would land.

Based on the way the left corner of her lip quirked up, he guessed it had. "I'm not innocent, remember?" she quipped, but her tone was tired—flat.

"Get some rest," he encouraged. "I'll keep watch."

Based on the dubiousness of her expression, she didn't trust him—he couldn't really blame her for that—but she moved toward the fire with outstretched hands, anyhow, seeking its warmth. No matter how seriously she took the vision in her Mirror of Death, no matter how hard she tried *not* to rest, Idris was confident that the adrenaline crash would knock her out soon enough.

He left her to her own devices, stalking back into the woods for his own gear, which he'd stashed in a log on his way toward the monster's commotion. When he returned to the clearing, he allowed himself a single glance in Anya's direction, pleased to see that she hadn't run but had curled up by the fire with her head on her pack.

Idris had a long night ahead, but something about the company enlivened him.

He wasn't sure whether that was a good sign or not.

13

A QUEST
BEGINS

ANYA

In spite of my best efforts to *not* fall asleep in the presence of my would-be killer, exhaustion had gotten the better of me.

I woke to cheerful birdsong, along with the clink and *thwap* of leather straps being fastened. I was still clutching the paring knife I'd found amidst the guards' cooking supplies; the joints in my hand creaked as I released the handle and pushed off the ground. My shoulders and chest muscles ached in protest, but despite the soreness of my body, I felt blessedly rested—almost hungover from the depth of my sleep.

It was embarrassing how quickly the warm fire and the adrenaline crash had swept me into the abyss of slumber.

Idris had kept his promise of not murdering me in my sleep, though. At least he had a sense of honor—and humor, dark as it was.

Perhaps I should've been surprised to run into him last night, but I wasn't. The mysteries I'd noted when he visited the Possum now made perfect sense. The armor. The Oath tattoo. The suspicious wound. His secretiveness and silent exit. What was more surprising was the existence of the grotesque monster he'd slain—but he'd seemed unfazed by that.

Familiar, even.

Sitting up fully, I took stock of my surroundings. A low fog filled the clearing, illuminated by sunlight. The grasses were gold, offset by the burgundy stems of wild rose bushes clustered around the edges of the hollow. Due to a slight undulation in the land here, I couldn't see the High Road, nor the wide valley that ran north to south alongside the Wend—but I could see the distant trees of the high eastern hills, spectacular red and orange foliage interrupting stoic green pines.

It was almost peaceful, if I ignored what I knew was behind me.

Yet when I turned, the wreckage and gore were...*gone.*

No more abomination. No more splintered wood. No more dismembered body parts. Even the grass—matted and muddy—appeared clear of the black slime and blood of last night. The only trace of what had occurred were patches of ash, and long drag marks leading into the Western Wood.

Fates, I must've slept like a fucking stone.

The crescent-shaped area between me and the edge of the forest was completely empty.

That is, except for Idris.

He stood with his back to me, fitting a saddle atop a tall draft horse. He coiled the leather strap of the cinch around one hand, fastening it tighter; the loose end slapped against the back of his wrist with a snap. The horse shifted, and he placed a big palm on its neck, calming it with gentle strokes. I hated that the hands destined to drown me were so...pleasing to watch.

And *capable*, judging by the overabundance of weaponry on his person.

His sword hung casually at his hip above black fitted trousers. Straps crisscrossed his shoulders and back in a harness that held more blades: knives of various sizes, plus a small axe. I wondered how often he used them all. His cloak, breastplate, and vambraces rested atop a rucksack nearby, and without their bulk on his body, I could plainly see the muscle beneath his loose-fitting black shirt. He wasn't lean like a ranger, nor functionally fit like the average knight; he was broad and powerful, burly like a...monster hunter.

I recalled our conversation at the Possum. *Are you a mercenary?* I'd asked. *Something like that,* he'd said, flashing me his tattoo.

"You're awake," Idris noted, swiveling toward me.

He sleeves were rolled up, showing off the veins in the backs of his hands and forearms. His puncture wound was bandage-less, still black but much improved; he must've been following Hattie's instructions with the salve.

"I'm awake," I confirmed, rising shakily to my feet; my right ankle was still sore, but I could put more weight on it compared to last night. "You found a horse?"

"His headstall was tangled around a branch not far off," Idris said. "I figured we'd make faster progress with a mount."

"Progress?"

He scratched the back of his neck in a manner that briefly drew my attention to his biceps. He'd tied his dark brown hair back, adding severity to the rugged bone structure of his face. His beard from the night of our meeting was gone, replaced by a day's worth of dark stubble; it shadowed his tentative half smile.

Hattie had been right. He *was* handsome. And considering he was my future maybe-murderer, I was an absolute *fool* to notice.

"I'm escorting you to your trial in Fenrir City," Idris said matter-of-factly.

All appreciation for his looks disappeared. "Absolutely not," I protested. "I'm going back to Waldron."

"And what do you plan on doing once you get there?"

"Running my inn," I said, but my conviction died with the words. Without Lord Haron's absolution, I'd be a fugitive; I couldn't run the Possum as a fugitive.

"If you go back to Waldron," he stated, "you'll return to jail, only to end up in another caravan." His smile was almost boyish as he added, "Traveling with me to Fenrir is preferable, no?"

"Not if you kill me."

His jaw ticked. "I already told you, I won't bring you any harm."

"But the Mirror—"

"Could be wrong," he finished. "Anya, I assure you, I have no nefarious intentions."

I ignored the flutter in my stomach at the breathy, patient way he'd said my name. "How can I be sure?"

"I would remind you that I did save your life last night. That has to count for something."

"You didn't know it was me until after the saving." I considered his offer. "This trip. What's in it for you?"

"If not the pleasure of murdering you?" He seemed amused.

I narrowed my eyes.

He handed me the horse's reins, then walked over to his pack to retrieve his breastplate. "It's my duty," he said. "All knights are, in one way or another, bound to protect the realm and its citizens. Seeing as the Mirror outed you as a vicious criminal, I can't in good conscience allow you to run free, wreaking havoc."

I folded my arms, scowling at his jibe, even as I wondered what sort of Order he belonged to.

Idris smiled, nestling the breastplate against his wide chest, his deft fingers making quick work of the buckles. The tooling around the plates's edges was surprisingly delicate, a silvery floral pattern etched into the black metal; it was unlike any other knight's uniform I'd seen.

With the ornate piece of armor in place, he returned to me, looking even bigger and more formidable. "Besides," he continued. "I have reports to deliver. I'm heading there anyway."

Monster reports? I thought grimly. Did the Lord of Fenrir already know about them? Idris certainly did, but was that what his Oath's duty pertained to? Questions piled like logs damming a river, rendering me silent.

"There's something you need to know before we depart." Idris fastened his silver vambraces onto his wrists, then pointed at the clearing. "What you saw last night—"

My heart leapt into my throat. "The monster—"

"*Bear*," he amended. "Rabid bear."

I shook my head. "I know what I saw, Idris, and that was no—"

"What you saw," he enunciated slowly, forcefully, "was a rabid bear. Nothing more."

I pursed my lips, considering the implications of what he was saying. In all my life, I'd never heard even a rumor about something resembling what I'd seen last night. It seemed Idris wanted to keep it that way, but *why*? Shouldn't people know about such horrors? Perhaps that's why Idris was going to the capital. To allow Lord Haron to decide what to do.

Idris took another step toward me, entering my personal space, and it took effort not to flinch at the pent-up energy radiating off him. Not threatening...but definitely not comforting. "Do you understand?" Idris asked.

I bit my lip, nodded. This close, I had to tip my chin up to meet his blue-green gaze.

Then my mind was racing, taking me back through the events of last night and the nights previous, the familiar whine of the "rabid bear" and the similar sound I'd heard the same evening Idris arrived at the Possum.

"Is Waldron safe?" I asked. "From...bears? I thought I heard one—"

"Let's just say I'm not the only bear hunter in these parts," Idris said. "Now, do you know how to ride a horse?"

"Of course, I do."

"Good," he said, turning away again.

I did *not* wish to travel with him, but he had a point: his company seemed preferable to being detained and imprisoned in another wretched caravan. At least I could keep an eye on my killer; perhaps even endear him to me and change my Fate, after all.

Reins still in hand, I held our horse steady as Idris fitted already-packed saddle bags, a roll of pilfered blankets, and both our rucksacks into place behind the saddle. In addition to burning the wagons and hauling the iron into the cover of the woods, he must've looted the camp while I slept, too. It was smart of him. Practiced, even.

Fates above, it was alarming how hard I'd slept to miss all that.

When he finished his preparations, he took a knee in front of me. It seemed for a moment like he was proposing, or perhaps offering some sort of fealty. I wasn't sure. With his head level at my sternum, he looked up at me through dark eyelashes, those riverlike irises catching the morning light. My gaze sank from his, catching on his full mouth, only to land on the thin black tattoo that ringed the base of his neck.

"Well?" Idris rasped.

I blinked, cheeks heating as I noticed he'd laced his fingers into a makeshift sling.

To give me a leg up.

Onto the horse.

"I'm assuming you need help up, what with all the..." He gestured at my skirts, which were indeed cumbersome. The draft was also quite tall, the horse's shoulder higher than the crown of my head. It was kind of Idris to help me up in this manner—to let me step on his hands, instead of hoisting me by the waist or bum.

"We're leaving *now*?" I asked, suddenly feeling quite physically and emotionally unprepared. "Can I—can I go off into the woods, first?"

Idris unlaced his fingers. "To run off?"

"No?" I said, drawing out the vowel in the hopes he'd get it.

He did not. "Why, then?"

"To"—my voice dropped to a whisper, as if that might make this less awkward—"do my business?"

"Oh." With slow effort, he rose to his full height again, towering over me. "Of course. Feel free."

I handed him the reins and scurried off into the woods to quickly relieve my bladder. Shrouded in the cover of the trees, I wondered if I ought to run off, after all—but aside from the fact that Idris would no-doubt hunt me down, I felt strangely *fine* in his presence. I didn't trust him, but didn't feel a warning twist in my gut, as I did around threatening customers at the Possum or when I had boarded the prisoner caravan and saw Beady Eyes.

That had to count for something.

When I was done with my business, I took a moment to wipe my teeth against my sleeve and re-braid my hair into one thick plait so the loose strands no longer tickled my neck. My dress was filthy with mud, grass stains, and red spots of blood that I didn't wish to ponder—but at least I hadn't gotten any of the beast's black sludge on it.

When I returned, Idris had donned his cloak and was loitering by the horse, his cheeks tinged the faintest mauve. "Apologies," he said when I neared. "I'm not accustomed to traveling with…"

"Women?" I supplied, as if my femininity were to blame for my basic needs.

"Anyone," Idris amended good-naturedly. "Now, a leg up?"

I nodded, gathering my skirts into a wad by my knees. Idris bent down again, and I stepped unsteadily into his palms with my left foot. He lifted me with surprising ease, and I gripped his shoulder—firm and warm, even beneath his cloak—with my non-skirt-holding hand, swinging my right leg up and over the horse's back.

I adjusted my seat, arranging my skirts into a bundle by the pommel. I probably ought to have changed into something less cumbersome, but the layers of my dress were warm and comforting.

Idris looped the reins over our mount's head and handed them to me. Then he stuck his foot into the stirrup.

"What are you doing?" I asked.

Idris paused. "Getting on?"

"We're riding…together?" When earlier he spoke about traveling together, I hadn't really considered what that meant.

"It's nearly a three-week journey to Fenrir City," Idris said, "do you really want to delay by having one of us walk?"

Before I could protest further, he swung easily up behind me. The horse shifted under the added weight, and I tugged the reins, keeping our mount still. Idris had found quite a large saddle, but it was still a tight fit with the two of us; the front of him pressed firmly against the back of me, seat to spine. I was glad his breastplate kept me from feeling the shape of his chest and torso underneath.

"You're not going to strangle me from behind, are you?" I asked, shifting awkwardly in the saddle, trying to alleviate a pinching sensation in my thigh.

"We'll find out, won't we?" The rumble of his voice was devastatingly close to my ear.

I tried not to shudder. "Very funny."

"I thought so."

"Don't Oaths prevent knights from lying?" I asked.

"I can't lie to my Lord," Idris drawled, "but I can lie to you all I want." Though he sounded positively devilish, his heart thudded quicker now that we were in such close proximity. I couldn't begin to guess why.

"That's not very reassuring," I said.

"Let's get one thing straight." His tone remained low, gusting over the shell of my ear, distracting my magic from the sound of his pulse. "My duty isn't to reassure you, or kill you, or befriend you. My duty is to escort you safely to Fenrir for trial. Got it?"

I jerked my chin in a quick nod.

When he spoke again, the intensity in his tone had dissipated, and he was back to his unique brand of congeniality—assured but unassuming. "Ready?"

"Yes," I choked out. "Do you want the reins?"

"I'll kick, you steer," he said, knocking his heels gently against the horse's sides.

I reined us toward the northeast, where the High Road snaked just beyond this secluded clearing. The draft horse's gait was long and languid, rocking us against one another. I could feel Idris's breath breezing against the back of my neck, warm enough to give me chills.

"What should we call the horse?" I asked, trying to distract myself from my own nerves and the sensation of the man behind me.

Idris seemed to consider my question seriously. "I'm not sure—but he does deserve a name, doesn't he?"

I stared down at the horse's wheat-colored neck and flaxen mane. A few light brown briars were tangled in the creamy strands, and I reached forward to pick them out. "How about Briar?"

"Briar," Idris repeated good-naturedly. "I like it."

And with that, our quest began.

14

OATH OF THE ORDER OF THE VALIANT

IDRIS

I dris would never forget the day he took his Oath. It had been springtime in Fenrir City, and uncharacteristically warm for the season. Lord Haron had a whole crowd of Oath-takers to get through, receiving the Oaths of each man and woman who knelt before him, then signaling for his squires to bequeath the customary magic-imbued armor and weapons.

Idris had snuck into the ceremony already wearing his brother's breast-plate, sweating profusely in the stuffiness of the chamber. The tall stained-glass windows that lined the long rectangular room emanated heat, casting colorful patterns on the marble tile. He kept his eyes down, waiting patiently in line as Oaths were taken, mouthing the words silently to himself.

I, Idris Togren, hereby take the Oath of the Order of the Valiant, pledging my life to the protection of the realm and the safe keeping of its secrets. I swear unyielding loyalty to the Lordship of Fenrir and the Kingdom of Marona. I will not stray from my duty; I will not falter from the Valiant path; I will not unveil that which seeks to fill the land with fear. I bear my duty with honor, compliance, and bravery.

By the Fates and the arcane power of this Oath, I swear fealty to the Order of the Valiant, never to forsake my duty except in the completion of my sentence or death, whichever comes sooner.

To the rhythms of the folks preceding him, Idris had mentally repeated the Oath some fifty times by the time he reached the front of the line. Staring at the Lord's spotless orange slippers—embroidered with pastoral scenes in red thread, with silly little bells on the toes—Idris had taken a knee to begin reciting.

But before he could speak, Lord Haron interrupted. "Where did you acquire that breastplate?"

Idris kept his eyes down, head bowed. "My brother, m'Lord."

"What is your name?"

"Idris Togren."

"Your name is not on my list."

Idris cleared his throat. "My brother's was—is—in the ledger," he stuttered. "Grinnick Togren."

"At ease," the Lord said.

Idris looked up at Lord Haron's face, almost childlike in its flawlessness. It was a face of high privilege. No sunspots or moles, no wrinkles or scars. His white-blond hair was perfectly styled in a swoop off his forehead. His overcoat was so laden with embroidery and gemstones it appeared uncomfortably stiff. Yet Lord Haron lounged comfortably in his chair, his hands at rest in his lap.

"Grinnick Togren," he mused, his shrewd voice carrying down the length of the chamber. The perfume he wore was an assault on Idris's nose.

Idris nodded.

Lord Haron gestured at a hooded figure to his left, who stood at a small podium that supported a thick arcane Oath Ledger, where members of the Order of the Valiant were magically tethered, recorded, and tracked. At the Lord's prompting, the ledgermaster flipped backward through the pages, presumably to find Grinnick's name. They eventually paused, hefted the book, and angled it toward the Lord to observe.

"It is as I suspected," the Lord murmured—presumably to himself—before waving a hand, dismissing the ledgermaster back to the podium. "I remember every name in my charge," he told Idris, not without a note of smugness.

Idris highly doubted that the Lord could remember the *thousands* of names bound to the Oath Ledgers, but he said nothing.

"The magic of this ledger," the Lord went on, "has not marked Grinnick as deceased, nor as having completed his sentence. Have you come to explain his whereabouts?"

"I've come to take his place."

"And why is that, *hmm*?" Lord Haron gestured at the podium with a callous-free palm. "Forsaking or breaking his Oath would've triggered the ledger's magic to record him as such."

"He is not an Oath-breaker," Idris ground out.

"Then where is he?"

"Dead." The force with which Idris said the word caused it to echo throughout the chamber, much as it had been echoing throughout the caverns of his heart since that fateful day.

"Oath Ledgers don't lie, Idris Togren," Lord Haron said, gesturing at the volume atop the podium. "If your brother were dead, he would be listed among the deceased."

Idris forced his gaze to hold firm. "He died in my arms."

The Lord shifted in his seat, eyeing him with more interest, now. "Breastplates are not passed down. Usually, they are lost. In rarer cases, they are brought by a fellow knight of the same Order to the royal forge to be repurposed."

Just the mere mention of the other knights in the Order of the Valiant had Idris clenching his fists.

"You say you were there when he died. What killed him?"

Idris couldn't bring himself to say.

"Never mind, I don't much care. But you *took* his breastplate, yes?"

"He gave it to me," Idris said, willing his voice steady. "It was Grinnick's dying wish that I take his place in the Order of the Valiant."

"*Ah.*" The Lord wagged a finger at him, putting pieces together. "The very act of telling you about the Order means that your brother *did* break his Oath—not by death or desertion, but defiance. That's the worst of the three." Lord Haron stroked his baby-soft chin and glanced at his ledgermaster. "*Curious* that the ledger didn't record death nor Oath-breaking."

The ledgermaster's dusky brown and gold robes shimmered faintly as they shifted on their feet. Their voice was reluctant, raspy. "Sometimes when the threads of magic are crossed, it causes an error in—"

The Lord waved a dismissive hand, clearly uninterested the particulars of how the Oath Ledgers worked.

He leaned forward, gripping the armrests of his throne. "You wish to take your brother's place *willingly*?"

"I do," Idris said.

Gasps rose from the crowd of other Oath-takers—but in his grief, it mattered not that Idris was about to enter one of the most dangerous and secretive Orders in the realm on his own accord. In fact, the threat made the dullness of his inner pain sparkle anew. He felt more alive now than he had since Grinnick died. To take his brother's place was to bring honor to his memory. To walk Grinnick's path was the only way for Idris to stay connected to his brother—and keep himself safe.

"I am pleased you feel that way. It makes this so much easier," the Lord said. "Rarely do I transfer criminal sentences, but these are extraordinary circumstances, aren't they?" He arched a brow expectantly.

"They are," Idris replied through clenched teeth.

Lord Haron's childish smirk was no better than the boys Idris had known growing up on the streets of Fenrir, boys who used to torment stray cats for fun. "Because your brother broke his Oath before a noble death could absolve him, and therefore did not suffer the proper consequences—all for *your* sake—it seems fitting to pass his full sentence to you," the Lord concluded. "Idris Togren, you are hereby sentenced to twelve years in the Order of the Valiant. Do you object?"

Idris's breath caught. *Twelve years*. His brother's full sentence.

When Grinnick died, he'd already served half his term. Idris would've expected to serve the final six, not the full twelve. But it was too late to object—and Idris didn't want to. Grinnick had encouraged him to take the Oath of the Order of the Valiant for a reason, and Idris was more than happy to oblige the urging of both his beloved brother and the Lord of Fenrir.

"I do not object," Idris said firmly, steadily.

"Wonderful." Lord Haron clapped twice, pointed at the ledgermaster—presumably to tether the magic by recording Idris's name.

Idris bowed his head again, reciting the Oath aloud this time, directly to the Lord of Fenrir's ridiculous shoes. As he spoke, he felt an odd pull toward the ledger, magic weaving between himself and its sacred pages.

When the Oath snapped fully into place, it was no more dramatic than a sneeze building and fading in the back of his sinuses. He felt a slight tingle along his neck as his magical leash formed into the customary tattoo that *all* knights—regardless of territory, Order, or the tenets of their Oath—bore.

While Oaths stemmed from the magic of the ledgers, they were tied to the territory for which a knight served. Lord Haron might've currently held Fenrir's ruling title—and therefore held all the knights' magical leashes—but the Oaths were ultimately sworn to the land, not the individual who controlled it. Idris was glad his Oath did not bind him to Lord Haron, specifically, but to the realm; the technicality of true fealty was a balm to his hot hatred for his new master.

As the odd sensation of his new tattoo eased, Idris was given vambraces and a hand-me-down sword—Halgren—by one of the nearby stewards and ushered into the lineup of other Oath-takers to await the Lord's final proclamation and the assignment of his training barracks.

Perhaps Idris should've been scared, but he wasn't; in his youth, Idris had already encountered plenty of hardship and suffering. At least as a Knight of the Order of the Valiant he'd be provided with resources, elite training, and a magic weapon. At least he could turn his guilt, grief, and misery into something useful.

Of course, back then, at barely twenty years of age, Idris hadn't fathomed the full extent of the Oath he'd taken that day. He'd reflected on it many times since then. His fellow Valiant Knights had questioned his sanity in those early days, but not once in the past fifteen years had Idris ever regretted his decision to take the Oath—and stay past his required sentence for further atonement.

Until now, he thought miserably.

Anya's full hips and rump rocked back against him with Briar's every stride, a sweet torture he hadn't experienced in all his years with the Order. The scent of her filled his nostrils with every inhale, bright and intoxicating. No matter how inappropriate it was to lust after a prisoner of the realm—one he was, by the honor of his Oath, responsible for depositing in Fenrir City—he couldn't find a way to master the thrill he felt at her nearness.

He was beginning to regret the horse, practicality be damned.

His Oath in no way hindered his freedom to take lovers, but he was forbidden from marrying, and given his isolated lifestyle, no self-respecting woman would tolerate his long absences and the secretiveness of his duty. He'd long since grown accustomed to a semi-celibate existence.

Now, however, he wondered if he'd simply been deluding himself.

Not that he thought of Anya as a potential lover. *Fates above*, after what she'd seen in the Mirror of Death, he felt guilty for even thinking about her in that way. No, the torture of this ride couldn't possibly be about *Anya* specifically, just...friction.

She wasn't impervious to the friction, either though. Reading her pheromones with his magic, Idris scented the faintest trace of... *Fates*. It was musky like desire, but sharper, almost agitated. The more he tried to understand it, the more confused he got, so he clamped down his magic and stared out across the rolling hills, jaw clenched.

"Please tell me you're hungry," Anya said, yanking him out of his wretched thoughts.

"Why? Are you?"

"Can't you hear my stomach grumbling?"

He hadn't noticed, what with his preoccupation with her scent. "There's jerky in my pack."

He twisted around, his leg pressing into hers and his breastplate pinching under his arms as he rifled through the exposed pockets of the saddlebags behind him. When he found the provisions he sought, he swiveled forward again, handing a few scraps of jerky over her shoulder.

He tore into his own meager bites, just for the distraction.

Anya snacked for a while in silence, then began to shift in the saddle, grinding uncomfortably against him. "*Ugh*, I'm uncomfortable," she complained. "I think my ass has fallen asleep."

Idris choked on his mouthful.

"Can we take a break?" Anya asked, leaning forward over the pommel in an effort to adjust. "You can't possibly be comfortable, either."

He wasn't, but: "The fewer breaks we take, the faster we get to the capital."

"What happens when we arrive, and I'm incapable of curtsying for the Lord because my legs don't work?"

"We'll rest at high noon," Idris said, pointing at the sun, which was still on the rise.

Anya tugged on Briar's reins, slowing their horse to a halt.

Idris knocked his heels gently against Briar's side, encouraging the horse forward.

Only for Anya to pull his reins again.

Idris was a Knight of the Order of the Valiant. Honorable. Dutiful. Therefore, he should *not* stoop to childish games. And yet—

He kicked his heels again.

She pulled.

He kicked harder.

Briar threw his head and stomped a foot, frustrated by the mixed signals.

"You're irritating the horse," Idris scolded.

"You're irritating *me*," Anya fired back. "Let me down."

"We aren't stopping," Idris said.

"Then let me *walk*."

"I'll walk," Idris countered.

"But *I'm* the one who's sore!"

"A gentleman shouldn't ride while a lady walks."

Anya barked a laugh. "*You*? A gentleman?"

Idris was mildly insulted. He might've been an urchin-turned-monster-hunter, but that didn't mean he didn't possess decorum—in fact, his background made him even more eager to prove his goodness. More than that, though, he didn't want Anya feeling threatened by him, thinking him uncouth.

"I think I've been perfectly kind so far," he protested, "what with the—"

"For the love of the Fates," Anya exclaimed, "would you *please* let me down? Else I'll be adding new crimes to my growing repertoire."

Idris sighed. He wasn't sure why he was acting so hurried. He supposed a noble knight would rush to the capital to share news of the encroaching monsters, but his haste wasn't just about duty. He was desperate to restore order to his life by getting Anya out of it.

Even so, it wasn't fair to take his frustration with his role out on her. He decided a gentleman wouldn't deny a lady, either.

Idris grunted. "Fine. Walk."

Anya needed no further permission. She swung her right leg over Briar's neck and slid to the ground. She landed with a thud and a wince, but stood tall, jutting her chin smugly up at Idris.

Idris settled into the cradle of the saddle with a sigh, grateful for the extra space—and relieved by the absence of her contact. The atmosphere was less heady without her so close, too. As much as he wanted to complete their journey efficiently, at least he was now free of the torture of her nearness.

Anya practically skipped down the road, clearly enjoying her freedom from his touch, too. Her dark auburn hair fired copper in the autumn sunshine, her tidy braid bouncing against her back with her cheerful gait. Her dress was still filthy, but she looked so...at ease, compared to the shell she'd been last night.

Her ankle must've been feeling better, too.

In spite of her irritable threats, Idris couldn't imagine her committing a crime of death, nor could he imagine her being found guilty—but Idris knew how the Mirror trials usually went.

He ought to put all that out of his mind, before his compassion made this trip even harder—but as he took up the reins and eased Briar into a slow walk, watching Anya frolic ahead of them, compassion crept in, anyhow. The weakness he'd felt building inside him in recent years only became more potent with her presence.

So what if her being on foot will slow us down? Idris thought indulgently. At least it would delay her inevitable sentence and his imminent return to his lonely charge.

15

FOOLISH COMFORT

ANYA

The day's journey took us over undulating hills, across modest valleys, through orchards and crop fields, and past livestock pastures. Though our path paralleled the Wend, the road and river were distant from each other, the water a mere strip of reflective blue to our right. Given what I'd seen in the Mirrors, I was glad it hadn't swung nearer to the High Road so far—it was hard enough being in such close proximity to the man Fated to drown me, even without the nearness of water.

After our long morning pressed together atop Briar, Idris and I took turns walking for the remainder of the day. He didn't seem to feel any particular way about riding together, but the closeness had grated on me—not just due to the normal discomfort of sitting in a cramped saddle for a long stretch of time, but the awful *pleasantness* of his strong body behind me.

I'd spent the entire time in that saddle cursing the Fates for making my would-be killer in any way alluring, and cursing *myself* for appreciating the gentle rocking of his armor-clad chest against my back and his hips against the base of my spine. It was ludicrous of me to fixate on the sensation, but it was impossible *not* to when my ass was pressed against him, and his heartbeat thudded against my magic in a steady rhythm.

I'd *had* to put some distance between us—so when he told me I couldn't walk, I'd gotten mad. The fact that he hadn't lost his temper but instead insisted on being a gentleman had only made me angrier. How dare he complicate matters by being *nice*? I still couldn't reconcile the man I'd seen in my Mirror of Death with the man I'd teased at the Possum, who traveled with me now.

Flustered was at the bottom of the list of things I should've been feeling. I should've felt heartbroken by Remy's callous rejection. I should've been terrified of the uncertainty ahead. I should've felt threatened by Idris. Yet there I was, enjoying Idris's presence in spite of it all. His calm and capable attitude throughout the aftermath of the attack and up through our first day of travel had been comforting in a way Remy had never been.

My would-be killer, a *comfort*.

Oh, I was frustrated with myself. I was not a frivolous woman, nor a romantic one, but apparently my foolishness made up for my lack of more whimsical flaws.

Walking was the only way I could escape my own raging stupidity, so walk, I had, until my feet ached and blisters formed. Then Idris—annoyingly astute—had suggested he walk while I ride. And so our mostly-silent travels had unfolded, switching places atop Briar until the sun sat low and a thick fog clung to the ground.

We made camp just as the light was fading, setting up in a stand of alders not far from a shallow offshoot of the Wend. While Idris fed and watered Briar, I wandered north along the stream in search of a private place to wash up. This was the farthest from Waldron I'd ever been, and each step felt both mundane and monumental.

Perhaps the shock of last night was making me sentimental; I wasn't sure the full reality of the gore I'd witnessed had fully sunk in yet.

With my pack slung over one shoulder, I found a mossy bank out of sight but still within hearing distance of Idris's soft mutterings. As I plunked down on the spongey ground, tugging off my boots, I lifted my magic in his direction, curious to hear what Idris had to say to our intrepid mount.

It turned out to be sweet nothings, mostly: about the shine of Briar's coat, the softness of his nose, his amiable demeanor, and how well he stood to be untacked and have the stones picked out of his feet. The one-sided conversation was dangerously endearing, so I plunged my feet into the icy stream and started scrubbing.

The night was fully upon us when I returned to camp refreshed and wearing one of the spare outfits Hattie had provided, a practical gray-blue woolen tunic with heavy underskirts. I sat on a log by the fire Idris had built, allowing the flames to banish the damp chill from my skin. Two small pots were nestled in the coals, one simmering with rose hips in water and the other burbling the warm aroma of spiced porridge and mushrooms. He'd already laid out our bedrolls, too; I noted that they were a respectful distance apart, one on either side of the fire.

Nothing was as homey as the Possum, but compared to a prisoner caravan, this...wasn't bad.

"Tea?" Idris asked, not looking at me as he crouched close to the fire and stirred the porridge. "You're welcome to help yourself."

So my future killer was thoughtful, too. *Great.*

A pair of mugs rested on the other end of the log, a sprig of mint inside each. I lifted the simmering pot off the fire and tipped it over one mug, then the other, spilling a bit as I clumsily poured the boiling water over the leaves. When the rose hips sloshed too hard into the second mug, it wobbled unsteadily, and I reached out to catch it before it fell—only to pour the boiling water directly onto my hand.

White-hot pain blazed over my skin, and I drew back, letting the mug and pot fall to the dirt as I yowled. "Fuck!"

Idris rose to his full height in an instant, startled by my outburst.

The back of my hand was already bright red, a streak of welts forming across my knuckles. I shook it as if that would dispel the sting, hissing through my teeth.

"You alright?" Idris asked, but I was already stomping off toward the stream to plunge my inflamed skin into the cold water.

By the time I got back, Idris had dealt with the upturned mug and laid out a meager medical kit. He was still standing as I walked up, concern etched into his features.

"How bad is it?" he asked.

"It's fine." I cringed.

He took a step closer. "May I see?"

I held out my hand, and he winced. "Here—" He swiveled toward the supplies, but I didn't want his help.

"I can do it," I interrupted.

He wavered. "I know you *can*, but—"

"I *will* do it," I amended. "Sorry about the tea."

He considered me for a moment. We stood a full stride apart, but given his height, he practically *loomed* over me. He'd removed his breastplate, weapons, and cloak. The laces at the collar of his shirt were undone, revealing the dark ring of his Oath tattoo and the harshly etched lines of his upper pecs.

The light of the fire cast shadows on the side of his face, illuminating the faint sheen of sweat on his forehead and catching on the vertical crease that formed between his eyebrows. He looked, for a moment, like he might argue—then his expression smoothed, becoming almost indifferent as he gestured at the remaining mug. "You can have it," he said, then went back to stirring the porridge.

Air gusted out of my lungs, and I plopped onto the log beside the bandages and salve. The little jar he'd set out was Hattie's, her handwriting on the label immediately recognizable. Come to think of it, *all* the supplies were from Hattie. For Idris's wound.

As he poked at the fire, I noticed the black streaks on his wrist were almost completely gone. Almost.

"Don't you want to save this for your infection?" I asked, lifting the jar of salve. "Hattie was specific in her instructions."

Idris didn't glance back. "I can spare it."

Yet another act of contradictory kindness.

I unscrewed the top of the jar and gave the salve a sniff. It smelled sweet, botanical—just like Hattie. Sudden tears pricked the corners of my eyes, and my injured hand lifted to my chest, feeling for the labradorite pendant tucked underneath my tunic. I missed my friend. I hoped she and Wicker were managing all right without me. The town, too.

I sniffled as I lathered a small bead of salve across my knuckles, then wrapped my hand in one of the fresh bandages to keep it clean. I was still struggling to tie the ends one-handed when Idris lifted our meal off the fire.

He sat on the opposite end of the log, a good three feet away. He arched a single brow as he watched me fiddle with the fabric. I felt silly and helpless under his gaze—not exactly the impression I wanted to give the man destined to murder me. He gave me another thirty seconds of fumbling before he grunted frustratedly, rose from the log, and lowered to his knees in front of me.

Wordlessly, he held out one big hand, face-up. I curled my injured hand against my chest, staring at the callouses and creases that roughed his palm. There was so much *life* written across his skin. So much experience.

It might've been a small thing, to give him my hand, but I *really* didn't want to undergo his touch more than I had to. To accept even a nominal amount of help from my future murderer felt...vulnerable. I already feared how *unafraid* of him I was, and given our tangled circumstances, his generosity only worsened my confusion.

"Don't be stubborn," he grumbled impatiently. "Let me do this for you."

16

FRAYED NERVES

ANYA

Even as he knelt in the dirt, Idris's expression was open—probably more patient than I deserved. It occurred to me that even a reluctant amiability between us would make our three-week quest far more bearable—so, with a resigned sigh, I held out my hand.

Idris's fingers grazed my wrist, featherlight in their search for the ends of the bandage. My eyes rose to the cobalt sky as he removed the fabric, realigned it across my burned knuckles, then wrapped it snugly and tied it in place. It took all of fifteen seconds, but with my eyes trained on the stars, I felt every brush of his skin against mine. His touch was gentle, perfunctory, but sent my nerve endings scattering.

"There," he said when he was finished. "Was that so hard?"

My gaze slid back to his. "Nothing about any of this is *easy*."

He chuckled. "Fair point."

His amusement shook some of the tension loose in me. At least we were both on the same page about our quest together being...fraught.

Idris stood and began packing up the spare bandages and salve. As I watched his injured hand gather up the supplies, a soft laugh of bemusement escaped me.

"What?"

I pointed at his wound. "We match."

"Your left and my right," Idris noted dryly. "Between the two of us, we have one functional set of hands."

"We're quite the pair," I said without thinking, then pinched my lips together with my teeth.

Idris didn't respond to the awkward comment. He dished up dinner in silence, then returned to his side of the log—far from me. "I only have one bowl," he said. "I did find an extra spoon, though." He handed both to me, then took up his own spoon and began eating straight from the cooking pot.

The fire crackled. Briar snorted. Wind rattled the branches of the trees. If I didn't think too hard about why I was out here, the night was almost peaceful.

Following Idris's lead, I dug into my supper. The porridge was surprisingly tasty. He'd seasoned it well, with warming spices like clove and ginger, along with a sweet flavor that complimented the mushrooms' earthiness. In between bites, I sipped the tea, relishing the sharpness of the rose hips and the freshness of the mint.

By the time I was halfway through the meal, I felt more like myself than I had in *days*, the warmth of the food and fire mending my frayed nerves.

Idris still seemed tense, though. Weary.

"This is really good, Idris. Thank you," I said—a peace offering after my cold countenance earlier.

He merely grunted.

"You must have taste magic," I continued. "The flavors are so well-balanced. What gives it the sweetness?"

"Maple syrup."

"Excuse me?"

At that, he glanced up. "Have you not had maple syrup?"

I shook my head. "Never heard of it."

Abruptly, he stalked over to where his rucksack rested by his bedroll. He pulled out a small bottle, uncorked it, and held it out to me.

I took it, careful not to touch his fingers in the tradeoff. I lifted the bottle to my nose. It smelled nutty and sweet.

"Go on, have a sip," he prompted.

I did—just a small one, but delightful, the thick liquid coating my tongue. It reminded me of honey, but better.

"Decadent." I handed the bottle back to him. "Where did you get it?"

Tucking the bottle away again, he then returned to his place on the log, lowering himself slowly—stiffly. "I made it," he said. "It's a northeastern delicacy. I learned about the process during my training—" He faltered. "Up in Porkirk." Seeming to want to skim past whatever he'd been about to say, he continued quickly. "In winter, you hammer a metal tap into the tree, and it leaks out a thin sap, which can be boiled down into a syrup."

It was the most he'd said to me unprompted since this morning. The conversation felt almost...normal.

"And to answer your question," Idris went on, "I possess scent magic, but it still translates well to cooking, as you might guess."

Scent magic. While everyone possessed one heightened sense, each individual's skill with their magic varied. In rare cases, scent magicians could not only discern fragrances with ease, but also pheromones. I hoped Idris wasn't the latter. It would embarrass me to no end to know that he could smell my fear—and other base urges.

I took another bite of porridge, feigning nonchalance. "I'm impressed. Although—Hattie could tell you—I'm not much of a cook, myself. It's why she manages the kitchen at the Possum."

While this morning my determination to clear my name and return home as soon as possible had motivated me, now, the thought of the Possum and Waldron filled me with a subdued, anxious yearning. Perhaps the long day had worn me down, and another sound sleep would restore my optimism.

But as we returned to silence—with only the snapping of the fire, the soft snuffling of Briar snacking on leaves in the underbrush, and the scraping of our spoons occupying the space created by the lull in conversation—dark thoughts crept in. It'd been easy to put the horrible monster out of my mind in the daylight, but now, the memory of last night's terrors clung to my cloak like the fog.

I looked at Idris, hoping more chit-chat would banish my rising fear, but he was focused on his meal, seemingly lost to his own musings. Usually, I found it easy to engage with others—to make small talk and ask questions and banter playfully. I loved the flow of good dialogue, the sparks of intrigue in getting to know someone. Behind the bar at the Possum, conversing came naturally—but I didn't possess the same dynamic here in the woods. This wasn't my domain; I wasn't in control.

Idris wasn't making this any easier, either. Tipsy guests were far simpler to engage than a stoic knight.

Still, his quietude wasn't agitated, just broody. Anyone who sweet-talked horses and carried around syrupy delicacies seemed unlikely to be a cold-blooded killer; he had a gentleness about him that was at odds with the Mirror of Death. Perhaps it was strange to try and befriend him, but friendliness had a way of softening edges—maybe even enough to alter Fate.

I tried again.

"My magic is hearing," I offered.

Idris's gaze remained trained on his porridge. Clearly, he'd exhausted his conversation for the day on maple syrup. But I was undeterred.

"It's not just a heightened sense for me, though," I went on. "I also possess the rare secondary ability of sound suppression and amplification."

His nod was the only proof he'd heard me. His resistance to my chit-chat only made me want to get a rise out of him more.

"Do you always speak to horses, or is Briar the sole recipient of your praises?"

That got him to look up. "You heard me?"

"Don't be embarrassed. We should all be so lucky as to receive mushy compliments from time to time."

"I'm not embarrassed," Idris said. "Just surprised you heard from so far away."

"As I said, my magic is sound. Lends itself to eavesdropping."

"I'll keep that in mind next time I want to sweet-talk the horse," Idris said wryly, returning to his meal.

I set my bowl aside. "So what's with the blue fire sword?"

He dropped his spoon into the pot with a clatter, then frowned down at it like it'd fallen into his dinner on purpose. Wiping some of the goo off the handle, he muttered, "Halgren."

"Huh?"

"My sword's name is Halgren."

"Swords have names?"

"Mine does," he said, taking a huge bite of porridge.

"I suppose if it glows blue fire, it deserves a name," I remarked.

He didn't acknowledge that.

"Is it magic, then?" I shook my head. "What am I saying? Of course it is. But what kind of magic? I didn't know weapons could be imbued with power."

He kept eating, clearly unwilling to answer.

"Must come in handy when fighting monsters," I needled. "That's what you do, right? Fight monsters? It explains your visit to the Possum with that gruesome wound, and your appearance at the caravan. And seeing as you didn't seem like you were about to piss yourself with horror last night, it must've been something you've seen before."

Idris stood. "Finished?" he asked, gesturing at my bowl.

"Not quite," I said, cradling it again.

Wordlessly, he carried his pot off toward the stream for washing.

Alone in the dark, I stared into the underbrush after him. Talk of monsters made me suddenly hyperaware of the possible existence of *more* of them. My magic flared, listening intently to Briar's contented nibbling, the steady trickle of the stream, and Idris's returning footsteps.

"Will you say *anything* about last night?" I asked when he reappeared in the firelight.

He tucked the clean pot into his rucksack. "No."

"*Can* you say anything about last night?"

He continued rummaging around in his pack without answer.

"A gentleman would comfort a lady, after such a disturbing sight."

"I told you this morning, it's not my job to reassure you." One corner of his mouth kicked up—the bastard. "Besides, I thought I wasn't a gentleman?"

"You seemed concerned with being one earlier," I said tightly. "Figured I'd give you a tip."

He pulled a small flute out of his pack and sat on the log again. "Noted."

A mix of anger and unease swirled through me, but I didn't want him to see the extent of my emotion, so I folded my arms across my chest and stared at the fire.

Idris lifted the flute to his lips and began to play a slow, wistful tune. The notes were crisp and lilting in the quiet night. His deftness with the instrument surprised me. While I didn't recognize the melodies, I found them lulling, my agitation gradually easing from my shoulders until my eyelids began to droop.

After a few songs, I gave in to my weariness. I laid down on my bedroll, tucking myself inside the thick blanket. I stared up at the night sky, watching the stars twinkle. Idris continued playing until the fire diminished to coals, then stalked off to wash my bowl. All the while, I listened to his movements; he seemed so mindful and at ease out here in the countryside. Far more comfortable than he'd been seated at my bar.

When he settled down for the night, I swiveled onto my side to regard him across the flickering embers. Without supper or music to occupy my mind, harrowing flashes from yesterday began to encroach on my mind like shadows encroaching in the absence of our campfire.

"Do we need to worry about...*them* tonight?" I whispered.

Idris's hulking shape turned toward me, mirroring my position. "No," he answered.

"Is that really all you'll say?" I asked, allowing the true depth of my worry to reach my tone. It felt vulnerable to admit I was scared, but it also felt vulnerable to be out here at all. I feared what I'd seen last night far more than I feared Idris.

"I can't—" He broke off. Restarted. "Can't say much. But we're safe. You can trust me."

"'Trust me,' says my killer," I quipped, even though his confidence in our safety did ease my worry a bit. He'd obviously faced many foes; surely, he'd survived for a better reason than mere luck.

"I am not your killer," he insisted.

"What makes you so sure? You've only seen a sliver of how truly irksome I can be."

He chuckled at my joke, and the sound made me smile. "I'm sure," he said.

"How, though?" I asked, propping myself up on an elbow. "How can you be so confident in your contradiction of *Fate*? How can you appear in my Mirror of Death and walk free unreported, when I appear in someone else's and am imprisoned? How can—"

A sigh gusted out of him. "Anya, I can't speak freely about these things."

"About killing me?"

Silence.

"About *monsters*, you mean?"

"Bears," he insisted gravely. "Rabid bears."

"What do 'rabid bears' have to do with you appearing in my Mirror? With a *knight* being exempt of Fated murder?"

"They have no Fate," he said—then sat up abruptly, coughing as if a strong spice had suddenly hit the back of his throat.

"I'm going to need you to elaborate."

"Can't," he choked.

"Won't?"

He heaved a breath, settling his coughing fit. "Can't."

Was that...his *Oath* preventing him from speaking?

It was a well-accepted fact that citizens were not permitted to know the exact tenets of Oaths—not even for the most famous Orders—but the public knew enough to understand that Oaths were spun from powerful binding magic.

That seemed like a logical explanation for Idris's apparent limitation in speech.

"Monsters...have no Fate," I mused.

The very *idea* of that disturbed me—deeply. The Fates were as natural as the seasons. As the sun and the moon. Soil and water. To be disconnected from Fate was to be...unnatural. Unpredictable. *Lawless*.

"But you aren't a monster," I said.

"Thanks."

"*Idris*—"

"To interact..."—he paused meaningfully, swallowed—"can warp one's Fate."

Proximity to monsters warped Fate? That explained my cellmate's insistence that the abomination wasn't how he was *supposed* to die.

"Is warping the same as a Fate that isn't fixed?"

I took his silence as a *no*.

"That's how you're exempt, then," I concluded. "That's how you can guarantee you won't—"

"With a Fate like mine, nothing is guaranteed."

"So you're saying you *could* kill me, after all?"

"Anya," Idris said exhaustedly. "Get some sleep."

17

AFRAID OF THE
DARK

ANYA

In my dreams, real memories turned into strange, altered visions. Wagons stained with blood and gore. Wood cracking and pained screaming and the bone-chilling whine of the monster. Red eyes narrowing on me. Maw dripping crimson. A male voice—*Idris's* voice—coming from the grotesque creature's thin lips to utter the words of my cellmate: "You have quite the mouth on you, don't you, love?" A snarl. "What else can it do?"

A shout tore loose from my throat, and I shoved off the ground, clutching at the firm body that hovered over me. My fingers curled against the open neckline of his shirt, my knuckles grazing warm skin. In my lingering terror, I buried my nose in the hollow of his throat, nuzzling close, seeking safety. A huge arm banded around my back, tugging me consolingly nearer. When I melted against him, his breath hitched.

"Anya." Idris's voice was all gravel, hot against my neck.

Idris.

Fuck.

I pushed against the hard chest I'd just been clinging to and scrambled backward on the ground, horrified that I'd just sought comfort in the arms of *him*. "Get away from me," I choked out, but it was the nightmare still crowding my vision that made my wrists tremble. Wild-eyed, I searched the forest behind Idris, half expecting a monster to leap out of the darkness.

Idris reached out again, gripping my upper arms so hard I thought they might bruise. Those blue-green eyes were wide in the moonlight. "Anya, you're fine.

You were having a nightmare," he said, shaking me a little, returning me fully to reality. "Deep breaths."

Sweating, panicking, I panted through my teeth, puffs of hot air curling into the cool night air. Having my killer this close wasn't helping me calm down. "Let *go*," I demanded, wrenching myself free.

He released me, holding his hands up in surrender. "Alright," he said. "Alright. Just *breathe*."

Fingers gripping the dirt at my sides, I forced a shaky inhale, then exhaled.

"Good," Idris said. "Keep going."

I breathed again, compelling my lungs to move slowly, even as my heart thundered in my ears. Gradually, as the panic subsided, I began to take in my surroundings again. The rumpled blankets of my bedroll. The ashen circle of our spent campfire. Briar tied to a nearby tree, ears swiveled toward us. And Idris, kneeling before me, his shirt askew on his shoulders but his features calm.

My hands relaxed, palms flattening on the ground.

It was just a nightmare.

I slumped, covered my face with my filthy hands, then began sobbing. Chest-quaking, uncontrollable sobs. Through the pitiful sounds I made, I heard the scuff of boots, Idris shifting his weight.

"I'm not going to touch you," he said. "I just want to...reassure you." His tone was wry.

"I thought reassuring me"—my chest convulsed—"wasn't your job."

"Yeah, well. You're keeping me up."

I lowered my hands. "Sorry to interrupt your beauty sleep with my terror."

"You think I'm beautiful?"

I glowered at him.

"There are no threats nearby, just so you know," Idris said. "Listen for yourself if you don't believe me." He rose and wandered back to his side of the fire circle, where he laid on his back.

I wanted to debate him, to point out that—according to Fate—*he* was my greatest threat. But then my gaze fell to the jut of his collarbones in his supine position, the tattoo at the base of his throat. I'd pressed my nose there just moments ago; he'd smelled like smoke and pine and the heady salt of sweat.

Last night, fearing his presence, I'd slept with a knife; tonight, I'd reached for him and had been soothed. *Get it together, Anya.*

I pulled myself off the ground, straightened my blankets, and slipped beneath their warmth again. A shaky sigh slipped out of my lips. I had no idea how I was supposed to sleep in the wilderness after what I'd witnessed.

"You can talk," Idris said, "if that helps."

"Not sure it would."

"Why not? You seem to like the sound of your own voice."

Annoyance flared in my sternum. "I like *conversation*," I argued. "*Mutual* conversation."

"I'm trying to help."

"By insulting me?"

"By distracting you."

I ground my teeth, irritated that his strategy had worked. "Maybe I'm not used to accepting help."

"From strange knights?"

"From anyone." I didn't like to feel indebted. Help always came with strings attached—my mother had taught me that—and Idris and my strings were already tangled enough. "I don't like to be a burden."

"It sounds like you don't like to be vulnerable."

I pressed my lips together, fighting a growl. "Contrary to the evidence of this quest of ours," I said, "I am not a helpless damsel."

"I didn't say you were," Idris replied. "We have a mutual interest in traveling to Fenrir. I have wilderness skills. It's only fair that I share those skills as we travel together. That's not a burden, that's just the facts of the matter."

"Are you always so practical?" I asked.

He chuckled. "Yes."

A pause spread between us, in which the sounds of night encroached: the squeak of bats, the creak of swaying trees, the rustle of a raccoon in the distant underbrush. My mind pulled toward darker images, imagining the mundane sounds as belonging to scarier beings. My heart kicked up, and I forced more deep breaths, riding the wave of fear as it rolled through me and subsided.

"I'm sure once we make it to the next settlement, your skills will take center stage," Idris said, drawing my attention once again. There was a note of teasing in his resonant voice.

"What exactly do you think I'm skilled at?" I asked dubiously.

"Making connections." He wasn't goading me this time—he was serious.

And he was *right*. I thought of Waldron and all my many beloved connections, relationships with friends and neighbors that I had worked hard to foster. But while I loved them deeply, genuinely, there was also a desperate fear in me that drove my craving for close bonds.

My mother had taught me the importance of connections. Her parents had cast her out for being an unmarried, pregnant burden, and yet Waldron had taken her in. After how the town had rallied around her before I was born, we were both indebted to Waldron's generosity, and had done all we could to show our gratitude over the years. We'd pulled all-nighters with the farmers during lambing season, helped repair the rotted-out boards of Waldron's fishing docks, dredged flooded wheat fields, and my mother had even filled in at the school when Whitney, the head teacher, had her baby.

It made us feel important to be at the center of the town's happenings, to pitch in.

Then my mother died, and my honorary grandmother, Aldah—the Possum's original owner, who'd taken my mother in when she came to Waldron—became my caretaker. Just as with serving my many neighbors, the purposefulness of helping Aldah run the Possum became yet another a buoy in my sea of grief. Even when the waves of my deepest sorrow calmed, that sense of purpose had remained.

When Aldah joined the Fates two winters ago, the town had rallied around me once again, further indebting me to their kindness. The philosophy of service that my mother had instilled in my childhood became my guiding light in adulthood. A reminder of her memory; a continuance of her gratitude; proof of my love for Waldron.

"Connection isn't a skill," I said, "it's an act of survival."

Idris snorted. "So is starting campfires, hunting, and everything else I do."

I touched the pendant at my chest, my mind lingering in Waldron. I'd used my folded cloak as a pillow, and my mother's heart-shaped pin was a cool imprint against my cheek. Precious items, made even more precious by distance.

"Want to try sleeping again?" Idris asked, misreading my pensiveness.

"I'm not sure I can, after what I saw," I said. "Every time I close my eyes…" I shivered.

"Have you always been afraid of the dark?"

"No, never," I said, nestling deeper beneath my blankets and staring up at the vast spray of stars overhead. "In fact, I love the night. Especially at this time of year."

Idris folded his hands behind his head. "Tell me more."

I knew what he was doing—still distracting me from my nightmare—but I welcomed the respite, now. "For starters, my birthday falls on Astrophel."

"Two months away," Idris noted.

"I'll be thirty."

He offered a low rumble of acknowledgement. "That explains some things."

I chose to ignore the topic of my fixed Fate, and was grateful when Idris did, too.

"Naturally, Astrophel is my favorite holiday," I went on, smiling as I allowed myself to get swept away by happier topics. "It's also Waldron's most cherished festival. We celebrate for an entire week, night after night of merriment and togetherness. There's a craft market and apprenticeship fair, lantern-lit boat rides on the river, and nightly bonfire dances, plus a myriad of foods only made for the occasion—special herbed chèvre and sausage rolls, snowflake candies, and spiced fermented cider—all culminating in an all-night party to celebrate the longest night of the year."

Idris was quiet for a beat, and I half expected him to call the festival silly and quaint, as Remy had, but when he spoke again, his tone was reverent. "That sounds wonderful, Anya."

"It really is."

When I was a girl, my mother had worked her way up to become one of the lead organizers of the festival—yet another act of service to the town. Some of my fondest childhood memories were of braiding rosemary into my hair and dancing with my friends around the fires; kissing my first love, Peregrine, behind one of the craft tents, the taste of cloves on his lips; and following my mother as she darted between tents, checking on each vendor, knowing everyone by name.

In adulthood, I found myself drawn to the sense of importance that came with being a part of the orchestration of good cheer. I still had all the ornaments my mother and I had selected from the craft tents, baubles we hung on our bed frames as tokens offered to the Fates, in hopes they might answer our dreams for the coming year.

"My mother used to claim I was given the gift of hearing because of the music during Astrophel," I told Idris. "Apparently, I heard the drums from the womb and began kicking wildly. She said I came early because I wanted to hear the music for myself."

"I believe it," Idris said.

I glanced over at his profile. "Have you ever been to a proper Astrophel celebration?"

"No," he said. "I grew up in Fenrir City. Astrophel isn't as big a deal there as in the townships."

"I've never been to the capital, but somehow I still can't picture you in a city."

He laughed. "City life never suited me."

That seemed like an understatement.

"Well, if you end up *not* murdering me, you ought to attend Astrophel in Waldron," I said proudly. "Nothing beats a small-town festival."

Seconds passed, and it dawned on me that I'd just invited him to my hometown. *Idris.* Drowner. Veritable stranger. Knight of a secret Order. I *really* needed to get some sleep—get my head right. Cringing, I waited for Idris to rebuke the ridiculous idea.

But then he lowered his hands from behind his head and regarded me across the dark expanse between us. "Careful, Anya. I might just take you up on that."

18

THE RIVER

ANYA

The following three days unfolded similarly. We crisscrossed through end-less farmland and fallow fields, over rolling hills and down through pretty valleys. We slept in secluded glens, the evenings sparkling with starlight and frost. We shared Hattie's salve until both our injuries had faded. Idris and I took turns atop Briar, silent in the sunshine, then—after dark—sharing stilted conversation over supper. Nightmares plagued my slumber, but I didn't wake up screaming again, and if Idris was aware of my tossing and turning, he didn't comment.

On our fifth day, the sun slipped behind a large cloud bank, the light dim-ming and the wind picking up. Though Briar was a gentle giant, he was still a prey animal, and without a herd, he grew antsy and insecure in the wild weather. Our progress was therefore slowed, which in turn tipped Idris from taciturn to downright irritable.

By midday, all three of us were tense. The High Road—barely a two-carriage muddy track in this pastoral part of the Fenrir Territory—hooked right, bring-ing us at last to the River Wend.

I heard the river before I saw it. Up until now, we'd been traveling on the western side of the Wend; as we came out of a thin forest of alders, it seemed the road was meant to cross the river and continue northward on the eastern side. But the old stone bridge ahead was crowded with village folk, a carriage blocking our way.

From my elevated view atop Briar, I craned my neck to see what the commo-tion was about. The carriage was tipped harshly to one side.

"Broken wheel?" Idris asked from his limited viewpoint on the ground.

I stood up in the stirrups. The back wheel of the carriage was not broken, but in fact had fallen *through* a huge crumbling hole in the stone. There was no way to cross the bridge; the carriage was angled such that the narrow pathway was completely blocked.

"Broken bridge," I told Idris.

He tugged Briar forward, grumbling as we approached the scene.

Eight people were unloading goods from the carriage and transferring them to a wagon on the far side of the river, where a team of horses waited impatiently. Briar whinnied to his fellows, announcing our arrival. A few of the villagers looked in our direction, but none paused in their efforts.

"Hello there!" I called. "Do you need assistance?"

An older gentleman leaned over the stone railing of the bridge, peering at us from around the blockage. "No, no, we have it well in hand! Though it'll be another hour 'til we get this cleared—and even so, this bridge is as good as no bridge at all."

"Is there another bridge nearby?" Idris asked.

"Five miles south," the man answered. "But it's safe to cross 'ere, especially on that draft. The riverbed is shallow enough."

Idris looked over his shoulder at me. "Looks like we'll have to share Briar across."

I eyed the Wend's slow-moving waters. Its surface reflected the turbulent gray sky, reminding me of the Mirrors. When I glanced at Idris again, my Fated death flashed across my vision.

"You take the saddle, I'll ride behind," I said, scooting up and over our saddlebags to seat myself on Briar's rump. While I could easily squeeze into the saddle as we had on our first day, the river made me want to keep my distance—even if that meant just putting some gear between us.

Idris stared at me for a moment but didn't object. I leaned back, giving him ample room to swing his leg over the saddle. Then he gathered Briar's reins and angled us toward a flat, rocky shoreline a little way south of the bridge, where there was a gap in the bordering reeds.

Briar was reluctant, dancing sideways as Idris encouraged him to enter the water. I couldn't blame the horse. The current was gentle here, but the river's depth was uncertain.

"It's okay, Briar, walk on," I soothed, patting his rump.

"Easy, buddy," Idris added, knocking his feet against Briar's sides.

Slate-gray clouds were swelling overhead. Thunder rumbled in the distance. I continued speaking to Briar, scratching his butt, doing everything I could to distract him from the commotion on the bridge and overhead.

Eventually, Briar clopped into the shallows, his dinner-plate hooves slapping loudly. With no saddle between my legs and the horse's body, I felt how bunched his muscles were, how much tension he held in every step. But he was doing well, trusting Idris to guide him safely.

That is, until a splitting crack filled the air.

It came from the carriage on the bridge—perhaps an axle finally snapping, or a trunk slipping out of someone's arms to break open on the stones—but I didn't have time to deduce the exact source, because Briar lunged out from under me, racing for the opposite shore.

I fell backward into the river with a hard splash, water filling my open mouth. My vision filled with bubbles and the debris of vegetation. A memory cleared in my mind: of Idris, looming above the surface, pushing me down.

I kicked my legs and pinwheeled my arms, frantically trying to find the bottom so I could orient myself. The river might've been calm and relatively shallow here, but it still had some push, and it tumbled me sideways over the rocks.

Finally, in all my flailing, I managed to find purchase and popped up, completely disoriented, coughing and gulping for air. My hair was plastered to my face, and I wiped it away with a shaky hand, shivering with cold and adrenaline. A shadow passed across my blurred sight—Idris, looming as he had in the Mirror of Death.

With icy water still up to my neck, I scooted backward, feet slipping on slimy rocks.

"Anya!" Idris called, wading closer, the river sloshing around his upper-thighs. "Take my hand!"

Behind him, I saw a crowd of villagers lined up on shore, one of them holding Briar's reins. Witnesses.

Logic finally eclipsed my fear. I stared at Idris's proffered hand, then his eyes, seeing his genuine concern. The chill was beginning to clutch my lungs, a different sort of shock setting in. Idris took another labored step forward, keeping sturdy footing as he reached for me, grabbed me under the armpits, and lifted me bodily out of the water.

Instinctively, I clutched at his breastplate, his arms, as my feet found purchase underneath me. Water swirled around my waist, my soaked dress weighing me down—but Idris's grip was firm and steady.

"Are you alright? Can you wade to the other side?" he asked, sounding rather frightened. "Should I carry you?"

I shook my head. "No, I can walk," I said, but I clutched his arm as I made my wobbly way to the other side of the river.

On the far bank, I flopped down in the mud to catch my breath. Villagers crowded around, asking if I was hurt—"Just my pride," I managed—and offering dry blankets and assistance. As I sat there, cold and dazed, I reached for my mother's cloak pin at my throat, ensuring it hadn't fallen off in the river; I was relieved to find it still fastened in place, with Hattie's necklace still tucked beneath my sopping clothes.

While the gaggle of strangers fussed over my wellbeing, Idris loitered nearby, arms folded, his expression creased but unreadable. Eventually, someone handed Briar's reins back to him, and without removing his eyes from me, he patted the horse's neck reassuringly.

A woman—not much older than my mother would've been today—knelt beside me. "Who knew the day would hold so much excitement?" she asked breathlessly. "I'm Ida. Me pub isn't far from 'ere. Why don't we get ye warmed up?"

I was beginning to shiver uncontrollably; all I could do was nod.

An hour later, I was swaddled in another spare outfit from my pack, plus a blanket from Ida, and seated beside the fire in her pub with a cup of tea in my hands. Briar was in the stable, getting looked after by Ida's teenage son, while Ida's daughter was off washing our soiled, soggy clothes. Idris—after I insisted he help the villagers clear the carriage from the bridge—was now sipping an ale in the upholstered chair beside mine. Both pairs of our boots were arranged in front of the fire to dry.

"We really ought not to delay," Idris said to me, but his tone lacked conviction. It was raining, now, and he looked relieved to be out of the weather.

"Ida already said we could sleep on her floor tonight. Let's just accept the kindness and enjoy the respite, shall we?" I said. "We have plenty of cold nights spent out in the elements to look forward to, what with inns being so few and far between in these parts. As much as I look forward to clearing my name in the capital, there's no need to suffer to save ourselves a day. Allow yourself a little indulgence while it's here."

He grumbled at my speech, but I knew he was glad to luxuriate in a warm pub. Who wouldn't be?

That night, we were given hearty stew and extra blankets to cushion our bones from the pub's hardwood floor, and the following morning, we rose before the sun, revived.

"Ye sure ye don't want to stay for a proper meal?" Ida said as Idris and I stepped out the door in our mostly dry boots. "I've got blood sausage and freshly baked rolls!"

Idris shook his head. "We ought to be going."

I shot Idris a warning glance, willing him not to be rude. Then I gave Ida a quick hug, grateful for her generosity and the cheer of her feminine presence. "You've already given us so much," I told her.

"Then what's a little more, eh?"

I grinned. "If you insist—"

"Oh, I do—"

"—then I'll take a few sausages for the road," I said.

Ida was thrilled to oblige, and as we left the small village and continued north through a haze of rain, I happily snacked on sausages in the saddle.

Idris glanced back at me from his place walking beside Briar. "Those smell good," he commented.

"They are," I said. "We could've both enjoyed them by the fire in the pub, but *no*, you thought it best to ride out."

He faced forward again. He'd shaved last night, and his lack of facial hair made the clench of his jaw obvious.

"Are you jealous that I took Ida up on her kind offer?" I asked.

"No."

"Do you want one?"

He glanced back again, hope sparking in his eyes.

"If you want one, you'll have to ask nicely," I said.

He huffed an aggravated laugh, shaking his head. He walked beside Briar for another while, then finally said, "Anya, may I please...?"

"May you please what?" I goaded.

"May I *please* have one of your sausages?"

"Of course," I said brightly, passing one down to him.

He took it sheepishly, and when I laughed, he smiled.

19

BODY HEAT

ANYA

The wind was howling, rain spitting, when we made camp the next night. We'd found a semi-protected cluster of birch trees near a wide bend in the Wend and set up under their skeletal canopy. While I wrestled with the fire—the tender flame fickle in the wild weather—Idris strung a rope between two strong trees, flung a large sheet of waxed linen over the line, and anchored the corners, creating a tent. Then he disappeared in the direction of the river, a small net in hand.

I was still struggling to keep the fire lit when he returned with a fish, and I felt all the more useless when he crouched by my paltry flame, stuffed papery birch bark into the shelter of the larger logs, breathed life into the fire until it caught heartily, and cooked us the fish.

I wasn't much in the mood for talking, especially since our evening conversations continued to be rather one-sided—even when I steered clear of the topic of his Oath. *When* Idris deigned to converse with me, I found his dry wit and heartfelt interjections enjoyable. But over the past couple days, he'd seemed determined not to befriend me.

Not that I wanted to be his friend, either. All I truly wanted was to clear my name and return home.

The weather was poor, and the contrast between tonight's howling wind and last night's hearthside slumber was painfully apparent. Travel was wearing on me, and I was beginning to understand Idris's gruffness; if I lived like this day in and day out, year after year, I'd be gruff, too. I was gruff already.

"You're quiet tonight," Idris noted after dinner, holding his hands to the fire. His wound was no more than burgundy a freckle now, the black webbing entirely gone.

I was clutching a mug of rose hip tea, which Idris had poured this time. He'd added chamomile, which was a favorite of Hattie's. Inevitably, the thought of her made me think of Wicker and the Possum and town, which led me to remember my Fate, which reminded me of why I was out here in the wilderness instead of Waldron. It was a vicious cycle of worry and heartache, but at least the tea was warm.

"You must be relieved," I told Idris, still staring into my mug.

The wind gusted through the trees, leaves and small twigs falling with the spitting rain.

"It's rather disconcerting, actually."

I eyed him. The dark waves of his shoulder-length hair were ruffled, tan cheeks flushed from the cold. He looked...wind-swept and wild.

"I expected you to be more tough," he went on, "but it seems the discomforts of the road have dulled your edge."

His words angered me, my inner fire flaring, even as our campfire waned in the wet weather. "It's not the discomforts of the road, but the tiresomeness of the company," I snapped. "Not to mention the ominousness of our mission. I *am* a prisoner of the realm, after all."

I expected Idris to balk or protest at my tart reply. Instead, he huffed a soft laugh. "There's that edge."

"You're goading me," I realized.

"I'm making conversation."

"Badly."

"I'd beg to differ," he said. "I'm quite enjoying this."

I growled and sipped my tea, hating how effective he was at taking my mind off the awfulness of our trip. "No flute tonight?" I asked tightly.

"Thought I'd listen to the music of the rain, instead."

I found I shared his sentiment; it was something I myself might've said.

Fondness sprouted in me like a seed; I didn't care for it. To think fondly of him was to *like* him, and that was dangerous. He might've been kind to me now, but could I really trust his kindness to last? Fates aside, everyone knew that a knight was loyal to his Oath above all else.

I sipped my tea. The rain was light enough that we could linger out in the open by the fire. As we listened to its music—as Idris had called it—I couldn't help but rouse my magic, amplifying the patter of droplets on the surrounding leaves. Here beneath the mostly bare branches of the birches, the tough, ever-green foliage of the underbrush plinked with the melody of water. Joining the percussive rainfall, the trickle of the Wend provided a sweet harmony.

Idris's eyes widened as I plucked at the threads of sound. I wasn't the symphony, but its conductor, uplifting the natural elements around me. I rarely wielded my magic so freely, but it felt good to *enjoy* the bad weather for a few moments. To relish its beauty, even as its damp chill seeped into my tired bones.

"That's..." Idris cleared his throat, not finishing his thought.

But his observation of my play snuffed its spark. My magic dissipated, until all that remained was the rain, back to its normal pitter-patter.

"Why'd you stop?" Idris asked.

"That was indulgent of me," I said, embarrassed.

"Why not allow yourself a little indulgence?" Idris asked, echoing what I'd told him in Ida's pub. "It's a beautiful skill, Anya."

The compliment warmed me more than my tea had. I downed the rest and abruptly stood. "I'm going to check on Briar," I said, and left the firelight.

We'd tied Briar to one of the birches anchoring the tent. He seemed content under its meager canopy, head hung, butt to the wind. His ears perked when I approached, and he nickered softly. I handed him a hard oat cookie from my pocket—a gift from Ida's son, who'd grown attached to Briar during our brief visit.

Briar chewed, then nosed me for more. "That's all I've got," I lied, because I wanted to save the remaining treats for the coming days. "You're a good boy." I patted his muscular neck, wet with rain, and leaned closer to his ear. "I want you to know: I don't fault you for my tumble into the river. We all get frightened sometimes."

He pressed his huge head against my torso, which I took to mean that he understood, even though the more likely explanation was that he was trying to wipe the rainwater from his eyes.

I chuckled at myself. Just like Idris, I was enjoying a conversation with the horse. Briar seemed to be a good listener, and suddenly I understood Idris's urge to praise him. I, myself, felt compelled to do the same—in addition to telling Briar all my secrets.

But the wind was picking up. Briar braced against the gusts, calmer now than he'd been yesterday. Perhaps the cover of the trees comforted him. I scratched the downy fur underneath his forelock, then gave his velvety nose one last stroke. He lipped at my fingers, checking for treats, then hung his head as the rain surged.

I lifted the hood of my cloak and returned to camp, hunching in the increasing downpour. The fire was extinguished with no hope of relighting. Idris was tucking our packs inside the tent and checking the stakes that secured the corners.

It was then that I fully grasped that we'd be *sharing* the tent. The *tiny* tent.

The rain slanted through the tree branches, icy and biting. As much as I wanted to protest the intimacy of sleeping together under narrow cover, it was clearly our only option. I might've been foolish, but I wasn't completely dense.

When Idris spotted me, he straightened. The right corner of his lips slanted downward in a knowing, apologetic frown. Something about the self-deprecating expression—his comprehension that I did not relish such close proximity, nor did he—removed the worst of my hesitation.

I ducked inside, out of the deluge. He'd laid our bedrolls side by side, folding the blankets lengthwise in half, like two books resting spine to spine, a fabric buffer between us. Our packs rested along the edges, presumably to insulate us from the cold. His thoughtfulness in this setup further eased my feelings of awkwardness. While he waited outside, I quickly removed my boots and my outermost layers and tucked myself under the blankets. Then Idris crawled in, repeating my movements until he rested on his back beside me.

Wordlessly, we listened to the weather raging outside. I felt bad for Briar, barn-less and exposed to the elements. But he'd seemed in good spirits—and plenty warm—when I'd checked on him.

"Have a nice talk with Briar?" Idris asked, seeming to sense the direction of my thoughts.

"You heard me over the rain?"

"Not your words, just your voice," he said. "I thought I was the only one who enjoyed talking to him."

I *humphed*. The faint tremor of my muscles caused my shoulder to brush against Idris's through our blankets. It really was *tight* in here. I could tell he was trying not to rub up against me too much, but that was a losing battle.

Idris cleared his throat. "I want you to know that I take no"—another cough—"pleasure in this. The tent is pure necessity."

"It's quite clear you take no pleasure in my company, Idris, so you don't have to defend your gentlemanly intentions."

"Do you really think that?"

"Think what? That you'd rather travel alone? Absolutely."

He shifted under his blankets, relaxing his big shoulders somewhat; his arm came in firmer contact with mine, but I resisted moving away. There wasn't much *away* to move to, and besides, I didn't want him to think that I was repulsed by him. On the contrary, I found his solidness...not unwelcome. It was the Mirror's vision that tainted our closeness.

"My solitary existence is not by free will," he said, seeming to choose his words carefully. "I am required—" He broke off abruptly and didn't continue.

I turned my head, regarding him in the dark. I couldn't see much more than his silhouette against the light backdrop of our linen cover, but that was enough to spot the bob of his throat.

On the morning our quest began, he'd mentioned *reports* he needed to deliver to the capital, his duty to *protect the realm*. What else was he required to do—or not do? While many knightly Orders were well-known and respected, the Oaths knights took were highly secret. And seeing as I'd never heard even a frightened whisper about the monsters Idris fought—not even a *hint* of such abominations from the farthest-flung guests who passed through the Possum—it seemed logical to assume his Oath was somehow tied to their existence. *Warped Fate.*

We were skirting too close to his Oath again. While I wouldn't hesitate to ask personal questions, an Oath went deeper than personal secrets.

I looked at the trembling rope that held up our ceiling. "You don't have to explain yourself," I said. "But beware, I can't promise my own gentlemanliness; I'm a natural snuggler, and my nightmares persist. Apologies in advance for how that combination will manifest."

His tone was warm with humor when he said, "Thanks for the warning."

Indeed, as the night aged, I found myself inching closer to Idris—for warmth and security. Cold leeched up through my blankets from the hard ground, chilling me. Grim dreams sent my heart racing. I'd nod off, only to find myself pressing into his side, desperate to steal his heat and safety; I'd readjust with more space between us, but it was no use against my instincts in slumber. It felt like my first nightmare all over again—I could still recall the hardness of his chest beneath my clutching fingers.

Meanwhile, Idris remained stone-still beside me, his hands folded on his stomach beneath his blanket—either asleep, or politely ignoring my delirious invasion of his personal space. Eventually, I turned my back toward him. But as the night wore on, the cold worsened, and I began to shiver, teeth chattering. I tried to magically keep the sound low, so as not to disturb him, but when fitful sleep weakened my hold on my magic, the clacking of my teeth and the hiss of my quick breaths returned to their normal volume.

Late in the night, Idris sighed long and low, roused by my shivers. I poked my nose up out of my cocoon, about to apologize for keeping him up, but I was cut off when he peeled back my blanket, exposing my body—still clad in my travel clothes, sans tunic—to the cold air.

"Fucking Fates," I swore.

But Idris wasn't being cruel; he was rearranging our blankets: flattening mine against the ground and using his to cover us both—our barrier gone. He added Briar's saddle blanket on top, its thick woven material insulating us further.

Idris resettled on his side behind me, tucking my shivering body against him. It was reminiscent of sharing a saddle, only without the breastplate between us. He curled against me, his chest enveloping my back, hips fitting firmly against my ass. His warmth was...delicious. Compared to my chilled skin, he was an inferno. I was too cold to be embarrassed by the contact; I nestled against him gratefully.

"Is this alright?" he murmured, his breath heating the tender skin of my neck.

"*Warm*," I muttered appreciatively.

He let out that breathy laugh of his, another hot gust across my flesh. He reached for the edge of the blanket and lifted it higher, until only the top of my head was uncovered. He continued to breathe down into the blanket, and so did I, our exhales gradually banishing some of the chill. Meanwhile, he rubbed my upper arm, bringing heat into my skin through the thin linen of my underclothes. The rough pressure of his touch rocked me against him, but I was too frigid to feel self-conscious about the rhythm.

I relished not just his warmth, but his care. Back in Waldron, I was always helping others—fixing fences, lending an understanding ear, validating and assisting. Even with Remy, I had always been the one to provide free drinks and a free stay. After how thoroughly Waldron had welcomed me, it felt like the least I could do, and while I drew immense joy from being useful, occasionally I did feel a little...*used*.

Nowadays, it was a rare thing, for me to be cared for.

So as Idris looked after me, I felt not just my muscles melt, but also my resolve.

Long after my shivering subsided, he kept on rubbing my arm, his movements slowing the drowsier I got, until eventually, I fell asleep in his embrace.

20

REGRETS

IDRIS

If it hadn't been for the piss-poor weather, Idris wouldn't have held Anya so tightly.

That's what he told himself, at least.

The problem was that he was telling himself a lie.

Sure, he'd rearranged their blankets out of necessity. Anya had been shivering uncontrollably, and it wasn't right to leave her to suffer hypothermia for the sake of avoiding contact. The wilderness had a way of stripping away superfluous etiquette; it brought beings of all kinds into closer contact with necessity. It'd been *necessary* that Idris do away with propriety to help her warm up.

Unfortunately, his heart had done away with propriety, too. Even now, in the emerging dawn, he *enjoyed* holding her—and not just because the tasks of his Order starved him of human touch. He enjoyed holding *Anya*, specifically. Her body fit perfectly against him, plush against the hard angles of his own. All night, that lemon and rose scent had taken him away from their dreary camp, into lush gardens under warm sunlight.

He'd *basked.*

With his arm banded around her, he still did.

But physicality aside, it was her straight-shooting humor that allured him most. Her ability to make jokes even in her misery. Her desire to see the good in people, to *connect.* Even to him, her would-be killer.

Over the past few days, he'd found himself continually struck by her ability to weave topics and paths of thought. To appear vexed one moment, amused the next, keeping him on his toes. To befriend villagers and relish indulgence. Unapologetic in her delight (had Idris *ever* delighted in something guilt free?).

In short, he quite liked her company, even though he ought not to. Even though the Mirrors insisted upon their doomed future.

Monsters or no monsters, Idris wasn't interested in tempting Fate—yet he found himself already dreading the end of their journey. Aside from the inevitable return of his regular duty, criminal trials rarely favored the tried in Fenrir; the sinking feeling in his gut made him wonder if he was marching Anya to a grim end, after all. His guilt was fighting a losing battle with his duty, but as his fondness for Anya grew, the margin between the two narrowed ever closer. Even now, his arm tightened protectively around her waist.

The rain persisted into the soft gray dawn. It was cozy inside the tent, and Idris found himself lingering, relishing Anya's curves tucked against him, the softness of her skin. As his body roused, awakening more fully to another long day, his desire stirred, too. It was a deep curling sensation low in his stomach, the rushing of blood to his groin. It became imperative that he rise—before his erection did further—so he peeled his body away from hers and crept out into the chilly morning.

Outside the tent, the small grove was strewn with twigs. The wind had died down, leaving the air peaceful and still. Briar—who'd taken liberty with his long tether to munch on grass by the Wend, nickered to him in greeting. Idris took a moment to look over their horse, pressing a hand to his chest to test his body heat. Remarkably, Briar seemed to be in good spirits, despite last night's miserable weather; perhaps he was relieved that the worst of it had passed.

After murmuring to Briar his due praises, Idris wandered off to relieve his bladder and collect water for their morning porridge. He then stoked a modest fire, squinting against the assault of smoke that wafted up from the wet firewood. The scent of ash permeated his senses, mingling with Briar's wet-horse musk. Even so, such strong smells weren't enough to overpower Anya's sweetness still clinging to his shirt. The lingering garden scent was yet another blow to his resolve.

For months, he'd been growing weary of his task, no longer thrilled by the hunt and slaughter of the realm's greatest threats, nor as steadfast in his devotion to his Order. The principles of his youth had faded with age and wear. He wasn't sure exactly when cynicism and disloyalty had crept into the dark corners of his heart, but they *had*, infesting him with thoughts of apathy and—in his darkest moments—outright treason.

Anya—with her fun-loving lightheartedness and biting allure—had only worsened his temptation.

What he needed—he realized as he stirred their bubbling breakfast—was to remember why he took the Oath in the first place. Grinnick had sacrificed *everything* for Idris. Scraped and strived and worked himself to the bone. Idris's beloved brother—his elder by barely two years—had stepped into the role of both parents when no family was left. He had done his best.

In Idris's eyes, Grinnick's crimes—stealing food, cheating in the gambling halls, participating in illegal fighting rings for extra coin—had been acts of honor, responsibility, and love. But in the eyes of Fenrir, his crimes were simply crimes, and warranted his sentence.

"This is your path to absolution," the Lord of Fenrir had told the criminals arranged in the hall the fateful day Grinnick took the Oath.

Idris had scaled the outer and inner wall of Castle Might and wedged himself in one of the stained-glass windowsills, peering through a thin clear panel to witness his brother—the only person Idris had left to love—enter an Order that would guarantee his doom. The Lord's words had sickened Idris. His brother did not need absolution; he needed money, mercy, a fucking *break*. They both did.

At barely sixteen, Grinnick had looked small inside the too-big shell of his black breastplate; the greataxe they'd given him had appeared cumbersome in his young hands. He'd looked—Idris had thought—like a boy playing dress-up as a knight, rather than a real one.

It had filled Idris with dread.

The memory had stuck with Idris over the years—the beginning of the end. His brother had been so strong for the both of them: through the death of their father and abandonment by their mother, through long hard years on the unforgiving streets of Fenrir, through a grim sentence with a Fates-forsaken Order, until his untimely death.

A death the Lord himself had deemed dishonorable.

Grinnick deserved honor, if only in memory. It's why Idris still lingered in the Order of the Valiant, following in his brother's footsteps if only to hold onto the feeling of walking beside his brother in life.

Yet here he was, wishing to cast all his principles aside after just a few nights on the road with a *woman*. His weakness was despicable.

Idris was still scolding himself when Anya emerged from the tent, her sunset hair rumpled with sleep, her brown eyes impossibly bright. There was not enough campfire smoke in the word to choke out the scent of her. She was beautiful to all his senses.

It made him angry with himself.

Oblivious to his inner turmoil, she plunked down on the fallen log beside their fire and regarded him with cheerful eyes. She was well-slept; had she realized that her nightmares had dissipated with Idris's touch? She seemed unabashed in her appreciation for his company this morning. If he'd been uncertain about her reaction to his nearness last night, he knew now: she'd enjoyed it, too.

The realization sparked hope in his chest—which he promptly smothered with more self-reproach.

"I'm glad the weather's eased," Anya said, her pretty lips curving. "I was dreading forcing Briar to trudge through more wind and rain, but he seems revived."

Idris merely grunted, not wanting to encourage more chit-chat.

But that had never deterred Anya before. "Thank you for not letting me freeze." Her cheeks colored with bashfulness, pink as a spring sunrise.

Idris felt miserable with want.

"How did you sleep?" she asked politely.

"Fitfully."

She frowned. His comment had obviously stung. "I'm sorry to hear that."

Idris lifted the pot off the fire and dished up their breakfast, hoping his gruffness might deter her from being so...pleasant. For making this harder than it needed to be.

But she kept on. "You must know that I didn't *intentionally* keep you up, Idris. I—I was cold, and I thought—"

"That I'd *enjoy* being woken up?" Idris bit out.

Anya caught her lips between her teeth, pinching them shut. Her cheeks were fully red now. Idris's self-hatred intensified, now for another reason. He didn't want to hurt her, but he *did* want to push her away. Maintain enough distance not to get attached. He feared he was already far too attached.

Tense silence stretched between them as they packed up and moved out. Idris allowed Anya to ride Briar—not just out of kindness, but because when he walked beside the horse's shoulder, *she* remained out of his immediate view.

21

CONCOCTAILS

ANYA

The day unfolded grimly.

The clouds hung low and heavy over fields of slumped grasses and tilled earth. The road was muddy and puddled with rainwater. Mist showered down, clinging to our cloaks, stinging my cheeks. Everything on my person—from my clothes to the saddle to my boots—was damp and cold.

Grimmest of all, however, was Idris's mood.

I hated how hurt I was by his sourness this morning. Because I hadn't felt unsafe, as I probably should have in the face of my potential killer's ire—I'd felt *rejected*.

I'd wanted to protest. To point out that I *knew* he'd enjoyed spooning me, too, at least physically. His hardness pressing into my backside, followed by his swift exit, had been proof enough of that. And I'd thought—*Fates spare me*—I'd thought he'd enjoyed it emotionally, too. In spite of the potential ruin between us, I'd savored his closeness last night; in the light of day, it was hard to excuse my feelings as merely a symptom of being cold.

Now, I didn't know where I stood.

And so the day unfolded, with both of us stewing quietly, save to announce our occasional needs to relieve ourselves or procure a snack from Briar's saddlebags.

We steered off the High Road early that evening, so that Idris could go hunting. The sprinkling rain hissed on the surface of the Wend. It seemed we'd need a tent again, so I set it up on the mossy riverbank between two weeping willows. Then I lit a fire using small twigs and fallen leaves and set a pot of water atop a sturdy log to boil tea. After that, I scuffed Briar's withers, checked his feet for stones, and fed him another oat cookie, before allowing him to forage for grass along the bank.

Idris was still gone when twilight purpled the edges of the sky. The willows cast long shadows along the ground, their thin branches rattling in the breeze. When I was a girl, I found willow trees to be impossibly romantic: what better place to rendezvous with a lover than underneath the pretty shelter of their boughs? Here, I found them slightly unsettling, their constant movement in the breeze drawing my eye ever toward the darkness, alert.

Desperate for something less sinister to occupy my attention in the growing night, I grabbed my pack and sat on one of a few small boulders by the fire. With the harrowing events and quick pace of our travels, I hadn't had much of a chance to audit the tinctures Hattie had packed for me. Aside from clothing, unknown bottles had been clinking in the bottom of my bag for days, and now seemed as good a time as any to inspect what she'd given me.

I pulled out the clothes, first, of which I was already familiar. First, my party dress from the Fate Ceremony. In addition to the gray-blue tunic I currently wore—which had dried overnight at Ida's—Hattie had packed extra under-garments, too, along with trousers and another tunic in a rich charcoal color, stitched prettily with cream thread. There was the bar of soap I'd already used, plus a coin purse, a bottle of ink, and a few folds of paper, too, plus Hammond's instructions and the sealed character references for my appeal.

When I finally reached the bottles, I pulled them all out, laying them in the dirt at my feet and stuffing everything else back into my pack. There were ten in varying sizes, plus a small jar of antibacterial salve. The excess of Hattie's glassware made me grin; it was just like her to supply me with plenty of tinctures—impractical, given the weight, but also thoughtful and clever and demonstrating of her fierce love.

Six of the vials were tiny and intended for medicinal purposes: one for menstrual pain, another for stomach upset, my monthly anti-pregnancy tincture, a sleep aid, and two different tinctures for staving off infection (including one that was the same as what she'd given Idris for his wound).

The other four, slightly larger bottles elicited a laugh. They were what Hattie referred to as "concoctails"—concoctions to avail merriment. At the Possum, she was famous for mixing distilled spirits with sweet syrups and herbal tonics to create tasty alcoholic beverages worth sipping and savoring. In my pack, she'd included one with raspberry syrup, another with citrus and juniper, and two consisting of brown liquor, honey, lemon, and a dash of anise bitters.

It was silly of Hattie to assume that on my journey I'd require such a decadent way of getting drunk. But—bless her—this was *just* what I needed tonight. A chance to get my mind off of my confusing burgeoning affection for Idris, my coming trial, the bad weather, and all the other things that plagued me.

I was still chuckling to myself as I pulled the cork off the raspberry bottle.

"What's so funny?" Idris asked, materializing out of the darkness beyond the firelight.

I scowled at him, meeting his petulance with my own.

But even as I did, I couldn't help but marvel at his hulking form. A hare and quail dangled from his belt, the results of two successful snares. He still wore his breastplate, the menacing black reflecting the orange glow of the fire. Halgren hung ominously on the other side of his belt, its weight—and his familiarity with it—apparent. Indeed, one huge hand rested upon its hilt, as if it were an old companion.

A flash of *knowing* streaked through me like a comet as I remembered that same hand stroking warmth into my skin. Pulling me from the river. Pouring maple syrup into my porridge. His were hands that wielded flaming swords and set snares and would—supposedly, one day—drown me, and yet my experience with them had only ever been positive.

"Care to elucidate what's making you frown like that?" Idris asked.

I hadn't realized my lips had turned downward in thought. "You," I answered honestly.

His mouth quirked up in a half-smile, and he smothered the doting expression with a palm, scratching his stubbled jaw with a *humph*.

I wondered what he saw of me. What features he noticed, which ones he liked. He had a bashful-looking nose, with a bridge that angled downward from middle to tip, as if the Fates had pressed it down. What opinions did he have about my nose? Did he find it cute, or too protruding, or did he not think of it at all? His lips were full, almost obscenely so; did he wonder what mine tasted like?

Fucking Fates, Anya, I warned myself. *Don't go there.*

When he lowered his palm from his face, he was still smiling a little, his efforts to contain the expression failing. The moment passed, and he removed his armor and weapons, then busied himself with our dinner, taking the hare and quail off into the nearby shadows for cleaning and gutting—another task his hands knew.

While I sat there, alone again, it occurred to me how abrupt his contempt had been this morning. What if our closeness *hadn't* irritated him? What if, in fact, he'd felt the opposite? What if his Oath demanded that he keep to himself, even if he didn't wish to?

It was a lot to assume.

I sipped my concoctail, relishing the sweet sting of Hattie's genius. For an inn and pub owner, I didn't drink hardly at all, as I was usually busy supplying alcohol to my customers. This meant that the spirit went immediately to my head—not helped by my empty stomach.

By the time Idris returned, I was a third of the way through the bottle and already swaying a little on my rock. I stared openly at him while he removed the boiling pot of abandoned tea from the fire, added a couple logs, and laid out our prepared skewers of meat for roasting.

He sat on a boulder across from me, avoiding my eye contact for a few minutes before finally giving up his grumpy charade for pure curiosity. "Whatever are you drinking?"

"Concoctails," I said with a hiccup. "Alcoholic mixtures that Hattie squirreled away in my bag. Want one?"

He eyed me dubiously. "Are you...drunk?"

"I'm *tipsy*," I corrected. I leaned forward, dropping my voice to a conspiratorial whisper. "Does that make you want to be ungentlemanly?"

Idris rasped a surprised laugh. "No?"

Was it possible for a single syllable to be…flirtatious? *No*, it must've been my semi-inebriated imagination.

"Can I see the bottle?" he asked.

I handed it over, and he took a swig.

"Hey!" I exclaimed. "Drink your own."

He hissed and wiped a hand across his glistening mouth. "*Fates*, Anya, that's strong."

I giggled. "Here," I said, handing him the citrus and juniper one.

He took the bottle by the neck, lifting the label to the light to see its ingredients.

"Come on," I goaded, "live a little, would you? The weather's been miserable, and *you've* been miserable. It's perfectly harmless to take the edge off."

He quirked a brow.

"I know you quite like *my* edge," I went on, "but yours is insufferable."

He tipped his head back and laughed heartily. The sound fizzed in my ears, intoxicating in its own right. His dark waves fell away from his face, showing off his cheekbones, his jawline, and—without the obstruction of his breastplate—a bit of chest hair and his Oath tattoo. There was a rather deep hollow at the base of his neck, just beneath the black line. I suddenly had the inexplicable urge to press my tongue into it.

Maybe Hattie's concoction was stronger than I realized.

Oblivious to my inappropriate thoughts, Idris uncorked his own bottle and sipped. Then scowled. "This one is different."

"I should've known you'd prefer the sweet one. Here, we can switch."

We traded bottles across the fire, and when he drank again, his mouth pulled into a pleased grin which, this time, he didn't bother to hide.

A half hour passed. While I drank, he fiddled with the strips of meat, sprinkling them with seasoning from a small jar he'd procured from his pack, and turning them every so often so that they cooked evenly. I was salivating by the time he handed me a skewer.

Of course, it was delicious. Annoyingly so.

"You're *such* a good cook," I said around a huge bite of quail.

"I like to cultivate simple pleasures," he said. "Good meals are one of them."

"What other pleasures do you enjoy?" my drunken mouth asked.

His pupils expanded, darkening his blue-green gaze, filling it with firelight. But he merely shook his head and drank from his bottle, unwilling to engage.

Tipsy as I was, I now saw his reservation as a game—a *challenge*—rather than a deterrent. "Does your Oath require you to be so shut off, or is that a personality defect?" I asked.

Idris practically choked on his bite of dinner. "Wow."

"Amazed by my sharp observation skills?"

"That's one way to put it."

"How else would you put it?"

He paused for a beat. "I'd say I'm surprised you don't have more tact, given your public-facing profession."

"Most of my guests find my straightforwardness refreshing," I said tartly, then grew more serious. "You didn't deny that your Oath limits you."

He stilled. "I did not."

"That doesn't disprove a personality defect, though."

"I'd prefer it if you refrained from calling me *defective*," he said. "Hurts my fragile ego."

I stared into his eyes, wishing they'd burn me with their fire. "You hurt *me*, earlier." The drink was making me loose tongued, but I didn't care. I was bursting with frustration. Over what, exactly, I wasn't sure; I just wanted to make it *his* problem instead of mine.

He lowered his bottle, regarding me with genuine apology. "I'm sorry. I was an ass."

Thinking about what he'd said of our night together, I asked—somewhat out of context—"So did you really?"

"Did I what?"

"Sleep fitfully?"

"Yes," he said—roughly. He didn't sound annoyed this time but stricken. "Did you?"

"I slept like a dream." I aimed my honesty like an arrow at his armor. "It's rare that someone bothers to look after me."

Idris leaned forward, resting his elbows on his knees. Where his shirt gaped from his neck, I saw the jagged white streak of a grizzly scar, and I wondered where it led.

"You're...not unpleasant to look after."

The deep register of his voice sent desire pulsing through me. I probably ought to have laid off the drink, but instead, I drank long and deep.

"If you can't tell me about your Oath," I said—back to a safer topic, at least for me—"can you tell me why you took it?"

He drank quickly, eyeing me over his bottle. "My brother."

"Is he also in your Order?"

"Was," Idris said, wincing at that. "I took his place."

I touched my hand to my heart. "I'm sorry for your loss."

He nodded, then he drank. "Did you always want to be an innkeeper?"

"I grew up at the Possum," I said. "When the original owner died, it became my inheritance—my everything."

"Seems we both know loss. I'm sorry."

I shrugged, minimizing the pain so that I didn't get choked up. "Loss is a part of life. Besides, there are lessons in the hurt. Grief has made me more appreciative and intentional about the things I love."

His mouth was wet from his drink, glistening faintly. "And what do you love?" His deep-river eyes held mine.

He'd said it—*love*—so softly, like velvet. The intensity of his gaze had me glancing coyly away, out through the willow branches toward Briar.

When I considered his question, the answers came easily. "Hattie, Wicker, and the Possum," I said. "Festivals with snowflake candies. Bonfires with music and dancing. Sweetbreads and gossip. Sunrises over Stone Hill."

He lifted his bottle high. "Cheers to Waldron."

I hefted my bottle in response, my eyes pricking with the overwhelming feeling of homesickness, and being understood. "What do *you* love?" I dared to ask.

His gaze dropped to his clasped hands. "Memories."

I didn't know what to say to that, so—feeling raw, myself—I said nothing.

If things in the capital went sour for me, everything I loved would become memory, too. I wanted to ask Idris about the likelihood of that outcome. I wanted to ask him what'd happened to his brother, about the things he'd loved that were now locked in his past—but even with the alcohol in my system, I thought better than to pry into old wounds. We were more alike than I'd realized, and I knew how delicate those kinds of scars could be. How difficult it was to cherish something and face the possibility of giving it up.

The fire crackled. An owl screeched. Silence gradually washed away the heaviness of our conversation, and with a few more sips, I found myself settling into pleasant tipsiness once again.

"So, this crime of yours," Idris said, recovering himself, too. "Is it me you kill?"

I laughed, surprised by his bluntness—but also glad for the twisted levity of more rude questions.

"Some sort of instant revenge?" he continued playfully. "Double murder?"

"If *only*," I said.

"So, who, then?" he asked. "It must be a man."

"Why's that?"

"You seem like you'd happily kill a man."

If it weren't for the drink, I might not have found the comment funny—but I did. "Do you find me threatening, Idris?"

"Endlessly," he said darkly.

I giggled.

"Does it have anything to do with the man at your inn? What was his name?"

"Remy." Just saying it aloud left a bitter taste in my mouth, so I took a quick sip; the suction of the bottle popped at my upper lip as I lowered it.

"Remy?" Idris prompted.

"I have plenty of reasons to murder Remy," I said, "but I *wouldn't*."

"He was a...paramour?" Idris sounded vaguely as if his mouth was filled with honey—slow and strangled.

"I'm not sure what he was, to be honest."

Presently, I found I didn't much care. He'd never given me his full attention; why would I be jealous of him giving it to someone else? His daughter certainly deserved his love more than I did. My only regret was that I hadn't been more candid with him—and myself—about what I'd wanted from our relationship.

"You're astute, you know that?" I said. "Seems wasted on the squirrels and the trees. You should be in towns, telling fortunes and trading gossip."

"Reading minds is tiresome," Idris said, playing along. "I much prefer the solitude."

"Do you?" I challenged.

He stared out through the sheet of willow branches toward the Wend, pensive. When he looked at me again, his eyes were dark. "Actually, I don't," he admitted.

He shifted closer, knuckles grazing the side of my neck—the closest exposed skin. "You don't feel freezing," he accused. His fingertips dipped briefly under my collar. "You feel...warm."

I swallowed thickly, buzzing with need. I could blame the drink, but it was clear the alcohol had only intensified cravings that were already simmering beneath the surface. But these feelings...they were wrong. *Futile.*

Resisting the urge to press backward into him, I did the opposite, scooting on my side so that an inch of chilly space separated us. "No need to warm me, then," I said briskly. "We don't need you sleeping *fitfully* again."

The hand that had been stroking my collarbone slipped away. "Is that what you want?" His voice was honey poured over stone. Smooth, delicious, but hard underneath.

I wasn't sure either of us could handle hearing what I wanted aloud, but the concoctail let slip the smallest truth: "No."

His hand returned, this time to my shoulder, rolling me toward him. Idris tucked me against his chest, under his chin, his huge arm wrapping around my waist to hold me firm and close. He pulled the blanket up to my cheek, shrouding me in warmth. His stubble grazed my temple.

My sense of right and wrong dissolved. With my head nestled against his shirt, I could smell his pine-smoke scent, and it fortified my nerve. "Are *you* cold?" I asked.

"Freezing," he deadpanned.

I inched closer, sliding my fingers underneath the hem of his shirt. I grazed the hair dusting his abdominals, then banded my arm around his waist, pressing my chest to his, splaying my palm on the bare skin of his back. His heart began to patter in time with the rain outside.

He hissed. "Anya," he murmured, half warning, half...something else. He ghosted his knuckles across the side of my neck again, then cupped my jaw, sinking his fingertips into my hair. He tipped my chin up to look at him in the dark.

22

SLIPPERY SLOPE

ANYA

We drank our concoctails and laughed into the night. I told Idris stories about my wildest customers: the man who kept me up all night by barking in his room like a dog, the woman who demanded we provide *two* mattresses for her to sleep on, and even the story of Hattie's arrival. He met my stories with rapt interest, and shared tales of his own adventures in the wilds: seeing the green streaks of the northern auroras, a sketchy frozen lake crossing in the heart of the Bone Mountains, and an unfortunate (hilarious) run-in with a raccoon whose cave he'd had the audacity to wait out a snowstorm in.

By the time our bottles were empty and the fire had cooled, it was late, and the rain had picked up considerably. We couldn't avoid sharing the tent any longer, and as we ducked inside, the promise of his touch sobered me; it seemed to sober him, too. The remaining hiccups and giggles died on our tongues in the darkness of our shelter.

The air wasn't as cold tonight, but the ground was still hard and damp. Earlier, I'd arranged the blankets for sharing, thinking it an unfortunate necessity. Now, I wondered if I should offer to reinstate our blanket buffers. But as I slipped underneath the fabric, an anticipatory thrill pulsed through me—a sensation that kept me quiet.

Idris wordlessly wedged in behind me. Was it chivalry or genuine desire that caused him to curl so close?

"Are you cold?" he whispered.

I wasn't. In truth, I felt itchy and constricted in my clothes.

"*So* cold," I lied. "Freezing, in fact."

Airless with anticipation, I watched as his lips parted ever so slightly. Would he kiss me? Was that a terrible thing to want? I felt as if I were teetering on a high precipice, craving and dreading the fall.

"*Fates spare me,*" he swore, releasing me roughly.

"Spare you from what?"

"You know what."

Feeling as if I'd been toyed with, I turned with my back to him again, suddenly ready to focus on sleep.

But his voice cut through the dark again. "How do I do it?"

I knew immediately of what he spoke. "You drown me."

He huffed a laugh, but it was devoid of mirth.

I closed my eyes, assuming that he'd keep his distance, now.

But he settled behind me again, resting a careful palm on my hip. Hot breath warmed my shoulder as he inched closer, then his chin grazed the exposed skin of my neck, where my shirt gaped. He pressed a single kiss there, chaste, and completely unexpected, sending a rush of awareness up and down my body. His mouth was there and gone in a moment, leaving me humming with energy.

While he remained close, his touch wasn't charged as it had been. But it still tormented me long after the drink wore off.

The next morning, I rose before dawn—before Idris—to bathe in the river. I hadn't had many chances for a proper wash, and I figured I ought to take any fleeting opportunity that came. More importantly, I hoped the frigid water might douse any remaining heat that lingered in my core from another night in his arms.

Perhaps tonight we'd come within reasonable range of an inn, where we might enjoy the reprieve of separate rooms. Maybe then I'd gain some sense and stop lusting after my killer. My quiet, funny, unexpectedly *caring* killer.

I ducked out of the curtain of willow branches and carried my pack toward the water. Pastel clouds dappled the sky in shades of periwinkle, baby pink, and lemon, the Wend reflecting its splendor. Birds sang, water trickled, and nearby, Briar munched grass in a cheerful rhythm.

Once I reached a secluded area out of view of camp, I unpacked fresh clothes and Hattie's rose-scented soap, then stripped down to my chemise. As much as I'd craved Idris's touch last night, in the light of day, my drunken behavior embarrassed me; I shouldn't have come onto him as I had, and I didn't want him to catch me naked now, so I decided to make do in a semi-dressed state.

The river rocks were slick as I waded into the shallows. I stepped carefully, my toes stinging with cold. When the water reached my knees—just below my hemline—I bent, wetting my old shirt to use as a wash rag. I started with my underarms, humming to myself as I worked my way down and underneath my chemise, scrubbing away the sweat and grime of travel. My magic lifted the sounds of nature to meet my little tune, filling my head with a sweet melody, and—

"Morning."

Too busy orchestrating my own song, I hadn't heard Idris approach. With a startled shriek, I jumped—feet slipping on the wet stones—and fell into the Wend for the *second* time on our trip, landing on my butt with a splash.

As water sloshed against my chest, I pouted up at Idris. "You did that on purpose."

"I most certainly did not," he said seriously, rushing to the water's edge, offering his hand.

I eyed it, thinking about the last time I fell in the river. I realized I didn't fear him this time; our conversations over the past few days had diffused much of my suspicion. In fact, when my gaze followed the length of his arm up to his concerned face, I forgot the Mirror's vision entirely. Maybe his warped Fate had changed mine, after all. Maybe I'd changed my own Fate, just by trusting him.

Either way, it wasn't panic that I felt now, but mischief.

I reached out, but instead of taking his hand, I flicked the surface of the water, splashing him heartily.

"Whoa, hey!" Idris exclaimed, leaping back as droplets peppered his trousers. His heels collided with the small ledge of grass that met the rocks of the bank, and he stumbled, falling onto the soft ground.

Laughter spilled out of me, filling the quiet morning. Idris laughed, too, his cheeks flushed with bewilderment.

I rose clumsily to my feet, still chuckling. "Revenge is sweet!" I declared.

Idris's gaze dipped, and his laughter died.

I glanced down at my soaked chemise, the dark circles of my nipples easily visible through the fabric. When I looked up again, he met my eyes, looking like he wanted to devour me and felt *very* guilty about it. His throat bobbed; I could hear the thick gulp from ten feet away.

But before I could say anything, Idris stood, storming off toward camp. "Get a move on, would you?" he called over his shoulder. "We've a lot of ground to cover today."

This time, his sourness was painfully transparent. I tossed my wet braid over my shoulder, chuckling to myself as I shucked my useless chemise onto shore and finished bathing in peace.

20

GOSSIP

The night following the *second* river incident, the rain had cleared, and the weather had warmed, so Idris laid their blankets across the fire from one another. Separating himself from Anya seemed to be the right move, given how close he'd come the previous night to giving fully into temptation.

What was worse: Anya had seemed tempted, too. When had her fear of him shifted to...something else? It *must've* been the alcohol that made her so flirtatious; he couldn't imagine a world in which someone as vibrantly funny and sexy as Anya had any true interest in him. It was clear she possessed a rare willingness to see the good in people—even under extraordinarily contrarian circumstances—but that was all the more reason for Idris not to take her behavior last night too seriously. Even if she *did* want him, his Oath would never allow him to give her what she deserved.

Besides, he had his own Fate to contend with.

If Anya took offense at the unspoken signal of tonight's separate sleeping arrangement, she didn't show it. In fact, she'd been perfectly pleasant all day, and her apparent lack of self-consciousness remained intact throughout the evening, easing Idris's tension.

From his bedroll across the fire, Idris found himself telling Anya about the bird he'd cared for in the Bone Mountains (careful to omit that he'd thought of her similarly, at first); she, in turn, told him about the colony of violet-green swallows that nested under the Possum's eaves every summer. Their night of drinking had broken a barrier of some kind, and now that they knew each other better, it seemed no amount of space could keep him from seeking connection to her. It felt like a different sort of indulgence.

In the two days that followed, she remained chipper, buoying his mood even when he tried his best to anchor it in reality—but her amiable small talk and stories from Waldron-on-Wend amused him. By the afternoon on their tenth travel day together, Idris knew all the names of the townsfolk, and was embarrassingly invested their lives.

This was one thing the wilds truly couldn't offer him: good gossip. Serious as Idris saw himself, he *loved* gossip. The interplay of people's whims and wants was endlessly entertaining—and this seemed to be yet another opinion he and Anya shared.

Walking beside Briar, Idris found that his pace quickened slightly with intrigue as they discussed a bit of gossip Anya had heard from Martha, Waldron's baker. "Wait, so the cobbler's daughter—"

"Illian," Anya interjected.

"Right, Illian," Idris said, "was seen kissing the *jeweler's* son? I thought she was all but engaged to that Benny fellow?"

"She *was*," Anya said. "But truth be told, I'm not sure she ever loved him as much as he loved her."

Idris snorted. "Sounds like self-sabotage."

"I think it's the restlessness of youth," Anya said thoughtfully. "It's not uncommon for small-town youngsters to want...*more*. To travel, to meet new people, to set out on their own. So, when they're faced with the real prospect of settling down, they act out."

"Is that how you felt in your youth?"

"No, I've always been too responsible for my own good."

"Somehow I doubt that."

He was walking in line with Anya's stirrup, and she nudged him in the arm with her boot. "I *was*," she insisted. "I—well—my mother got sick when I was thirteen. After she died, I ended up caring for the owner of the Possum, my honorary grandmother, in a rather intense capacity. It gave me purpose during a dark period—but it didn't leave me much time for daydreaming about adventure."

Idris's heart twisted; he knew intimately what it felt like to lose family at a young age, and it pained him to imagine Anya experiencing the same. "Have you dreamt of adventure since?"

"My wildest dreams are in Waldron," she said, not without a hint of wistfulness. "Even before my mother died, I *loved* small town life. I still do. The connections, the community, the sense of belonging—it all gives my life meaning."

The twisting sensation in his chest screwed tighter, this time with...longing. Had his life ever possessed meaning, beyond the tenets of his Oath? He'd been so focused on his brother's legacy that he'd never much considered his own. It unsettled him and filled him with envy for what Anya had: a welcoming home to return to, when all was said and done.

"I'm sorry about your mother," he said sincerely. "I lost my parents when I was a boy. My brother, Grinnick—" Idris's throat tightened, but he pushed through. "He looked after us for a time. Died when I was twenty."

"*Fates*, Idris," Anya said. "That's awful."

He kept his chin up, facing forward, hoping she didn't catch the sudden color that stung his cheeks.

"So that's when you took your Oath?" she asked.

"Thereabouts."

What he couldn't divulge was that, unlike voluntary Orders such as the highly respected Order of the Mighty or the well-known Order of the Mirrors, the Order of the Valiant was a *sentence*. He hadn't taken Grinnick's place out of mere honor, but because Lord Haron had forced his hand. It didn't hurt that the monsters had a volatile effect on Idris's own disturbing visions in the Mirrors of Fate—but he put that out of his mind now. It was a mental path not worth walking—ever.

"What happened with Illian?" He prompted. "Did Benny find out?"

She hesitated a beat, no doubt noting his clumsy attempt to change the subject. "I'm not sure," she answered finally. "I was—well, not long after I heard about Illian, I ended up here."

Idris glanced over his shoulder at her. "Oh. Well. I guess you can look forward to hearing more about it when you return home."

She smiled weakly. "I suppose so."

They walked for another while in amiable silence, the sun poking out from behind the clouds. Soon, they crested into a shallow valley that was neatly bisected by the Wend. A town was clustered around the river on both sides, poplars and chimney smoke rising over the thatched cottage roofs. The wilds of the Western Wood swept inward from the left, dark and tangled branches reaching toward farmland; to the east, verdant hills were dotted with white sheep, black cattle, and late-season crops.

They'd reached Brine-on-Wend, their halfway mark.

"*Blessed be the Fates,*" Anya breathed, urging Briar into a faster walk. "Can we stay at an inn tonight? I'm dying for a hearty stew and a soft mattress."

The past handful of days had seen them through the most spread-out parts of the Fenrir territory—mostly empty countryside and the occasional homestead nestled against distant stone fence lines. The relief and longing in Anya's words was apparent, and Idris found it difficult to find an excuse not to stay the night in Brine.

"Very well," he relented.

"*Really?*" she asked. "No grumbling protest? No cranky speech about unnecessary indulgences?"

"Are you trying to talk me out of it?"

"I'm just surprised you're being so *amenable.*"

He glanced up at her again. Clearly enlivened by the mere *hope* of a proper bed, she appeared revived—reborn. She sat taller, her rosy cheeks puckering with glee. He thought of the sorrowful story she'd shared; a modest inn in Brine would do nothing to erase past pain, but if he could offer Anya even a temporary balm, Idris felt pulled to do so.

The pull was made stronger by seeing the way her body swayed with Briar's quickened strides. Idris hated that he now knew what her breasts looked like and could now picture their perfect shape at any moment. It made him miserable with desire. It made him desperate to please her. Perhaps a night away from her was *just* what he needed—a chance to get ahold of his resolve without her charm undermining his efforts.

"Enjoy it while it lasts," Idris said wryly, solidifying their plan.

"Oh, I will!" Anya clapped her hands, bouncing in the saddle.

Idris looked quickly away, hating how happy her happiness made him.

24

Don't Look a Gift Goat in the Mouth

Anya

Brine-on-Wend was deserted.

At least, it seemed that way at first. The outermost homes appeared empty, blinds drawn, with no stirrings that my magic could detect inside. No shepherds walked the fields, but the sheep seemed healthy enough; all storefronts were shuttered, but the planter boxes outside were well-kept, even for late autumn. Brine reminded me of an abandoned Waldron-on-Wend, if slightly bigger and less welcoming.

But as we neared the main thoroughfare, a cacophony of voices rose up from the center of town. It became clear why our arrival was lacking in initial witness: it seemed the entire population had crowded into the cobblestone square. As we rounded the corner into fuller view of the congregation, I was overwhelmed by the volume of angry shouts, pained sobbing, and strained pleas and opinions.

A stone statue of a goat was located at the far end of the plaza, and a well-dressed man with a huge mustache and wild gray hair stood atop the statue's square base, his arm clinging to the animal's neck for balance. He was speaking to the crowd—or rather, he was trying to, his raspy voice overpowered by louder citizens.

"What do you *mean* it had six legs?" someone demanded.

"The Fates have come to punish us!" another yelled in shrill terror.

"How many more deaths must we endure?" someone else wailed.

"Leave it locked in the barn and let it perish of starvation!"

"Set the barn on fire!"

"And risk the creature escaping?"

"Settle, settle!" the man atop the statue shouted. "This is a town meeting, not a riot! Have some decorum so we may come to a clear-headed conclusion!"

I halted Briar at the back of the crowd, Idris—on foot—tucking himself close to the horse's neck.

I leaned out of the saddle to whisper, "I think there's a bear in someone's barn."

He glanced back at me, expression grim. "Impossible," he ground out, even as his hand gripped Halgren's hilt.

"You have to help," I insisted.

I expected him to deny it, but he didn't. "Wait here."

Idris shouldered his way through the throng. He was taller and broader than most here, and his form—armor- and weapon-clad—was rather intimidating as he pushed his way to the front. He went straight to the town's leader, who—still standing atop the statue—wasn't even eye-level with Idris.

Idris leaned closer, whispering into the other man's ear. The crowd was too raucous for my magic to pluck out Idris's voice, so I could only watch as the town leader listened intently, nodding his head and stroking his mustache thoughtfully. Finally, he patted Idris's shoulder in a gesture that appeared something like gratitude.

When he piped up again, his voice rang out clearly. "We have a volunteer!" he said, then unceremoniously hopped down from the statue.

A hush swept over the crowd, then murmurs followed.

From my vantage atop Briar, I watched as Idris bent, whispering in the other man's ear again. He gestured toward me, and the older man craned his neck, nodded heartily, and waved me over.

I clicked my tongue at Briar, urging him forward slowly, offering my apologies to the folks who had to step out of his way. When I reached the statue, I hopped down, and the town leader introduced himself.

"Percival Penning," he said, holding out a hand. "Mayor of Brine. I'm sorry you've arrived at such a...tumultuous moment. I assure you, under normal circumstances, our community is far more genteel."

He was shorter than I was, and when I shook his hand, I found that his palm fit neatly into mine. "No apologies necessary," I said. "I'm Anya Alvara. I own the Pretty Possum in Waldron."

"Oh, the Possum! I've stayed there a time or two."

"Have you?" I had no recollection of him—and he seemed hard to forget.

"Stayed there on my honeymoon, in fact," Percival said, stroking his mustache, "though that was probably before you were born."

"My grandmother ran it before I."

Idris cleared his throat, bringing our brief and pleasant exchange back to reality.

Percival straightened and waved over a lumbering, light-haired man with a deep-tan face and cracked lips. "This is Len, the farmer whose barn is currently...plagued."

Len bobbed his head in greeting.

"Let's find us a private place to talk, shall we?" Percival asked. "My wife, Petunia, can tend to your horse."

At the sound of her name, Petunia, a tall and buxom older woman who'd been hovering nearby, smiled warmly at me. "We've a stable at the Lark, our inn and pub," she said, handing Briar a nub of carrot from her pocket. "He'll be in good hands there."

After passing Briar's reins off to Petunia, I fell in step behind Percival, following him out of the square. As I passed the goat statue, I noticed a neat script had been chiseled into its base: *Brine: Beloved billy goat, finder of this fair valley, our most cherished four-legged founder.* How utterly delightful that the town had been settled and named after a goat who wandered here? The insight left me with a friendly impression of the place.

With the rest of the crowd still debating the issue and shouting after Percival, we all ducked into a stately stone building that must've been Brine's official town hall. The main floor was filled with pews all facing a stage at the front, complete with a podium and throne-like chair.

Percival locked the door behind us—just in time for folks to start banging on the wood—and led us down the central walkway. Stepping up onto the platform, he flopped into the fancy chair; his legs didn't reach the ground from his seat, but he still appeared quite distinguished in his tailored waistcoat and proud posture.

"So, you say you can help?" Percival said to Idris without preamble. "You certainly look the part, what with that armor and formidable weapon, and I'm *certainly* not one to look a gift goat in the mouth—but I must say, I find it surprising you'd volunteer without more insight into the, uh...perils of what we're facing."

"It seems there's a rather unbelievable creature that's made itself at home in Len's barn?" I ventured.

"So, you've some idea," Percival said, lacing his fingers together.

More than you know, I thought darkly.

"Rowdy as everyone seemed in the square, they told no lies. Their fear is earned." Percival extended a hand to Len. "Tell them what happened, Len, from the beginning."

Len fiddled with the ends of his scarf, staring down at his hands as he spoke. "Took me pigs," he said, his country accent thick. "Just a few to start. Thought wolves were to blame at first. Then three nights ago, I forgot to close me barn door for the night. Just slipped me mind. When I went out the next morn..." He looked up at us, then, his eyes red-ringed. "Massacre."

I winced, aching for the poor frightened animals that'd met their end by the teeth of a monster.

"He managed to trap it inside," Percival supplied. "Came to me straight away. We mustered up a brave party of fighters yesterday to slay the creature." His gaze fell to the floor, mustache drooping with a sorrowful frown.

"Me neighbor, Farmer Gill..." A small sob escaped Len, and he clapped a weathered hand over his mouth.

The thought of the citizens of Waldron organizing like that, only for their efforts to end in tragedy...my chest ached. I met Idris's eyes for reassurance, but his expression was dark—all hard lines angling downward.

I went to Len, squeezing his forearm. "I'm *so* sorry. How awful."

"Vile thing," Len spat. "Never seen anything like it. Reckon I'll have nightmares for weeks."

I knew how he felt. My nightmares had ebbed as of late, quelled only by the knowledge that Idris was near, and capable, and seemed to have a sixth sense for whether or not such creatures were lurking. Len did not have the privilege of a knight looking after him. My eyes found Idris, and the corner of my mouth kicked up, a new facet of appreciation taking shape.

"What did it look like?" Idris asked. "Can you be specific?"

"'Bout the size and shape of a wolf, but..." Len drew a spiral in the air above his head.

"Antlers," I supplied.

He looked to me, wide-eyed, and nodded. "And too many legs."

"Is it still trapped in the barn?" Idris asked.

Len nodded. "After Gill...we nailed the door shut. Heard it whining last night, scratching at the wood."

Idris's jaw feathered.

"You probably think we've gone mad," Percival said, "but there've been similar sightings along the Western Wood for months. At first, I thought they were merely the tall tales from the homesteaders west of here—those lonesome folk can be superstitious, you know—but then..." He shook his head. "I blame myself, for not taking it seriously much sooner."

"How in the Fates can you eradicate such a thing?" Len asked Idris. "I couldn't bear to look upon it a second time."

"You won't have to," Idris said firmly.

"You seem mighty confident," Percival said, narrowing his eyes. "You sure you know what you're up against?"

I considered telling them that he'd slain monsters before, but I didn't want to divulge more than his Oath allowed. "He's a formidable fighter," I assured them instead, even as my heart lodged itself in my throat at the thought of Idris facing another monster on his own.

"'Tis no average predator," Len said darkly.

Idris's face—shadowed in the dim gathering hall—gave away nothing of his confidence. "Take me to the barn."

25

MONSTER HUNTER

IDRIS

For fifteen years, it had been Idris's solemn duty to protect the towns of Fenrir from the monsters of the western wilds. Over time, through experience and the magic of his Oath, he'd grown sensitive to the movements of abominations—their paths, their patterns, their methods of spreading. His very purpose was linked to the wretched creatures, to the keeping of their secret and their eradication.

But today, as he followed Percival and Len toward a big red barn on the outskirts of Brine-on-Wend, he felt like he'd failed.

Of course, he was not the only Knight of the Order of the Valiant. He encountered others from time to time—to share news, commiserate, feud, and, in his younger years, track and kill large creatures together. He'd watched great men fall to their final Fate by the teeth and talons of the monsters they hunted—including Grinnick. When Idris fought, he fought for his brother and his realm, and also for the brave souls who'd fought before him.

The collective responsibility of his Order did not lighten Idris's sense of blame now—it made it heavier. The wolverine by Waldron and the bear at Anya's prisoner caravan were disturbing enough, but a monster venturing so far east as to encounter true civilization, a *town*? That had never happened before, and the news was deeply unsettling. It seemed that in spite of the Order's efforts—*his* efforts—the abominations were undeterred. This made Idris not just a single failure, but a small part of a failing enterprise, which was all the more disconcerting.

Discouragement, however, was not an option at present. What better way to expel his pent-up guilt than to eradicate Brine's current and dire threat? It might've been the duty of Idris's Oath to prevent further citizen deaths, but it was his anger—with his own weakness, his own disheartenment toward his life's duty—that motivated him now.

As Idris trudged up the hill, his boots crunching through the semi-frozen overgrown grass, his tongue still stung with the bitterness of his Oath's warning, the secrecy he was bound to. He'd never expected to confront the limits of his Oath by conversing with folks who *already knew* the heart of what he could not say. Anya had helpfully, gracefully assisted him in navigating their conversation with Percival, but he wondered now if having witnesses to this fight also contradicted the tenets of his Oath.

Then again, to let the abomination run free was *also* a contradiction of his Oath, and—in Idris's opinion—much worse than the spreading of information he himself hadn't even confirmed.

Besides, it was folly to hope to eradicate the creature without witnesses; as Anya had reiterated in her gossip from Waldron, in small towns, word traveled fast. Indeed, by the time their intrepid foursome reached Len's barn—halting some fifty yards from its entrance—the crowd from the town square were already halfway up the hill behind them.

To mitigate risk and rumor, Idris concluded he would have to fight the monster inside the barn, with the door shut.

"Keep them back, would you?" he asked Anya, his heart already tripping into a faster beat, the rancid scent of the nearby monster stinging his nose. "No matter what you hear, don't allow *anyone* to enter the barn."

Anya reached for him, her delicate fingers squeezing his forearm just above his silver vambrace. "Please be careful?"

This was yet another reason not to get attached. When he had no hope or worldly desires other than to serve his brother's memory and the tenets of his Oath, he was fearless; when he had something personal to lose—such as more time with the woman in front of him—the danger was illuminated in greater contrast.

"Don't tell me you're worried about me," Idris said, making light of her concern.

She smirked. "I've become rather accustomed to your aggravating ways." Real worry laced her carefully playful tone.

He stared down at her, surprised by her transparency, even in humor. Her brown eyes were flecked with gold, her pink cheeks freckled. A strand of hair that'd come loose from her customary braid now caught on her wet bottom lip.

Fates, she was beautiful. But more than that, she was quick-witted, which Idris was finding to be a real weakness of his.

He covered her hand on his arm. "I'll be fine," he promised, then he gently removed her grip.

"You truly wish to go in alone?" Percival interjected. "It seems—well, forgive me, but—it seems rather foolish to face it one-to-one."

"I agree," Len added.

Idris gave them both a tight-lipped smile, repeating, "I'll be fine."

"I can't say I condone the risk," Percival said, "but you are your own man."

The crowd was gathering into a half-moon behind them, eyes wide and voices hushed. Children hugged their parents' legs fearfully. A few brave men and women held pitchforks and shovels. Percival's expression was resolute, but thin as ice, a cold terror visible under his smooth surface.

It was not Idris's job to comfort the people of Brine; it was his job to protect them. Without another word, he turned and strode toward the barn.

The sliding door was nailed shut with shoddy boards and bent spikes. Idris retrieved his small axe from its holster on his back and used it to wedge the boards free. It took a few minutes of anticlimactic fiddling, in which he felt painfully aware of his audience. But then he wrenched the boards free, squeezed through the door into the shadows, and closed himself inside.

The barn reeked of death. Overpowering the familiar scents of hay, grain, and manure was the iron-tang of flesh and blood, along with the cloying rot of monster. No sound emanated from the darkness. For all their snarling viciousness, abominations could be surprisingly silent—perhaps the extra legs lent them stealth.

Idris unsheathed Halgren, the metal singing into the quietude as he stepped forward. "Here, kitty, kitty," he called tauntingly, feeling the energized calm of adrenaline hit his bloodstream. He took a sick sort of pleasure in the killing of these creatures, all his vengeance and frustration funneling into a focused hatred. An outlet for his pain.

Two red eyes appeared in the darkness ahead, glowing with inner evil like two coals in a bed of ashen fur. The wolf-faced abomination hissed low and from the throat, a guttural vibration that Idris felt in his core.

His Oath didn't just hold his tongue and power his sword; it offered him heightened awareness that was separate from his sensory magic. A creature moved, and if Idris was close enough, he felt a reverberation against his skin like ripples in water. It was this sensitivity that rendered him unsurprised when the creature leapt out of the darkness.

Idris dropped to the ground, rolling across the blood-crusted straw out of the creature's path, only to hop to his feet again on its other side. Halgren caught fire, illuminating the barn with its blue flame. Idris's will and the monster's proximity activated the sword's magic, charging it like lightning in a thundercloud. Confronted with Halgren's crackling fire, the creature whined and snarled.

This was where it got fun.

Idris swung, catching the tip of one of the wolf's spindly forelegs, spider-like and protruding from its shoulder. It *screamed*, black blood spurting across the straw floor. Idris used its surprise to his advantage, swiping at its other wretched foreleg and cutting it off at the joint. The beast reared back, the tangle of its short, deformed antlers crashing against a crossbeam in the barn's ceiling.

Dust sprinkled down from the rafters, and the walls shook. Idris heard shrieks and gasps from outside.

The abomination backed away, recovering from the surprise of Idris's blows. It was in such pauses that he saw the animals that the monsters had once been, a flash of innocence behind the red glow in their eyes. He pitied the poor creatures. Whatever sickness took over—evil infecting their blood, bodies expanding in size, bone shoving through temples, new legs forming—it always seemed to leave a bit of *awareness* inside, as if the soul of the animal kept the disease alive.

It felt like mercy to kill them.

Idris let out a growling cry, swinging Halgren in a practiced arc. He caught the monster in the crease of its neck, but its flesh was tough. It wrenched free of his blade, snapping at Idris's sword-wielding arm with a furious snarl. Teeth nicked Idris's shirtsleeve, but didn't manage to catch skin, for which he was glad—he was running low on Hattie's salve.

Outside the barn, Idris heard the vague scuffle of concerned voices, a child crying out. He imagined the sounds he and the monster were making were alarming.

Sweat formed on his temple and along his spine. He lunged at the creature again, slicing at it in a quick series of blows that strained his old shoulder injury. Rather than backing off, the monster snarled at him, swiping out with an uninjured paw, its unnatural claws as long as Idris's forearm.

Idris ducked, dropping hard on his knees. He found himself practically under its chest, and without enough space to stab up into its heart, he swung Halgren from the side, hacking at the wound he'd already started in the creature's neck.

More slimy, caustic blood rained down, stinging Idris's cheeks. He kicked his legs, scooting backward across the floor; he needed to get his feet under him.

But then a metal track whined, and light sliced through the barn door at his back. A child appeared, screaming, *"Daddy!"*

The child, hysterical, tried to rush further inside—but he was caught by a hand on his collar.

Anya.

Her red hair flashed in the light of Halgren's flame. He saw her mouth round into perfect shock as she hauled the child back. Her presence was just distracting enough for Idris to falter, missing his Oath's warning when the monster pounced.

Anya cried out in terror, her vocal cords cracking at the pinnacle of her shriek. *"IDRIS!"*

The monster's teeth collided with Idris's chest. Grinnick's breastplate re-pelled the beast with a force, searing it with magic. The abomination wailed, stumbling backward.

"GO!" Idris boomed at Anya.

There was more commotion behind him, arguing voices and the door screeching shut again, the child crying uncontrollably.

Idris didn't have time to worry that the child had witnessed the monster. He was on his feet again, burying Halgren into the side of the beast's neck. This time, he hit something vital, and the monster yelped. Teeth snapped; another paw swiped at him. Idris growled again, leaning all his weight into one final swing. The killing blow.

The monster went down with a thud, Halgren's edge buried deep in its spurting neck.

Idris gritted his teeth as his tattoo hummed, magically reporting the kill to the Oath Ledgers—then he yanked his sword out of the abomination's flesh. Halgren's flame flickered out, and he wiped the steel on the wolf's fur before sliding the blade into its sheath.

Idris took stock of the rest of his body. His breastplate was dented, but it'd done its magical duty; his chest still buzzed with the sensation of the blow, an unpleasant vibration of force and magical energy. The muscles in his arms felt strained. The joints of his knees ached. Aside from the tear in his shirtsleeve, he was unscathed.

As his eyes adjusted to the flameless dark, he finally had a chance to observe the destruction of the creature's presence. Body parts of pigs were strewn about, rotting and caked with black sludge. One corpse had the beginnings of new forelegs and antlers, but the wolf had torn a hole in its side. The floor was wet with old blood; the air smelled not just like death, but cloying disease and ominous rot.

Idris wiped his cheek on his sleeve. Then he retrieved a piece of flint from his pocket and struck sparks in the hay at his feet. The monster's black blood was flammable, and caught quickly, igniting the body and the surrounding splattered beams. With its abominable form engulfed, Idris turned and walked out into the late afternoon sunshine to face the crowd.

26

HERO TREATMENT

IDRIS

I dris's duty had always been a thankless one, and he possessed no desire to stoke his ego with illusions of glory. His was an Order of punishment, after all. But as he stepped out of the flaming barn, the crowd erupted into cheers, and for the first time in his hard life, Idris felt like a victor.

A hero.

Making his way toward the townsfolk, Idris tried to construct a narrative in his head that might control the rumors. Would they believe a rabid wolf was to blame? Anya certainly hadn't believed his rabid bear excuse, but she'd seen far more than the citizens of Brine. Rumors of antlers and mangled forelegs would be hard to explain away, but by the will of his Order, he would have to at least *try* to diffuse the inevitable talk with a sensible explanation. Perhaps he could convince them the deformities of the monster were mere tricks of shadow...

Idris was still turning over ideas in his mind when Anya broke from the crowd and stormed toward him. The sight of her—cheeks flaming, hair disheveled—halted any further consideration of the abomination.

She appeared rather...angry? Her eyebrows were pinched, lips set in a determined line. It stopped Idris in his tracks, but *her* approach did not falter as she entered his personal space. Her body collided with his, her hand gripping the back of his neck, bringing his mouth down to hers.

All thought left him, save for the scent and sensation of Anya.

Her kiss was furious. It reminded him of a hard rain, cutting through his layers, soaking him through. Delayed by his bewilderment, Idris's arms finally encircled her, crushing her softness against him. Who was he to deny her? Who was he to deny *himself* in this gloriously confusing moment? He was principled and strong, but not enough to resist *her*.

She tilted her head, lips pleading under the hungry press of his own, mouth opening for one thrilling brush of her tongue.

Then she yanked free of his embrace.

His body rocked forward in her absence, pulled by her magnetic force.

He met her eyes, and in them he saw anger and fear and relief. *How dare you almost die*, they said, and in spite of all self-restraint, he felt fucking *smug* to have gotten such a rise out of her. To have perhaps impressed her with his heroics.

Fates, was his ego already so inflated?

They didn't have a chance to linger in their charged standoff, for the crowd was rushing in, patting his back, offering him free ale at the Lark, asking him impossible questions about the creature, overwhelming him with attention. Anya disappeared into the chaos, and Idris didn't have a chance to question her passion—*surely it was just an expression of relief, nothing more?*—as the townsfolk bombarded him.

His body buzzed not with adrenaline now, but the lingering effects of her attention, a ravenous excitement he hadn't felt since his adolescence. He was mildly ashamed of how distracting his desire was, how quickly he'd forgotten everything else happening around him, and how his body still clung to the ghost of her brief but passionate touch.

He realized he *wanted* the kiss to mean something more than just the hero treatment. And that went against everything else he stood for.

"Please, people, please!" Percival said, elbowing his way through the crowd to Idris. "Give our hero some *space*, would you?" He offered Idris a grandiose bow, one toe pointed, his arms outstretched. "You've Brine's most sincerest gratitude. We are in your debt!"

"No debt," Idris said.

Percival leaned in close, rising on his tiptoes to whisper, "However did you manage this feat? What *was* that creature?"

Idris fixed his face into what he hoped looked like casual certainty. "Rabid wolf."

Percival didn't seem to believe him. "But the other men said it had—"

"Illusions of light and shadow," Idris interrupted. "Fear plays tricks on the mind."

There, he thought to himself. *I've done my duty.*

Idris spotted Len nearby and broke from Percival's attention to address the farmer. "I'm sorry about your barn, but inside was—"

Len patted Idris's shoulder, his eyes shining with the glow of his burning barn, which was now fully engulfed in flame. "Couldn't imagine stepping in there again," Len said. "You did me a favor. I know the whole town wants to treat you to an ale, but…"

It was clear that there was no evading the town's gratitude; was it so wrong to enjoy his duty, for once? Idris smiled. "They can get in line behind you, I reckon."

Len's answering grin was a little wan, but he patted Idris again heartily, then started down the hill. Idris walked alongside him, cutting through the crowd. Hands reached out toward him, patting his back appreciatively.

Then Idris spotted the boy who'd interfered with the fight. He paused again.

The child was tucked safely against his mother's leg, his face tear-streaked and blotchy. She didn't appear much better, her eyes red-ringed and puffy, her hand gripping the boy's bony shoulder. The dead farmer's family, Idris deduced. He thought of the husband she'd lost, the father her boy would grow up without, the sorrow and uncertainty of their lives now.

Idris knew that pain. It felt like the sun disappearing from the sky, dire and disorienting.

"My sincerest condolences," he told the widow, knowing the inadequacy of his words even as he spoke them. "Your husband did a brave thing; he died more a hero than I."

She bowed her head.

Idris crouched down to the boy's level. His eyes were watery, but his jaw was set; he was trying to be brave. It reminded Idris of himself, the fear and loss that had plagued his own boyhood. He held his hand out toward the boy; after a hesitant moment, the boy took his palm, and they shook.

"You have your father's bravery, I see," Idris told the boy. "Remember it, when you find yourself missing him or doubting yourself."

The boy sniffled, curling his fist against his chest.

Idris rose to his full height again and turned to Percival, who'd been following on his and Len's heels. "You say you are in my debt?"

Percival bobbed his head.

"Look after them," Idris said of the mother and child. "Ensure they never go cold or hungry. That is all I wish."

By the standards of the competitive city streets of Fenrir—where another person's success was nearly a direct threat to one's own—Idris's request would've seemed extravagant. But Percival didn't hesitate.

"We will—we already *are*," the mayor said. "Brine is not just a town, but a community. We look out for one another." He said it like it was obvious—a given.

The sentiment seemed so far outside Idris's own experience with civilization that he was momentarily struck. He swallowed thickly, then rested a palm on Percival's tiny shoulder and shook it approvingly. The moment passed, and he started down the hill again, leading the entire crowd toward the tavern in the square.

Idris resisted the urge to glance over his shoulder in search of Anya; he had the suspicion that if he did, he'd get flustered all over again. It took enough willpower just to set the moment aside in his mind.

"I insist you stay the night in Brine," Percival continued, jogging to keep up with Idris's purposeful strides. "For free, of course. You'll suffer no expense! It's the least we can do for you, in thanks for what you've done."

Idris thought of Anya's earlier request, about staying a night in the comforts of an inn. It was not for himself, but for her, that he said to Percival, "I gladly accept."

27

NIGHT AT THE LARK

ANYA

Brine's revel for Idris extended into the night with fresh bread, hot stew, and free-flowing ale. The only moment of peace he seemed to get was when the innkeeper, Fiona, showed him his room; he returned downstairs with wet hair and a clean face, clad in fresh clothes; without his armor, he appeared more approachable, but no less heroic, his broadness and musculature proof enough of his power.

As soon as he reappeared, Idris had been swept up in the merriment, folks slapping his back, shaking his shoulder, and pressing fresh tankards into his reluctant palms. I tried not to glance in his direction as I nestled deeper into my corner seat by the fireplace, nursing a hot mulled cider.

Surrounded by half-drunk townsfolk, I couldn't help but relish the camaraderie around me. It reminded me of the Possum—I half expected to hear Hattie giggling behind the bar, spot Martha and Hugh and Vera at a nearby table, to glance down and see Wicker at my feet. Just the thought of Waldron made my heart clench, tight as a fist.

I took another long sip of my cider, a part of me wishing I'd ordered something stronger.

Across the pub, a string of men had slung their arms across each other's shoulders, with Idris in the middle. They were singing an old soldiering song, swaying from side to side. Idris clearly didn't know the words, and his lips moved reluctantly during the long verses, gaining confidence with the repetition of the chorus. He was clearly uncomfortable—bemused, even—under such enthusiastic attention, but he seemed appreciative, too. Given his secretive life, it must've been overwhelming to suddenly be at the center of a celebration.

I found his reluctant acceptance of their praise endearing. Most men—especially those in the rural stretches of Fenrir, who fancied themselves tough—would've *preened* under such revelry. Chests puffed, flirtatious comments on the tips of their tongues. But from the moment Idris had emerged from that burning barn, smeared with pig's blood and the black splatter of his foe's gore, he hadn't raised his sword in triumph or declared himself a hero. He'd simply looked like himself, huge and capable, but also humble and kind. A man of hard edges and a soft center.

It was another tally in the growing list of reasons that his appearance in my Mirror of Death seemed...wrong.

His humility was *not* the reason I'd kissed him, however. It'd been the hysterical relief flooding my veins. The acute desire to touch him, just to prove to my harried heart that he was all right.

All throughout the fight, the crowd had been whispering their doubts, their discouraging words penetrating my sensitive heart. Confident as I was in Idris's capabilities, it had been impossible not to feel the collective sense of doom as we waited. Horrible, frightening noises had come from within the barn.

It seemed the widow's son possessed similar gifts as mine, because when he heard the grunts of Idris's efforts and the monster's returning snarls, he'd become *convinced*—blinded by grief—that it was not Idris but his own father fighting the monster inside. When the boy darted across the grass, I'd anticipated it. I'd raced after him, fearing not just for the child's life, but Idris's, if the boy's interference caused a distraction.

And it *had*.

We'd arrived in time to see Idris on the ground, his flaming sword held awkwardly aloft as the huge, wolf-like abomination stalked toward him. At the critical moment, Idris had taken notice of us, his blue-green eyes finding mine.

Seeing the horrible monster leap toward him, mouth open wide, ready to consume him—it had filled me with an ice-cold dread similar to what I'd felt for my own life the night Idris had rescued me. Even now, safe inside a merry pub, a warm drink in my hand, I did not feel fully thawed. But as I watched him swaying with the other men, the dark waves of his hair brushing his cheeks as he rocked from side to side, desire heated my blood once more.

Try as I might to convince myself that the kiss had been a one-off—merely an impassioned moment after Idris had put himself in harm's way and survived—I knew myself better. Tension had been simmering between us since our first night in the tent, and now that I knew what it felt like to have him crush me against his chest, *hungry* for my mouth...well, it only made me crave *more*. What had once been a spark in my belly was now an inferno, and the longer I spent with him, the less I cared if I got burned.

I *should* care. I should keep my eyes firmly on the path ahead. Because beyond the creature comforts of a *man*, what I really wanted was to clear my name and return to Waldron and forget this adventure ever happened. But was forgetting even possible, now that I knew what lurked in the Western Wood? Could I go back to normal life, now that I knew what Idris tasted like?

I downed the rest of my cider, frustrated with my inner contradictions. *He's your future killer*, I reminded myself sternly, but even my inner voice sounded halfhearted tonight.

All afternoon, I'd been ruminating on the rumor from Brine, about the old man's altered Fortune. Had the proximity of monsters been the cause of his warped Fate? Were the tangled threads of that story and today's events enough to prove the possibility that Idris's Fate could negate mine? Or was I simply grasping for excuses to trust him, to justify my attraction?

I can lie to you all I want, Idris had said on the first morning of our quest, but at no point during the past ten days did it seem like he had followed through on that threat. At least, not on the topics that mattered most.

The singers had started a new tune about a brave man on the road, dreaming of his lady love. I hummed along softly, chuckling to myself when Idris fumbled the words, only to sober at the reminder that I, too, was merely a brave soul on the road, pining for home.

I stood, suddenly ready for solitude. I carried my glass to the bar, thanked Fiona for her hospitality, and slipped upstairs.

My room was at the end of the hall. When I slipped inside, I was pleased to find it pleasantly toasty, the hearth already crackling. The room wasn't as nice as the Possum—the furniture plain, the curtains a bit dusty—but the bed was spacious and inviting.

The one thing the Lark *did* have on the Possum was a working chimney. I sighed heavily, resolving to clean ours if I returned home. *When* I returned home. I bit my lip, turning away from the fire even as I wondered if Idris was any good with chimneys.

A tub in the corner had been filled, and I swirled a finger in the water, finding it tepid now, but not too chilly. After unpacking my things, I decided to wash up; compared to my icy river baths, this was decadent, and I went so far as to scrub my hair and soak in the sweet-smelling water for a while, my cheeks warmed by the nearby fire.

When I was done, I threw an extra couple logs on the coals and bedded down, nestling into the comfort of the soft mattress and excess of blankets. The pillows weren't as fluffy as the Possum's, but I was just grateful for a pillow that wasn't my wadded-up cloak. Cozier than I'd been in two full weeks, the merry sounds of the party downstairs lulled me to sleep.

I awoke to a loud thud outside my door.

I peeked one eye open, irritated. The room was dark. Voices still floated up from downstairs, but they were diminished now. I glanced at the hearth and found that it had died down, signaling the lateness of the hour. Midnight, perhaps.

I closed my eyes again, chalking the thud up to a drunken guest stumbling to their room. Peaceful seconds passed.

Then another thump sounded, this time like a heavy fist hitting my door.

I lifted my head, peering at the threshold. The dim light of the hall illuminated the gap underneath my door, but the strip of yellow was darkened by twin shadows: feet.

"It's me," Idris grumbled from outside.

At the sound of his gravel-ridden voice, two sensations occurred in my chest. First was a flood of annoyance that Idris would interrupt my precious night in a proper bed. Second was a fluttery, thrilling sensation, like a murmuration of birds trapped inside my ribs.

I decided to focus on the annoyance.

I flung the covers back and shuffled over to the door, opening it a crack. "What?" I enunciated harshly.

He rested a hand high on the doorframe, his bicep mere inches from my face. A goofy smile spread across his lips. "Hi."

He was drunk.

"May I help you?" I asked.

His eyes fluttered closed, and he lifted his chin. "I hope so," he slurred. "Will you let me in?"

With a sigh, I opened the door wider, stepping to the side. He stumbled into my room, carried forward by the momentum of inebriation. I closed the door and swiveled round to face him, finding him near. He swayed toward me a little, and I steadied him with my hands on his stomach.

His very *solid* stomach.

"Whoa there," he said, straightening.

"Seems they lavished you with ale," I said, taking a healthy step back and resting my fists on my hips.

His eyes meandered down my body and back up again, apparently noticing that I was, unfortunately, wearing the same chemise as that of the morning he caught me bathing in the river. He didn't seem to think it unfortunate, however. Drunk as he was, his eyes darkened. "What I wouldn't give to lavish *you*," he murmured.

"With...?"

His eyes narrowed, like he hadn't quiet followed.

I laughed a little, even as the fluttering sensation in my chest threatened to lift me off the ground. "Do you mean *ravish*?"

"Whatever you want," Idris said, with the grave seriousness that only a very drunk man could pull off.

He didn't seem like a grabby drunk, nor a dangerous one—rather, he seemed like an honest drunk. My favorite kind.

I smiled sweetly at him. "And what do *you* want?"

Those blue-green eyes bored into me. "Something I can't have."

My breath caught, but I recovered quickly. "What can I help you with, at such an hour, Idris?" I asked, lacing my tone with impatience. "Knowing you, you'll demand we leave at the crack of dawn, and this late into the night, I can't imagine you'll have enough time to sleep off the barrel you've drunk."

He huffed a laugh, then said on a sigh, "I just wanted to know why."

"Why what?"

"Why you did it."

He was speaking of the kiss, obviously. But I played coy. "Did what?"

He took a step closer, looming over me. I wanted to put my hands on him again—and not just for the sake of keeping him from falling. "Why you *kissed* me," he whispered, sounding utterly pained.

In the dark, the sharp angles of his face took on a shadowy quality, the effect intensified by the dark stubble on his jaw. The only soft thing about him, it seemed, were his eyes—looking at me so longingly—and his barely parted lips. I knew his hands could be soft, too, but they were currently in fists at his sides.

"Because I wanted to," I answered honestly.

A crease formed between his eyebrows. "But only the one time, right?"

I couldn't bear to answer that—not with the way he was looking at me, like a flower he was trying not to pluck for himself. I saw in his eyes the answer to the question *I* had been wondering all afternoon, and it scared me.

Slipping out from his personal space, I opened the door for him to leave. Even drunk, he knew how to take a hint, and walked heavily into the hall. With his palm on the doorknob opposite to mine, he glanced back at me.

"I hope you sleep well, Anya," he said, then shuffled into his room and closed himself inside.

28

CONTROL

ANYA

Idris did not speak much the following day.

He didn't seem embarrassed by his drunken visit to my room, just horribly hungover, and out of pity, I let him ride Briar. I preferred to be on foot, anyhow. The events in Brine—the monster, the kiss, his visit to my room, along with the proof that I truly need not worry about his appearance in my Mirror of Death—all filled me with an excess of energy that was best walked off.

We reached a tiny village just before nightfall, no more than a cluster of homesteads among fields of agriculture. The air was still and had turned bitter, the sky clear and unforgiving. Briar's hooves clattered on the frozen mud of the High Road, and as soon as the sun slipped behind the tree line, frost formed on the grass in a sparkling crust.

Idris wanted to pass through the village and travel through the night, to make up for our late departure from Brine—but when one of the villagers spotted us, he flagged us down and *insisted* we stay the night, out of the cold. Apparently, tales of Idris's bravery had already spread ahead of us, and the folks here thought it an honor to host the famed hero of Brine.

A half hour later, we were seated on the common room floor of the village's largest home (a modest four-room cottage) with eighteen members of their total population of twenty-five. The congregation included our host—Bren? Wren? I hadn't caught his name—his wife Tura, their five children, their closest neighbors, and *their* children, along with a few stragglers.

Throughout supper, they peppered Idris with questions, which he managed to evade with varying levels of finesse. I didn't know the exact rules of his Oath, but I knew secrecy was involved, and as the night wore on, Idris appeared more and more run-down from the tediousness of avoiding questions he couldn't answer.

I tried to interject on his behalf when I could, but many of the questions—especially those regarding the monsters' existence, like where they came from and why no one had ever heard of them before—were ones I harbored, myself, and I found it hard to disregard them. Idris stuck to his rabid wolf story, but even he seemed wretchedly unconvinced.

After our bowls of root vegetable stew were emptied, the neighbors had gone home, and the children had been tucked into bed in the other room, Idris and I sat across from each other at the family's worn oak table, cradling cups of peppermint tea while our hosts prepared dessert in the conjoined kitchen.

Idris looked worse for wear. Dark circles shaded his tired eyes. His mouth drooped in a lopsided frown. His forearms rested limply on the table, candlelight catching on his knuckles and the veins in the backs of his beautiful hands like sunlight setting over rugged ridgelines.

The cheerful commotion of welcoming strangers had me feeling quite the opposite of the way he looked. I was revived, bolstered by this home away from home—but, then again, I hadn't drunk my bodyweight in ale the previous night.

"How are you faring?" I whispered, keeping my voice low so that our hosts didn't eavesdrop from the other room. From what I'd gathered from the story of how they'd met—the humorous tale relayed to us two hours ago—they both possessed sight magic.

Idris sighed through his nose, causing the curl of steam above his mug to scatter and reform. "It's *exhausting* being a hero," he said. "And it's been a long time since I was this hungover."

My mouth quirked, and without really thinking, I reached across the table to trail my fingertips along his wrist. "You poor thing," I teased.

His attention snapped to our hands. Perhaps my consoling touch had been a mistake. I made to draw back, but Idris caught my fingers before I could, tugging at them with his own in a silent signal that the touch wasn't entirely unwanted. When his tired eyes found mine, they were inquisitive.

But before either of us could speak, our hosts returned, and we both let go.

"What's this?" I asked politely as they arranged four tiny plates of jam and fluffed cream on the table.

"Tura's specialty," the husband—I still hadn't confirmed his name—said, pulling up a chair. "The cream's from our beloved cow, Chicken—the kids named her that," he added with a laugh. "And of course, Tura made the jam, too. Sweetest blackberries in all of Fenrir, I say, due to the thicket's proximity to the Wend."

"Wren exaggerates," Tura said modestly, taking her seat as well.

"What a decadent treat," I said brightly, picking up a spoon, "you're spoiling us."

Idris lifted a brow at my overly polite tone. The excitable energy of the last few hours was subsiding, easing into a somewhat awkward quietude in the presence of these strangers; I didn't want them to take Idris's weariness personally.

"I think I missed where you two were headed," Wren said, taking a tentative sip of his own tea. "Seems a rough time of year for travel."

"We're heading to the capital," I said. "We've some...business to attend to there."

"Fenrir City!" Tura exclaimed. "I should've known the famous Hero of Brine would have important business there."

"What sort of business?" Wren asked—an innocent question if it weren't for his prying eyes dipping to Idris's Oath tattoo.

"This and that," I answered for him.

Wren didn't even glance in my direction. He was still staring excitedly at Idris, clearly spellbound by the idea of having a knight at his table. "What sort of knight are you, anyway?" he asked, leaning his elbow on the table. "Not sure you said earlier."

"He didn't," I cut in.

Idris looked up from his dessert. A bit of cream clung to the stubble on his chin, and for a moment I imagined climbing across the table and licking it off. Catching my expression, Idris cocked his head to one side, a familiar wry smile ghosting across his lips. Heat prickled across my cheeks, and—too flustered to keep looking at the man seated across from me, even after he wiped his mouth with the back of his hand—I dropped my focus to my plate, fixating on the task of spooning up the perfect bite of jam and cream.

It had been a strange twenty-four hours, filled with fateful revelations and harrowing heroics, and that kiss that made the tip of my tongue tingle even now, just thinking of it. As much as I basked in the hospitality of Brine and this small village, I found myself suddenly missing the solitude of the road, where I had Idris's attention all to myself.

Then again, the idea of having those blue-green eyes fixed on me now, with no distractions, sounded akin to standing with my toes to a fire—too intense for more than a few seconds.

"*Wren*," Tura scolded, her sharp tone shaking me loose from the fantasy of my own thoughts. "You can't ask a knight about his Order."

"He doesn't have to answer," Wren argued, swiveling his arm on the table—only to knock Tura's plate into her lap.

"*Fates*," she swore, jumping up from her seat and sending the plate and spoon clattering across the floorboards.

A brief scramble ensued, in which Wren sprung to gather the dishes from the floor while Tura quickly wetted a napkin in her tea to dab at the jam covering the front of her pale blue dress.

"Oh, that's going to stain," she said miserably, rubbing furiously at the purple splotch. She was clearly trying to hold it together for our sake. "Wren, you can be such a ninny sometimes."

My gaze shot to Idris, who promptly lifted his mug to his lips, eyes wide over the rim.

"I'm so sorry, my sweet, so sorry," Wren kept saying, bustling around her unhelpfully.

Tura didn't say more, but her cheeks were the bright pink of a woman truly upset. "This is my favorite dress," she murmured, still scrubbing at the stain. Her tone was impossibly light, bemused, almost humorous—which told me she was on the verge of hysterical tears.

"I can help with that," I said, rising from my chair, too. "We can make it like new."

When she looked at me, tears were wobbling along her lower lashes. "Oh, you're just saying that to make me feel better. It's clearly ruined."

"No, truly," I said, laying a steadying hand on her arm. "Back in Waldron, I run an inn, so I've battled many a stain." I made a cringing face, and Tura chuckled. "I have a trick I can show you. Do you happen to have any snowberries growing near here?"

Tura visibly cheered. "There are a bunch along the barn, in fact. Let me get changed and I'll show you."

The next hour went by in a flurry, the four of us collecting berries in the frosty dark, bringing our foraged treasures into the kitchen, and working the berries' juice—which could be frothed into a soapy lather—into the stain in Tura's dress.

Silly as it was to take pleasure in laundry, it felt good to remove Tura's pain and embarrassment and turn the mishap into something sweet again. After feeling so helpless on the road, I'd forgotten how much I enjoyed bettering peoples' lives. And given the grim uncertainty of what awaited me in Fenrir, it was nice to clean up a tangible mess, to feel *accomplished*.

When finally, Wren and Tura retired to their bedroom, Idris and I laid out our bedrolls on the common room floor. A faint smile played across my face as I replayed Tura's expression in my mind, watching as the stain faded away, her whole demeanor lightening. I was still distracted by it while I blew out the candles on the table, which were no more than soft piles of wax this late into our long evening in this nameless village.

Darkness consumed the unfamiliar room, and I shuffled across the floor, feeling my way toward my makeshift bed with my feet. My toe caught on the edge of something firm, and Idris—supine already—reached out, staying me with a hand on my bare ankle.

I halted, teetering more from his touch than a lack of balance. His grip sent a pulse up my leg straight to my core.

"Please don't step on me," he said.

I looked down at him, unable to make out much in the dark other than the vague shape of his body blocking my path. "Please don't trip me," I replied.

His palm slid under the hem of my dress, cupping my calf. Fingers brushed against the back of my knee. Ever so gently, he guided my leg up and across his chest, setting my foot safely down on the other side.

For a moment, I stood over him, my ankles bracketing his waist. The air felt charged with a sudden, heady tension. As my vision adjusted to the dark, Idris's eyes looked like the two brightest stars in the night sky, giving me the odd sense that the floor and the ceiling had switched places.

Wobbling slightly, I continued my path across the obstacle of his body and lowered myself to my bedroll a safe two feet away. Then I spent far too long folding and refolding my cloak into a pillow. By the time I rested my head atop it, I half expected—*hoped*, really—that Idris would be asleep; he'd had a long couple days.

But as I stilled, settling into my blankets, he piped up quietly. "I think you made Tura's whole week."

"Oh, please, you were the main draw this evening," I said. "I just saved us an awkward night of listening to their hushed argument in the other room."

He chuckled. "You really do enjoy helping people, don't you?"

"Yes," I said.

"You're good at it."

I turned onto my side to face him. "Thank you."

"Far more natural at it than camping," he teased.

I chuckled. "Being useful is one of my favorite things. After feeling so useless on the road, it felt nice to turn things around tonight."

"Why is that, do you think?"

"In Waldron," I said wistfully, "I'm the one everyone turns to for help. I guess it gives me a sense of security. I like feeling like people need me."

"Hmm." His tone had a slight edge to it—judgement.

"What?"

Idris—still on his back—rolled his head to the side to appraise me. "Tonight was like watching you disappear."

"Excuse me?"

"The *helper* version of you is...different. More polite. More bubbly in your response to things—like Tura bringing dessert—and more calculated with your quips, like you were trying to manipulate her feelings."

"You take issue with my being a gracious guest?" I asked tightly. Feeling defensive, I added, "I was trying to make her feel *better*."

And here I'd been proud of how I'd saved the night.

"I'm not articulating this right," Idris said, scratching his jaw.

"Did it ever occur to you that I'm my normal self with others, and I save all my rude, sharp edges for you?"

He pinned me with his celestial stare—not cool like the river tonight, but molten. "You seemed relieved to have a role," he said. "Relieved to lose yourself in fixing her problem."

"Why wouldn't I be?" I snapped. "When it feels like my problems are unfix-able?"

The statement was like a collapsing bridge, hard stone damming the river underneath, halting all flow of conversation. Idris didn't speak for so long that I eventually gave up on waiting and turned over to face the opposite direction.

But before I fell asleep, his voice rasped against my senses, coarse as sand. "For the record, Anya, I like your edges, best."

29

WELCOME

ANYA

"You were right," I said to Idris around noon the next day.

The morning had been frosty, both between us and before us. Ice glittered on the hills ahead, crunching under Briar's hoof-steps. The cloudless, pale blue sky had left me feeling exposed, nowhere to hide in the heatless sunshine.

The silent miles following our departure from the village had allowed me plenty of time to ruminate on Idris's comments from last night, plenty of time to draw parallels between his observations and Hattie's continual chiding for the ways in which I overextended myself.

I'd eventually come to the conclusion that Idris hadn't been criticizing me for what I'd *done* for Tura, but the *way* I'd helped her, eager to jump into that old familiar role, to lose myself in someone else's problem. It had been a comfort, to feel in control. To pretend I was capable. He'd seen through that veneer, and I'd gotten defensive.

"Last night, I mean," I clarified.

He glanced up at me from where he walked beside Briar. "I was an ass."

"You were hungover, tired. But you weren't wrong."

He faced forward again, giving Briar's neck a firm pat. "Don't make excuses for my tactlessness."

I laughed. "To be honest, you sounded like Hattie."

That earned me another glance, this one wry. "I'm going to take that as a compliment."

"You should," I said. "She lacks tact, too, but she's almost always right."

That time, we both laughed.

From there, the day unfolded with more amiability, Idris and I trading off in the saddle as we ventured through the rolling countryside. The air was bitter, stinging my cheeks and making the tips of my fingers and toes ache, but at least there wasn't any wind.

Rural folks waved at us on occasion, no-doubt recognizing Idris's breastplate from the rumors from Brine. We passed the occasional traveler along the High Road— merchants, messengers—but other than that, it was just us again.

The contrast between the past few nights socializing with excitable townsfolk and villagers made me realize how *at ease* I'd become in Idris's presence. By managing the logistics of our travels, Idris had given me the opportunity to worry about *myself* for a change—and worry, I *had*. The closer we got to Fenrir, the more wracked with worry I became—but the weight of that worry wasn't so heavy without others' worries heaped on top of it.

I found I quite liked being cared for, looked after. Even if Idris was doing it mostly out of duty to the realm and not out of any deeper affection.

Fates, I think I wanted his affection, though.

As night fell, Idris grasped Briar's reins and led us off the High Road into a cluster of small pines and old madrone trees. I'd been expecting another night on the cold ground—dreading it, really, after two consecutive nights cozied up indoors—but as we passed through the shelter of bristly branches, we ended up in a clearing with a small rectangular shape up ahead.

Peering into the haze of dusk and not quite believing what I saw, I asked, "What's this?"

"A secret among knights," Idris said. "We call it the One Week Cabin, as it's located seven nights from Fenrir."

"Clever," I quipped. "Are you sure I'm allowed to be privy to such secrets?"

I swung out of the saddle, pins and needles lancing up through my frozen shins when I landed. I stumbled forward, and Idris caught me by the waist, steadying me.

Then he stepped back, gesturing at the single-room structure. "It's not that much of a secret," he admitted. "Just a waypoint for knights on the road. It's mostly reserved for Knights of the Order of the Mighty, because they're fragile city dwellers unaccustomed to nature, but I have an in."

I lifted Briar's reins over his head and led him toward a small corral attached to the south side of the cabin. "Does your *in* know you think of them as a fragile city dweller?"

Idris grunted a laugh, breath clouding his face. "I tell him every chance I get."

I pursed my lips, trying to imagine this friend of his.

He circled Briar to begin unfastening the saddle bags. From over the horse's back, his eyes roved over my expression. "What?"

"Just never thought of you having a *friend*," I said.

Idris un-cinched the saddle, next, and rested it on the railing. "I'm full of surprises."

Once Briar had been tended to, Idris and I walked up the two creaky steps to the cabin and opened the door.

The place was small and pleasantly cozy, with a worn rug on the stone floor and a four-poster bed piled rather luxuriously with furs and blankets. A table and two chairs were arranged under the single window by the door, and a lantern rested atop it.

"This is...*nice*," I said, dumping my pack by the door and walking father into the space. "Nicer than I expected."

"Mighty Knights consider *this* roughing it."

"Sounds like you have quite the feud."

"Impossible to have a feud when there's a clear winner."

I chuckled, walking over to the woodstove to get a flame going for some heat. With the sundown, the cabin was downright frigid—but thankfully, there was already a stack of wood on the floor, ready for use.

While I stoked the fire, Idris lit the lantern, then removed his cloak, breastplate, and weapons, taking special care as he laid Halgren across the worn wooden tabletop. I stole a glance or two as he organized his gear, watching the corded muscle of his back and shoulders shift beneath the dark green linen of his shirt. The laces along the neckline were undone, and the collar gaped, allowing me a glimpse of his tattoo around his collarbones and the gnarly-looking scar across his right pectoral. Not for the first time, I wondered how he got that scar, how he survived it.

When he was done, he sank down on the bed, palms resting on his knees. "Are you hungry?" Idris asked.

We'd eaten just an hour earlier, on the road, finishing off an excess of hand-pies that Tura had given us this morning. "No, mostly just tired. You?"

"Same. Tired." He jerked his chin in the direction of the woodstove. "Thanks for doing that."

I brushed the ash off my hands and went to my pack, busying myself with my own gear. "It's freezing in here."

"Not for long," he said gratefully.

Sitting with my back to him on the opposite side of the bed, I pulled the tie from my braid and shook out my hair, then began unlacing my boots.

Silence spread.

Without a tent to set up or dinner to distract me, there wasn't much else to do but take note of the cramped proximity of the cabin, the single bed we'd have to share. This wasn't like camping, with the constant trickle of the river and the scuttling of nocturnal animals to fill the gaps in conversation. In here, the loudest sounds were the fire in the woodstove and *us*—our voices, our breaths, our hearts beating.

This felt far more intimate than camping.

"It must be a relief not to have to field questions from excitable villagers tonight," I said—a painfully obvious observation. Normally, my conversational skills were better than this, but he was right, the tiny room was heating up fast; I felt flushed all over.

"You have no idea," he said with a chuckle, removing his boots and then—*Fates spare me*—his shirt, too.

I heard him do it: the whoosh of fabric. I peeked over my shoulder and saw the wide expanse of his back, a rugged topography of muscle and pale scarring—then I promptly faced away again, blushing furiously, biting my lips together with my teeth.

Get it together, Anya.

While he slid underneath the covers, I stood, buying myself just a moment's more distance by extinguishing the lantern. The room filled with shadow, save for the beam of silver moonlight that streamed through the window. I then circled round to my side of the bed again, and quickly removed my outer clothes, leaving my chemise on. Finally, with unnecessary delicacy, I lifted the blanket and settled in beside Idris.

We both rested on our backs, bodies rigid. We did not touch, but I could feel the heat emanating from his bare skin mere inches away. My own skin tingled with the urge to feel how firm and warm his body was. But I kept my hands where they were: resting awkwardly at my sides.

I couldn't stop thinking about the kiss. I wondered if he was, too, alone with me in the dark for the first time since Brine.

Normally, I didn't feel so self-conscious around the opposite sex, but our foolhardy attraction wasn't like the casual, straightforward dalliances I'd had before. The complication of our tangled Fate hadn't pushed us apart but—inexplicably—had brought us closer. *Forced* us to be vulnerable, to be honest, and to see each other for who we *were*, not for the people we wanted to be.

After weeks on the road together, I had developed a craving for his nearness that now resembled something close to desperation. I could hear the rapid beat of his heart, as if he were running miles in his head, too; ignoring such a sound all night was going to be torture.

What I wouldn't give to lavish you, he'd said.

Do you mean ravish?

Whatever you want.

His drunken words might've been honest, but that didn't mean that in his right mind he intended to act on them. I wanted him to act on them, though. I wasn't sure when I'd become so desirous—perhaps when I watched him almost die in that barn—but I burned with urgency now, and I had to know if these feelings were at all mutual.

"Idris?" I whispered.

"Yes?"

"How much do you remember of our night at the Lark?"

He became even stiller than he already had been. With my magic, I heard the uptick of his heartbeat, a song growing in fervor.

"I wasn't so drunk that I don't remember our conversation," he said, then sighed at length. "I'm sorry. I had no intention of making you uncomfortable."

"You didn't."

"Well, as for tonight"—he cleared his throat—"I have no intentions to…" He trailed off, leaving the rest unsaid. "I mean, I know you don't want—"

"How do you know that?" I rolled onto my side, propping my head up to regard him more fully. "What did I say to make you think—"

"Anya," he said patiently, dotingly. "I was in your Mirror."

"You said yourself that our Fate can change—*warp.*"

"I did. It can. But that doesn't mean we aren't…doomed."

"Are you saying you plan to murder me, after all?" I meant it lightly, but my tone betrayed my heartache.

He chuckled, though, mercifully. "No, I don't." His tone sobered. "But there are plenty of other reasons that two people can be wrong for each other."

Wrong.

I rolled onto my back again, facing the ceiling, blinking rapidly. The sense of rejection I'd grown so accustomed to with Remy—always keeping me at an emotional arm's length—was a familiar clamshell closing over my heart now. I might've pretended Remy's distance didn't bother me, but the truth was, I'd spent all that time wondering *why.* What was it about me that made him not want to commit? Plenty of men had taken interest in me over the years, but as soon as I was ready to get close to one, I was pushed away.

But then Idris turned to face me, elbow bent, head resting on his fist. Studying me. I could *feel* his gaze roving over the tightness of my mouth, the wateriness of my eyes. I suddenly felt so stupid. Coming onto my killer, only for him to reject me. *Oh,* how this quest had reduced me.

With my magic still open to him, however, I heard his heart pound even faster.

He cleared his throat again. "I think you've mistook my meaning," he said. "My Oath…"

I looked at him in time to catch the slight clench of his jaw.

"I live a solitary life, Anya."

"Is yours an Oath of celibacy?"

He spluttered. "*Fates*, Anya, *no.*" He rolled onto his back and scrubbed a hand over his face. "I'm just trying to be a gentleman." He sounded frustrated—not with me, but himself.

The reference to our inside joke encouraged me. The stampeding of his heart did, too. Maybe he wasn't pushing me away; maybe his responsibility was holding him back. Desire against duty.

I turned onto my side again. "Suppose you *weren't* a gentleman, though," I ventured.

His hand—which had been covering his mouth, scratching his jaw—fell to the bedspread. He regarded me, pupils blowing out his irises. I couldn't tell if the dark expression was warning or ravenous. Maybe both.

Either way, it made me *ache.*

"I'm *trying* to do the right thing," he said.

"What if you stopped trying?" I whispered, my own heart racing in time with his. "Just for the night?"

30

WAR

Idris

Idris regarded Anya in the dark. Her hair was mussed, fire-bright eyes intent. Her mouth—with its perfect curvature, her upper lip ripe for biting—was parted slightly in wait. With the blankets draped over her as they were, her fulsome hips and the angle of her waist were accentuated—an undulation he longed to traverse. Her springlike scent was a haze in the room, punctuated by the sharp pheromones of her desire.

There would be no *just for the night* if he gave into temptation. How could there be?

You should never *underestimate me*, Anya had told Idris on the first day of their quest. Perhaps this was his punishment for not taking her warning more seriously.

From the moment she had come into his life, Idris had felt off-balance. That should've been omen enough, his weakness like war horns announcing the army on his doorstep. As he stared at her from across the pillows, he felt like he was staring out across the battlefield at his opposing general.

He didn't stand a chance against Anya. He never had. His sense of right and wrong was teetering on the edge of *her* blade, not his. Dread swirled through him like a wintry wind, but it did nothing to extinguish the inferno of desire building in his body. The pounding of his heart became his marching beat, sending him into the fray.

"Anya..." Idris said cautiously. "Be serious."

"I *am* serious. Forget the repercussions, forget Fate. Think only of us alone in this cabin together." Anya smiled like she had him at sword-tip. "What would it look like for you to not hold back?"

His fingers curled against the bedspread, clutching the fabric, aching to clutch *her* instead. A war was raging inside him, too—Idris against Idris. Because of course he wanted her, wanted *this*. He'd brought her to this cabin to give her a respite from the cold, but he'd forgotten the single bed; he'd been dismayed when he saw it, when faced with a night trying to resist her.

Even now, it took all his willpower not to grab her and pin her to the mattress and take her until she was pliant and shaking beneath his hands, moaning and begging him for more. The problem was that he was spending all his willpower resisting his *own* urges, and didn't have any strength left to deflect hers.

And she knew exactly what she was doing with her goading conversation.

"In your wildest, most debauched dreams," she dared him, "what would you do to me?"

The question was like a physical blow, cracking his armor. Idris swallowed thickly, his lower abdominals tensing. Would it be so wrong to forfeit the fight? It was almost laughable how quickly she'd gotten under his skin.

But his fortifications were in place for a reason. His was a dangerous Order, but it wasn't just his sense of duty or the hazardousness of his Oath keeping him from reaching across this bed—it was the damned Mirrors. The threat of a fraught future. Idris took comfort in knowing the abominations' influence on his Fate, but it wasn't a guarantee.

And it wasn't just *her* Mirror they'd have to contend with.

To be with Anya was to endanger her, and he'd promised her that he wouldn't bring her harm.

"Someone has to be the voice of reason, here," he rasped. "Us, together. It's more dangerous than you realize."

"The *world* is more dangerous than I realize," she argued. "Can't it be more pleasureful, too?"

Idris tried to draw a steadying breath, but all it did was intoxicate him on the scent of lemon and roses and *her*. He stared into her eyes, hoping she could see in them the direness of their potential union—see past what his Oath would not permit him to say.

Anya reached out and slid a slow, tantalizing finger over the sensitive skin of his neck, right along his Oath tattoo. "What would you do to me?" she pressed, breaking through his final defenses with her wicked words. Her voice went husky. "What would you do, if you knew that I *ached*—"

"I would put my hands on you," he said roughly.

"Where?"

He growled, exasperated.

"Where?" Anya demanded.

"*Everywhere.*"

"Be specific," she taunted, breathless. "Would you touch my neck? My breasts?"

"Anya," he said—no, *pleaded*—giving her this final chance to change her mind.

She narrowed her eyes at him, seeing the truce he was offering, the opportunity to turn back. Then she said, "I want to hear you say it."

Cursed Fates be damned, that was *it*. Battle over.

In this war, her victory was his, too.

"I would worship you so thoroughly that the Fates themselves would scorch the realm with envy," Idris said.

"Show me."

31

WORSHIP

ANYA

He was already moving by the time I made my demand, pushing me back, sliding his rough palm up the side of my neck. His fingers scraped into my hair; his thumb pressed hard under my chin. The touch was controlled yet commanding.

But he did not kiss me—yet. His forearm rested on my collarbone, pinning me to the mattress. The delicious pressure of him holding me down made my stomach flip. For a few excruciating moments, his lips hovered over mine and we shared breath.

"That's more like it," I said, challenge still in my tone.

I tried to close the distance, but he held me firm. He wasn't even on top of me; the bulk of him remained on the mattress, his chest angled above mine but still not touching. Just the promise of contact had me frustrated, thrilled, arching. The tips of my breasts grazed his chest through my chemise, and he sucked a breath in through his teeth. His grip on the side of my neck tightened slightly, his thumb pushing my chin up higher.

"You're insatiable," he scolded.

"You're a tease," I retorted.

He laughed a single, staccato *ha*. "*I'm* the tease?"

I narrowed my eyes at him and nodded, thoroughly enjoying this game.

His grip slacked ever so slightly, a flash of his earlier resistance entering his gaze. I knew he was thinking about the Mirrors when he whispered, "Are you sure...?"

I couldn't decide which I liked more: his genuine care or his possessive grip. Maybe it was the combination I found so intoxicating.

Either way, I was getting impatient. "Fucking *Fates*, Idris, would you just—"

He closed his mouth over mine, swallowing my order.

The kiss was meant to scorch—and it did. Trapped in his hold, all I could do was give in, and—*fuck*—that's all I wanted. His lips devoured. His stubble scraped. His fingers that had been tangled in my hair splayed on the mound of my stomach, my waist.

I arched again, desperate to feel his chest against mine, and this time he acquiesced, rolling fully on top of me, hips pinning my hips. The air rushed out of me, and I moaned it into his mouth. He groaned in response, the sound rumbling through me like thunder.

He buried his face in my neck, kissing a hot wet line from my jaw to my collarbone. "You smell so fucking good," he growled, like he almost hated me for it, but his lips were soft, pliant, worshiping. He cupped my breast through my chemise, squeezing.

He *must've* possessed pheromonal magic. This time, I didn't feel so self-conscious at the thought. I *wanted* him to know how much I craved him. I wanted him to smell it on me as plainly as I heard the pounding of his pulse.

I ran a hand up his arm, over his pec, my fingers catching on the thick scar that looped over his shoulder. "You *feel* so fucking good." To punctuate my statement, I wedged my other hand between us, skidding over his firm stomach and down, palming his erection through his trousers.

"You're going to be the end of me," he said.

"How the tables have turned."

He laughed, pressing his lips to mine again. I deepened the kiss, sucking and biting. I was fierce as I slid my mouth over his. Starved. Hungry. He was right: I *was* insatiable.

But he was, too. He cradled my face in his big palm like I was a sacred thing, our tongues sparring. Meanwhile, the hand on my breast moved downward, skating over my waist, belly, leg. He found the hem of my chemise and slid his hand back up my bare inner thigh. I practically shook with anticipation.

But the bastard paused.

"What are you doing?" I asked.

He swept his thumb across the crease of my hip, torturously close to where I wanted him. "Just altering the power dynamic," he said. "You were a little too smug earlier." He palmed my thigh, squeezed sensuously.

I squirmed underneath him. "Are you going to make me beg?"

He smirked, seeming to consider that idea. Then his expression heated. "Not this time."

He dipped a finger into my wetness.

Both our breaths caught.

He sunk his finger deeper, only to draw the slickness up to my clit. He circled it, his eyes trained on my face, reading me in the dark. When he hit the right spot, I jerked, and he smiled down at me like he'd learned a coveted secret.

He made the same move again, crossing the pad of his finger over my most sensitive place. A needy little whine slipped out of me, surprising even to my ears, and he bent, kissing the crease of my neck, right by my collarbone.

"I think you're right," he murmured against my skin. "I'm not a gentleman."

With the way he was touching me, pleasure coiling through my belly, I could barely follow his words. I was helpless to his touch.

"If I were," he continued, "I wouldn't feel so greedy to hear you make that sound again."

His fingers repeated the motion, picking up speed, blessedly consistent. I was so close to the edge now—teetering, really, my limbs both heavy and weightless, ready to fall at any moment. I was silent in my anticipation, focused—but apparently that wouldn't do, because Idris wrenched his hand away. I lifted my head, disgruntled and fearing he'd stopped altogether, but he was ducking under the covers, replacing his fingers with his mouth.

The world disappeared, everything narrowing on the sensations between my legs: the flick of his tongue, the softness of his lips, the stubble scuffing my skin. He gripped my thighs, anchoring me with his strong hands, even as I arched my pelvis up to meet his mouth. His movements were somehow both messy and exact, dizzying me and making my legs tremble.

I whined again, lost in my enjoyment of his touch; he groaned into me in response. Hearing his enthusiasm was my final push. Pleasure swelled in my belly, then burst with a flood of tingling heat. My inner walls convulsed, and I curled forward off the bed, crying out. My hand found his shoulder, and I held on as the sensation rolled through me like a wave.

He kept on feasting, riding out the full extent of my pleasure until I collapsed back against the bed. Only then did he lift his head, and the look on his face—

He looked more victorious now than he had after the heroics in Brine.

I sat up and yanked off my chemise. His victorious expression morphed into one of hunger, dark and predatory.

"Take those off, would you?" I said, nodding at his trousers.

"Anything for you."

He climbed out of bed and started unbuttoning. I watched unabashedly, eyes widening when he stepped out of his clothes. Everything in me clenched at the sight of him. His body was...big, powerful, perfect.

When I looked at his face again, his smirk was back.

He returned to bed, and I urged him to sit upright with his back against the headboard. He acquiesced, watching me with rapt attention as I knelt between his legs, gripping his hard length in my hand.

I bowed my head, taking him in my mouth. It was my turn to relish his sounds: rumbling, guttural, thunderous. He was always so *controlled*, and I took pleasure in how *undone* he sounded as I gave to him what he'd just given me. His fingers curled in my hair, not gripping or even guiding, just holding on—that is, until he tugged gently, a signal to stop.

"Come here," he rasped.

He was still seated upright. I climbed up his body until I straddled his lap, knees bracketing his hips. My breasts grazed his chest; the dusting of hair across his pectorals was coarse against their sensitive tips. His cock pressed into my thigh, dangerously close to my slickness.

Idris cupped my face in both his hands, staring into my eyes meaningfully. "How did I end up here like this with you?"

"Fate," I said.

He chuckled as his hands cascaded down my shoulders, gripping my waist. A shiver followed his hands, pebbling my skin.

"You're the most stunning woman."

A coy smile spread across my lips. I'd never been complimented like this before, not in a way that made me feel so savored. I didn't know what to say, so I let my desire lead. I reached between our bodies, gripping him in my hand, guiding him—

"I don't have an anti-pregnancy tincture," he said quickly, as if the thought had just occurred.

"I take one monthly," I told him. Bless Hattie for putting this month's dose in my pack.

He released a relieved breath.

"May I proceed?" I asked politely.

"I beg you do."

I angled him toward my entrance, then paused. "Beg, hmm?"

"I am not above begging you."

I arched a brow, but since I was still staring down at where our bodies were almost joined, the haughty expression was likely diminished. I still could hear his heart beating, a wild, primal drumming in my ears. I gripped him a little tighter, and his abdominals rippled with tension. Anticipation.

I sank onto him. Stars swarmed my vision, and when they cleared, it was his blue-green eyes I saw, staring at me in wonder. I felt impossibly full, stretched.

He gripped my hips and began to rock me against him. I twined my arms around his neck, pulling myself closer to his chest, riding his lap. In this position, my clit ground against him with a delicious friction. Pleasure pulled through me, taut as a bowstring. I picked up speed, chasing the sensation. Idris matched me with his own thrusts, holding me with a hand on my back, the other cupping my breast. He bowed his head, taking my nipple in his mouth, biting down.

The orgasm shot through me like an arrow.

Unlike earlier, he didn't give me any respite. In one quick, dizzying move, he swiveled me underneath him. I squealed in surprise, clinging to him from my new position on my back. Caging me with his arms, he brought his mouth down on mine, the kiss rough and claiming.

Then he was pumping hard. I hooked a leg over his hip, steadying myself and giving him a deeper angle. He reached between us, placing his hand on my lower abdomen, his thumb pressing my clit. The outside pressure made me feel even tighter inside, heightening the sensation of every thrust.

His movements were becoming less controlled, more fevered. Knowing he was close—it was enough to send me over the edge again, making me scream. His satisfied grin was a lightning-flash in the dark. Then a low, animalistic groan tore out of him as he followed my pleasure with his own. I felt the sound in my core, my extremities; the remnants of it seemed to ring in the silence that settled over the room as we stilled.

I wrapped my legs around his hips, keeping him firmly in place inside me, not ready to let go. We were both panting, shuddering, and sensitive. He rested his forehead against mine, then kissed my nose.

The heady moment dispersed, and then he was leaving to clean himself up. My body felt heavy, warm—but more than that, my heart felt *full*. It wasn't just desire and satisfaction, but genuine affection, flowing out of me like an overfull glass.

One night together, and I was already dangerously attached—but I no longer cared about would-be danger. The threat might've been foretold, but it wasn't what stood before me now. The man climbing back into bed, drawing me into his arms, crushing me against him like he was afraid to let me go—he seemed quite the opposite of dangerous.

Idris was *safe*.

32

WEAKNESS

IDRIS

Idris had long ago accepted his miserable lot in life. It'd started with the loss of his parents, like the first storms of autumn, harsh and destructive. He had grown colder with the hardships he faced as a boy on the streets of Fenrir, turning glacial when Grinnick died. For the past fifteen years as a Knight of the Order of the Valiant, Idris had been frozen. Numb. Resigned. Isolated in an endless winter.

Last night, Anya had cracked him open.

Now, his blood flowed like spring melt, swift and urgent. When once his most vulnerable emotions felt dormant, they were now awakened, emboldened, like bulbs pushing through hard ground. Possibility warmed him like precious sunshine.

In the span of one night, his seasons had changed. He'd *thawed*.

Lying with Anya in his arms—her soft body boneless with sleep—a new sort of fierceness now swept through Idris. His loyalty toward his Order still clung to him like frost—but a new devotion was taking shape. He squeezed Anya a little tighter, relishing her closeness and the delicate, dreadful optimism of her presence.

This complicated things. How could it not? Sleeping with her didn't change the fact that he was duty-bound to a life of solitude; wanting to be with her didn't diminish his loyalty to his brother's memory; *caring* about her didn't change the unpredictability of the Mirror's vision. How could he, in good conscience, let this continue without being forthright about his limitations, his failures, and the danger of his mere presence? How could he explain that which he was not permitted to voice?

Anya made a squeaky, satisfied sound, nestling closer to his chest. Idly, he kissed her temple. It was early morning, and the chill of last night's freeze permeated the walls of the cabin—but here in bed, they were warm. Impervious to the cold.

Anya slid her hand up Idris's torso, from his abdominals to the base of his neck. She traced the hollow dip beneath his throat, then pressed her delicious curves against him, stretching up to kiss him in the same place, right on his tattoo. He tipped his face down, brushing his lips across hers softly, then pulling back far enough to stare into her pretty amber-brown eyes. The depth of them—flecked with gold, star-like around her pupils—seemed endless. A land he could wander for an eternity.

"You're quiet," Anya said, brushing her hand over the stubble on his cheek, up into his hair.

He leaned into the scratch of her fingernails. "I'm always quiet."

"You weren't last night," she teased.

He chuckled into her hair.

"What's on your mind?"

"You."

She scraped her nails lightly down his neck, over his chest. Sensation pulsed in his groin.

"Good things, I hope?" she asked.

He growled long and low, then gripped her jaw. The scent of her—the sweet tang of her fresh arousal—told him she liked his commanding hold. "Not good, no."

She pouted, but her pupils had expanded. "If not good things, then...?"

"Wicked things," he murmured, biting her lower lip.

"I see." She grinned against his mouth. "And here I was worried I'd disappointed you."

Idris rolled on top of her. "Never."

33

HONESTY

ANYA

I was quickly learning that in the religion of our sex, there were many forms of worship. Last night had been heated, frantic, hungry; this morning was slow, needy, and indulgent, a push and pull that had me wound up and strung out.

When our bodies were once again sated—gray light streaming through the single window in our cabin—I wondered, idly, what other forms of reverence he'd yet to show me. I looked forward to finding out.

Idris was still panting slightly when he settled on his back. I curled toward him, pressing my bare body against his side, and resting my head on his collarbone.

He blew out a long breath. "That was...*fuck*," he said appreciatively.

I laughed. "It really was."

A half-smile kicked up the corner of his mouth. "You don't regret...?"

I shook my head. "Do you?"

"Absolutely not."

I released a breath, more relieved than I anticipated. While we'd played a game of tease and hesitation last night, it'd come from a real place—an awareness of the circumstances that complicated this budding *thing* between us. In the light of day, the complications were still present, but I was glad he found this worth the risk.

I know I did.

My hand, which had been resting on his stomach, meandered up his strong torso, relishing every ridge. When my fingertips reached his scar, I traced its path from where it started on his chest to where it disappeared over his shoulder and back down again. The surface of it was smooth, but the skin was dense and gnarled underneath, like a tree root draped in silk. The wound must've been deep.

I wondered what'd left such a gruesome mark. I imagined the monster in the grove the night he rescued me, how frightening and terrible it had been. The one in Brine had been no less horrifying. How many had he slain over the years? Tens, hundreds? What sort of life did he truly live when he wasn't escorting innkeepers to the capital?

The pad of my thumb found the widest part of the gouge, just to the left of his nipple.

Idris squirmed. "That tickles." He stayed my hand, enveloping it with his and holding it against the center of his chest.

"If I asked you about your scar," I said, "could you even tell me?"

His grip tightened, like he didn't want to let go. "No, I couldn't." He turned his head and stared into my eyes, his expression earnest. "But I want you to know that I don't delight in withholding things from you."

"You must delight a little," I teased.

He kissed my temple. "Only in jest."

I threaded my fingers through his. I found it hard to reconcile that the man who'd worshipped me last night was magically bound to something I couldn't know and didn't understand. That the hands that'd brought me so much pleasure were the same hands that wielded a flaming sword and fought unspeakable evil.

It was...*hot*, in a frightening sort of way. A reckless sort of way.

"Can you truly say nothing of your Oath?" I asked.

He didn't speak—didn't even shake his head.

"What *can* you say, then?"

"I keep only the secrets I am bound to keep, secrets that are not mine to tell," Idris said. "But ask me anything you like, Anya, and if I am able, I will answer."

I eyed his scar again. "Does it hurt?"

"Sometimes. Especially in the cold."

"When did it happen?"

"Fourteen years ago. I was twenty-one."

"Had you already taken the Oath?"

He quirked a brow, as if to point out my proximity to that which he couldn't say.

"I'll take that as a yes," I said, trying not to shudder at the thought of a monster's claw doing such damage; no wonder Idris hadn't seemed alarmed when he came to the Possum with that puncture wound. "Have you ever been in love?"

He released a surprised puff of air, then his brow furrowed as he considered his answer. "I thought I was, once. In my youth." He toyed with a tendril of my hair as he continued. "She was the daughter of the baker that Grinnick and I stole from on occasion. She caught us rummaging around in the garbage behind the bakery one night and gave us a fresh loaf.

"For the next month, she fed us the failed bakes—breads that hadn't risen properly or had too many air pockets. We formed what felt to me like a friendship, something I hoped would become more. Then I overheard her father telling a customer about his beloved only daughter's engagement." Idris shook his head. "As a sixteen-year-old, it was devastating. But it was only puppy love."

"She was kind to you," I said.

"I mistook her kindness for true feeling," he agreed, releasing another soft laugh. "A valuable lesson for a young boy, I reckon."

"My first love was named Peregrine," I mused. "He was an idiot. So was I. Maybe that's the point of puppy love."

"Have you ever been in love?" Idris asked.

I stared at our entwined hands on his chest. "A month ago, I might've said yes. But now I think true love requires more reciprocity than what I've experienced in the past."

"Sounds like they didn't deserve you," Idris said, his tone surprisingly cool—protective.

"No, but I should've been clearer about what I wanted."

His tone took on a gravelly quality. "And what *do* you want?"

"I thought I was the one asking the questions?" I teased, then—in the spirit of learning from my past mistakes—I decided to answer him, anyway. "I want commitment. I want to feel like I'm not the only one giving."

Seconds passed.

I began to fear I'd been too forward. That he'd interpret my words as expectations rather than transparency.

But then Idris said, "So you want to be the one *taking*." He squeezed me closer, kissing my neck. "That can be arranged."

I laughed, grateful for the levity. It was too early for me to expect anything from him other than *this*.

"Alright, alright," I said, "back to you. What's your favorite color?"

He lifted a brow. "Really, that's your next question?"

"Thought I'd reward your sad puppy story with an easy one."

"Sad puppy." He huffed. "Glad that's what you took from that story." He tipped his chin up, staring at the ceiling. "Let's see, my favorite color..." After some thought, he met my eyes again. "It's the shade between red and orange. Sunsets, fall foliage"—he tugged on the strand of hair he'd been playing with—"the color of your hair."

I shoved his chest. "Empty flattery."

"I already fucked you—why would I offer empty flattery now?"

His cheekiness surprised me, and I laughed heartily. "To fuck me again?"

He waggled his eyebrows. "Is it working?"

"No," I said, but my face heated.

He brushed his thumb across my flushed cheek. "I like this color, too," he murmured.

"What else do you like?"

"I like the smell of first snow," he said. "I like Hattie's concoctails. I like being honest with you."

My flush intensified and I glanced away.

When I met his eyes again, I asked, "Do you like living in the wilds on your own?"

"I've made my peace with it." His brow creased. "Or, rather, I've found ways to make it tolerable."

"You can put maple syrup in your porridge without sleeping in the woods."

"Tastes different on the road, trust me," he said. "The forest is the closest I've ever gotten to feeling like I belong. And I like the sense of purpose."

"Isn't it lonely, though?"

The arm he'd wrapped around me pulled me closer. Then his fingertips grazed the nape of my neck, sending tingles down my spine. "Not currently."

"But usually?" I insisted.

"Usually? Yes."

"Last night, you said this was wrong."

His jaw clenched. "I was just trying to protect…" He trailed off, restarted. "To reiterate the risks of further entanglement. It's one thing for me to escort you to the capital; it's something entirely different for us to—" He broke off abruptly.

"Entangle?" I supplied.

"Exactly."

"Do you look forward to the end of our quest, then? Going back to normal?" I nudged him playfully. "Finally being rid of me?"

He let out a long, lung-rattling sigh. "In truth, Anya," he murmured, hugging me close, "there's nothing I dread more than the end of our quest."

34

SWEAT

IDRIS

The next four days were a dream: beautiful, unbelievable, something that couldn't possibly last. Knowing that at any moment he could wake up, Idris enjoyed every waking second.

By day, he relished the *ease* between them. He played his flute, and she sang along to the familiar tunes. Conversation spilled from Anya like a mountain spring, her stories flowing over him in an endless stream of lilting laughter and small-town intrigue. She gestured animatedly with her hands as she described escaped pigs and funny misunderstandings. He asked about her mother and grandmother, and her voice became wistful, sharing stories about the women who'd raised her and shaped her.

He even told her more about Grinnick, happy memories he hadn't thought about in years: the time Grinnick unknowingly met the Lady of Lothgaim in a crowded market and tried to bed her; the pranks he pulled on Idris when they were boys; the books about mythic heroes their father used to read to them, and how they acted out the fight scenes with stick-swords; the taste of their mother's molasses cookies, Grinnick always taking the biggest one. They were memories he'd forgotten on purpose, but now—in the joyful retelling—they didn't sting so harshly. Anya squeezed his hand when his voice broke, and laughed heartily at the moments that made him smile.

It amazed him how similar they were—not just their love of music and gossip, but also how their lives had been ruled by loss. Yet where Idris had withdrawn, Anya had flourished. She'd taken the pain of her grief and wove it into deeper connection and community—overextending herself at times, she admitted, but doing so out of genuine fondness.

Idris—who had avoided further heartbreak at all costs—found Anya incredibly brave for facing her grief head-on. Instead of retreating from her pain, she had opened herself more fully to love.

The ease between them only deepened by night, exploring, and *lavishing*, and *ravishing* until Idris lost track of all foreboding. Inside their tent or under the stars, with the heat of her bare skin against him, their bodies were impervious to the cold. To what loomed ahead.

As the days and nights unfolded, the bulb-like feelings in his chest grew taller, and he wondered, puzzlingly, if this was what the beginnings of love felt like. It wasn't the same as the puppy love he'd described, a youthful infatuation. This felt deeper. Truer. More rooted.

But how could he, Idris, be capable of such a beautiful thing? Such a disastrously *hopeful* thing? In the cabin, Anya had all but told him that the commitment she wanted was something Idris—so long as he remained in his Order—couldn't offer. And yet, with Anya in his life, he felt capable of *anything*.

He knew it was premature to feel so strongly, yet the intimacy of life on the road had fostered a deeper *knowing* than time suggested. *No*—it hadn't been the road. It was *Anya* who had opened him up like this, bit by bit, across campfires and from Briar's saddle. In the cabin, he'd told her more than he'd ever told anyone—including Grinnick, who didn't even know how hurt Idris had felt after the baker's daughter, Nina, had cut him off. Traveling with Anya had created shared experiences, but it was the connection they'd forged *together* that made him feel so overcome now, so bold in his desire of a life beyond his Order.

He hadn't been lying when he told her he feared their Fates were doomed. Now that he knew what she felt like, sounded like, *tasted* like—the fear had only grown. So, yes, with Anya in his life, he felt capable of anything—but he also felt more vulnerable than ever.

This was the danger of falling in love, Idris knew. Love, he'd long ago learned, was the ultimate weakness. And Anya...well, she'd stolen all his strength the moment she'd opened the door to the Possum and invited him in.

⁂

On their final full day of travel, Idris and Anya rode Briar in tandem. All the sensations Idris had tried to ignore the first time they rode together had become things to relish: her scent in his nose, the persistent rocking of her backside against his groin. Idris had banded one arm around her stomach, brushed her hair away from her neck, and pressed kisses behind her ear. He'd been half-hard all day.

As the miles passed, the land morphed, becoming flatter and more verdant the closer they got to Fenrir City. Winter crops dotted seemingly endless fields to the east, while the wilds Idris typically roamed became a distant smudge to the west. Orchards and livestock were interspersed with quaint homes, and they encountered more and more people on the road: farming wagons, merchant caravans, casual travelers, and messengers clad in the Lord of Fenrir's customary crimson and orange.

According to Anya, some folks they encountered murmured about his breastplate and Brine, but the rumors were more spread out, now, and seemed less dazzling to the more populous areas they were passing through. Knights of all kinds were more common here, which made his armor less remarkable the closer they got to the city.

By dusk, they came within sight of the capital. It was built into the foothills of the Shield, the largest and southernmost mountain in the Axe Range, which spanned the northeastern reaches of Fenrir Territory. They were still half a day's ride away, yet the mountain's size made it seem closer, rising high into the sunset sky. At its base, the pale stone buildings of the city reflected the light, making the capital—which Idris knew to be harsh, grimy, and old—appear welcoming and grand.

Fenrir was the smallest territory in the Kingdom of Marona, but as they halted on the final rise overlooking the sprawl of hamlets and farmland outside the city walls, the land appeared vast. Beautiful.

"Quite the sight, isn't it?" Idris said.

Staring out at the capital from over Anya's shoulder, Idris saw it through her eyes, anew. The Wend ribboned out from its hidden source in the Bone Mountains to the west, gold and shimmery. Smoke rose from the cottages clustered on its banks. Poplars reached their branches toward the dimming sky. Shadows purpled in the twilight.

"Quite," Anya agreed breathlessly. Idris wondered whether she was breathless with worry, awe, or anticipation—perhaps a mix of the three.

Soon, she would face trial before the Lord of Fenrir. Idris hadn't allowed himself to think that far ahead, but now, a sense of dread sickened him. Trials rarely ended well—why would they, when prisoners could take Oaths and benefit the Lord?—but Idris couldn't imagine Anya's trial turning sour when proof beyond the Mirror's telling was nonexistent and she carried with her countless references.

She also had a Knight of the Order of the Valiant looking after her, willing to vouch for her. *That has to count for something*, Idris thought.

So, Idris refused to get swept into worry. There was no room for criminal convictions in their already-complicated futures. He had not lied to Anya when he told her he was lonely, that he didn't want their time together to end, but he did not yet know how to be with her and still live out his duty. Perhaps he could focus his monster-hunting territory on the lands surrounding Waldron-on-Wend? Perhaps his stretches of duty-bound absence would be tolerable to her, so long as he always returned?

He was still stewing on such concerns as they made camp for the night. They found a small, woodsy grove about a quarter of a mile off the High Road and laid out their bedrolls side by side within the trees' protection. While Anya busied herself with Briar's care, Idris slinked off into the young wood to forage for dinner (but not without first planting a kiss on her lips).

As the sounds of camp faded, Idris tuned in to the rustling of night. Mice and other small mammals scurried into their small hideouts. A chilly wind rattled the branches of the trees. Leaves and twigs crunched under Idris's boots, the leather straps of his gear groaning as he moved.

He opened his power to the grove, scenting animal musk, sap, and decay. His nose led him toward the dark mound of a fallen tree, where he was certain he'd find mushrooms he could cook for dinner—but then an out-of-place smell reached him, hitting the back of his palate: stale pipe weed, wool, and man-sweat.

A man he knew.

Idris halted, his hand finding Halgren's hilt.

35

ORDER

IDRIS

A lanky form materialized from a stand of alders ahead, his plain black breastplate glinting faintly in the starlight. "It's a wonder your mouth-breathing hasn't gotten you killed," the familiar voice said. "I could hear you from a half-mile away."

"Heris." Idris exaggerated a sniff. "I'd point out your need for better hygiene, but I have a feeling past lovers have already brought that to your attention."

The other knight laughed mirthlessly as he stalked out of the shadows, halting about six paces away from Idris in the small clearing. Heris was tall and rangy, with sharp cheekbones and a narrow, angular jaw and chin. The black void of his missing right eye added further harshness to his appearance. At court, Heris took to wearing an eyepatch, but out in the wilds, Idris knew he preferred to let the scar breathe.

Idris hadn't seen Heris in years. He'd done his best to avoid the man responsible for his brother's death.

"To what do I owe the displeasure?" Idris prompted.

The world quieted, then—an effect of Heris's sound magic. Like Anya, he could dampen sound, insulate their conversation to keep their secrets contained. It was an eerie thing, to be so immersed in the music of night, only to have it go suddenly silent.

"As usual, Idris, you are the cause of your own peril."

Idris scoffed, even as his palm on Halgren's hilt tightened. He lifted his gaze to the longbow strapped to Heris's back, its elegant curve rising high above the knight's head. On someone else, the weapon might've appeared graceful, even beautiful, but in Heris's possession, it looked just as thin and wicked as its owner. Of course, to survive the Order for as long as Heris had was the true mark of wickedness.

Idris wondered what his own longevity said about him. Perhaps the same.

Idris widened his stance, both impatient and defensive. "Speak plainly or go."

Heris lifted his chin. "Your stunt in Brine could prove costly."

"What do you know of Brine?"

"*Please*," Heris said, "you know how fast rumors travel."

In villages, sure, but not among knights of the wilds. Idris thought about the movements of monsters and the machinations of the Order. Heris usually favored the northern forests, and therefore rarely traveled as far south as the capital, let alone to Brine; it was why, in recent years, Idris had stuck to the more central stretches of the Western Wood. Heris's knowledge of Brine suggested he'd been roaming much closer, as of late.

"Did the mountains become too taxing for your old bones?" Idris quipped.

"You've seen it yourself. Abominations are no longer keeping to the fringes. I hunt where the hunting's good."

"Then you cannot fault me for doing the same," Idris said. "Brine was not a stunt, but a mercy, just as all other kills we are charged with."

Heris scoffed. "Brine provided a choice: uphold the secret of our Oath or go for the glory of a public kill."

Idris opened his mouth to argue, then faltered. "You knew of the abomination in Brine?"

"I'd been tracking it for the better part of a week."

Idris thought of the innocent man who'd died trying to eradicate the monster from the barn—the husbandless wife, the fatherless boy—and swore. "I should've known it was not chance but *incompetence* that drove it into a township," he growled. "How could you know of its presence and not act? How could you do nothing when the tenets of our Oath *require* us to—"

"How dare you question my loyalty to the Oath," Heris snapped, "when you yourself have all but broken yours."

Idris went rigid. "I have done no such thing."

"You have done something far worse than a forfeited kill." The dark socket of Heris's eye narrowed. "You violated the secret of our Order."

"By saving a town from death?" Idris might've tasted the Oath's warning once or twice in Brine, but it hadn't broken. His tattoo was still intact. He waved a dismissive hand. "The secret of which you speak was already out."

"The secret of the monsters, perhaps, but history is laden with tall tales of frightening creatures roaming dark forests," Heris said. "By slaying it as no ordinary person could, *in broad daylight*, you revealed yourself as something *other*."

"That is hardly the same as breaking the Oath," Idris stated, but inside, his assuredness faltered.

Why hadn't he thought to slay the creature after dark, in the dead of night, when no one was around to witness? He could've been stealthy about it, but the embarrassing fact of the matter was that he hadn't even considered it. *You have to help*, Anya had insisted, and Idris hadn't even questioned it. He'd just...stepped forward.

It wasn't Anya's fault, of course. It was *his*. He'd allowed himself to get swept up in playing a hero for her. After rescuing her, he'd forgotten the full extent of his Oath's demands. It had been a relief to spend time with someone who understood even the smallest fraction of the reality of his life. But even Anya's *awareness* of his Oath had been too much, too revealing—he might not have told her his secrets outright, but he'd allowed her to come to conclusions without proper mitigation. In the comfort of being seen, he'd been complacent.

Anya truly *had* become Idris's weakness. More than he'd realized. More than he wanted to admit.

Heris must've noticed Idris's shift in mood because he smiled wolfishly. "You're just like your brother," he said. "Brash. Clumsy. A hopeless fuckup, undeserving of absolution. A traitorous Oathbreaker—"

Idris was on Heris in a heartbeat, fists swinging. But Heris expected the outburst, sidestepping the violence, slimy as an eel. Idris's fist met only air, and anticlimactically, he turned away from the other man. Scrubbing a hand over his jaw, Idris gathered himself. Gathered his anger. Shoved it down.

He was glad Heris had silenced their conversation from Anya's potential eavesdropping—not only had Heris shielded her from the secrets of their Order, he'd spared her from witnessing Idris's embarrassing temper, his lapse in control.

"I'm doing you a favor," Heris snarled. "I offer you the same merciful warning I offered your brother. Keep your head down, stay in line, and do your duty. Say nothing more of Brine, and your Oath will remain intact."

Idris kept his back to Heris, still seething. The older knight spoke of favors and warnings, but it was not mercy that drove Heris—it was greed.

Their Order was not made up of heroes, after all, but criminals. For the lucky few prisoners who fit the criteria to become a Knight of the Order of the Valiant, the choice was simple: face dungeon time (or execution, if the crime was bad enough) or take the Oath. The Lord played it off as rehabilitation, but at its heart, their Order was a sentence.

Magic and rewards kept the criminals in line.

The Oath's magic was bitter and strong, preventative of most small offenses, such as saying too much in mixed company. But forsake the Oath entirely, and the magic would report it to the Oath Ledgers, enacting the original punishment of dungeon or death. Even former knights who'd long-since earned out of their sentences could—in their newfound freedom—break that last thread of their Oath and face their original consequences.

In short: the secret of the Order was one a knight bore for eternity.

Rewards helped sweeten the deal. Compete for most kills in a year—which were also tracked by the ledgers—and knights would be rewarded with money and sometimes even shortened sentences. And since most Valiant Knights were nefarious and disloyal in nature, in-fighting and competition were common—if not expected and encouraged. For the good of the realm, of course.

It was riches and potential freedom that drove Valiant Knights like Heris to form smaller factions within the Order, no better than dungeon gangs pretending to have autonomy in their powerless existence. Hunting parties could track and take down monsters more reliably, and they gamed the reward system to favor the hierarchy of the faction.

Knights like Grinnick sent monetary rewards home to family; knights like Heris amassed wealth for the sake of power—of exactly what sort, Idris still did not know, only that Heris had made it his mission to earn as much as possible. Rumors claimed he'd earned out of his sentence altogether, yet he chose to remain, taking money over freedom for some secret end.

Idris didn't much care what Heris aspired to. It was Heris's faction—referred to as the Bad Blues, renowned for their strategies and wealth within the Order of the Valiant—that had brought Grinnick to his doom, and as far as Idris was concerned, no crooked goal of Heris's was worth Grinnick's untimely death.

"Mercy," Idris growled, still facing away from Heris, unable to look upon the bastard. "Is that what you call orchestrated murder?"

Heris laughed cruelly. "Your brother had it coming, but we both know it came from *you*, not me."

Idris's fists tightened. His chest felt packed full of hot coals, aching and steaming.

Grinnick had never spoken to Idris about the Order, of course, but he'd visited Idris plenty over the six years of his tenure. That—along with what Idris had learned when he snuck into Grinnick's Oath ceremony—had allowed Idris to infer quite a lot. As a knight, Grinnick fought secret foes to protect Fenrir. He'd joined a faction of fellow knights who offered him camaraderie. And he was good at it, earning more than double Idris's meager wages as a garrison at Fenrir Castle, and sending the vast majority of it home to Idris.

But what Grinnick earned in rewards was matched in jealousy from other knights. Grinnick's stories were vague, but Idris read between the lines, and as the years went by, he became worried about his brother's safety within the Bad Blues. When Grinnick told Idris he was going on a particularly treacherous journey with his "fellows," and would not visit for a month, Idris feared the worst. With the foolishness only a little brother could possess, he decided to tail his brother into the wilds.

Not long into the trip, Idris learned the full truth of his brother's charge. Idris witnessed his first abominations, overheard the extent of the in-fighting in the faction, and saw Heris—their leader—for who he was: a greedy criminal.

Idris also saw just how skilled Grinnick had become at killing abominations. The Bad Blues had been tracking a massive parent-monster—called a Morta—and had felled numerous lesser abominations in its wake. The blue glow of Grinnick's battle-axe had arced gracefully through the air to strike down three out of four in only a handful of days.

But in a group where killing blows were predetermined by rank—not skill—Grinnick's success disrupted the hierarchy. It had only taken a few nights of eavesdropping for Idris to understand how things worked within the faction. Grinnick was *supposed* to injure the monsters and allow Heris and other higher-ranking members of the Bad Blues to make the final kill—and therefore reap the monetary rewards—but in the chaos of the fights, Idris had seen Grinnick step out of line to take the kills for himself.

The other men ribbed him for "stealing" rewards from the higher-ranking knights. Their jests were chummy but tinged with contempt. Grinnick—clearly high on a sense of belonging—didn't hear the disdain in his fellow's jests around the campfire.

But Idris had.

Before dawn on the tenth day, Idris revealed himself to Grinnick, and begged him to abandon the chase, lest his comrades betray him out of resentment—but Grinnick wouldn't listen. He scolded Idris for following, told him it risked his Oath for Idris to learn their ways, and demanded Idris go home.

Idris would not abandon his brother, though. He followed the hunting party from a greater distance, catching up when he heard the sounds of battle. Idris arrived on the scene in time to watch Heris parry Grinnick's killing blow, pushing him in line with the monster's swiping claws. Idris rushed from the underbrush, screaming a warning for Grinnick—"watch out!"—and as Grinnick turned, the monster's claws opened his belly just below his breastplate.

He fell, while Heris took the kill for himself.

Idris held Grinnick while he bled, while his brother's so-called friends fled the scene.

As the light faded from Grinnick's eyes, so, too, did the black line of his Oath tattoo. Grinnick used his dying breaths to tell Idris everything—not just to spare

Idris of the confusion of never knowing the true nature of his brother's role, but to warn Idris about the others. It was the knights' duties to contain the secret, and now that Idris knew the existence of monsters and had seen the magic bestowed upon them by their Order, they would turn their sights on hunting him down and silencing him.

Grinnick urged Idris to sneak into the next ceremony and join the Order to protect himself, and at the moment of Grinnick's final breath, a small gap formed in his tattoo, right at the base of his throat. At the time, Idris hadn't known what it meant; he didn't truly understand his brother's broken Oath until his own Oath ceremony.

In Idris's eyes, Grinnick had always been too good for the world. Rakish at times, and over-confident, but also kind and playful and feeling. After six years in the Order, Grinnick had come to love protecting the realm; but he'd taken his love and loyalty for *Idris* to his grave. On the edge of death, Grinnick had broken his Oath to warn Idris of the Order's wrath; he'd protected his little brother one last time.

But Grinnick's logic was flawed.

By breaking his Oath to Idris, his death was not recorded. It was this, as well as Idris's possession of Grinnick's breastplate, that drew the Lord's attention. It's how Idris had been punished with his brother's sentence, unable to leave the Order willingly but by the laws of his brother's crimes. And it's how Idris had ended up here: spending his life in his brother's shadow, seeking absolution for Grinnick's memory, lest his grief and guilt swallow him whole.

Yet Idris had found purpose in his brother's old charge. It was impossible not to take at least some pride in the role. The Order allowed the guilty to repent, and his Oath became the perfect way to punish himself for Grinnick's dishonor, retreat from further heartbreak, yet still do some good for the world.

Since his own taking of the Oath, Idris had done his best to remain separate from the worst factions of the Order of the Valiant, but he'd never forgotten Heris's betrayal. Nor had Heris forgotten Idris's role that day.

Idris turned, facing Heris again. "Why involve yourself in the matter of Brine? Why take issue with my Oath? After all this time, what's in it for you?"

"I am a mere messenger," Heris said coolly—but his shoulders had stiffened.

Idris must've hit a vein. "You're too selfish to be a messenger. We both know the Order is failing, and in the name of our Oath, you seek to keep that fact a secret," Idris said. "You don't honor our duty but hide behind it. Why?"

"Our Oath, our *duty*," Heris spat, "is a sentence. Not everyone is a masochist like you, entering the Order of their own free will—"

"You would've killed me for what I learned—what I knew." Idris had needed the magic of the Oath to level the playing field between himself and the Valiant Knights who hunted him. He hadn't had a choice.

Unless...

Idris couldn't believe it hadn't occurred to him before: Heris *must've* heard Idris trailing them on that Fates-damned hunt. "Why didn't you kill me when you first heard me?"

"Finally figured it out, did you?" Heris grinned. "It was better for morale that I not foil him. Better it be you."

The rage in Idris's chest flared. "But you blocked his killing blow!"

"A mistake in the melee," Heris said with a dismissive wave. "*You* distracted him outright."

Idris's temples ached—with tension, with memory, with self-hatred and regret. He'd been so, *so* naive. Heris had *used* him to murder Grinnick. Had Idris not followed, Grinnick might've lived.

Idris deserved every ounce of misery he'd endured in this Fates-forsaken Order. He deserved never to leave its painful clutches.

"Order or no, every citizen in Fenrir has to claw for the life they want," Heris went on. "You blame me for your brother's death, but did you ever think to question why we hated him so thoroughly? He was just as ruthless as the rest of us."

"Take that back," Idris growled.

He wanted to knock the other knight's yellowed teeth out, but for all the years Idris had dreamed of settling the score by beating Heris senseless—even taking Heris's life—no amount of revenge or violence would bring his brother back.

"You call me a masochist," Idris said, "yet you remain in the Order of your own free will, just as I do. So, I ask you one last time: if you despise your sentence so much, why not end it? Why concern yourself with mine?"

"We all love to feel like good guys, Idris," Heris said with a smirk. "Even me. The Fate of the realm rests on the continued secrecy of our charge. Not just to prevent the inevitable panic of Fenrir's citizens, but to conceal the Lord's hand in this conspiracy."

Idris frowned disbelievingly. "The Lord would never—"

"The Lord is a fool—and I know you don't disagree. But if the Order of the Valiant fails, so, too, does the order of Fenrir itself. Remember your duty, Idris—not just for the sake of your vengeance, but for the greater good."

"You know nothing of what's good."

"I know as much as you do, I reckon," Heris said. "But if you truly care about that pretty thing you're traveling with, you'd do well to stay in line. She already knows too much."

At that, the sound barrier dropped, and the sounds of night pressed in again—a cacophony compared to the silence Heris had willed.

The mention of Anya had Idris running back to camp.

36

FALSE HOPE

IDRIS

I dris feared the worst: that one of Heris's subordinates would already be standing above Anya's limp body, her life already spent. But when he broke through the trees, he found her seated by the fire, warming her hands contentedly.

Her eyebrows darted together at the sight of him. "Are you all right, Idris? You look like you saw a monster."

I did, he thought wretchedly, but refrained from revealing any more than he already had. *She already knows too much*, Heris had said, and he didn't dole out empty threats.

Idris sank onto the fallen log beside her, almost sick with relief that Anya was alright. "It was nothing."

She stared at him, clearly trying to decide whether to challenge his answer or accept it—then she sagged and rested her head on his shoulder. He kissed the side of her forehead. The smell of her hair, the weight of her head, the closeness—another jolt of protectiveness shot through him.

But *how* could he protect her when his nearness was what jeopardized her wellbeing? If Heris and his subordinates had already taken note of her, how long would it be before they saw her as a problem worth dispatching? How long would she be willing to put up with Idris's secrecy, before succumbing to the draw of the unknown and digging into his treacherous truths, just as Idris had done with Grinnick?

This was the exact outcome he'd been trying to avoid. By allowing himself to get close to her, he'd put her directly in harm's way. It seemed that simply to care about her—to *want* her—was to endanger her.

Then again, to push her away now would be to forfeit her protection, too—because without him, she'd be on her own in the capital. He had the power to vouch for her during her trial; it would be cruel to withhold his sway. As nominal as his status was, he was Oath-bound to speak honorably in the presence of the Lord, and that had to count for something—it could, in fact, mean *everything* for Anya, and therefore he had to try.

Besides, it was his duty to escort a prisoner of Fenrir to the capital for trial. There was no getting out of that.

But say she was absolved—then what? For the past few nights, he'd been imagining a future with Anya. A life with a purpose not solely rooted in his Oath.

It was the first time since Grinnick's death that Idris had pictured a brighter future. And yet...there was a reason the vast majority of Valiant Knights lived in complete isolation. It was too painful, too dangerous, too lonesome for their loved ones to endure the reality of their charge. Idris himself knew the agony of loving a Valiant Knight, counting the days between visits, worrying he might not return. Anya deserved someone who could be there for her. Commit fully.

The easiest way forward, of course, was to see her through the trial, then set her free—just as he had with the little bird in the mountains. He could monitor the wilds outside Waldron for a while, just to make sure Heris didn't pose a lasting threat, then Idris could return to serving Grinnick's memory, sequestered far away from Anya and the risk of her safety.

Idris tipped his head against hers, knowing he was kidding himself. Now that he'd experienced something better, there'd be no returning peacefully to his old ways.

There was another option, though. The thought shuddered through him like a cold wind howling down a forbidden path. A dark path.

Due to the effect of monsters on his Fate, Idris had long-ago discounted what he'd seen in his Mirrors. A different death every time, but always the same disturbing Fortune: shallow blue-green water, and his own two hands pushing someone under. In the vision, the reflection of the sky on the water's surface had obscured his victim's face, but the filthy fabric swirling around his arms had suggested a dress. A woman.

How could his greatest Fortune be the death of someone else? The Oath had spared him of fearing his Fate, and he'd long-since put it out of his mind.

So, it had startled him to hear that in Anya's vision, he drowned her. That first night he'd held her, he'd resolved not to tell her of his own Mirror's vision—not out of treachery, but because he couldn't bear to frighten her. Though the Mirrors suggested their tangled futures, his role as a Knight of the Order of the Valiant meant that he operated outside the bounds of Fate. As long as he actively served his Oath, there was a chance he could avoid the Mirror of Fortune's vision.

The problem was: Idris was no longer sentence-bound to the Order.

He'd taken up his brother's charge, yes, but he'd earned out of his sentence three years ago. Idris now bore the Oath of his own free will. He had stayed because the Order was all he'd ever known—the only way he'd ever felt useful, purposeful. He had stayed because he felt he *deserved* to stay, after Grinnick. He had stayed out of fear of finding love and losing it—he couldn't experience attachment or loss when he lived far, far away from civilization, hunting monsters.

But then Anya had come along and changed everything.

Idris could retire from knighthood and be with Anya fully, if he so chose. Be happy *and* watch over her. But *if* he retired, he'd lose control of his Fate, and put her at risk.

He'd never, within his power, do her harm. But without the Fate-defying nature of his Oath, he didn't trust himself. How could he, when so much of his life was ruled by his past mistakes? Besides, there was no sentence long enough to assuage Idris of the guilt for what he'd done. To forsake his Oath would be to forsake Grinnick, too.

A tearing sensation pulled through his chest, an inner conflict he didn't know how to solve. It seemed that all paths led to Anya in danger, whether she faced it at the hands of the Order, her trial, or Idris himself. Idris despised Heris, but there was one thing the other knight got right: Idris *was* a clumsy, hopeless fuckup. Responsible for his brother's death and disgrace. No-doubt Idris was the reason their mother left after their father died, too. And now Anya.

Warped Fate or no, Idris seemed destined to fail those he loved.

And he couldn't even *tell* her the majority of his predicament.

Which brought him back to this: as soon as he saw her well in the capital, Idris *had* to let her go. It would hurt her, perhaps, but not nearly as much as him sticking around. The decision juddered through him like a physical blow, because it hurt him, too.

"Do I dare ask what plagues you?" Anya asked, lifting her head.

Pulled out of his dark thoughts, Idris stiffened. "Better you not."

"Could you tell me if you wanted to?"

He didn't answer.

She made a small *humph*, then stood, wandering over to her pack. She procured the two remaining bottles of Hattie's concoctails and handed him one.

He tried a sip, then—at the delectable taste of whiskey and honey—drank deeper. When he lowered his bottle, she was still watching him.

"Why do I feel like you're trying to get me drunk enough to spill my secrets?" he asked, forcing levity into his tone. It was their last night on the road together, after all, and he wanted it to be...*nice*. For both their sakes.

She clinked the base of her bottle against his, feigning casualness. "I'm trying to get you drunk enough to bed me again."

"You think I'd need convincing?"

Her playful facade faltered, then fell completely. "Something's wrong," she said, brows creasing again. "Something you're not telling me."

"There's a lot I can't tell you."

"I heard a man, in the woods. Someone you knew and didn't like," she said. "Then I lost the thread."

Idris lifted his face to the wind and breathed deeply. He scented nothing but the soil and trees, a doe upwind. Still, he had the feeling of being watched. Of Heris and his goons lurking just beyond the reach of his magic, waiting for Idris to reveal too much to her.

He stared into her fire-bright eyes again, ashamed of his powerlessness.

After a few seconds, Anya pursed her lips and nodded. "Can you at least tell me it'll be all right? Can you tell me I'll return to Waldron-on-Wend?"

Of course, she was thinking about the trial. What she wanted most wasn't *him*, but to return home.

He smiled at her. "You'll return to Waldron-on-Wend."

"Do you truly believe that?"

"Anya." He set down his bottle and reached for her, brushing his knuckles over her soft cheek before taking her face in his hands. "I'll do everything in my power to make it so."

When he kissed her, she met his mouth with openness, her tongue sliding against his. She tasted of honey, and he deepened the kiss, chasing the sweetness like it was something he could capture.

Like it wasn't fleeting and already half-gone.

37

STRENGTH

ANYA

On our final night on the road, we lay side by side, the nearby campfire keeping the frost at bay. Our bodies found each other in the dark, warming and wanting. Naked on my back in our private grove, I shuddered as Idris buried himself deep inside me. His face blocked the stars above, and yet I stared up in wonder, my heart aching with the uncertainty of my future and the unbearable pleasure of *now*.

Afterward, he nestled behind me under our blankets and pressed a constellation of kisses into my neck and shoulder. I allowed myself to believe him when he said I'd return to Waldron. I allowed myself to *hope* that when I asked him to return with me—to carry out his Oath nearby if he could—he'd say yes. After years of getting strung along by Remy, I would ask for what I wanted. And what I wanted—what I'd *always* wanted—was to feel like I belonged unconditionally.

In our short time on the road together, Idris had done that for me. He'd laughed at my sass and jokes, asked riveted questions when I told him long and meandering stories about Waldron, and never once made me feel like my worth to him was contingent upon my usefulness. While I loved to be helpful, it was freeing to feel like my helpfulness wasn't the primary reason he cared about me. His affection—even after a mere three weeks—felt steadfast.

So—in spite of his pensive nervousness on our last night, no-doubt Order-related business he couldn't tell me—I allowed myself to believe Idris's words: *You'll return to Waldron-on-Wend.*

Come morning, as the weak sun rose above the frost-covered hills, I donned my Fate Ceremony dress, wanting to appear presentable in case the Lord saw me immediately upon our arrival. We packed up camp, mounted Briar, and set out.

As the High Road unfurled through farmland and larger hamlets, Idris played happy songs on his flute to the beat of Briar's steps. Soon, the road met up with the Wend, paralleling it toward the city. With Idris's presence behind me in the saddle, I felt strong against the uncertainty ahead. Determined to follow the Wend's current back to Waldron once my business was sorted.

After a few hours of travel, the Wend hooked west, skirting around the outside of the city walls and disappearing into the foothills of the Bone Mountains. We crossed the river via a wide, flat stone bridge, and then the sound of the water left my ears altogether, replaced by the commotion of denser civilization: voices, bells, squeaky wheels, livestock, footsteps, and so much more.

We'd reached the capital's doorstep.

The High Road was congested here; we found ourselves in a long slow line leading toward the city's gatehouse. Teams of city guards trotted by on tall, graceful war horses. Farmers drove wagons brimming with produce. There were single travelers on foot, some pulling small carts behind them, others leading oxen loaded up with goods. Idris and I became merely two of many seeking entry.

As the hubbub increased, so did my anxiety. By the time we reached the gatehouse, I was coiled as a spring. The curtain wall rose impossibly high above us, the pale stone much grimier up close. At the portcullis, a pair of guards were asking questions and ushering folks inside one by one. Seeming to sense my tension, Idris's hand spread across my low belly, hugging me close against his breastplate.

I pulled back on Briar's reins when we arrived at the front of the line.

"State your business," one of the guards said gruffly, staring up at me with shrewd eyes.

I stammered, tongue tied.

Idris flashed his tattoo. "Order business."

Without another word, the guard lifted his hand, gesturing for us to pass through.

Idris clicked his tongue, urging Briar forward. We rode through a short tunnel in the wall and into the city.

The drawings I'd seen of the capital didn't do its scale justice. It had been built into the rocky skirts of Mount Shield in a series of five plateaus, all rising to eventually reach Castle Might at the city's apex. The mountain's snowy peak loomed high, high above, ringed with wispy clouds.

There were people *everywhere*, and I had to steer Briar carefully through the throngs by Idris's instruction, following the main road's zigzagging, uphill trajectory. Two- and three-story buildings edged the way, interrupted by the occasional tower topped with the orange and crimson flags of Fenrir. Poverty and splendor mingled confusingly, with well-kept shopfronts neighboring dirty alleyways, and well-dressed merchants rushing past beggars hunched on stoops.

The sounds of the city overwhelmed my ears with a constant assault, from the squeaks of rats racing underfoot to the cacophonous calls of hundreds—no, *thousands*—of voices bartering, arguing, laughing, shrieking. Hinges squealing, doors slamming, glass breaking, and the sharp clatter of metal against stone.

Gentle fingers brushed the side of my neck and were then replaced by Idris's soft lips; he'd shaved this morning, and his skin was smooth against mine. His touch brought me back to the moment, to simpler sensations: Briar's steady gait, the press of Idris's hips against me, my own breathing.

"Thank you," I murmured.

"*Mhmm*," he breathed into my ear, the low register sending a shiver down my spine.

I leaned forward and patted Briar's neck, his fur silky under my fingertips. I'd braided his ivory mane last night, and he looked rather gallant and celebratory. A horse fit for the streets of Fenrir City.

A pair of young boys rushed across our path, one shouting for the other to slow down, their clothes tattered and faces dirty. Briar tossed his head in surprise but kept walking as the kids scurried past. I wondered if that was what Idris and Grinnick had looked like, two grimy urchins running through the streets, doing what they must.

"I can't imagine you growing up here," I said. "It's so…"

"Loud and smelly?"

"Yes," I said. "It must've been frightening."

"Not with Grinnick around," Idris said. "He always looked after me."

I leaned my head back against his chest, the metal of his breastplate cold and hard. "You said you took your Oath because of him—to take his place. Why did he join your Order?"

I asked the question not fully expecting him to answer—to even be able to. But after a moment, his lips found the shell of my ear again, and he said, "Everything Grinnick did, he did for me. To look after me. To shelter me."

"And then?"

"And then he died."

I looked over my shoulder, finding Idris's blue-green eyes. "You blame yourself?"

A muscle pulsed in his jaw, and he glanced away. "I blame myself."

There was a deep pain in his tone, like a bottomless lake with wretched creatures slithering in its depths, threatening to drag him down. I wanted to buoy him, help to keep him from sinking.

I squinted up at the pale castle for which we were headed. "Well, I don't."

"You know nothing of what happened," Idris said with an edge of disbelief.

"But I know you," I said, "and I can't imagine any scenario in which you'd willingly hurt someone you love."

With his mouth so close to my ear, I didn't need magic to hear his breath catch. But even so, I opened my hearing to him, just to listen to the beating of his heart. His good heart.

"Blame doesn't care about good intentions, Anya," Idris said.

"But I do."

He grunted—not like he didn't believe me, but like he didn't want to.

38

NOBLE KNIGHTS

ANYA

Passing through the gates of Castle Might was much the same as passing into the city, but with no line and more guards. Still, it took Idris only the flash of his tattoo to grant us passage, and then we were riding through the twin guard towers of the barbican gate and into the bailey.

I glanced over my shoulder as we left the chaotic streets behind, dizzied by the height of the city's final plateau. The castle overlooked what felt like the whole world: the huge stair-like steps of the city, the flat grasslands beyond the city wall, endless agriculture clustered along the thin thread of the Wend, the east and western forests a mere fuzz at the edges of the fertile hills rolling southward.

I was still staring as the portcullis closed, blocking my view. Then Idris was swinging off of Briar with a metallic thud. He lifted his hands toward me, and though I could climb off a horse by myself, I allowed him to deposit me on the ground. My legs wobbled with worry, but more than that, I wanted to feel his hands on me as much as I could before I had to stand on my own for trial.

Idris took Briar's reins in one hand and my shoulder in the other, leading us farther into a huge rectangular courtyard, grassy and crisscrossed with stone pathways. Guards and other personnel scuttled back and forth between the low-lying buildings on either side of us, paying us no mind, save for the occasional fleeting acknowledgement: a look, a wave, a nod. Ahead of us, Castle Might's keep stood resolute in the afternoon sunlight, its imposing architecture square and regal.

Idris did not gawk or meander; he walked confidently, as if he knew the way—though I noticed a slight stiffness in his gait. I knew he was a knight, but it hadn't really occurred to me what that truly meant. He was...noble. He served the Lord. He'd probably been here countless times. Without him, I probably wouldn't have gotten past the gatehouse of the city, let alone the castle—certainly not without shackles.

I stared at his profile, seeing the last two weeks with him from a new angle.

Idris glanced at me sidelong. "What?"

"I'm realizing how important you must be, to be able to waltz in here without questioning."

He looked forward again. "Make no mistake, Anya. I am but a dog wearing a collar and leash in my master's home."

The disdain in his voice made me flinch. Why would he take an Oath if it felt like a collar and leash? And what sort of dog did he see himself as? A hound hunting monsters? A guard posted on the edge of civilization, small towns like Waldron mere herds of sheep to him? Having seen Idris's formidable skill and power, the fact that he saw himself as a dog at all was...troubling.

He lifted his chin, and suddenly I saw the tattoo that ringed his neck in an all new light. I followed his gaze forward, realizing he wasn't staring at the keep but something closer.

In the center of the yard stood a large marble statue of a man on bent knee, head hung. He held a round shield, and his carved cape flowed backward off his hunched form as if kicked up by wind. In his right hand, he gripped the round pommel of a sword, its point nestled into the ground. A knight of Fenrir, leaning on his weapon, about to rise after a stunning blow.

As we got closer, I realized the sword was *real*—and too huge for an average man. At least seven feet long. The steel shined brightly in the afternoon sunlight, its edge still razor-sharp. Until this moment, I would've thought Idris—with Halgren—was the most formidable-looking knight in Fenrir. But whomever the statue immortalized made even Idris's imposing form appear diminished.

I approached the statue, halting at its base. Idris came up beside me, slackening Briar's lead so the horse could nibble grass at our feet.

"That's Noble the Mighty, the first Order Knight," Idris said, "and his sword, Killhammer."

The Order of the Mighty were the most famous and well-respected Order, with knights scattered throughout the seven territories and Marona—but I'd never heard of its founder. "His name truly was Noble?" I asked, finding it too perfect for mere coincidence. I wondered if Hattie's crush had been named after this Mighty Knight.

"No," Idris said with a chuckle. "His actual name was Nolan, but legends have a way of twisting word and fact."

"What did he do to become the talk of legend? Aside from being able to wield such a gigantic blade?"

Idris quirked a brow at me. "Do you find Killhammer more impressive than Halgren?"

"Who wouldn't?"

Idris clutched his breastplate, as if I'd wounded him. "So quickly have I fallen from your esteem?"

I rolled my eyes. "Killhammer is at least a foot longer than Halgren."

"It's not the length of the sword, but how a knight uses it, that matters."

I scoffed at the cheap joke, even as my face flushed with memory—with desire.

Idris bent down, his lips grazing my ear. "Have you forgotten that mine glows blue?" he whispered almost inaudibly, his voice teasing and seductive.

"Are we still talking about Halgren? Because otherwise, you really ought to see an apothecary about that."

Idris tipped his head back, laughing heartily.

I faced the statue again. "So, what legendary tale precedes this statue?"

A new voice joined our conversation from across the courtyard, drawing both our attention. "Six hundred years ago, in the War of Wraiths, an alchemist's apprentice named Nolan from Fenrir enlisted in Marona's Royal Army. He worked his way up the ranks, and eventually founded the Order of the Mighty, the first Oath-bound Knights, which led the charge at the Battle of East Hammer. His victory marked the end of the war."

The speaker halted a couple paces away. He was tall and broad, with golden hair and a kingly jaw. Based on the regality of his appearance, I would've thought him the Lord of Fenrir, except that he wore gold armor and possessed an Oath tattoo. A red and orange cloak was draped over his shoulder, and a dazzlingly ornate double-headed battle-axe was strapped to his back, the rounded blades glittering behind his head like a deadly halo.

At the sight of him, Idris took a knee, bowing deeply. "Oderin," he said, chin tucked.

Following Idris's lead, I lifted my skirts and sunk into a low curtsey.

"Rise, you ass," Oderin said to Idris, striding forward. He clapped Idris on the back, then pulled him into a quick hug, their metal armor clacking together. When he released Idris, Oderin turned his golden-brown eyes on me. "Who do we have here?"

"This is Anya Alvara," Idris said.

I rose, staring up at the golden warrior.

"She's here for trial before the Lord," Idris added.

Oderin's warm smile faltered, his brows drawing together. "A criminal?"

Idris procured a folded paper from his pocket and handed it to the other knight. Oderin unfolded it quickly, eyes darting over the page. "A *hypothetical* criminal," he amended, not without a hint of pity in his tone. He waved the paper. "This prisoner caravan was meant to arrive two days ago."

"She was the lone survivor," Idris said. "It's why I'm here."

Oderin's tan skin visibly paled. He handed the paper back to Idris. "Seems there's much to discuss. Come. Let's get you inside." He turned on a heel, marching toward a low building off to the right.

Idris tucked the paper back into his pocket. It must've been a crime record he found while cleaning up the mess after he rescued me. It was a reminder that, no matter what had happened between us on the road, our quest had begun with Idris's sense of duty toward the Lord—a directive that was still intact.

Idris pressed his hand into my back, guiding me quickly forward, with Briar on his other side. While we walked, he whispered into my ear again—not sultry this time, but forceful. "Say nothing of what you've seen."

It turned out that "much to discuss" didn't include me.

Once Briar had been handed off to a stable hand, I was deposited in Oderin's single bedroom inside the barracks. Apparently, he was a rather high-ranking Knight of the Order of the Mighty, overseeing the Royal Guard. Which explained Oderin's gold armor, glamorous weapon, and Idris's immediate, respectful bow.

What I hadn't gleaned on our short walk to Oderin's quarters was how he knew Idris and why they were so chummy. Oderin *must've* been the friend Idris had mentioned, the reason he knew of the One Week cabin.

Their friendship certainly boded well for me. Oderin had deposited me in his *bedroom*—not a dungeon—in spite of my technically being a prisoner of Fenrir. As far as temporary holding cells were concerned, this was quite cushy. As I stared out Oderin's single window, overlooking the eastern foothills of the Axe Range, I wondered how else their chumminess might benefit me.

Feeling restless, I turned away from the window and went to my pack. Underneath the spare clothes and Hattie's tinctures were the numerous letters I'd carried from Waldron. It comforted me to look upon them, count them, remind myself of the community I had back home. Each letter was secured with Mayor Tomilson's seal pressed into the wax—proof of their legitimacy. I'd already read through Hammond's instructions, too, just a few sentences about etiquette (such as remembering to curtsy and not looking at the Lord until prompted). I knew nothing of Mirror Trials, but the advice of a Mirror Knight and the character references from my closest friends and neighbors—combined with my connection to Idris and now Oderin—*had* to mean something.

I had expected to grow more and more anxious the closer I got to facing the Lord, but a quiet hope was building in me instead, a fortress made entirely of my community, each person a pillar of support. Bolstered, I allowed myself a moment to indulge in imagining my trip home. Riding Briar with Idris wedged into the saddle behind me. Frosty nights snuggled up in our tent. Cresting the hill into Waldron. Folks crowding Swan's Row, waving excitedly. Wicker bounding over the cobblestones and into my arms to lick my face. Introducing Idris to the town.

With a sigh, I tucked the letters carefully back into my pack. I was getting ahead of myself.

I glanced out the window again, noting the position of the sun. Almost an hour had passed since I'd been deposited here, and I was getting bored of my own thoughts. I could take a nap, but it seemed weird to sleep in Idris's friend's bed—and besides, I was too antsy to rest.

Seeking other interests, I sank into the wooden chair by Oderin's small writing desk. The surface of the desk was littered with papers: maps, records, and lists of names. I brushed a finger over the uneven edge of a particularly precarious stack and casually read the top: a news report from the remote western town of Yar-on-Gray. As I skimmed the words, a cold prickle of dread prodded at the base of my throat like the steely tip of a dagger.

Abomination.

Massacre.

Few survivors.

I swallowed. Reread. The report was rushed, barely two sentences.

I lifted the sheet off the stack, hoping to find further explanation underneath, but the disruption caused the papers to slide sideways across the desk. I fumbled, catching the slow topple and steadying the pages lest they spill onto the floor. But as I pushed the papers into a pile again, the stack remained unsteady, balanced awkwardly atop a small but rather thick book.

Carefully, I leaned the stack against my arm and slid the book out from underneath their weight, setting it aside as I straightened the papers back into balance. Once the almost-mess was contained, I picked up the book. Perhaps it would entertain me while I waited for Idris and Oderin to return.

The book was bound in red leather, its edges tooled with a pretty triangle pattern. In gold debossing, the cover read: *Orders.*

A hungry curiosity swept over me, and I flipped through the pages, my attention gobbling up as much as it could. As its simple title suggested, the book was a log of all Orders: their histories, what they entailed, with details about the magical bindings, including the words knights recited to take their Oaths.

My first instinct was to search for Idris's Order, but I knew so little, beyond his charge to fight monsters. And I saw no mention of "monsters." Remembering the news report, I began skimming for the word "abomination," but in my frenzy, I didn't spot that, either. The word I did see in great repetition was, perhaps, more presently disturbing: "sentence."

As in *criminal* sentence.

I found it on the pages for the Order of the Shrewd, the Order of the Fierce, the Order of the Valiant. I'd never heard of such Orders before, but each and every one of them had the same final line in their Oaths:

By the Fates and the arcane power of this Oath, I swear fealty to the Order of [that which the Oath pertained], never to forsake my duty except in the completion of my sentence or death, whichever comes sooner.

Was the Lord using some Orders as a form of imprisonment? Punishment? It was a known fact of Fenrir that countless Orders existed, some famous and lauded, others secret. It was the same as the factions in Fenrir's army, the cavalry a known entity, while no-doubt there were spies and other groups carrying out more clandestine dealings. I'd never thought much about who took the Oaths and how—or why. Over the years, a few young men had left Waldron with their sights set on enlisting in one way or another, but I'd never taken much interest in how folks served the Lord. It'd never concerned me.

Now, it concerned me.

A dog with a collar was a prisoner of sorts, no? Did the leash not imply that the dog would run, if given the freedom?

A loud clang outside the door had me snapping the book shut and shoving it underneath one of the smaller piles on the desk. I smoothed my hands over the front of my Fate Ceremony dress, wiping off my sweaty palms. Twenty or so voices filled the hall with a sudden, nervous chatter, as if a meeting were letting out.

I went to the door, pressing my ear to it to eavesdrop. I elevated my magic, sifting through the confusion of numerous, echoing conversations happening at once as the group passed.

"—Mirror Criminals seem like the least of the Lord's problems when—"

"—you hear the rumors from Yar? What if—"

"That can't be possible, it's too—"

"—wonder if the incident is related to—"

"Do you think it's possible for an Order to fail?"

"If so, it's a sobering thought."

The voices diminished as swiftly as they came, the group disappearing down the hall. I turned the doorknob slowly and poked my head out to look after them, curious who they were—Royal Guard? Other knights of some kind?

I'd barely caught a glimpse of annoyingly unidentifiable red and orange rounding the bend when a voice called out from the direction from which the others had come.

"Anya?"

I startled, blinked, not truly believing who I saw.

Hammond was standing at the end of the hall with a tall, dark-skinned woman who wore the same Mirror Knight attire as he. Given the delays Idris and I faced on the road, they must've *just* beaten us to the capital after the Mirrors' tour across Fenrir.

"I'll catch up with you," Hammond said to his fellow knight, and with a nod, she turned on a heel, disappearing around a corner.

Then Hammond was rushing toward me, his bootsteps echoing in the now-quiet hallway. When he reached me, Hammond glanced at both ends of the hall before pulling me into a quick version of one of his bone-crunching hugs.

His eyes were wide when he released me. "*Fates*, Anya, I thought you were—" He covered his mouth with a hand.

"You heard about the prisoner caravan," I guessed.

He nodded, then glanced at the placard on the door. "What are you doing in the Major's quarters?"

"Oderin deposited me here," I said. "He's meeting with my escort."

"Your..." Hammond's eyes widened even further. "*Fates*, Anya, you truly are full of surprises." He gripped my shoulders, whispering quickly. "What *happened* out there? There's been some speculation among the ranks, but—"

I shook my head. "I'm not sure I should say, Hammond."

His hands slid off me, and he straightened, regarding me quizzically. "Is that so?"

Apparently, my avoidance of his question was telling enough. I thought of Idris's Oath, his warning: *Say nothing of what you've seen.*

"Tell me, how is Ellie?" I asked quickly.

His eyes narrowed, seeing my evasion plainly, but the topic of his wife was one he could never resist. "Morning sick," he said, "but she glows more radiantly than sunlight on snow."

"Throwing up all day can do that, I hear," I said.

He chuckled, then shrugged. "Every time I call her beautiful lately, she says I'm blinded by devotion, but I wouldn't have it any other way."

I smiled at him, warmed by the hint of normalcy. Of love and humor and the hope of growing families.

"I best be going," Hammond said, pointing a thumb over his shoulder. "Has your trial been set yet?"

"I'm not sure. We just arrived. I was told to wait here."

"Oderin is a good person to have on your side," he said. "I'll do my best to be there for your trial, too."

"Really?" I asked, touched.

"My presence won't do anything for your case, but perhaps a familiar face..."

Bootsteps echoed nearer from an unseen hallway, but I didn't care. I stepped into another tight hug, relishing Hammond's kindness. "Thank you," I said against his chest.

A throat cleared, and we parted to find Idris approaching. His nostrils were flared slightly—and not in a way that suggested magic, but...jealousy? I smirked, finding it rather silly that he'd be so on edge around *Hammond*, of all people.

"Idris," I said, waving at him. "Do you know Hammond? He's a Mirror Knight I know from—"

"The Lord will see you now," Idris interrupted tightly.

39

TRIAL

IDRIS

Idris had always hated Castle Might.

He'd hated growing up hungry and impoverished in its opulent shadow. When he'd snuck over the wall to spy on Grinnick's Oath Ceremony, he'd hated the exclusivity of the castle's compound: the neatly landscaped bailey, the pretty statues, the greater knights who walked the grounds. When he himself had become a Valiant Knight, he'd hated the elegant architecture of the throne room, that the doom of countless individuals had been sealed in such an airy space.

He hated the wealth and control and ruthlessness the castle represented, so far removed from the struggle of the city below. The struggle inside his heart.

Idris considered himself lucky to live in the wilds, no matter the grim duty that kept him there. He only had to come to Castle Might every year or two, mostly to attend the introduction of new recruits when it was his turn to assist in training, and the rare intelligence briefing. The only thing he *liked* about coming to Castle Might was the chance to see Oderin, their bond forged in their early knighthoods and strengthened by many a night commiserating over ale.

Oderin was one of the few knights Idris respected—one of the few who actually lived up to the title of his Order. And even *he* couldn't spare Anya from her trial.

Idris had tried to convince him—he really had. The Order of the Mighty was the only order entrusted with the full intelligence of lesser orders, and Idris had been able to speak plainly with Oderin about the prisoner caravan—but when it came down to it, Anya was a prisoner of the realm. Mirror Criminals had to be tried, no exceptions.

Idris's only hope, now, was that Lord Haron would be amenable to Idris vouching for her—and wouldn't ask too many questions about the monster attack. Idris knew firsthand how sensitive the Lord was to criminals knowing too much.

So, as Idris escorted Anya down the long corridor toward the throne room, his hatred for this Fates-forsaken place grew to new heights.

What was worse: the Mirror Knight—Hammond, Anya had called him—followed on their heels. The man seemed nice enough, and Anya obviously knew and liked him, but his presence prevented Idris from speaking freely to her; Idris didn't trust that Hammond would keep his mouth shut, if pressed. That was the whole point of Oaths, after all—to guarantee loyalty. To keep the leashes tight.

Had Idris known how abuzz the castle was with talk of the missing caravan—further spurred by whisperings about "unknown" horrors in Yar-on-Gray, which Oderin had informed him of the moment they'd been alone—he would've warned Anya to avoid the topic altogether. If only there had been time today for Idris to prepare her for her audience. His Oath prevented him from advising she lie to the Lord, but had they had a moment alone together—*Fates*, he could've said *something*. Or, at the very least, comforted her before this culminating moment.

But now, he remained silent. Anya—clutching her letters tightly against her pretty embroidered bodice—kept looking up at him for reassurance, but all Idris could do was smile down at her like he wasn't leading her toward a trial that could prove more complicated than he'd originally anticipated.

Toward her possible imprisonment.

When they reached the end of the long corridor, Idris halted before the two guards stationed outside the door to the throne room. "I come with Anya Alvara, for trial, as requested."

One of the guards cracked the door and whispered to the pair stationed on the other side. The small gap was enough for Idris to smell the stink of the Lord's perfume clouding the throne room; nobody knew Lord Haron's sensory magic—it was a mystery he delighted in maintaining—but Idris was willing to bet it wasn't scent.

Another thing Idris hated about this place: the tedium.

Idris glanced down at Anya, aching to touch her, but holding himself back. He didn't want to seem overly biased toward her in mixed company, but her fear was plain on her face now, creasing her usually open expression, her light brown eyes darting from the guards to the tapestries on the walls, to Hammond standing behind them, only to land on Idris pleadingly.

He *had* to say something, so he whispered the only thing he could: "Remember what I told you." He hoped she knew to what he referred: *Say nothing of what you've seen.*

She stared up at him, lower lip wobbling—then the doors opened, stealing her attention.

"Walk ahead of me," Idris murmured.

She did as she was told, her footsteps echoing off the marble. She held her head high; her hair hung in a single braid down her back, exposing the long, proud line of her neck. Witness to her courage, an overwhelming sense of respect spread through Idris—only to be eclipsed by a sinking sense of dread as he followed her inside.

Not much had changed in the imposing space since the last time Idris had seen it, but never had he felt so knotted up with fear upon entering—not even when he took his Oath. Anya was far more precious to Idris than his own future had been to him at the time; wracked with grief over Grinnick, he hadn't much cared about what he'd face in the Order of the Valiant. It was that lack of caring that had *kept* him Oath-bound even after his sentence was complete, lingering grief and self-hatred affixing him to the very thing he despised.

But now, things were different. Now, he cared very much about what the future held.

The Lord of Fenrir was seated on his raised throne at the other end of the chamber, framed by his robed-and-hooded ledgermasters, a few attendants, and four Royal Guards. Oderin had already seated himself in the area reserved for witnesses—a cluster of chairs off to the left, empty except for him—and Hammond broke off to sit beside the other knight.

Idris continued on Anya's heels, seeing her all the way to the Lord. "Six more steps, then halt and bow—low," he whispered, his words mere breath to his ears, but he knew Anya would hear him.

She followed his instructions, lifting her skirts in one hand and curtsying as low as she could without dropping her numerous letters. Her dress had been a good choice. It was rather simple compared to the ostentatious fashion of the Lord's court, but it showed effort, which the Lord would appreciate.

"Rise," Lord Haron said, his voice just as gratingly nasal as Idris remembered. He wore a flamboyant pink and green waistcoat with a white ruffled shirt, and a matching version of those silly pointed shoes he favored. Sometimes Idris got the sense that the Lord wore ridiculous things just to see the trend sweep noble society, to test his subjects' blind devotion.

Anya rose, but kept her chin tucked, not looking the Lord in the eye.

"My, my, you are a pretty little criminal, aren't you?" Lord Haron said.

Idris clenched his teeth. The Lord loved to bait his subjects into speaking out of turn. Idris should've taught Anya some basic court etiquette in preparation for her audience—but it was too late, now.

Thankfully, she didn't respond to the Lord's question.

After a beat, the Lord chuckled, a menacingly haughty staccato. "Do you know why you are here?" he asked. "You may speak freely, Anya Alvara."

Finally, she lifted her gaze to the Lord, holding her chin high enough that Idris—standing a pace back and to her left—could see the fluttering of her pulse on the side of her neck.

Yet, in spite of her palpable nervousness, her voice was steady and clear. "I am here for my Mirror Trial."

"Very good," the Lord said, as if he were speaking to a child. "What did you bring me? Letters?" He held out a beckoning hand.

Anya fell for it. She stepped forward, and the foursome of gold-clad Royal Guards flanking the Lord's throne all moved as one, brandishing the long daggers they kept at their hips. Anya stopped short, startled; a few letters slipped out of her grasp, fluttering to the floor. Idris stooped without thinking, realizing only after he'd handed Anya one of the escaped letters that he'd made a mistake, too.

When Idris rose to his full height again, Lord Haron had his chin propped on a fist. He was smirking.

"Hand them to Xina," the Lord ordered Anya, pointing at one of the squires.

Anya settled the letters into the squire's outstretched arms, her cheeks flaming. The Lord clearly relished seeing her squirm—but not as much as he relished seeing through a charade.

As the squire deposited the letters into the Lord's hands, his shrewd eyes flicked to Idris. "You always were a sentimental man, Idris, but caring about a Mirror Criminal?" The Lord tisked, sounding endlessly amused. "Even *I* wouldn't have guessed."

A multitude of sarcastic comments came to mind, but Idris kept his mouth shut. To reveal any emotion would be to play into the Lord's hand.

His show of affection toward Anya was bad enough on its own. Any favorable word Idris spoke of Anya was now debatable at best, invalidated at worst. The Lord would no doubt use it against him if the opportunity arose.

The Lord gestured at one of the squires, who approached the throne carrying a gold platter with a creased piece of paper resting atop it. "Tell me, Anya, are you a criminal?" Lord Haron asked as he lifted the sheet off the tray.

"No," Anya rushed out. "In my case, the Mirror must be wrong. I would never—"

The Lord raised his hand, cutting her off. He held the paper aloft. "Here in my hands is the testimony of a one Daisy Merchold. Do you know a woman by that name?"

Anya shook her head, but Idris saw the clench of her fist at her side.

The Lord took on a high-pitched, feminine tone. "'My husband left for Waldron-on-Wend seven weeks ago and never returned. He said he had an attachment in Waldron that he needed to sever.'" The Lord lowered the paper. "Ringing any bells now?"

Anya simply stared.

Was she surprised by the *testimony*? Or the fact that Remy hadn't returned to his wife? Had she known he *had* a wife? *I have plenty of reasons to murder Remy,* she had told Idris, *but I* wouldn't.

The Lord licked his lips and continued reading in that insulting voice. "'It is my belief that my husband Remy—a merchant under the crown's esteemed banner—was murdered by his mistress after he ended their dalliance.' Blah, blah, blah." The Lord set the paper back on the squire's tray and flicked his wrist in dismissal. "It is not uncommon for women to become hysterical upon rejection."

Anya shook her head again, a strand of hair by her face coming loose from her braid. "Who's to say he isn't just late returning home? He was never a particularly trustworthy individual—*clearly.*"

The Lord arched a brow. "*Was?*"

Anya closed her eyes, clearly realizing the potential implication of her phrasing. But when she opened them again, a fierceness had come over her. "If he has not returned by now, perhaps he perished in the attack on my prisoner caravan."

Fuck. She mentioned it.

Idris's heart went from steady drumbeat to stampede—loud enough for Anya to tip her ear slightly in his direction, taking note. *Say nothing of what you've seen. Say nothing of what you've seen.* If he thought the words loud enough—Idris wondered illogically—would she hear his plea?

"I have no record of Remy Merchold being convicted," Lord Haron said.

"He came to see me that first night on the road," Anya explained quickly. "He followed the caravan and sought me out after sundown to break things off. How could I kill him from inside a cell?"

That was a surprise. Idris glanced at Oderin and Hammond; both men were wide-eyed.

"That's quite a yarn you're weaving," the Lord said. "Why would—"

"It is no yarn," Anya insisted.

The Lord narrowed his eyes, angered by the interruption. "Give me one good reason why I should believe you."

Anya glanced back at Idris; she wanted him to jump in, but he couldn't. Not when the Lord was so agitated. Not when the Lord suspected that Idris held affection for her. It wasn't the right time.

A single tear slid down her face. "I—I have character references," she said, gesturing at the stack of letters on the Lord's lap.

He made a show of lifting one aloft and ripping it in half. "Friends of murderers are hardly to be believed."

Another tear fell from Anya's cheek, wetting the fabric of her dress, a dark splotch right over her heart.

Her letters, his knighthood. They'd both been so optimistic about her trial. How had this gone so wrong? Idris would be hard-pressed to believe the wife of a merchant would be worried about his absence when the travel alone took six weeks round-trip; inclement weather, a broken axel, a horse with an abscess—there were any number of reasonable explanations for Remy's delay.

Was it possible the Lord had commissioned the testimony? Had the Lord already suspected that Anya knew too much? No information in Fenrir was *illegal*, but a conviction for something else would certainly silence her.

And Anya had played right into the Lord's scheme—perhaps better than the Lord could have anticipated. Because by her admission, if Remy died in the attack, there was no risk of him showing up later to disprove Anya's "crime." With Remy gone, the Lord could *easily* pin the blame on Anya.

But how had the Lord caught wind of Anya's knowledge in the first place? *Heris.*

It was just like the other knight to have the *Lord* do away with Anya over murdering her himself. The question was *why*? Why would Heris wish to contain the rumors from Brine, but tell the Lord about Anya?

Idris couldn't take it anymore—he had to defend her. "If I may, my Lord—"

"You may not," the Lord bit out.

Idris tasted the warning of his Oath on his tongue, the bitterness that'd ruled his whole adult life. He clenched his jaw again, molars aching.

Lord Haron swung his cruel eyes on him. "Actually, there is something I'd like to know from you, Knight."

A sour feeling spread through Idris's gut.

"Does she know too much?"

Anya, trembling now, glanced at Idris again, eyes red.

Idris couldn't outright lie to the Lord—his Oath prevented it. Thankfully, the Lord was sloppy with his phrasing. Overly subjective.

Idris inspected his own fingernails, assuming a bored tone. "Anya is an innkeeper from Waldron-on-Wend," he said. "She knows little of the world." It pained him to say it, but he hoped the dismissal would appeal to the Lord's already-dismissive attitude. He didn't look at Anya to see his statement's impact. He lowered his hand and met the Lord's eyes. "Hardly nefarious, if you ask me."

"That wasn't what I asked, though," the Lord said. "All day, my halls have hummed with rumors about a prisoner caravan that never arrived at the capital. A caravan filled with Mirror Criminals. By her own word, Anya was on that caravan—a fact which was confirmed by the record you brought. No others have turned up, and yet here *you* stand. A Knight of Fenrir, doing your duty to deliver her to my doorstep for proper trial."

The acid in Idris's stomach intensified, burning up his chest, into his throat. He swallowed.

The Lord leaned forward, gripping the armrests of his throne. The many rings on his fingers ground against the wood as he gripped it tighter. "How is it that she survived when no other prisoners did? When not a single one of my guards returned?"

The prisoners had died by the claws and jaws of the abomination, but the guards...Idris had seen a few of them run off. He wondered now if Heris or one of his subordinates had silenced them before word returned to the capital.

It seemed believable enough: if Heris had been motivated to contain the news from Brine, he would've felt similarly about the caravan—especially in the aftermath of whatever had gone wrong with the Valiant factions in Yar-on-Gray, which didn't reflect well on the effectiveness of the Order.

But Anya had been a loose end—too difficult to kill with Idris hanging around. So perhaps Heris had changed tactics, deciding to tell the Lord about the caravan, after all—and using the intelligence to put himself back in the Lord's good graces after the Bad Blue's failure in Yar.

It wasn't too far-fetched. In fact, it sounded *exactly* like something Heris would do.

Idris's head swam as Lord Haron continued his tirade.

"Answer me this. What in all the seven territories of our beloved Kingdom of Marona has the power to eradicate three prisoner wagons and eighteen trained prisoner guards?" the Lord asked, finally reaching his point with a cruel thrill in his beady eyes. "Think on it for a moment, Idris, then tell me: Does. Anya. Know. Too. Much?"

Anya tipped her face toward Idris, her cheeks slick with tears, her mouth parted.

For a single, reckless moment, Idris considered abandoning his Oath. But to lie would only confirm that which the Lord sought to know. And to refuse to answer would have a similar effect—and could also break his Oath, depending on how the Lord chose to wield the magic against him. The Lord's question was unavoidable; Idris was entirely trapped.

He could not save Anya.

A landslide of devastation swept through him, big heavy boulders and suffocating mud burying him in shame. He should've never expected the Lord to take his word seriously, to assume a dog had sway over his master. He should've anticipated that there would be Order politics at play. He should've known that his presence would ruin things. He should've remained outside the room. He should've retired his Oath and done away with this Fates-forsaken place long ago. He should've...*stayed out of it.*

Heris had been right about one thing: Idris was nothing but a clumsy, hopeless fuckup. Even without a fixed Fate, it seemed Idris was forever destined to fail the people he loved.

40

RATS

I stared at Idris, waiting for him to tell the Lord that I knew nothing, that I was innocent, that I was no more threatening than a field mouse captured in Waldron and set loose in this chamber.

His jaw—dusted with a faint stubble this late in the day—feathered. A crease formed between his brows. He looked as if he were fighting an inner battle—not just weighing options like potential threats but sizing up a real limitation.

His Oath.

I looked to Hammond and Oderin in the audience. They were both stiff, the slightest grimaces pulling on their set mouths as they watched the scene unfold.

Idris wasn't looking at me; he was still facing the Lord. His blue-green eyes were unwavering, resolute. Tension passed over his lips, the faintest flash of a pained frown. Then his expression fell in what I could only interpret as defeat.

"I will not ask again," the Lord said in a low, scolding register.

No matter how much he cared for me, Idris couldn't lie. He couldn't forsake his Oath.

But I was not bound by such limitations.

"I saw a rabid bear," I blurted, remembering what Idris had insisted after my rescue. "It came from the woods, mouth frothing, and destroyed the wagons—clearly hunger-crazed." I swallowed, hoping my palpable fear for the Lord's wrath translated into a convincing show of fear for the memory of the attack. "I cowered under some wreckage and kept my eyes shut. I didn't open them until Idris found me."

"I did not ask you," the Lord said impatiently, scowling at Idris. "I asked one of my loyal knights. Whom I will remind now that it is not just his duty but *his brother's* that will be impacted if he does not *speak*."

What the fuck did that mean?

A chair groaned, drawing attention to Hammond rising from his seat. "My Lord," he said, confusion furrowing his features. "Please excuse my ignorance, but what does a bear attacking the caravan have to do with the vision in Remy Merchold's Mirror of Death? It seems to me that—"

"I have been clear!" Lord Haron screeched, starling everyone in the chamber. "About whose opinion I have sought! And it is not yours, Mirror Knight!"

Hammond sank into his seat once again, his cheeks bright pink.

Was Hammond—a respected Knight of the Order of the Mirrors—truly not privy to that which we spoke? *Fates*, no wonder Idris was always so tongue-tied. The monsters truly were a hard-kept secret.

No wonder the Lord seemed to want to use my Mirror Crime to condemn me—to silence me. I shook my head disbelievingly; the back of my nose stung. This clearly wasn't going to end well.

"I did find her cowering, eyes shut," Idris said.

The Lord pursed his lips with thinly veiled fury over Idris's vague statements. He waited, obviously intent on not asking again.

Silence filled the hall. Oderin and Hammond sat uselessly. A squire near the Lord shifted uncomfortably on her feet. The Royal Guards framing the Lord were motionless, save for their eyes, which danced from me to Idris to the Lord and back. The Lord himself was still scowling, those thin lips of his pale from being screwed up so tightly.

Finally, Idris regarded me. His eyes were impossibly soft—*pitying*—as they roved over my face. Our gazes waged a silent war. Of pleading. Of powerlessness. Of regret.

When he broke our stare and faced the Lord of Fenrir once more, I *knew* that Idris was about to betray me.

"She knows of that which I cannot speak," Idris ground out.

Even though I saw it coming, I gaped at him, open-mouthed. Hot tears streaked down my cheeks, my body giving into fear even as my mind hung on Idris's words, not believing that he'd really said them aloud.

The Lord clapped his hands. "Well, that settles it! Take her away."

Panic seized me just before the guards did. "Wait!" I shouted, desperate now. "Wait, I'm innocent! Tell them, Idris!"

But Idris had stepped back. Surely his Oath did not prevent him from arguing, for fighting for me? Yet he was *allowing* this to happen.

I bucked against my captors' holds, their fingers pinching my arms, bruising my skin as they held me firm. "I know nothing! I know nothing!"

"Whatever do you mean?" Lord Haron said innocently. "You are being sentenced for the murder of Remy Merchold. By the law of Fenrir Territory, what you *know* has nothing to do with—"

"But my Fate isn't yet fixed!" I argued. "It can still change!"

Idris didn't even flinch at my desperation; ice filled my veins at the sight of his blank expression. He'd shown up in my Mirror of Death, and yet by some cruel double standard, he was untouchable by the very thing that would ruin my life.

"This isn't fair!" I shouted as the guards dragged me toward the door. I wrenched one arm free and pointed at Idris. "My Fate could be warped, same as his! I'm—"

The Lord laughed. The sound was so cruelly amused that I broke off.

"No, no, go on," the Lord prompted. "Please, by all means, give us all further proof that you know far more than you ought. Dig a deeper hole for the knight, too."

My vision blurred with tears. I heard the squeal of chairs across marble, of Oderin and Hammond speaking over each other, imploring the Lord to reconsider. But I was focused on Idris's form; he looked like an immobile black smudge to my eyes. No better than a statue. "Idris..." I cried pitifully.

He didn't move or speak.

I kicked my feet and flailed my arms. I screamed at the top of my lungs, my vocal cords burning with strain. Finally, a guard smothered my mouth with a rough palm, his hand tasting of sweat and metal, but I continued to shriek into it until I grew hoarse. My heels dragged on the marble as I was yanked through patches of dull, multicolored light coming in from the stained-glass windows. The last thing I saw as I was carried away was Idris, still in the chamber, standing with his back to me.

Hours later, I sat on the floor of an empty stone cell far underground. No light permeated the darkness, save for the single lantern hanging at the top of the stairs, a flame that caused a faint silvering of the edges of my iron bars. The dungeon reeked of urine. I heard the scuttling of rodents, the trickle of moisture, and the faint echoes of other prisoners in the deeper depths of the underground tunnels.

My throat was still raw from all the screaming, my ears still rang from the sound of my own terror, and the skin underneath my eyes stung with the dried salt of my tears. I felt hollow, alone.

How could the trial have gone so wrong? I'd had references. I'd had a knight on my side. I'd done nothing *wrong*! And yet, just by witnessing a monster, I was doomed? What of the people of Brine who'd fought a similar foe? Would the Lord send out a regiment to collect them, too? Was the secret of the monsters' existence really worth such trouble to contain? Was it not better to alert the vulnerable towns of Fenrir to the imposing threat, rather than keep them in the dark?

And *Remy*.

Fates, did I hate him in this moment. His cowardice. His selfishness. Of all the people who could've absolved me from this mess, it would've been him. He could've easily written me a character reference—and he hadn't. Because, deep down, he'd thought me capable of killing him; he'd thought himself *worthy* of such vile jealousy, that I'd rather see him dead than be with anyone else. It was laughable how highly he thought of himself; it was shameful how oblivious I'd been to his low opinion of me.

Even so, I didn't know why I'd used the word "was" with regard to Remy in front of the Lord. A slip of the tongue, perhaps, as his role in my life was now firmly in the past. But then I'd blabbered about his presence the night of the attack. I'd been shocked to hear that he hadn't returned home—seeing as he'd run off into the woods—but perhaps in the chaos the monster had found him, after all. Or perhaps he ran out on his wife and daughter, too, escaping Fenrir altogether to start anew in a different territory.

No matter what had happened to Remy, I *hadn't* murdered him. But now, it seemed too late to convince the Lord of that fact. Short of locating Remy—which would be nearly impossible if he'd fled and truly impossible if he was dead—there was nothing I could do. Nothing I could've done.

Which brought my thoughts back to Idris.

He'd simply...stood there. Watching. Frozen as they took me away. His face had been void of emotion, and it was his lack of expression that hurt the most, a blade of betrayal shoved into my side. Even Hammond and Oderin had eventually risen from their seats, arguing with the Lord—but it was Idris's name I'd called, and it was Idris who had turned away, not answering.

Just the thought of him now was a twist to the phantom blade; the pain of it was so visceral that I gasped. The pitiful sound repeated as it echoed off the walls of my cell.

Logically, I knew he was bound by Oath not to lie to the Lord. All knights were. But could he not have spoken about my character? Could he not have insisted that, though I knew too much of the monsters, I could be trusted not to mention them? Could Idris not have done more to curb my sentencing?

In truth, I had no idea. Because I didn't really know him, did I? Not when his Oath withheld so much of him from me.

And what did a sentence even mean? The Lord had not been specific about my outcome. Would it be dungeon or death? Or could it be...an Oath of my own?

I considered what I'd read in the book on Oderin's desk. Had *Idris's* Oath been a criminal sentence? Was that why he wouldn't—*couldn't*—forsake his Oath to save my Fate? Because he didn't have a choice? The thought comforted me over the alternative: that he'd actively chosen his Oath over me, betraying me in the process.

The problem was: I couldn't tell which possibility was reality. This was damning in and of itself. Proof that the connection we'd forged had been built on an uneven foundation, destined to crumble. I couldn't trust him as I'd thought. As I'd *hoped*.

The Mirror of Death had been right, after all. Not in method, but in action. Idris *would* be the death of me—by trial rather than by drowning, but still. Rather than making excuses for him and giving him the benefit of the doubt, I should've listened to that voice in my head: the one that'd told me I was a fool for falling for him.

Because now...now I was here.

Would I ever see Waldron-on-Wend again? Would I ever see another sunrise over Stone Hill? Would I ever sink my fingers into Wicker's soft fur again? Hear Hattie's laugh again? Serve another customer in the Possum, or plan another festival, or celebrate another Astrophel? Was this truly my legacy—my Fate? To be carted off to the capital, never to return home?

I'd thought myself fully out of tears hours ago, yet new ones began to fall, searing my cheeks. A soft wail slipped through my lips, and I hugged my knees closer, bowing my head, holding myself in the loneliest embrace.

If I could pick up a weapon and fight my current reality—fight it to the death—I would. But I was unarmed.

Another while later, the low register of men's voices permeated the door at the top of the stairs. I lifted my head from my knees, a pitiful part of me hoping it was Idris coming to explain, to set me free.

The conversation grew louder as the door was unlocked, light spilling down the dusty steps and into the long hall of cells. I used my magic to pluck out the tonal differences of the voices, to identify the speakers. There were two I recognized from being deposited here: the dungeon guards.

And then there was Hammond.

"Thank you," I heard him say, his pitch hitting the walls of the dungeon such that I could picture him already turning from the guards, approaching the stairs.

I crawled over to the iron bars at the front of my cell in time to see him lift the lantern off its hook. Then he and the light were descending, warming me with their presence.

"Anya?" he called—too loudly.

A terrifying cacophony of shouts erupted up from the dungeon's depths. I was located on what seemed to be the first level, a holding cell not far from the base of the stairs; I was alone in this block. Past my cell and into the darkness, another, narrower set of stairs descended. It was from there that the grotesque sounds rose, like a cruel and tortured beast lurking. Their cries made me shiver.

"Anya?" Hammond repeated, quieter as he reached the landing.

"Over here," I rasped.

He blinked and lifted the lantern a little higher, its brightness making me squint. When he spotted me, he rushed over to my barred door, his forehead furrowed with a mix of horror and sympathy.

He lowered to his knees and extended a hand inside.

I took it, relishing the simple kindness of his touch.

"I came to make sure you were all right," Hammond said.

"How can I be all right?" I croaked. "Look where I am."

"I'm so sorry this is happening to you," Hammond said. "After you were taken away, Oderin and I tried to appeal, but..." He shook his head.

"What of Idris?" I asked, unable to help myself.

"We were asked to leave, but it sounded like he got a good dressing down from the Lord."

"That's all?"

Hammond frowned. "Knighthood is a serious business, Anya. There are tenets we can't challenge."

"He betrayed me."

"I don't know which Order he serves," Hammond said delicately, clearly circumventing his own limitations. "But if it's the one I'm guessing...then his betrayal isn't as straightforward as you might think."

"Best case scenario, I waste away in this dungeon until rats consume me," I said sharply. "Fates forbid I die by the hands of them." I pointed toward the second stairway, leading to the lower levels. "And you tell me his betrayal isn't *straightforward*? Complicated or not, it does not matter to me when my life is over."

"You do not yet know your sentence," Hammond said. "That's the other reason I'm here. I came to...well, I came to offer you some advice."

I huffed a dejected laugh. "Unless it gets me out of here, I don't see how—"

"That's just it," he insisted, gripping my hand tighter. "It might."

41

AN ALTERNATIVE FATE

ANYA

Hammond released my hand and stood to retrieve a stool from the base of the stairs. He placed it in front of my cell door and sat, his long legs spread wide. The lantern—which rested on the floor by his foot—glinted off his rose-gold vambraces, accentuated his ever-flushed cheeks. Without his hand to hold through the bars, I shifted positions so that I sat cross-legged, my skirts spread across my lap like a blanket.

Once we were resettled, Hammond rested his forearms on his knees and regarded me seriously. "How much do you know about the Mirrors of Fate?"

Unsure of how this was relevant, my face scrunched. "As much as anyone, I suppose. That they've been around for generations, are housed in Fenrir City, and tour the Kingdom annually to show people their Fortunes and Deaths."

"Do you know of how they came to be?" Hammond asked.

I shook my head. "Not much, other than that they were forged in the Well of Fate."

He clasped his hands and leaned closer. "The story starts seven hundred years ago, when a prince of Fenrir, Sharmond the Third, was engaged to marry the King of Marona's daughter as part of the alliance that brought Fenrir under Marona's rule. Back then, the fertile hills in the south had not yet been conquered, and Fenrir was mostly known for its ore. Prince Shar—rather a romantic, even by my standards—wanted to craft a wedding gift for his beloved bride: extravagant gilt frames, inside which their royal portraits would be displayed."

"All due respect to your charge, Hammond," I said, voice feeble, "but what does the history of the Mirrors have to do with my sentence?"

He held up a palm, bidding me to be patient. "At the time, Kelebraim-on-Gray was a small but well-respected city of craftsmen near one of the larger mines. The frames were forged of the purest Gildium, a rare metal found only in certain parts of the Bone Mountains. They were tooled in Kelebraim by the most skilled artisans in Fenrir and plated in gold and silver to represent the prince and his bride."

In spite of my impatience, I thought of the frames' sun and moon carvings, and how well the motifs matched the purpose of the Mirrors. Confused, I said, "But they're labeled with an *F* for Fortune and a *D* for Death."

Hammond smiled, seeming pleased by my observation. "Consider the traditional marriage vows of Fenrir."

I'd been to many a wedding in Waldron. Raging affairs spanning at least three days, with ten-course meals, endless music, and plenty of dancing. As much as I loved the party, I always found the ceremony—occurring on the second day of three—the most touching. "'Our marriage, forged in fortune, broken by death,'" I recited.

"Fortune and Death."

"Yet the frames were originally meant to contain portraits?"

Hammond nodded. "You see, the fine work of the artisans in Kelebraim took time, and they were not keen to be rushed. The royal gift wasn't finished until four nights before the wedding—and Kelebraim was a five-night journey to Fenrir City, where the ceremony was to be held.

"Prince Shar demanded the shipment be rushed, insisting the Royal Carriers travel a faster but more treacherous route out of Kelebraim, a northern pass that led through a maze of geothermal pools. Not only was the terrain full of hidden sinkholes and boiling geysers—it was rumored that the waters there were...peculiar."

"How so?"

"Magical. Cursed. Haunted," Hammond said. "Ancient accounts don't agree on which words to use, only that the pools were strange—granting odd powers and visions. Only one pool was unanimously foretold to bring new creation, but its location was disputed—and its blessing was not worth the risk of touching the waters of the wrong pool and ending up cursed. Most folktales from Kelebraim were warnings for children not to venture to the pools at all. Not even to look upon."

It reminded me of Waldron, where children's folklore warned against entering the western forest. People don't have to *understand* the dangers of a place to know it's dangerous.

"The Royal Carriers were not to stop, even at night," Hammond continued. "They were not inexperienced travelers, though. They entered the geothermal passage at the top of the second day, and made it through successfully by nightfall," he said. "But that second night, as they skirted the final pool—their path opening up to trees, forest, and a more easily traversable terrain, with the worst of the journey past them—a geyser at their backs erupted, spooking the horses. The wagon containing the royal cargo was jostled, and the frames fell into the pool.

"When the men fished the frames out of the water, their faces had turned silver and reflective."

"Mirrors," I whispered.

"The men saw strange visions inside the frames," Hammond said, "including one carrier who saw his death on that very journey. A day later, when he fell from his horse and hit his head on a stone, just as the Mirror of Death predicted, the men swiftly covered the Mirrors, fearful of what else might be foretold.

"When the frames reached Castle Might, Prince Shar was told of the incident and warned of the frames' strangeness. Curious about how the man's Fate had been predicted, Shar looked anyway, and saw his Fortune and Death: a great life laid out before him, ending in peace, surrounded by kin.

"He believed the Mirrors were a wedding gift from the Fates themselves and had them brought before the revelers on his wedding day. It was during the ceremony that he showed the citizens of Fenrir his Fortune and Death, and had his new wife do the same—her life mirroring his in its splendor. So inspired they were by their visions, and the apparent accuracy of the Mirrors, they enacted a decree for all citizens to have the opportunity to look upon their Fates. And so, the traveling of the Mirrors was begun."

Hammond sat back, seemingly satisfied with the tale. Without his voice filling the dank hall, I was reminded of where I was: on the ground, in a cell, facing a Fate filled with grimness and uncertainty.

"That's a nice story, Hammond, but again, I ask: what does this have to do with my imprisonment?"

He glanced up at the stairs, then dropped his voice to the faintest whisper. "The pool."

"The...pool," I stated. "The one the Mirrors fell into?"

His nod was solemn. "Known to you—and most—as the Well of Fate. It's said to have the power to change one's Fate if it so chooses. For hundreds of years, royals traveled there to plead with the Fates to have their outcomes altered."

"Why have I never heard of this practice?"

"The custom was known only to royals and Mirror Knights during that time, then eventually fell out of fashion and was lost to legend."

Not lost to Mirror Knights, though. I wondered why Hammond's Order was no longer bound to keep that secret. Perhaps because the practice was just that—a *legend*. A false story borne out of the real history.

"Even if I could ask this magical pool to change my Fate," I said dubiously, "you forget that it was *Remy's* vision—not mine—that got me into this mess."

Hammond appeared proud of his suggestion, energized by it. "I admit the idea is unorthodox, but what other hope do you have? Perhaps the Lord would allow you to visit the pool under guard and prove your innocence?"

As he spoke, the lantern caught his excitable gestures and cast odd shapes on the walls, making his shadow-arms appear overly long and spider-like—not dissimilar to the appendages of the monsters.

The recollection of them made me shiver. What I should have told the Lord was that I wished never to think or speak of the wretched creatures again.

I regarded Hammond, truly considering his idea and concluding it was too good to be true. "This can't be real, Hammond," I said with a shake of my head. "If it were, surely your Oath wouldn't allow you to tell me all this. Today's royals would be just as eager to alter their Fate as their forebears—and keep the Well of Fate's gifts a secret." I paused. "Unless...there's a reason it fell out of fashion? A reason no one ventures there now?"

Hammond's excitement fissured, then, his forehead split by a troubled crease. "Historical accounts are varied, but most cite a royal who became obsessed with her outcomes, visiting the pool over and over until she went mad. That...dissuaded others." His face pinched further. "And...well, Anya, that which you cannot know or speak about—the secret that has brought you here—is said to spawn in the surrounding geothermal pools."

A tired, hopeless laugh rushed out of me. "I see."

So, Hammond *did* know about the monsters. I wondered if that was a privilege of his Oath or a leak among the ranks of another Order. Either way, he clearly didn't understand the full extent of the danger he was suggesting I face.

"Look, Anya," Hammond said. "The Lord will have a final audience with you tomorrow to dole out your sentence. No matter what, your Fate is...uncertain."

"You mean that no matter what, I'll die," I said bitterly.

Hammond visibly swallowed. "Of all the possibilities, the Well of Fate could be your best shot."

"It sounds like a death wish," I countered.

"Giving up is also a death wish," Hammond replied, standing. He returned the stool to its place by the landing, then reached through the bars to grasp my hands again.

At the feeling of his skin—his palms so smooth, compared to Idris's callouses—I broke down into tears once more.

"It's just an idea," he said, releasing my hands. "An alternative to consider." He took up the lantern and shuffled back upstairs, leaving me to ponder my miserable future.

42

ALL PATHS LEAD TO DEATH

ANYA

I dipped in and out of sleep. The stone floor was cold and unyielding—but it was my dreams that haunted me. Filled with visions of Mirrors and flowing water and yawning dungeon caverns with sharp monster teeth ready to swallow me up.

I startled awake at the arrival of another visitor. This time when the door to the dungeon opened, only the faintest light permeated from the hall outside, suggesting that it was after nightfall. Judging by how my body ached from hours curled on the floor, it was probably close to midnight, if not edging into the following morning.

There was only one person who'd come to see me at such an hour.

I didn't get up when he came into view. I remained on my side, staring blankly at the bars of my cell, the grit on the floor illuminated by the light of his lantern. Boots paused at my door, and then he lowered into a crouch, blue-green eyes finding mine. They were red-ringed with sleeplessness, or perhaps a worse sort of torment. He had a bruise on his cheekbone and a split eyebrow that was barely scabbed, and in spite of my anger and hurt, I wanted to know how he got it. I wanted to strike the bastard who'd done it, because—

Fates help me.

—because I loved Idris.

What other emotion could possibly explain the magnetic pull of him, even now? Even after what had happened? My shock, panic, and fury had been dulled by the night, and now all I wanted was to tuck myself into his strong arms. To believe there was an explanation for why yesterday had gone the way it did.

Why he couldn't save me.

His betrayal isn't as straightforward as you might think, Hammond had said.

I *had* to believe that my trust wasn't in vain. That the care and affection he'd shown me—on the road and across campfires and as I lay naked in his arms—was still *real*. What emotion, other than love, could make me so desperate to uncover a satisfactory reason for his duplicity?

It was genuine exhaustion—and perhaps a touch of stubbornness—that kept me on the ground as he regarded me. I might've loved him, but he'd still hurt me.

"Anya." His voice was as rough as the stubble on his face, raw as the cut on his brow. "Talk to me, please."

"Unless you have the keys to release me, what is there to say?" I mumbled, allowing my hurt to show.

Idris swallowed thickly, a sound I felt in my own throat. Loose stones ground under his boots as he lowered himself to the floor, sitting parallel to my door with his long legs outstretched, one arm reaching through the bars.

"Come here," he begged, holding out his hand. "Please, Dearest." His voice cracked on that last word.

It was the term of endearment—never uttered before, so unexpected in this dark place—that had me moving. I pushed up off the floor and crawled over to him, sliding my arms through the iron between us to nestle into his embrace. His arms were gentle as they pulled me against the bars; his mouth was hot on my temple, my tear-torn cheeks, my trembling lips. The metal was a cold press against my face as we kissed through the door—the perfect embodiment of the distance I felt from him even now, my heart barred off and wary.

He ran a thumb across my cheek, the callouses of his palm rough on the sensitive skin. His hands were so *big*, and I leaned into the cradle of his touch, both burning and soothed. Ashen and sparking.

Then the moment of tenderness passed, and I pulled out of his grasp to sit on the ground beside him. I tried to rest my head on his shoulder, but the bars of my cell were too narrow, forbidding me from the comfort. But Idris snaked his arm through, resting a palm on my thigh, clutching at the heavy fabric of my dress.

Dearest.

I grazed a finger just below the bruise on his cheekbone. "Who did this to you?"

"It's nothing."

Having seen him face monsters, his statement about the minor injury was objectively true. But I wanted to know who'd managed to injure a knight who, to my eye, was all but untouchable in his fighting skill.

"Idris," I prompted.

"I was disobedient," he said—not embarrassed, pitiful, or angry—just stating fact.

So, he'd *let* them do this.

"Disobedient *how?*"

He quirked a brow.

My laugh was devoid of mirth. Maybe he truly *had* been powerless during my trial.

"Your verdict is tomorrow," he stated.

"Do you know what my options will be?"

He glanced sidelong at me. The speckled purple on his cheek looked like a spray of twilight, a sprig of lavender. "If he offers you an Oath, you should take it."

The plainness of his words surprised me—then made my gut clench. "And end up like you?"

He winced. "Is that not better than being down here? Never seeing sunlight again?"

I moved away from him, out from under his palm on my leg. His hand fell to the stone as I stood. "That's your plan? For me to give up—give in? Is there truly nothing you can do to help me?"

He rose slowly. "My leash is short, Anya."

"A couple nights ago, you said I would return to Waldron-on-Wend—when all the while, you *knew*." My voice shook. "You *knew* you were marching me to my end, didn't you?"

A sigh gusted out of him, and he rubbed a hand over his face—flinching when it passed over the barely scabbed cut. He began to pace, agitated as a pent-up animal.

His lack of response was answer enough. My anger flared, branding me with decision. "More than *anything*, I want to go home," I told him. "I will settle for nothing less. Hammond told me of an alternative, the Well of Fate—"

He wheeled toward me, gripping the bars. "You mustn't."

"Why not?"

He growled frustratedly.

This time, my laugh was ice. "If you can't tell me—"

"Anya," he pleaded, "it's certain death. Trust me."

He appeared genuinely terrified by the idea, wild-eyed and gravely serious.

But my anger was a gale, gusting over me with a reckless force. "How can I possibly trust you?" I shrieked.

Shouts sang from the depths of the dungeon, answering my outburst with horrible whines, howls, cries.

Idris jerked his attention toward the stairs leading down, and I saw the moment he pictured me there, another wave of fear quaking across his strong features.

I pointed in the direction of the wails. "I would rather face a thousand monsters than live out the rest of my days down there."

"Then take—" He broke off abruptly, licking his lips like he tasted something vile.

An Oath, he'd no-doubt been about to say.

But that was its own prison—clearly.

I sank to my knees, resettling into the potential for a real conversation. "Can we be honest with each other, Idris?"

He slid his palms down the iron bars until he, too, knelt. His voice was feather-soft as he repeated the sentiment from the cabin. "Ask me anything you like, and if I'm able, I'll answer."

So, we would play our old game, then.

I started boldly. "There was a book on Oderin's desk," I began, "detailing the nature of Orders, both widely known and secret."

Idris raked his fingers through his hair. "*Fuck*, Anya."

"You said you took Grinnick's place. Was his a criminal sentence? Is *yours*?"

I knew he couldn't answer that, but the way he paled in the light of the lantern told me everything I needed to know.

I pressed my lips together and nodded. "I read of quite a few criminal Oaths while I waited," I went on. "Order of the Shrewd. The Order of the Fierce. The Order of the Valiant."

He flinched when I named the last one.

I smiled joylessly. "You are quite valiant, Idris."

He shook his head in—was it disagreement? I had the sense that it wasn't a contradiction to which Order he served, but the word itself. Why did he think so little of himself? What experiences had beaten down this incredibly kind, brave man so thoroughly?

"What was your crime?"

"Loving my brother," he answered gruffly.

"So, he died, and you took his place *willingly*," I concluded. "What was *his* crime?"

"Loving me."

I felt his words like a punch in the gut. It didn't take much of a leap to understand what'd happened. Two boys, alone on the streets. Idris had stolen bread and fallen for the baker's girl. What had Grinnick stolen, and how had he been caught? As the older brother, I didn't doubt that his crimes were larger than baked goods. I thought of Hattie, not my younger sister by blood, but by bond. Like Grinnick, I would do any number of illegal things to keep her safe.

"If yours is a sentence, when does it end?" I asked.

Idris's eyes darted away from mine, to a random corner in the hallway. He made a fist, bit his knuckle.

"Your sentence is...already over?" I guessed.

When his eyes found mine again, he nodded, his brows tipped up with regret.

"Your Oath is *over*?"

"No," he said.

My voice became shrill. "But you are no longer *required* to keep it, to—"

"I saw you," he blurted, sounding miserable. "In my Mirror of Fortune. I saw you."

I stiffened, aghast.

He ran his hand over his face again, this time reopening the wound above his eye. It began to bead and weep, the crimson sparkling wet in the lantern light, but he seemed oblivious as he continued. "What you saw in your Mirror of Death," he said slowly, his lower lip wavering on his words, "*I* saw in my Mirror of Fortune."

"Your Fortune is my Death?" I asked, disbelieving.

"I didn't see a face in my vision," he said, eyes holding mine. "Only water, and a filthy dress, and my hands—" He broke off, staring down at his hands as if he couldn't believe what they were capable of.

"But the monsters warp your Fate," I said—then realized what that meant. "If you give up your Oath, your Fate is no longer warped."

Which meant his Fortune could come true. I could see his logic, but...*my* Fate wasn't yet fixed. That had to count for something.

"I don't believe it," I said, shaking my head.

"Do you really want to risk—"

"Not that," I interrupted. "I can't say I'm completely surprised that our Fates are more entwined than I originally knew. What I can't believe is why you didn't fucking *tell me* when you realized—" Now it was my turn to wipe my hand over my face, to gather myself. My gaze found his and held, unflinching. "What I can't believe is that you *could've* given up your Oath to help me, and you chose not to."

"I can't retire my Oath if it means killing you."

"You're already killing me."

His face quaked. It took him a few seconds to recover. "Even if I had broken my Oath during your trial and lied to the Lord about what you saw, he would've known the moment my leash snapped," Idris said. "And to break it dishonorably—without ceremony—could risk the Lord restarting—" He broke off again, clearly running up against his magical limitations, but I knew what he meant. "It wouldn't have boded well, either way," he finished lamely.

"And you didn't think to retire the Oath after we—" My voice faltered. "You knew that you wouldn't be able to lie to the Lord about what I saw. You *knew* that the Lord would take issue with it. You must've seen this coming, no? And you chose your Oath—a life of loneliness and danger—over me."

"The Mirror..."

"No," I said. "No, I don't buy that. You could've left years ago, before you met me. Which means this is about your brother. About your Fates-damned guilt over whatever happened to him."

He seemed struck, taken aback.

I shuffled forward on my knees and gripped the bars of my cell, needing to be closer to him to ensure my next words were heard. "I didn't know your brother," I said, "but as someone who's looked after countless people I loved, I can say with certainty that—no matter what happened between you—he wouldn't have wished you further suffering. It sounds to me like he did all he did to *save* you from suffering. By embracing the very thing he'd tried so hard to shield you from, you disrespect his efforts. That's not an act of valiance or love, Idris, but self-punishment. If you truly wish to honor Grinnick, why shackle yourself to his memory? Why not *live* the life he wished for you? Live the life that was taken from him?"

His eyes glistened. His next words were firm, but breathless. "Everyone I've ever loved has either left or died because of me." He hung his head, the dark waves of his hair falling forward, obscuring his face. "You are better off without me."

"Wait." The word was weak, watery. I couldn't keep the heartbreak out of my voice as I clarified, "You...don't wish to give up your Oath? Not *ever*?"

"The Mirrors."

"Fuck the Mirrors," I said. "You wouldn't even consider it?"

He lifted his gaze to mine, but barely.

"Was it all a lie?" I whispered.

"Anya..."

"Be honest with me."

"It's for the best that we part ways. That you—" His jaw ticked. "That you never see me again."

My hands slipped from the bars, and I rose to my feet, needing distance. "Now that I'm in a cell, you're *leaving*?"

He claimed this was for my benefit but—maybe I was the exact sort of burden to him that I feared. What else could it be? His leaving now—when I needed him most—was proof that I wasn't worth the effort. I was only worth what I could offer. And I couldn't offer anything from a cell.

"You really aren't going to help me?" I went on. "After your actions contributed to this *mess* I'm in?" I bit my lips together with my teeth, eyes lifting to the ceiling. "It's not your Oath standing in the way of us—of my entire future—it's *you*, Idris."

"I am nothing more than a danger to you," Idris argued.

"You are so much more than a danger to me." The words came unbidden, laced with tender implication. "So much more," I whispered.

His gaze darted away from mine, a rejection in and of itself.

My nails bit into my palms. "I thought you were a man who kept his promises."

"I am," he said, narrowing his eyes on me again with unmovable resolve. "I promised you I would not do you harm, and I am determined to keep that promise by staying far, far away."

My heart was splitting open, molten rage exposed. *And what about the harm of breaking my heart?* I wanted to ask, but my mouth wouldn't form the words. My shame was too potent. He was leaving. He didn't want me. Or, at least, he didn't want me enough to stay—to *try*. For the second time, I was being left by a man on the other side of iron bars.

"You're better off taking an Oath," he said levelly, "serving your time, and—"

"*Better off?*" My fists balled tighter, tears streaking down my face. "I will not."

My anger was fueled by heartache, but I *refused* to feel heartbroken now. Not when anger lent me strength. Not when heartbreak was the least of my concerns.

"Anya—"

"Fuck you."

"*Please*, Dearest—"

"Don't call me that."

"*Anya*," he pleaded, his voice cracking. "You can't go to the Well of Fate. It's a breeding ground for—for—for—"

He was bumping up against his Oath. It was easy to deduce what he meant. But I was done trusting Idris Togren.

"If you won't help me," I said, "then I have to help myself."

"You'll *die*," he insisted.

"And yet you insist I die alone."

He glanced away.

"All paths lead to death," I went on. "So, I might as well take Fate into my own hands and die on my own terms."

Idris opened his mouth, but I held up my hand, halting whatever he was about to say. Anger was my buoy.

"It's funny," I mused, "how this feels so much like a betrayal, and yet you haven't broken a single promise. I have to hand it to you, Idris, you are clever."

"I can't give you what you want," he said tightly.

"You're right," I said bitterly, goading him. "We didn't make any commitments to one another. *Just for the night*, right?" I spread my arms. "You are absolved from all post-fuck guilt. You don't owe me a Fates-damned thing."

He looked miserable, stricken. *Good.*

"Anya, what we shared—"

"It doesn't matter what we shared. You're leaving." I pointed at the stairs. "If you wish to break my heart and go," I said, "then fucking *go.*"

He stared at me, a mix of tender yearning and harsh determination on his face. A part of me dared to hope—even now—that he was about to change his mind.

Flashing in his blue-green eyes, I saw the future I had imagined for us, one surrounded by verdant hills fed by the waters of the Wend. Late nights curled up by the hearth at the Pretty Possum. Introducing him to the town and watching them fall in love with him as I had. I imagined a future in which he didn't drown me in the river. In which I didn't die in a nest of monsters as I sought absolution. In which I didn't rot in a cell.

As I stared into his eyes, I imagined a future filled with promise and love and *hope*.

Then he tore his eyes from mine and sulked back up the stairs, leaving me and that future behind.

43

SAVE YOURSELF

IDRIS

Fog slid down the face of the mountain toward the courtyard, a slow-motion avalanche of air. The rising sun cut a path through the cloud cover, beaming down on the face of Castle Might's keep. Glorious, godly, the light seemed oblivious to the cruelty that ruled within the stone walls.

Idris had not been permitted inside Anya's second hearing. After she was dragged away the previous afternoon, he'd appealed—*shouted*—at the Lord to set her free. He'd gotten on his knees to beg, only for the Lord to pick up one of the ledgers and hit Idris square in the face with it. Just a master kicking his dog. Idris hadn't spoken after that—by the Lord's word, the magic of Idris's Oath had rendered him completely silent for six hours afterward.

Those six hours had granted him perspective. He'd foolishly let himself believe that his role as a knight would mean something to the Lord, but all he'd really done was set Anya's trap. Idris had allowed the Lord to use his Oath—his inability to lie—to corner her and condemn her, and he hadn't even seen it coming.

It had been selfish of him to get close to Anya.

The moment he could speak, he'd gone to her to tell her what he should've told her to begin with—that she was better off without him. Even now.

Everyone I've ever loved has either left or died because of me.

Perhaps that wasn't directly true of his father, who'd died in a garrison accident after taking an extra shift for extra money for his family—but Idris's mother? She'd left because, without her husband, her boys were a burden. Idris being the younger, he had no doubt been her push. And, of course, Grinnick was all his fault. And now, Anya: no matter which path Idris chose, he would endanger her. The only thing he *could* do was leave.

So, sure, maybe he remained Oath-bound after his sentence in self-punishment, but he also did it to escape his Fate—not just what he'd seen in his Mirrors, but the wretched pattern of his existence. Love, endanger, lose.

It was his love for her that convinced him to let her go. To stay far away, lest he ruin things further. The irony was not lost on Idris that after years of avoiding love and loss through the duty of his Order, the only thing to ever make him *want* to retire—Anya—was the one reason he couldn't.

Now, as he paced the courtyard, all he could do was hope that she'd come to the same conclusion that he had. She had been too furious with him last night to see it, but with time, she would come to understand that his leaving was the only possible mercy.

At the sound of double doors clunking open, Idris turned, and saw Oderin swiftly exiting the keep. He was flanked by two Royal Guards, who—after a quick word from Oderin—broke off. Oderin sped straight for Idris, his tan face flushed.

Idris fell in step with the other knight without pause, and together they crossed the yard toward the barracks.

"She goes to the Well of Fate," Oderin said.

Idris swore, even as his stomach seemed to bottom-out with dread. The pool was located in the foothills of the Bone Mountains. It was a literal breeding ground for monsters—and not the small, secondary spawn Anya had seen previously. He'd tried and failed to communicate the danger to her last night.

All abominations came from the bite of a Morta, parent-monsters that spread their scourge by infecting animals. Knights of the Order of Valiant did not hunt Morta alone. They were grotesque creatures—huge, skinless, made of twisted sinew and bone, with poison in their veins and venom in their teeth. The geothermal pools outside the ruins of Kelebraim are where the Morta multiplied, and there were not enough Valiant Knights in all of Fenrir to infiltrate their nest.

For Anya to venture there by herself—it was unacceptable.

"The Lord truly agreed to it?" Idris asked Oderin. "What were her other options?"

"Dungeon."

"No Oath?"

Oderin arched a brow and pursed his lips. "I suspect the Lord withheld that option after the scene you caused yesterday."

Just when it seemed impossible for Idris to hate himself any more, he found himself in deeper loathing. "Fuck."

They'd reached the side door to the barracks, and Oderin held it open for Idris, patting his back consolingly. "She asked to travel to the pool, and the Lord agreed."

"He agreed because he knows she won't return," Idris said, his disdain echoing off the walls of the narrow hallway.

"You know how he delights in…unique alternatives," Oderin said. "And in the unlikely event that she *does* return, well, that's valuable information for the Lord, too."

So, the Lord wanted to know if a path to the Well of Fate still existed and was willing to gamble Anya's absolution—her *knowing too much*—to prove the theory. Idris shook his head, sick to his stomach over the Lord using Anya in this way. Nobility might've traveled to the Well of Fate hundreds of years ago, but there was a reason the practice had ended: at a certain point, those who sought the pool stopped returning.

"Why you serve him willingly, I'll never understand," Idris said.

Oderin unlocked the door to his quarters and closed the two of them inside. "I serve the great territory of Fenrir and the Kingdom of Marona," Oderin said with intensity, "*not* the disposable headpiece who calls himself Lord. There's a reason Oaths are controlled by whomever holds the *title*, and not the individual ruler."

"So long as Haron holds the title, though, he also holds your leash. Do you not feel complicit in his cruelty?" Idris asked.

"Do you?"

"I'm different."

"We can both walk away anytime we want." Oderin dug a large rucksack out of his armoire and began shoving clothes into it. "We all have our reasons for remaining. I can do more good for the realm working from the inside."

Idris pressed his fingers against the bruise on his cheek, just to check its tenderness. "What could I have done differently?" he asked his friend.

"You could've *not* fallen in love with her."

Idris stiffened.

Oderin shot him a quick glance over his shoulder. "Don't look surprised that I noticed. Your feelings are all over your face."

Idris tried to smooth his features into the bored neutrality expected of knights, but Anya had stripped him all pretense weeks ago. He was afraid for her. Terrified for her. It was impossible to pretend otherwise.

"You really told her about the warped Fate of the Valiant?"

Idris was glad Oderin had his back turned; he felt exposed enough by the question. "She saw me in her Mirror of Death," he ground out. "I didn't want her to fear me."

Oderin's glanced back again, this time with wide-eyed shock. It took a lot to surprise the Mighty Knight, and apparently Idris had succeeded. "Fuck, Idris," he said. "You know I'm no stranger to dubious conquests, but even *I* know that was a bad idea."

"She's not a conquest," Idris said flatly.

Oderin stuck his head inside the armoire again, rummaging around for something—a mess kit—only to shove it into his bag. "At least her Fate isn't yet fixed, by age or by proximity to your charge."

"Not yet." Idris leaned against Oderin's small writing desk, the wood groaning under his weight. In many ways, he himself felt like the desk—too brittle for what he bore. "I should've retired my Oath long ago."

"*Should* is nothing more than mental torment." Oderin fastened a strap on his bag with a quick jerk.

Finally taking note of his friend's quick actions, Idris asked, "What are you doing?"

Oderin turned, rising to his full height. His hair was tousled from having his head in the closet, giving the regal Knight of the Order of the Mighty a boyish air. Idris knew from countless nights drinking with Oderin that his friend often used that boyish charm to lure unsuspecting men into his bed. He was quite successful at it—and proud of it. Oderin was the most stereotypical wielder of touch magic Idris had ever met—completely insatiable.

Oderin raked a hand through his hair, then folded his arms, assuming a more authoritative posture. "I ought not say what I'm doing."

"And why's that?" Idris asked, letting the implication of the question—Oath or general secrecy?—remain unspoken.

"The Lord didn't trust Anya to walk the path to the pool alone."

"You were...assigned to escort her?" Idris asked.

Oderin shook his head.

"You *volunteered*." Idris would've felt heartened by his friend's gesture, if it weren't for how wretched he felt over the prospect of Anya going there at all.

"The least I could do for an old friend," Oderin said, clapping a hand on Idris's good shoulder. "Besides, I still owe you for helping me get my promotion. I get laid twice as often as a Major."

Idris had happened to be in the city for an intelligence briefing the same week Oderin was to take his Major's exam, and Idris had spent three sleepless nights helping him study. It was not a true debt between friends, but he appreciated Oderin's attempt to ease the tension of the current moment.

Idris smiled, but it didn't last. "It's a dangerous path," he warned. "Shouldn't a Knight of the Order of the Valiant accompany you?"

"The Lord wouldn't allow it."

"But he would risk a Major Knight of the Mighty?"

"I am to escort her only to a point, then she must go alone," Oderin said. "If she returns, she will have a chance to view her Mirrors before the Lord; if they are changed, she will be absolved. If she does not return—well, her sentence will be complete in a different way. He made her take an Oath of Proving to ensure she completes her mission with no assistance."

Idris covered his lips with his fingers and shook his head. Oaths of Proving were woven of lesser magic, not nearly as complex as Order Oaths, which possessed enough power for the Lord and his ledgermasters to directly control behavior, such as lying. An Oath of Proving was tied to a single matter; complete a mission, and it dissolved.

"The Lord only agreed to this plan because he trusts the honor of the Mighty," Oderin said. "The Valiant have not given him much reason to trust them as of late."

Idris lowered his hand. "She won't make it, Oderin. No one in recent history has sought the Well of Fate and lived." He wanted to murder Hammond for putting such a useless hope in Anya's head. He wanted to murder the Lord for letting her go on this fool's mission. He wanted...he wanted to protect Anya, and he couldn't.

His friend turned away to continue packing. "She won't make it in the dungeon, either, Idris. At least this way, she has a shot."

"Not without a magic weapon," Idris said, voice rising. "Not surrounded by Morta alone, defenseless—"

"Get her bag ready, would you?" Oderin said, clearly not interested in further debate about that which they couldn't control.

What would Grinnick do? Idris wondered. Grinnick had always been the more gallant of the two of them. "What if I—"

"Even a *hint* of interference," Oderin interrupted, "and her Oath of Proving will consider her bid null. The best thing you can do is stay out of it, Idris."

To hear Oderin confirm it—Idris wasn't comforted. He was powerless, *useless*, to assist the woman he loved. Idris growled with frustration, even as his chest ached.

"Her *bag*," Oderin repeated.

Anya's things still rested where she'd left them at the base of the window. With nothing left to say, Idris pushed off Oderin's desk to do as he was asked. The wood squeaked, briefly drawing his attention. His eyes landed on a small but thick book nestled amongst the mess of papers. *Orders.*

Idris had been shocked to hear Anya guess his Order last night. Hearing her say it aloud had been an unexpected and dreadful thrill, like a child losing a game of hide-and-seek. Finally *found*.

While Oderin's back was still turned, Idris lifted the book from the desk and slipped it into her pack. If he couldn't explain to her the tenets he followed, perhaps the book would elucidate his limitations. Provide the answers he himself could not.

He was securing the top of her pack when Oderin pivoted. Idris handed Anya's things to his friend, feeling like he was passing off a piece of himself.

"Do you wish to communicate anything to her?" Oderin asked.

Idris shook his head. "I broke things off with her last night. She's better off if I stay away." He winced at the echo of Anya's shrill, angry voice in his head: *Better off?*

Oderin only nodded. "Good. I'd hate for you to follow us. You know I'd be forced by my Oath to fight you off."

Idris snorted. "Not to worry. I know how you hate to lose."

Oderin rolled his eyes, then gripped Idris's shoulder and shook it a little. "You're doing the right thing."

Idris pressed his lips together, then nodded. "When do you ride out?"

"An hour," Oderin said, slinging Anya's meager supplies over his shoulder. "It'll take us three days to reach the path, and Anya another day to find the pool on her own. If she is successful, I am to escort her back to Fenrir City for an audience with the Lord to verify her new Fate. Stay in the city. You'll know within eight days whether or not she succeeds."

44

FIGHT

IDRIS

Hunched over the bar counter of Fenrir's Ire—a tavern popular among knights, located just outside the castle walls—Idris finished off his third ale. Twilight had come and gone, the sky turning purple as the bruise on his cheek, then black as the dread in his heart. With every breath, he thought of Anya. Alone. Hunted by monsters, only to perish on the cusp of freedom.

If you wish to break my heart and go, then go.

Her heart—broken, because of him. He should've never let it get that far. It didn't matter that his heart was breaking, too. He would break his heart a thousand times to protect her. But breaking *hers* to keep her safe? He did not regret his decision, but seeing the pain in her eyes, hearing the desperation in her voice, knowing how they'd left things and where she was headed now...not an entire barrel of ale could drown the wretchedness he felt.

Idris waved at the barkeep, signaling for another. Lord Haron had ordered none to meddle in her quest to the pool. If Idris interfered, things would only get worse for her. *Eight days*, Oderin had said. Idris could drink a lot of ale in eight days. Perhaps if he stayed drunk, the waiting—the *agonizing*—would be easier.

With a fresh pint in front of him, Idris took a long pull, downing half in one go. He set the glass mug down with a clatter. Fizz rose in the amber liquid like sparks. It was almost the color of her eyes, and backlit by the sconces behind the bar, the drink glowed almost as fiercely. Almost.

Idris swept his thumb across the condensation of the glass. The more he drank, the harder it was to get Anya's words out of his head. They echoed as if she herself had magicked them there. Words about Mirrors. About their future. About Grinnick.

He wouldn't have wished you further suffering. That was true. It was *Idris* who wished Idris further suffering. He deserved it, for what he'd done to his brother.

What had he done to deserve his father's death, though? His mother leaving? The scorn of the baker's daughter? The poverty and death that followed? It seemed that just by existing, by wanting love and connection, Idris had been a burden.

After so much abandonment and loss, the fight had left him, and Idris had given in to his grim reality. At least the Oath made him *useful*. Avoided his dangerous Fate. What a cruel irony that his proximity to monsters was what kept him from becoming one, himself.

She's better off without you, Idris told himself.

He downed the rest of his fourth ale and clutched the empty mug, tempted to order a fifth. His head was beginning to spin, but the buzz hadn't lifted his misery the way he'd wanted when he sat down—it'd only dragged him lower.

With a sigh, Idris fished a few coins out of his pocket and left them on the counter. Out in the cool night, an endless spray of stars above, Idris made his way down a side street. The frigid air sobered him, reminding him of the woods. He craved the fresh scent of trees and decay: the green sharpness of pine needles, the earthy sweetness of rotting leaves. He craved—*fucking Fates*—he craved *Anya*. Lemon and rose and the indescribable scent of her skin, that sweet-smelling nook between her neck and shoulder.

Idris glanced back, half tempted to return to the Ire and drown that craving in another drink. But at the other end of the alley was a figure striding purposefully toward him. They wore a breastplate that shimmered in the starlight and the hood of their cloak shielded their eyes.

Idris squared himself to the figure, sensing immediately that he was in danger. Even so, he was still surprised when he saw the blade flash. Slowed by bemusement and ale, Idris didn't have a chance to draw his own weapon.

He ducked, feeling the wind of the figure's sword by his cheek as he evaded the blow. He kicked out, his boot colliding with the attacker's leg to knock them off balance. The hood of their cloak slipped, revealing long hair and dark eyes.

The woman recovered quickly—but so did Idris. When she swung at him again, he met her sword with Halgren. Their blades clashed with a wretched *clank* that echoed down the alley. Pigeons roosting along the rooftops took flight, wings thwacking as they scattered into the night.

Idris had plenty of experience fighting monsters, but it'd been a long time since he'd fought another knight. He'd left his breastplate at the barracks and—drunk as he was—he felt sorely disadvantaged. But where his opponent was faster and mentally sharper, he was bigger and more muscled. He used his weight and strength to slide Halgren sideways, shoving the woman's weapon away. His shoulder injury protested with the sudden force, but like most things that pained him, he ignored it.

His attacker let out a grunt as she rushed him again, thrusting her sword out. He parried the blow, shuffling sideways on unsteady feet. He was just about to take his own strike at her when a blunt but awful pain shot through the back of his knee. He buckled—hard—as another knight joined the fray.

Idris landed on his hands and knees, palms bloodied, head spinning with the surprising throbbing in his leg. On the ground, the scents of the alley reached his nostrils. The mineral dust of stone. The sweet reek of vomit. Idris blinked, gathering himself.

"This is a gift from Heris," the newcomer growled, and kicked Idris in the side.

Something cracked—a rib. Idris reached for Halgren's hilt on the ground, swinging wildly. He managed to slice the newcomer—a short, stocky man that Idris didn't recognize—in the thigh. He wailed and toppled as Idris scrambled to his feet.

Idris found himself surprisingly steady. His leg would be bruised, but the discomfort was fading. The sting in his ribs, on the other hand, made him wheeze—but it also sobered him more than the cold ever could.

Idris turned toward the woman, who was braced in a fighting stance, sword outstretched. Gritting his teeth against the inevitable agony, Idris swung at her with a guttural groan, pain screaming through his torso. She only barely blocked his blow, eyes wide. She must've thought this would be easier.

Idris lunged at her again, slashing and stabbing in a fruitless onslaught until finally the woman stumbled on an uneven cobblestone and went down. Idris leveled Halgren's tip against her throat and glanced over his shoulder. The other man was still on the ground, clutching his thigh, blood gushing between his fingers.

Idris faced the woman again, recognition forming. The years had made the catlike bones in her face stand out in stark relief, her features no longer girlish but harsh. She had a new scar across her upper lip that added to her vicious appearance, a pale streak across tawny skin. Her brown eyes, on the other hand, were just as dark and deceptively doe-like as they'd been the day Grinnick died.

"Can't say I'm glad to see you, Mariana," Idris said, staring down the long length of Halgren's blade at her face.

Her eyes narrowed. A lock of black hair had fallen across her face, a dark slash bisecting her features. "Heris sends his regards."

"So, I've heard," Idris replied, tipping his head in the direction of her felled partner.

Idris had first learned Mariana's name from Grinnick. She was a deadly thief-turned-Valiant-Knight who'd worked her way up in Heris's ranks, and back then, the affection for which Grinnick spoke of her had worried Idris. Mariana had been yet another stone on the scale that had tipped Idris into following his brother into the Bone Mountains. She and Idris had crossed paths a few times since then. He had no real reason to hate her other than her association with Heris, but that was plenty.

"Tell me why I shouldn't run you through," Idris said with cool calm, pressing Halgren's tip against her throat enough to see the skin dip.

"Because you're a good person," Mariana taunted. There was a hardness in her gaze that even Idris did not possess.

"Where is he?" Idris demanded.

A rustling sound on the ground behind him drew his attention. Mariana's partner was blood-slicked and crawling toward his weapon, which rested at Idris's feet.

He kicked the blade away and refocused on Mariana, pressing Halgren against her neck with more force. A spot of blood beaded and slid down her throat and under the collar of her shirt. She lifted her palms in surrender, panting through her teeth.

"Where. Is. He?" Idris repeated.

"On the road." Her grin was wicked.

He knew immediately what she meant. Heris was going after Anya.

"Why?" Idris ground out.

"She knows too much."

The caravan attack. Brine. Those were hardly secrets held only by Anya. "So do others. So do many. Why *her*?"

Mariana bared her teeth.

Idris increased the pressure on her neck, twisting Halgren slightly to open her wound wider, draw more blood.

Mariana spoke through quick shallow breaths. "Most know—only one slice—of the greater scheme. She knows"—Mariana hissed in pain—"more than any other civilian. She threatens—the uprising."

"What uprising?"

"Run me through, Idris," Mariana said. "I'll say no more."

Idris lifted his sword from Mariana's skin and sheathed it. "Don't follow me."

She didn't bother wiping the blood from her neck. "I don't take orders from you."

"Don't do it for me. Do it for Grinnick."

For the briefest of moments, her face softened, the girlishness she'd once possessed sweeping over her features.

Mariana's expression loosened something in Idris. She missed Grinnick, he realized. And yet she still worked for Heris. She had been there that day. She'd seen it. Yet she'd run off with the rest of the party, into the woods, far away from the mess they'd made. She served Grinnick's killer to this day.

Her actions made Idris want to despise her, to kill her, but that flash of innocence, of true grief, gave him pause. It pleased him to know that he was not the only one who missed his brother. Not the only one who thought of Grinnick—even if only from time to time. Grinnick's memory bound him to Mariana in some twisted way. But he'd be damned if he made the same mistake she had.

Idris would not choose his Oath over love. Even if he was Fated to lose Anya, he wouldn't lose her without a fight.

Clutching his aching side, he stepped over Mariana's partner and strode down the alley, back toward Castle Might. He knew she would not follow.

Idris breathed shallowly as he returned to the barracks, doing his best to ignore the ebb and flow of pain in his ribs as he moved. He donned his breastplate and gathered his things, then crossed the moonlit yard to the royal stables. He walked the long empty corridor between stalls, searching for a familiar face.

A soft nicker of greeting rumbled from the end of the walkway. Briar's golden head poked out of a stall window, and Idris went to him, stroking the draft's soft forehead. Briar's tack was heaped on the ground outside his door, and Idris gripped the pommel of the saddle and carried it inside. He swung it onto Briar's back, tightened the cinch, and secured the saddlebags.

You are quite valiant, Idris.

He clung to Anya's compliment as he led Briar out into the night. He didn't believe her—not yet. But he was determined to prove to her and himself that what she'd said was true.

He would give up his Oath for her. He would risk Fate for her.

But first, he'd use Halgren's blue glow to clear all obstacles and light her path to absolution.

45

AUTONOMY

ANYA

I f even the smallest part of me had wondered if my affection for Idris had grown due to proximity of travel, and not true emotional connection, my first half-day with Oderin dispelled all concern. It was not that Oderin was a *bad* travel companion. He was Idris's friend, after all, and I felt safe under his guidance.

It was his *chattiness*.

In a single afternoon, I'd heard far more about his love life than even I—normally quite an enthusiastic gossip—would've cared to know. There were the young castle apprentices, the brawny coastal merchants, the thief who'd stolen his heart and the dress dagger he'd been given by the King of Marona. There was the time Oderin woke up in a literal pile of shit after going home with a stablemaster, and a rather exciting secret tryst with a nobleman from the southeastern territory of Lothgaim. The only men who were off-limits, Oderin had stated proudly, were his regiment.

Who would've guessed that a Knight of the Order of the Mighty—the most highly-respected Order in the realm—could be so...*horny*? Touch magicians were notorious for their pleasure-seeking, but Oderin was beyond the stereotypes of his skill. I supposed his title granted him some magnetism, but did it not also demand restraint? His conversational momentum—so counter to my first impression of him: regal, grand, perhaps even a little stoic—and his general outgoingness made me wonder how he and Idris had gotten so close. They were two opposites: Idris, taciturn and dryly humorous; Oderin, downright boisterous.

Come to think of it, Oderin's conversational momentum was a little bit like...*mine*. Had Idris felt this exhausted while traveling with me?

To be fair, under normal circumstances, I probably would've delighted in Oderin's wild stories—but seeing as I was a prisoner marching off to possible death, I wasn't in a place to be amused. Though I appreciated his efforts to lighten the mood, I found myself missing the quiet contentment of Idris's presence.

Oderin was also a stickler for the rules.

I had been given my own horse for the journey, but as a criminal, I had not been permitted to steer the mare myself. Instead, Oderin had knotted my reins to the pommel of his saddle, leading my horse from atop his mount. The two animals didn't get along. They pinned their ears and swerved constantly, making for a bumpy ride. And seeing as my hands had been shackled since the moment I was led from my cell, all I could do was hold on tightly, unable to even brush the strands of hair from my face lest I lose my balance.

By the time we stopped for the night, my butt-bones ached, and my wrists were raw. These were not the rolling green hills along the High Road. Here, the terrain was rocky and harsh. Jagged stones rose up all around us, black and crusted with pale green lichen. Scraggly bushes and stands of twisted fir trees provided some cover, but the Bone Mountains—even the foothills—were known for their frigid winds and arid scenery. Once we reached the River Gray, the western forest would provide more cover, but darker dangers than the elements haunted that path.

It took Oderin twice as long as Idris to start a fire, and with my hands still bound, all I could do was watch in silence as he struggled with the flint. I hadn't even been able to change clothes before we left Fenrir City, so I still wore my ridiculous party dress—warm, but laughably out of place. I considered asking Oderin if I could change, but even the thought of briefly exposing my skin to the chill of night made me shiver.

So, I simply sat there on the ground with my back to a nearby boulder. Once the weak fire was lit, I held my palms up to the flames, waiting for our meager dinner to simmer. Unlike Idris, Oderin didn't add any salt, syrup, or spices.

I hated that I missed Idris. I hated that Fate and Oaths and differing opinions had pulled us apart. *He left you*, I reminded myself. *He chose his lonely, miserable, Oath-bound life over you. He chose it over...literally anything else.*

Underneath the hurt, *that's* what I didn't understand. Why Idris would stay in an Order for criminals when he himself could walk free. Because if the Order of the Valiant wasn't *voluntary*, then the charge—hunting monsters and who knows what else—must be work that few would carry out unless forced. How grim. How awful. How insulting that he'd stay.

His admission about his Mirror *had* been a surprise, though. Regardless of what I'd said to him last night, his Fortune—the perfect reflection of my doom—*was* a compelling reason for him to keep his Oath. I just...had trouble believing that Idris would murder me. The Fates worked in mysterious ways, but then again, so did our hearts. Did my unfixed Fate mean nothing to him?

What did *any* of Idris's thoughts or decisions matter when I was about to face a nest of monsters? Whatever strength of nerve I'd felt this morning during my audience with the Lord was gone now, lost to the howling winds. I couldn't turn back, but I didn't see a clear path forward, either.

"Dinner's up," Oderin said, lifting the pot from the fire and dishing out our meal. "Fair warning: Idris's cooking is far better than mine."

The steaming bowl he placed in my outstretched hands was wonderfully hot, stinging my cold-numb fingers. I breathed in the steam, finding myself starving in spite of its bland scent. The heel of moldy bread that'd been tossed into my cell early this morning had hardly filled me up, seeing as I'd picked off nearly half of its bulk, the rats rushing for the scraps.

I took a tentative bite of soup, struggling with the logistics of eating with my hands shackled; it meant I had to lift the bowl toward my face along with the spoon, which was awkward and caused me to dribble some down my chin.

Oderin wasn't wrong—Idris's cooking *was* better.

"Idris is better than me at pretty much all things related to camping," Oderin went on good-naturedly, seating himself on a boulder to my right.

I fished a chunk of mushroom out of my broth. "He has more practice, I reckon."

Oderin chuckled. "That he does."

"When we stayed at the One Week Cabin, he told me Mighty Knights are fragile city dwellers unaccustomed to nature."

Oderin's chuckle morphed into a chesty laugh. "Glad to know the wilds haven't diminished his sense of humility."

"Why did you volunteer to do this?" I wondered.

"When clearly I don't enjoy camping, you mean?"

"It seems beneath your station," I clarified.

"Does it?" Oderin seemed pleased by my comment. "Why do you say that?"

"You're a Knight of the Order of the Mighty," I stated. "Escorting a prisoner to her death in the woods doesn't seem particularly...mighty of a task."

"You'd be surprised by how un-mighty my life is most of the time," he said with a chuckle. "When there are frontlines to travel to, I can fancy myself a gallant knight, but usually, my role involves scheduling my regiment, training new recruits, and lots of paperwork."

"Don't tell me my potential doom is a welcome break from the ordinary."

Oderin fixed me with his keen brown eyes. "Idris cares about you," he said, as if that explained it all.

If he cares about me, I wanted to ask, *then why did he leave?* Instead, I fumbled another bite of watery soup.

Our little camp was tucked within the shelter of a rocky outcrop, which served as somewhat of a wind break. A vast smattering of stars lit up the sky, which was completely clear, save for a few tiny, fast-moving clouds. I heard the horses shifting their weight nearby, the scuttle of small animals, and the faintest hint of distant—breathing? I tried to pluck the sound out of obscurity, but the wind gusted, dispersing it. I was probably just imagining things.

"Do you really think you're marching to your death?" Oderin asked.

I had to hand it to him, he was far more direct than Idris. That, I liked. "At the moment? Yes."

"Then why did you suggest this path?"

"Autonomy," I said, tipping the bowl up to my lips to finish the broth. I set the bowl aside. "You probably wouldn't know anything about that."

"Ouch," Oderin said, but he didn't sound offended. "I'd argue that my Oath gives me a better understanding and appreciation for autonomy than most."

I thought of the Oath of Proving I'd taken today. I'd been surprised it had a taste, almost herbal on my tongue as I'd finished reciting it to the Lord and it'd snapped into place. It didn't feel particularly restrictive, but I could sense its *hold* on me even now, like a leather strap tied around my neck. A pressure that didn't go away.

I couldn't wait to be rid of it.

"Why anyone would take an Oath—unless forced—is beyond me," I said.

"No, it's not," Oderin replied. "I'm sure you can imagine a hundred scenarios in which someone would willingly bind themselves to an Oath—or stay in an Oath." I didn't miss the hint at Idris. "It's human nature to crave security. Boundaries, rules, Oaths—these offer stability. Direction in a directionless world."

"Security and imprisonment are two very different things."

"I agree with you," Oderin said. "I'm just pointing out that it's easy to confuse the two—especially for those who've never known true safety."

I had to hand it to Oderin—promiscuous as he was, he had depth. This was the first serious conversation we'd had all day, and I was grateful for his openness—even if I disliked the point he was making about Idris. The *reasonableness* he brought to the heated emotions that—last night—had me insisting Idris leave the dungeon. Leave me to my sentence to fix the mess myself.

I settled back against the rock behind me, rubbing the raw skin of my wrists underneath the heavy iron shackles. "How'd you and Idris even become friends? You seem so..."

"Different?" Oderin supplied. "He helped my baby sister overcome her fear of horses."

I frowned.

"Annoyingly sweet, isn't it?"

"Yes, actually," I agreed. "How'd that even come to be?"

Oderin waved a hand, as if this was classic Idris. "Oh, he was up in Fenrir recovering from that gnarly shoulder wound. He found me arguing with Phina outside the stables. I was twenty—the youngest of three noble brothers, newly admitted to the Royal Guard—and Phina was sixteen, but that day, we were no better than two bratty children making a scene. My mother had tasked me with reintroducing Phina to horses before the summer parade; she had suffered a bad fall the previous year and had refused to ride a horse since. When Idris found us, I was at my wit's end, shouting at Phina while she screamed bloody murder, refusing to get on."

I laughed at the mental picture he was painting. Though I didn't have siblings, I'd witnessed and heard about plenty of brotherly and sisterly feuds in Waldron.

He rolled his eyes, smiling. "It was ugly, to say the least. And at some point, in our shouting match, the horse had tugged his lead out of my hands and wandered off. Idris found the gelding nibbling grass not far from the barn and came over to return him to me. He always had a way with horses—all animals, really."

A wistful smile tugged at my mouth as I thought of Idris whispering to Briar—but I smothered the grin before it took over, unwilling to think of him with wistfulness when I was still so hurt and heartbroken over our last conversation.

"Long story short, he offered to teach my sister to ride," Oderin said. "Of course, she immediately agreed. Even in his youth, Idris was all dark hair and broody glances, his quiet countenance impossibly mysterious and alluring—and with that sling over his arm, he appeared all the more valorous. To this day, she insists she accepted his help to rankle me, but it was a girlhood crush through and through."

"It's hard not to accept help from someone like Idris," I said. "He's too earnest. He doesn't make you feel like a damsel."

Oderin tipped his head, a smile quirking his lips. Suddenly embarrassed, I glanced at the fire, hoping he didn't see the way my cheeks heated.

"Well," Oderin said, continuing. "I was grateful to pass the thankless task off to some poor unsuspecting knight. Of course, he had her up on that gelding and cantering around by the afternoon." Oderin's smile spread wide. "He's a good man."

"If only he'd make good decisions."

Oderin snorted. "I like you. I hope you survive this."

"Thanks," I said on a sigh. "Me, too."

Later that evening, we settled our bedrolls a respectable distance apart. Oderin—unused to camping as he was—still managed to fall asleep within minutes, his soft snores lifted away by the howling wind. Behind our outcropping, the breeze was minimized, but the chill remained harsh. Astrophel—the longest night of the year—was quickly approaching, and I found myself wondering who in Waldron was making the preparations in my stead. Did they still expect me to return? How long after my absence would they begin to assume I wasn't coming home?

Don't think like that, Anya, I told myself harshly. *You're not dead yet.*

The rocky ground poked at my hip bones, my knees, my ribs. With my hands bound, I tossed from side to side, unable to get comfortable mentally or physically. Around midnight, frustrated, I sat up and grabbed my pack, hoping my spare clothing might provide some additional padding underneath my body. But when I reached inside, my fingers found something hard—a book.

I pulled it out, shocked to see its cover. There was no way Oderin would've put this in my bag, which meant—

My lips quaked, unsure whether to smile or frown. I swiveled away from Oderin's slumbering form, using the remaining glow of our fire to illuminate the pages. I flipped immediately to the section on the Order of the Valiant, half-expecting to find a note of some kind from Idris—but the chapter was unmarked. Even without confirmation, I knew what this was: his best attempt at helping me understand.

The Order of the Valiant is reserved for the rehabilitation of skilled criminals. It provides the opportunity to use their sentence to fight the evil of our realm and keep its guarded secrets. It is for this reason that Valiant Knights must live solitary lives in the wilds, visiting towns only for supplies and the Capital only by request of the Lord or in the name of duty. Valiant Knights swear unyielding loyalty to their territory and the Kingdom of Marona, never to unveil that which seeks to fill the land with fear. Kills are tracked by the Oath Ledgers; desertion results in a broken Oath. Sentences are absolved by time or death; broken Oaths reset the original sentence of dungeon or death. In retirement, Valiant Knights may never speak of their former charge; if they do, their dormant Oath will activate, and their sentence will be reset.

I continued to read, my forehead pinching. There was information about monetary rewards, the training of new recruits, even their magical weapons, but nowhere did the book use the words *abomination* or *monster*. There was no information about them at all—only that the unnamed "evil" remain secret.

While I read, I looked for clues as to why Idris would stay shackled to his Order. He didn't seem greedy or wanting enough to seek monetary riches. He didn't seem to enjoy being alone, nor killing monsters.

I flipped back to the beginning of the chapter, thinking about Grinnick and how it was *his* sentence Idris had taken. Last night, I'd accused Idris of self-punishment, but in my anger, I hadn't truly considered what that could mean. If a sentence was absolved in death, then Idris wouldn't have *needed* to take Grinnick's place, which meant...

Grinnick had broken his Oath.

For Idris, no doubt.

Had Idris been there when Grinnick died, then? Had he...*learned* something he was not permitted to know? Perhaps that would explain the Lord mentioning Grinnick during my trial. Had that been a threat to reset the sentence, even though Idris had already earned out? I wracked my brain, trying to sort through the disparate threads of Idris's story—the parts of him he couldn't let me see—trying to untangle the knots.

There was no scenario in which I could fathom Idris being responsible for Grinnick's death, but...well, I could see now how messy the secret-keeping of the Oath could be. And if the Lord was willing to imprison me simply for *witnessing* monsters, there was no doubt in my mind that countless others—perhaps even Idris himself—had been sentenced for the same thing. Apparently, the Lord saw Oath-controlled criminals as a resource to do his dirty work. It was cruel, but I could see how it was effective for a ruler unconcerned with cruelty.

I could see how we'd all been caught up in it.

"But *why*?" I whispered to myself, flipping back through the pages.

What benefit was there to keeping the monsters a secret at all? It seemed like such a massive amount of work to contain. And what of Oderin? What of all the other knights who knew of the monsters' existence? How was it possible to keep a secret from the public when it was so widely known among the ranks? Were the Oaths they took really that strong? Were knights just...puppets of the Lord?

A raspy voice answered my question. "Power, Dear. It's all for power."

Caught up in reading, I hadn't noticed the silence that'd overtaken our camp—like a blanket snuffing out a crackling fire. A thin, lanky man stepped out from a stand of nearby pines into the dim light of the stars. A dark shadow remained on his face, though, where his right eye should've been. He held a longbow, and the tip of his arrow flashed in the moonlight as he took aim—at me.

46

DAMSEL

ANYA

Many things happened in the moments after my assailant took aim.

First, I lifted my magic beyond the bounds of his power, thrusting my shout in Oderin's direction to wake him. While I did, I covered my face with the book. An arrow thudded into the thick volume, knocking me back with force and nicking my forehead. The next arrow was blocked by Oderin's axe, the metal arrow tip pinging off the flat head of his blade as he deflected the shot.

I dropped the arrow-skewered book and scrambled back, using my sound magic to hurl echoes and shouts at my assailant's ears; it wasn't much, but it had an effect, distracting him enough for Oderin to stride forward and knock the longbow from his hands. Oderin then used the butt of his axe to strike the man's temple; my assailant crumpled, his head knocking against a rock as he landed.

With our enemy limp at his feet, Oderin rounded on me, panting. "Are you hurt?" he asked, dropping to his knees. He reached up, thumb wiping blood from the place above my eyebrow where the arrow had scratched me.

Oderin's attention dropped to the book. Its gold debossed title was illuminated by the dim light of our smoldering fire, plain to see.

"How in the *Fates* did you get your hands on that?" He promptly tossed the volume—arrow and all—onto the coals. Flames flared to life on the dry paper, eating the pages hungrily. "Never mind, don't tell me. I don't wish to be incriminated."

My wrists were quivering uncontrollably, rattling my shackles. "Who was he?"

My attacker's body was limp, his mouth hanging open. Blood from the gash on his head was trickling into his eye socket.

"He *is* Heris. The blow knocked him out, but I didn't kill him." Oderin produced a set of keys from his pocket and unlocked my shackles, then draped them over his arm as he approached the unconscious man. "He's a knight."

"Like Idris?"

"Only by Order," Oderin said sharply—then hoisted Heris up by the armpits and dragged him toward a nearby tree.

I rose on shaky legs, resting a palm against the natural stone wall to steady myself. "Why was he here? What does he want with me?"

"Obviously, he wanted to kill you." Oderin grasped Heris's floppy wrists, encircled his arms around the tree, and shackled the unconscious knight in place. When Oderin was done, he tossed the keys into the bushes, strode back to me, and began rolling up his blankets. "We need to get out of here."

"Why would he want me dead?" I insisted.

Oderin didn't answer. He got to work saddling his horse and securing gear. "You have hands now. Use them."

I pointed at Heris. "You're just going to leave him here?"

"I don't kill other knights, unless duty demands it," Oderin said, tightening a strap with a quick yank. "If Heris is here, so are others. He'll be found. He'll serve as a delay—and hopefully a warning to let us be."

At the mention of others, I glanced around at the black shapes of the surrounding trees. They were too tall to be human, but as their branches rustled in the wind, I found myself bracing for hidden threats.

"What is going on?" I asked quietly.

"I'll explain on the ride."

Oderin's explanation was lacking.

As we raced into the night, all he was willing—or able—to imply was that Heris was the leader of a powerful and ruthless faction amongst the Valiant

Knights, happy to dispatch threats to his own secret dealings within the Order. What those secret dealings entailed, Oderin wasn't sure, but apparently my relationship to Idris made me a threat. I also learned that Heris and Idris had a history, about which Oderin seemed to know plenty but was unwilling to provide details.

Heris was yet another yarn in the tangled situation from which I'd been trying to cut myself free. How I'd ended up in the middle of such a vast tapestry—threaded with monsters, politics, and nefarious factions within secret Orders—was beyond me.

All I wanted was to return home to Waldron. Quaint, uncomplicated Waldron.

The next two days and nights were strenuous. Oderin pushed our horses hard, keeping a pace meant to evade and escape any other knights on our trail. With my hands unbound, I was able to ride more deftly, but after weeks on the road, wracked with stress, my body was bone-cold, weak, and exhausted.

On the morning we reached the path that led to the Well of Fate, fog hung around us like a curtain. The pines of the western forest were a dark mass up ahead, their tips piercing the low mist like sharp teeth. With my senses on high alert, I opened my hearing to the thicket. Somewhere within, the River Gray flowed, its current swift and crisp to my ears. I heard no moans, no howls, no signs of any life at all.

I remembered the report I read on Oderin's desk. Yar-on-Gray—the town south of here—had been completely overrun. Was that a sign that the monsters had vacated this area, or had their numbers outgrown it?

We both dismounted. My mare danced nervously sideways, emitting a nervous keen as she eyed the trees. I patted her neck, urging her to be still as Oderin and I met silently between our mounts. Our breaths rose in puffs, disappearing into the mist.

"The pool is pretty much a straight shot from here, but the fog will make it hard to keep direction," Oderin whispered as he adjusted the cloak at my neck. "Move swiftly, and you should reach the River Gray shortly after nightfall. Cross at the old stone bridge, then continue on through the night. Idris said you have hearing magic?"

Touching my mother's cloak pin at my throat, I nodded.

"Listen for the geysers. They'll keep you heading in the right direction. You'll feel the air temperature warm up as you near the pools."

"What of the—" I pressed my lips together, willing myself not to cry as fear took hold. "I saw the report on your desk, about Yar-on-Gray."

Oderin's jaw clenched. "We are miles north of Yar. It would not be unreasonable to hope that the harbingers of Yar's tragedy are still preoccupied."

I marveled at his careful phrasing.

Oderin patted my cloak-wrapped shoulder. After tearing my spare trousers while riding yesterday, I was back in my Fate Ceremony dress, which was warmer than the tunics Hattie had packed me. I felt clumsy—not just due to the heavy fabric that swaddled my still-chilled body, but in my acute lack of fighting skill.

If I encountered a monster, I would be a goner.

Oderin released my shoulder and went to his horse's flank. An angular bulk wrapped in thin fabric was fastened there, behind his saddle; he unwrapped it to reveal a small crossbow with silver detailing. It was beautiful. Deadly.

He handed it to me.

The weapon was heavier than I anticipated, cumbersome in my reluctant grasp. Oderin knelt in front of me and wrapped a belt around my hips underneath my cloak. On the belt, he fastened a small quiver filled with bolts the length of my forearm.

When he stood again, he whispered, "Do you know how to use it?"

I shook my head.

He rested his palms atop my hands, guiding them into place. Wordlessly, he showed me how to lock the bow back with a separate lever, where to secure a bolt, and the location of the trigger. I committed his guided motions to memory, even as the weapon itself brought me dismay. What good would this be against an abomination?

Unless... I studied the crossbow a little closer.

Oderin must've seen the change in my expression. "This weapon is not the same as Halgren," he said with a shake of his head. "Power lies in our Oaths."

My face fell.

He ducked his head, meeting my gaze. "Do not despair, Anya. This crossbow can still do harm. Use it not to defeat, but to deflect." He lifted the crossbow from my hands and hung it on a two-pronged hook on my belt, tucking the lever beside the quiver at my other hip.

With the gear balanced across my waist, I felt further weighed down, but bolstered, too. "Thank you," I said, hoping my sincerity was clear in my voice.

Oderin brushed my hair from my face with the affection of an older brother. "Do me a favor, would you?" he murmured. "Don't die and break my friend's heart. I don't think Idris could stand to lose yet another person he cares about."

I rolled my shoulders back. "Death isn't the only way he could lose me." I glanced up at Oderin. "Do *me* a favor, would you?"

He arched a brow.

"Be here when I return."

Without another word, I walked into the Western Wood alone to face my Fate.

47

MIGHTY FRIEND

IDRIS

Idris stood atop a rocky crag overlooking the barren plains. From the rise, he watched Oderin and Anya—their distant figures no larger than the tip of his thumb from this vantage—disappear into the fog bank that clung to the edge of the western forest. It was not lost on him that the last time he followed someone he loved into the foothills of the Bone Mountains, they'd died.

But Anya was not Grinnick, Idris reminded himself, and Idris was not the boy he'd been fifteen years ago. Oderin had ridden hard and fast, and Anya was no-doubt exhausted by the journey. Even well-slept and at her best, she didn't stand a chance inside those woods alone. No one without the magic of an Order would. She needed him in a way Grinnick hadn't. That difference had to matter.

After scrambling down the back of the crag, Idris returned to Briar, whom he'd tethered to the gnarled stump. His ribs ached acutely as he climbed into the saddle and urged Briar into a trot. The empty shackles he'd found two days ago clanked with the persistent bounce of Briar's gait. The horse had been a faithful companion; Idris regretted bringing him here, where the land was harsh and the dangers plentiful.

He regretted it even more as they entered the fog, the world going soft and gauzy around them. Briar whinnied nervously into the mist, blowing any cover Idris had hoped to maintain. Idris stroked the horse's neck, shushing him even though it was too late. A horse up ahead—completely obscured by white—returned Briar's call.

Idris swallowed the sensation of a stone lodged in his throat. He rested his palm on Halgren's pommel and urged Briar onward.

Minutes later, the dark streak of the forest came into view, as did the smudges of two horses. It was nearly midday, the sun high, but the fog here had not yet been burned off. A brightly illuminated wall of opacity surrounded them. It made Idris uneasy. So, too, was the sight of only *one* person seated at the base of a tree not far from the tethered mounts.

"You're a Fates-damned fool, you know that?" Oderin called.

Idris swung out of the saddle, tied Briar with the other horses, and dropped the shackles at Oderin's feet. They landed with a clatter in the sparse grass.

"Care to tell me where Heris went?"

Oderin was halfway through whittling a small figurine of some kind. He set down his knife and peered up at Idris. "How did you know it was him?"

Idris tapped his nose.

Oderin sat forward, resting his forearms on his knees. "Do I look like I know where Heris went?"

Idris had been panicked when he saw the remnants of a hastily abandoned camp. The blood. The curled, charred leather cover of the book, with a hole in the middle and an arrow tip buried in the ash. The empty shackles with the key still stuck in the lock. The scent of Heris clinging to the bark of a nearby tree.

For two days, the lack of bodies and the tracks of Anya and Oderin heading west had been his only proof that they'd *both* survived whatever scuffle with Heris had occurred. That, and the drag-marks that suggested Oderin had shackled Heris to a tree before they rode off. He'd been impossibly relieved this morning when Anya and Oderin came into view across the plains.

"You should've killed him," Idris said.

"Please tell me you're here looking for Heris, and not because you plan to go after Anya," Oderin said blandly.

Idris was here on both counts, but he wanted his question answered first. "Why didn't you kill him?"

"How many tracks were there?"

"Two must've freed him," Idris answered. "The trio diverted south."

Oderin nodded as if he'd been expecting that news. "He looked surprised to find a Mighty Knight with her. I left him as a mercy and a warning to the others to back off."

"Heris deserves no mercy, and he will heed no warning. They're regrouping."

Oderin rose to his feet. "For what? Do you have any idea?"

Idris grumbled and shook his head. "I really don't," he answered honestly. "Two of his goons jumped me in an alley the night you left Fenrir. Spoke of an uprising of some sort, but I didn't stick around to torture more answers out of them."

"You should have."

"Why didn't you press Heris for answers? He's their leader."

Oderin folded his arms across his breastplate and arched a haughty brow—a reminder of his noble upbringing. "Quibbles between Valiant Knights are beneath me, you know that."

The statement was meant in jest, but Idris saw through the veneer. "You don't want to know what they're planning."

Oderin took great pains to manage the information he knew and did not know. The Oath of the Order of the Mighty was powerful, demanding transparency with the Lord. Of all Oaths, it was one that required complete loyalty to even utter. Those with nefarious intentions could die trying to take such an Oath—its bond to Fenrir was *that* strong.

Which meant that Idris wouldn't get more answers out of Oderin about *why* he did not wish to know about Heris's machinations. The fact that his closest friend wished to turn a blind eye to the situation intrigued him, though. Did Oderin know about the uprising Mariana had mentioned? Oderin despised Heris, but he didn't much care for Lord Haron, either—his loyalty was to Fenrir, and perhaps he wanted to see a clash. Sometimes a disease had to be cut out, even if the blade was dirty.

Oderin did not allow for more questions. His expression softened. "You would've been proud of Anya, she handled Heris well. She's lucky she had sound magic to counteract his stealth."

Idris hated the thought of Heris watching her, stalking her, determined to kill her. But the thought of Anya thwarting Heris made him smile.

"She's bold, I'll give her that," Oderin added.

Idris flicked his gaze to the woods. "Too bold."

"Do you know why Heris targeted her?" Oderin asked.

"My guess is he'd been tailing us since the incident in Brine. I thought he was after *me*, but turns out, Anya was the bigger threat—probably since she isn't Oath-bound." He wiped a weary palm over his stubbled cheek.

"What incident in Brine?" Oderin asked. "You told me nothing of Brine."

Idris lowered his hand from his jaw. "Heris warned me not to divulge to the Lord just how badly the abominations have encroached."

"And you *heeded* his warning?"

If the Order of the Valiant fails, so, too, does the order of Fenrir itself, Heris had said. Idris didn't trust Heris—but he didn't trust the Lord, either, especially in light of the ongoing failure of the Valiant. Idris didn't quite know why he still clung to his Order, when Grinnick was gone, and all his Oath did now was make him miserable. Keep him from Anya.

But something didn't sit right about the Order's possible demise. The landscape of Fenrir's secret Orders was shifting, like groundwater melting and flowing underneath his feet. Thinking practically, if the Order was dissolved, knights would be reassigned. That was the best case. Worst case, the Lord would reset sentences or dispose of well-established knights altogether—and who knows what would happen to retired knights. To dissolve an Order was to dissolve an Oath—and in the face of losing control, it was not a leap to assume the Lord would do something rash.

Knowing the truth that Oderin's role demanded—Idris wasn't sure how much to say. Though Oderin was Idris's closest friend, this was the wedge between them. Oderin would always be a Mighty Knight first and foremost, and though Idris trusted Oderin with his life, he wasn't sure he trusted his friend with *all* his information.

Oaths tended to get in the way of relationships. Just like what had happened between Idris and Anya.

"Idris, what happened in Brine?" Oderin prompted, taking a subtle step closer.

"Do you truly want to know?" Idris asked slowly, giving his friend a choice in the matter.

Oderin pondered that question for a moment—then a serious line formed between his eyebrows, and he nodded.

"I did my duty and was witnessed," Idris said.

"Witnessed?"

Idris lifted his palms in a small shrug.

"Wait—you're not—" It was Oderin's turn to wipe his face with a palm. "You're not the Hero of Brine? I thought those rumors were hyperbole. A lone traveler killing a rabid..." He trailed off, eyes widening. "What in the *Fates* was an abomination doing in a *town*?"

"Heris was tracking it. Let it get away. I cleaned up his mess."

"By making a *bigger* mess?"

"Oderin," Idris said, hoping his honesty might compel his friend to listen with his heart as much as his duty. "Something is afoot among my ranks. Something I am not privy to. The abominations are spreading, and—"

"Something is afoot with *you*, my friend," Oderin said—not threateningly, but with a haste that told Idris, *I don't want to hear the rest.* "What are you doing here, exactly? I thought I made it clear that my Oath will not permit me to let you go after her."

So, they'd reached their inevitable impasse.

Idris's palm tightened around Halgren's hilt. "I am aware."

"You would fight me?" Oderin sounded vaguely amused. "When I so often best you in the sparring ring?" He brandished his axe, Feldon, the double-blades glinting red with the sparks of his power.

"Our Oaths are at odds," Idris said cooly.

"No," Oderin said. "Not our Oaths. It is the will of my Oath against the will of your heart. An uneven match if you ask me."

"Which side do you reckon is favorable?"

Oderin simply chuckled. "You really are a brokenhearted fool, aren't you?"

"I do not wish to fight you, my friend."

"Nor I, you."

"Heart against Oath, you say?" Idris murmured.

He didn't wait for Oderin's reply. Idris swung Halgren—alight with blue flame—toward his Mighty friend.

48

THE TREACHEROUS ROAD

ANYA

A faint whinny reached my ears as I crept deeper into the woods. The fog remained heavy, clouding around my shoulders. As much as I wanted to stretch my magic back toward Oderin, investigate the reason the horses were roused, I resisted. Best to keep my ears focused on what lay ahead. Best to use my magic to muffle the noises of my own movements.

Anxiety was a cold hand on my throat as I crept on.

The path was narrow but oddly clear, well-trod but without obvious tracks. The gnarled arms of the trees formed a tunnel of sorts, a dense tangle above my head that blotted out the noonday sun. Undergrowth cast odd shadows. Fog twirled in eddies. This was a still place. A haunted place.

Fear nipped at my heels, urging me to move faster—to *run*—but I refused to heed its goading. Fear was not far from panic, and panic, I knew, would do me no good in here.

I kept my steps silenced and my power alert to my surroundings—but to quell the fear, I touched my mother's pin again, and the necklace against my sternum, using the items to focus my mind on Waldron. To remember why I was here.

Wicker's wiry fur. Hattie's laugh. The scent of the Possum: malt, woodsmoke, linen. Dipping my toes in the Wend's cool waters in summertime.

Dancing around bonfires at winter festivals; hanging baubles on our bedposts for luck on the night of Astrophel. Sheep bleating from the eastern hills.

As time went on, the forest gradually dimmed with twilight.

Martha's gossip. Hugh's compliments. Avoiding Farmer Quinn's son, Francis, at market. Goslings floating on the river in spring. Red and gold poplars, oaks, and maples in autumn. The taste of sweet buns. Vera's birthday bouquets.

With the darkening light, fond memories led me to less-fond places. The mold in the Possum's storeroom, the pine out back that needed felling, the chimney I insisted on cleaning myself. Such remembrances brought up an unexpected desperation in me—one that squeezed in my chest. What if they forgot about me? What if they realized they didn't need me anymore? What if I returned home to find that no one had missed me?

Cruel thoughts, I told myself. *Those are cruel, insecure thoughts. Nothing more.*

But as I thought back on a childhood spent *helping*, an adulthood filled to the brim with work for others, I realized the ugliness underneath all those "selfless" acts. Even my mother—the queen of favors—hadn't overextended herself the way I had in the years after her death.

The labor I did for my neighbors was not borne out of pure helpfulness, no. I wanted to feel *needed*. Needed, so that they couldn't leave me the way she had.

Idris hadn't needed you. He'd cast you away.

That's different, I argued with myself. *That's not your fault.*

The sudden self-compassion made my eyes well with tears, and my steps faltered, coming to a halt. I hadn't been able to help my mother recover from the grimflu, but by the Fates, I had helped everyone else in town. Everyone but myself.

Helpfulness had given me purpose, but it had also stolen true connection. Idris had been the perfect example of that—someone who didn't need my help, but had come to enjoy my company, anyhow. At least for a time. He'd left, but he'd left of his own accord—not because I couldn't help him, but because he believed *he* couldn't help *me*.

For better or worse, his actions had forced me to help myself.

If I died here, at least I'd die doing something for *me*. Hattie would be so proud.

I wiped the tears from my eyes and started walking again, my footfalls faster—not with fear, but determination. *You will not die here*, I told myself. *You will return to Waldron-on-Wend.*

I silently repeated the words in rhythm with my steps. The forest had blackened around the edges, the remaining dusk evident only in the strip of pale gray beyond the trees' canopy.

You will return to Waldron-on-Wend.

You will return to Waldron-on-Wend.

A series of twigs cracked, drawing my attention.

It was not my boots that made the sound—my movements were still muffled by magic. It was someone—some*thing*—else. Somewhere behind me.

I swiveled, eyes searching the brush crowding the path's edges. Oh, how I wished I possessed sight magic right about now. I couldn't separate shadow from shadow. I couldn't make out any movement.

I reached for the crossbow at my hip, hands shaking as I fumbled the lever into place and cocked the weapon. I fished a bolt out of the quiver and secured it into place. Taking aim at the gloom from which I'd come, I backed up slowly, continuing down the road.

There was a tree up ahead, shrugged right up against the path. When I reached it, I put its rough bark at my back. My arms shook uncontrollably, the hardware on the crossbow rattling—but the noise was overtaken by the sound of more twigs snapping. It sounded like a small tree crashing through the underbrush.

A thing of nightmares materialized out of the mist. Black bones, shredded muscle, skinless—a carcass come to life.

True terror compressed my windpipe.

The monster in the road did not resemble any animal. It stood on two legs like a human, but its brutalized body was hunched at a broken-looking angle. Crooked as its posture was, it was at least ten feet tall. Its arms were claw-tipped, a fringe of shorter appendages ornamented its sides, and its hind legs were bent with backward knees, like a dog's. Twisted black antlers crowned its head. Even from thirty feet away, its cloying scent hit the back of my palate, making me gag.

The abomination turned slowly, a wretched grinding echoing through the fog. When it paused, so too did the cracking, and I realized the sound was not twigs underfoot but the monster itself. Small bones and ligaments breaking and reforming. A creature of continuous pain.

Two cloudy white eyes lifted, their otherworldly glow landing on me.

A small whimper escaped my throat. The abomination cocked its head with a quick jerk. Thin lips of sinew spread over its bare jaw, revealing far too many long, needle-like teeth and a leech-like tongue.

The sound of splintering wood started up again as the creature stalked closer. An overwhelming sense of fear had my bladder threatening to release. Motionless under the monster's menacing white gaze, a small voice in my head told me to run—but I couldn't get my muscles to listen. I remained immobile.

Twenty feet away.

Fifteen feet away.

Ten feet away.

Confusion coalesced in my mind. I was in plain view, and yet the creature moved not like it was stalking but *listening*. It paused again and tipped its head further to the side. Vacant eyes narrowed in my direction but didn't seem to focus on my form.

Could it really not see me?

I scrambled to maintain a hold on my magic, to silence my breathing and shaking and rustling. I hefted the crossbow a little higher, aiming for the exposed ridge of bone between the creature's eyes—but no matter how hard I tried to keep my arms still, the fear was too great. It shook me.

Without warning, the abomination lunged.

I compressed the trigger of the crossbow, and the bolt flew wide, pinging off a stone somewhere in the underbrush. The monster's teeth snapped toward my face. I shrieked, dropping to my knees to avoid its deadly bite. Before it lunged again, I magically threw my voice into the underbrush behind the monster, creating an echo that pulsed through the mist. Then I gripped the crossbow with both hands, shielding my head against the creature's second attack—but the bite didn't come.

The abomination had taken the bait, darting off into the bushes.

So, it was blind, after all.

I didn't wait. I scrambled to my feet and *ran*, shrouding my footsteps with silence so the creature couldn't hear my escape. I might've wished for sight magic earlier, but now, I was almost *giddy* with appreciation for my ability to warp sound. My magic had just saved my life. *I* had just saved my life.

With the crossbow still clutched in one hand, I pumped my arms, racing down the path as quickly and silently as I could. I ran and ran and *ran*, adrenaline coursing through my veins, carrying me much farther than I could've gone without it. I ran until my muscles ached. I ran until I heard water. I ran until I reached the bridge.

49

HEART AND OATH

IDRIS

The forest reeked of abomination. Of rot and death and the sickly sweetness of the Morta, the grotesque creators of the lesser monsters Idris usually fought.

But that was not the only thing Idris scented as he strode down the road. He smelled *Anya*, clear and bright as a golden ribbon leading his nose deeper into the tangled cover of this cursed forest. The warm, indescribable scent of her skin was too pure for such a wretched place.

It belonged in a cheerful pub, surrounded by singing and merriment. Underneath a blanket of stars, mingling with campfire smoke. Nestled in a soft bed, tucked against his chest. It belonged wherever Anya wished it to, for that was her charm: the ability to befriend and *belong* just by being herself.

Instead, her scent was here. Surrounded by the stink of monster that Idris himself had surrounded himself with for the last fifteen years.

No more. No more of this for either of them.

The delicate salinity of her tears peppering the forest floor kept him moving as swiftly and silently as possible. Protectiveness pulsed in his heart with each step.

His body hurt. The tenderness in his ribs ached with every breath, and the old injury in his shoulder was stiff with strain from his fight with Oderin. The streak of blood across his bicep from his friend's axe was already coagulating, cooling in the night air; it stuck to his ripped sleeve and pulled taut with his movements, cracking open to ooze more blood each time he flexed. Had Oderin tried harder, the gash would be deeper—but Oderin's heart hadn't been in the fight, and Idris's had.

Heart against Oath.

Idris knew now which one was the winner. Oderin hadn't even bothered to hide his amusement as Idris had shackled him to a tree. "This isn't the first time I've worn cuffs like these," he'd said with a wink before Idris disappeared into the forest.

That had been hours ago.

The quiet of this place disturbed Idris. Under normal circumstances, even he wouldn't've entered the forest alone. The ruins of Kelebraim were famously overrun with Morta, and this was the road that led there. Marked with Anya's footprints. A place even the bravest of Valiant hunting parties had long ago given up on patrolling.

What had he been thinking, abandoning her to take this path alone? The Lord's theoretical consequences for interference in Anya's mission seemed paltry when compared to the real and present dangers of this road. With her Oath of Proving, she had to do this alone, but that didn't mean he couldn't help from afar.

Idris hoped he'd come to his senses in time. That it wasn't too late for Anya. He picked up his pace, using his long legs to eat up twice the distance as her reluctant strides.

The scent of her fright intensified as he went, hovering in the mist, unmistakable. It smelled vulnerable as a newborn; pungent as sweat. He hated it. He hated that it was getting worse as he walked, her fear tipping into terror.

A shriek pierced the air, perhaps a quarter of a mile ahead.

Idris broke into a run, a different sort of terror coursing through him—determined, singular, selfless. He left the path and wove through the underbrush in the direction of her voice, ducking under tree limbs and leaping over logs. A great cracking filled the air, but he did not slow, did not hesitate. He pushed through the pain in his ribs, the stiffness in his knees, barreling toward Anya—

—only to find that her scent had faded.

He realized what she'd done the moment he saw the Morta appear—she'd thrown her voice, thrown the abomination off her trail. The creature—blind, based on its eerie white eyes—had fallen for it.

But so had Idris.

The Morta jerked its head, triangulating Idris with its cunning ears. The creature was on the smaller side, a young one. It was rare for a Morta to be sightless, but given the state of its body, it must've fallen into one of the pools. The geothermal waters outside Kelebraim were known for their strange effects. One couldn't enter a pool without exiting it *changed*. Seems this abomination had found a pool that would make it even more horrifying.

Idris prayed to the Fates that Anya found the *correct* pool.

Idris wasted no time in sizing up his opponent. He unsheathed Halgren, blue flame licking over his palm and wrist as he gave his sword a few swings, warming up his arm. Idris was worn down, slowed by age and the wear of so many years fighting the lesser offspring of creatures such as this—but in this fight, he had both his Oath and his heart on his side.

He ran for the abomination.

The Morta matched his vigor, swiping out with a vicious claw, impossibly quick. It clipped Idris in the chest before he had time to register the strike, his breastplate repelling the blow with a zap of energy. He gritted his teeth, heaving Halgren down on the gray slab of muscle at creature's hip.

Black blood spurted. The abomination squealed in pain, baring its long and pointed teeth. Idris swung again, but this time, the creature sidestepped him, only to lunge a second later. Its claws slashed his thigh, the cut searing with the poison of its sickness. Idris's Oath granted him partial immunity from monsters' fluids, but it wouldn't take more than a few wounds from a Morta to slow him.

To bring him down.

Idris breathed deeply, going in for another few blows. Even without eyes, the Morta moved confidently, using its eerily long arms to swipe at him. It nicked a vambrace, the metal repelling it back as his breastplate had. Idris used the opportunity to rush the creature, dealing blow after attempted blow. He managed a slice across the face, the shoulder. The creature's body crackled with a bone-chilling, calamitous racket of tearing flesh and snapping ligaments, and it took all Idris's focus not to be cowed by the sound. It drowned out even the sound of his own breaths, his own thoughts.

Halgren was a blue blur in the dark, blazing against the shadows that surrounded him. With a lesser monster, the fight would've already been won—that gash he doled to the Morta's hip would've been deep enough to fell the creatures he usually fought. But this abomination was fierce—fearsome.

In an unrelenting onslaught, the abomination came at him with the vigor of ten monsters combined. Apparently, it did not need sight to make a formidable foe; even with the awful snapping of its own body, it seemed to hear Idris plainly, no-doubt using the *whoosh* of Halgren's flame and the clamor of Idris's footsteps to locate his ever-moving location. It managed another strike to his leg, then his arm, the cuts burning worse than vinegar in a wound. Idris was forced to retreat, walking backward across the uneven forest floor while swinging Halgren wildly.

Then suddenly he went down, stumbling backward over a fallen tree. The abomination leapt, its bony chest slamming against Idris's breastplate with a clatter. Halgren slipped from his fingers, and when he reached for the sword, the abomination pinned his hand to the ground with a claw, the sharp black bone piercing all the way through his palm and out the other side into the dirt.

The pain—hot, searing—traveled up his arm, spiderwebbing like lightning. His eyes pricked with tears of shock, and he squirmed underneath the abomination's weight. It snapped at him with its dreadful maw, and he gripped its face with his one free hand, pressing his thumb into a white, unseeing eye—but the monstrosity wouldn't back down. It leaned into his palm, hissing inches from his face, saliva burning his skin like hot rancid oil.

True fear swept through Idris. He would die here, pinned underneath a monster. It was just another way he was destined to fail someone he cared about.

Idris braced for the inevitable impact, the shredding of skin by that venomous mouth. He breathed through his nose, his senses filling with the awful, vomit-inducing stink of Morta—

—and the gold ribbon of something...else.

Something warmer, sweeter, purer.

The scent was faint, but it was nearby, half-buried in the loamy ground. Iron, wood, and feather, tangled with the scent of *her*. Pressing harder into the abomination's eye, Idris glanced sideways along the forest floor and spotted it: a single crossbow bolt, no farther than an arm's length away.

50

SOMEONE ELSE'S FATE

ANYA

A cacophony of cracking bone and wailing filled the forest behind me as I neared the stone bridge that led across the River Gray—but I did not allow the sound of monsters to distract me or steal my nerve. I focused my hearing on what lay ahead, keeping my movements shrouded in silence.

The river was a slash of whitewater in the dimness. The trees were sparser here, the river carving out a hole in the thicket. For the first time since I entered the forest, I caught a glimpse of the star-splashed sky, a waning sliver of the moon lighting the way.

There was an abomination up ahead, between me and the bridge. It was much larger than the first—the height of two men at least, with more muscle and smoother sinew. Its form seemed to consume the moonlight; it was all darkness, shadow, and pointed shapes.

This time, when I aimed my crossbow, I sent the bolt into the woods on purpose, amplifying the sound of the shot and sending the echo to the south, far away from where I was headed. The abomination took the bait, loping on two legs into the gloom.

You will return to Waldron-on-Wend.

I loaded the crossbow again, then hurried out of the tree cover. I crossed the bridge swiftly, the river Gray's gush filling my ears with music and my nose with freshness. A chilly spray rose off its shores to kiss my cheeks. As much as I wanted to pause, to rest here surrounded by the comforting notes of water, I didn't linger.

I continued on into the night, minutes turning to hours.

My feet ached. Blisters reopened on my heels and the balls of my feet, smarting with each step. My legs trembled and my shoulders were sore from sustained tension. I saw no additional abominations, but I heard them rustling around in the underbrush. Eerie squeals, awful cracking. Even if I did manage to escape this place, I wasn't sure I'd ever sleep again.

The temperature of the fog rose considerably as I went, faint whispers of sulfur reaching my nose. Soon, I heard the distant hiss and puff of geysers. In spite of my exhaustion, I walked faster, deeper into the mist, bolstered by the beckoning sound.

The forest's density lessened, then the trees fell away completely, opening up to a rocky glade. Without the buffer of branches, a crisp wind dispersed the steam rising off a small pool on the opposite end of the clearing. Aside from a few burbling puddles edging the path, it was the only pool here.

After the night I'd had, I felt almost incredulous to see it now. Dubious. I recalled what Hammond had said of the Mirrors' history, the cursed pools that the travelers had faced from Kelebraim before the incident with the Mirrors. The Well of Fate was the farthest east of them all, and seeing as I'd come from the east, I could only conclude…

I'd made it. I'd actually made it.

Sweating in the heat of the geothermal flat, I shucked my cloak onto the ground. I shoved my mother's pin into my pocket as I started down the path through the clearing, heading for the water. Fog spun in columns, slipping across the path, blurring my sightline, but I was so close now. I was almost there.

An icy wind sliced through the steam, clearing my vision once again—and revealing a man up ahead on the path, standing between me and the pool. In the lingering haze, I couldn't make out his face, but his features were familiar. Blond hair. Sturdy build.

I took a few tentative steps closer, recognizing lips I'd kissed countless times. The utilitarian dagger I'd gifted him for his birthday two years ago still fastened at his belt.

"Remy?" I called, my voice echoing.

Confusion twirled in my chest like the eddies twirling in the surrounding steam. For a moment, I forgot my anger toward him. All emotion was replaced by simple *relief* to see a familiar face after so many wretched hours of barely contained panic. I strode forward, moving toward him with purpose—only to halt again when I saw his eyes.

Red. Glowing faintly.

And his hands—they were claw-tipped. His skin was webbed with the black poison of whatever monster had bit him. Closer to him now, I spotted the short nubs of black antlers poking out of his mop of blond hair, the ridges of new appendages under his torn shirt.

There was no recognition in his gaze. Only hunger.

So, this is why I was Fated to kill him.

I would've been comforted by his vision in the Mirror of Death if it weren't for what I'd learned from Idris, that monsters operated outside the bounds of Fate. Monsters *had* no Fate. Which meant the outcome of this fight was yet unknown.

There was no time to waste. I lifted my crossbow and fired, the bolt hitting Remy's shoulder with a thud. He tipped his face up to the heavens and *screeched*, a sound so inhuman I stumbled backward, cold terror filling me.

I flung my voice right back at him, my scream skittering off the surrounding stone. With my magic, I plucked the echo out of the air and aimed it into the distant trees. Remy didn't fall for it. With his sight magic, he could see me plainly. He stalked forward with a singular focus, red eyes narrowed.

I fumbled with the crossbow, wrists shaking as I tried to cock the weapon—clumsy with fear, I couldn't get the lever in the right place. I breathed deeply, trying to calm my quivering muscles.

By the time I took aim again, Remy was upon me. He smacked the weapon from my hands, the contraption clattering off the path and into one of the bubbling puddles. I scrambled sideways, tripping on my Fates-forsaken skirts and landing on my butt. The fall jostled a few crossbow bolts free, causing them to scatter on the path. My grasping fingers found one, and with all my might, I plunged it deep into Remy's thigh.

He wailed again, grabbing at the bolt protruding from his leg, trying to pull it free.

With Remy distracted, I crawled toward the pool on my hands and knees, trying to escape him and get my feet under me.

Claws closed around my ankle, yanking me back. The joint cracked, pain searing through my leg. My chin hit the ground, teeth juddering, grit and gravel scraping skin. I kicked out with my free foot, clipping Remy in the jaw. Swiveling onto my back, I kicked again, freeing myself of his grasp—but not without his claws shredding the skin of my shin, my calf.

It was the worst pain of my life. I *screamed*, scrambling backward, breathing through my teeth, adrenaline numbing my muscles, making me clumsy.

Any normal man would gather himself before pouncing again—but Remy was no longer a man. The Remy I'd known had died long before this night. He leapt on me like an animal, clawing at my bodice, nipping at my face. My hand found another loose crossbow bolt, and I buried it into the side of his neck.

He howled, but he didn't stop his assault. Claw-tipped fingers fumbled with my arms, and he managed to pin one by my side. I shoved at his face, pushing him away, unwilling to succumb to his bite. His black tongue lolled out, licking my palm. A bit of splatter landed on my lip, and it stung like alcohol in a wound.

I grabbed the bolt in his neck and pulled as hard as I could. His head twisted with a sickening *grinding* noise, black blood raining down on my neck and chest. The movement forced him to ease up on my pinned arm, and I reached for the dagger at his hip, yanking it free. I angled the short but wicked blade up, burying it in Remy's side.

That time, he took the hint.

He scrambled off me. With dagger still in hand, I didn't hesitate. I surged to my feet and lunged at him. He held up a clawed hand as if to block my blow. I slashed across his face from eye to mouth. Then I swept straight across his throat, opening the artery through which that poisonous black blood pumped.

He fell, just as his Mirror of Death predicted.

What the vision in the Mirror hadn't shown, however, was the way I fell right after, my injured leg buckling.

With adrenaline still coursing through my veins, I dragged myself backward, fully out of Remy's reach. In the silence that followed, short, shocked gasps escaped my throat. My lungs heaved. My fingers shook uncontrollably. I couldn't believe it. I couldn't believe Remy had *turned into a monster.*

I couldn't believe I'd *killed* him.

As my gasps became breaths, a new sensation swept through me, one of tingling pain and paralyzing dread. I lifted my skirts to inspect my injured leg and—at the sight of torn flesh and pale bone—acid rose up my throat. I swiveled to the side and vomited on the barren path.

Still shuddering at the gruesomeness, I forced my gaze back to the injury, trying not to overthink the odd way my ankle was twisted. I pulled my clothing up farther, wincing at the damage, fighting another rise of bile. My leg was...*unrecognizable. Irreparable.* How I'd managed to make a final stand against Remy at all, I wasn't sure—it must've been the adrenaline, the numbness of desperation.

I clung to that feeling now, but it was like sand slipping from my fingers. I reminded myself of the direness of my mission. If I could just reach the water's edge...

With shaking hands, I hiked my skirts higher, seeing the pristine untouched skin of my thigh. With the full ruin of my leg on display, my vision swayed. Blood was pooling around me on the ground, hot and sticky. My body was quickly growing cold, all the heat leaking out through my shredded leg. I unfastened the belt at my hip and threaded the leather underneath my leg, moaning through my teeth at the excruciating pain of even the faintest of jostling. With a swift yank, I fastened the belt around my thigh, pulling it as tight as I could, trying to slow the blood loss.

I leaned back on my elbows, panting from the exertion, the shock. My lips shivered against my chattering teeth. The world was beginning to blur at the edges. I rolled my head over to one shoulder, peering into the mist. The Well of Fate was only ten or so feet away—but with the way my vision was darkening, it might as well have been miles.

Nausea clenched my throat again, and I closed my eyes, fighting the dizziness.

It's not too far, I told myself, forcing my eyes open again. The blue-green waters of the pool lapped the rocky shore of its basin. Long stocks of a formidable-looking grass crowded its edges, reed-like and lush from the heat of the water. *You're so close. You can crawl. You can...*

My arm buckled, and the ground rushed up to meet my cheek.

51

FORTUNE AND DEATH

IDRIS

R ed blood slicked Idris's punctured palm. Black blood soaked his shirt. Everything reeked, everything *hurt*—but he was singular in his focus.

He held Halgren in his non-dominant hand, using the blade's flame to light his way. The sword hummed with power, as if bolstered by the kill he'd made. A Morta, felled by Idris alone. It shouldn't have been possible, but he'd done it.

The temperature was warming, fog turning to steam. He heard the distant rumble of geysers, the trickle of water. His nose ached with the assault of monster stink and sulfur, but he kept his magic open to his surroundings, following the gold thread of Anya, fragrant and out of place as a flower. He clung to the scent with all the fortitude he had left.

The stars were fading when Idris reached the edge of the forest. A cobalt dawn twinkled above a vast, rocky, fog-filled clearing. The scent of monster blood was especially strong, but something else pricked his senses, something Idris didn't expect: the scent of man.

He hurried into the mist, eyes catching on a rumpled heap in the road: Anya's cloak. He held it to his face, burying his nose in the fabric, breathing in the proof of her presence here, even as his stomach sank. *Why isn't she wearing it*?

He continued down the path, the fog thicker in the slight depression of this geothermal flat. Small puddles along the trail burped their earthen air, clogging his magic with sulfur. Up ahead, a small crossbow was lodged in one of the springs like a tiny shipwreck. The metal tooling was fine—*noble*. That explained the life-saving bolt he'd found in the woods.

Idris broke into an uneven jog, his body protesting fiercely. Wind gusted, clearing some of the steam, revealing another dark shape in the road. A body.

A reluctant sort of hope filled him, and he ran faster, boots skidding on the grit of the uneven path. When he reached the figure, he turned the body over—

"*Fuck*," Idris cursed, jerking back.

He'd only met Remy once, but he'd recognize the man's smug face anywhere. It'd been seared into Idris's brain since the moment he saw Remy at the Possum, smelled the sex on Anya's body, and felt a swift and illogical jealousy course through him. Idris really had been smitten since the moment he saw her.

This was not the Remy of his memory, though. The small, gnarled horns protruding from his blond hair, his claw-tipped fingers, and the nubs of new arms growing along his ribs told Idris everything he needed to know. That, and the black blood leaking out of the man's slashed neck.

Anya was a Mirror Criminal, after all. She had done well.

So why was the clearing so quiet?

Idris forged ahead, into the gloom. It only took him another few paces to spot Anya crumpled on the ground.

Idris rushed to her and sank to his knees, hands grasping at her hip, her shoulders. She was limp, her face alarmingly serene and streaked with monster blood and grime. Her pretty dress was soaked with red, hiked up on one side to reveal—

Idris's eyes widened at what he saw. The damage. The *blood*.

He lowered his ear to her mouth, listening for the faintest of breaths. He palpated her neck, feeling for a pulse.

It was there, but it was faint. She didn't have long.

"Anya." Terror made his tone guttural. "Anya, Dearest, stay with me."

Carefully—oh, so carefully—Idris gathered her into his arms. Her leg dangled in an awful manner, her boot knocking against his thigh as he carried her into the mist. With her head nestled against his chest, he pressed a firm kiss on her forehead.

She made a small sound in the back of her throat, roused by pain or movement or maybe his presence, he wasn't sure, but the sound was everything to him. *Everything*.

"I've got you," Idris said. "I've got you."

In the stories Idris had heard about the old custom of the Well of Fate, those seeking an altered future would plead with the water's surface, perhaps touch it with their fingertips. But so close to death, Anya didn't just need a new Fate—she needed a miracle.

When Idris reached the pool, he didn't think about his Oath. He didn't think about his Fortune. He didn't think about her Death. He thought only of Anya's wellbeing as he waded into the strange, warm water.

When he was submerged up to his waist, Idris gently swiveled Anya in his arms, supporting her back and neck, keeping her head tipped above the water. Her eyes fluttered open, finding his face, wide with wonder. He only waited a moment, long enough for her to understand what was happening. Then, in the faint light of morning, with bloodied hands and fear in his heart, Idris pushed Anya—his love—beneath the blue-green surface of the pool.

52

REBORN

ANYA

It happened exactly the way the Mirror of Death showed me.

Idris, handsome and formidable, backlit by a splash of dimming stars and purple dawn. His shoulder-length hair, dark and tangled and drenched with the sweat of a fight I had not witnessed. His blood-soaked hands cradling me with extraordinary gentleness. His mouth—one that had whispered to me, worshipped me, lavished me with passion—set into a grim line. And those beautiful eyes. Blue-green as the river I'd grown up on. Shining tearfully in the twilight. Filled with concern and resolve and *love.*

Then: *water.*

Not the Wend as I'd thought when I first saw this Fate, but a magical pool hidden deep within a haunted wood. The water that created the Mirror in which I'd seen this exact vision.

As Idris submerged me, the numbness in my injured leg cleared, revealing a pain I thought I'd escaped. I cried out, water filling my mouth, muffling my scream, bubbles fizzing all around. I felt bone, muscle, and skin knitting back together again. Making me *whole* again.

Impossible. Excruciating. Brilliant.

I opened my eyes and underwater I saw the silver storm of a Mirror's surface. New visions played out before me. Wicker licking Idris's face. Hattie's nose wrinkling with amusement. Sunlight filtering through tree branches; lily pads on water. Blue-green eyes staring at me across a pillow, across a table, across the hill of my stomach. Wrinkled hands—*my* hands—tracing a faint round scar on a big, creased palm. The sound of my own laughter. The sound of his murmurs. A full life. A happy life.

Then I saw other Fates. Flashes of life and death all across this land.

Babies born, homes built, raging fires, freak accidents. Hordes of monsters streaming from the woods and knights of all orders marching out from the capital. I saw the Lord with a soot-streaked face, his silly robes tattered. I saw flaming swords and axes, blood and gore and mud. Stone walls crumbling and repaired.

I saw snowfall and clouds parting. Buds forming, flowers opening. The decay of animal carcasses, seeds sown and grown from their flesh. Forests and mountains burgeoning with growth.

Underneath the surface of the pool, I saw the Fate of *all* stretching out before me like a map of time itself. I saw the world turning from far, far away.

This didn't feel like drowning.

This felt like pressure and like weightlessness, like a new life unfurling before me.

53

CLEAN SLATE

ANYA

Rain pattered gently on the roof, a song that made me want to burrow deeper under the warm sheets that surrounded me. I turned my face into the pillow beneath my head, a soft moan of satisfaction escaping my lips. After so many nights spent on the ground, *this* was what I'd been missing. I curled my toes under the weight of countless blankets, then arched my back, straightened my legs in a delicious stretch, and rolled over.

Gray light streamed in through the window, casting the room in a gauzy pallor. Rivulets of water ran down the pane, obscuring the outside. An upholstered chair had been dragged right up next to the bed but sat empty. There was a dresser in the far corner, with countless tiny bottles scattered across its top. A woman wearing an apron stood before it, mixing tinctures, filling the room with an astringent herbal scent.

At the sound of my stirring, she turned. Her strong jaw and short blonde hair were vaguely familiar to me, but I couldn't place her. My memory felt foggy.

"Anya," she cooed, her voice like warm velvet. "You're awake."

The woman floated closer, her layered skirts swishing. She laid the back of her hand across my forehead, her skin cool but not drastically different in temperature from my own.

"Your fever has broken, well done," she told me, as if my slumber had been a feat.

Then again, maybe it had. My body felt weak with over-rest. "What...happened?" I croaked.

"Stay right there," she said with a wink, "and I'll get someone who can say."

She hurried from the room, the wooden floorboards squeaking. I heard her muffled voice, then a much deeper one, with heavier strides returning. The door flung open again, and this time Idris filled its space.

Darkness ringed his tired eyes. His face was clean-shaven but drawn. Yet at the sight of my wakefulness, his expression shifted from weary to uncertain to rejoicing.

He rushed over and sank into the chair positioned at my bedside. Then his scarred palm was smoothing my hair out of my eyes, cupping my cheek. I gripped his wrist, finding it warm and firm and *here*. With me.

"I'll give you two some privacy," the woman said, then the door snicked shut.

Idris's eyes searched mine, like he couldn't quite believe that I was awake—like he hadn't *expected* me to wake up. "Anya, Dearest," he murmured, and there was so much contained in the endearment. Pain and fear and suffering. Doubt and dread and anguish. Gratitude and affection and...something deeper, more passionate and possessive.

Memory swept across my mind like a storm.

Dungeon. Forest. Monster. Pool. Then flashes of the aftermath of my Death Mirror's vision: my head lifting above the surface again, blood rinsing off Idris's hands and dispersing, his arms hugging me close, his shirt sopping wet. His resonant voice pleading, "*Please* be alright. *Please* be alright. I can't lose you. I *won't* lose you. This can't be *it*."

The clouds of memory shifted, and next I saw the underside of Idris's scruffy jawline, tree branches and blue sky above his head. I heard Oderin's wry voice. Saw the golden sheen of Briar's fur. Felt the juddering of hooves. Heard the squeak of hinges. Smelled fresh linens. Tasted tinctures.

As it all came rushing back, I stared at Idris here and now, wondering what had happened between my blips of consciousness. In the moments I couldn't remember. My lungs rattled with a long sigh.

Idris's thumb brushed my temple. "How do you feel?"

I knew his question was about my physical being, but as I stared at his concerned face, I answered with the first word that came to mind: "Safe."

His forehead furrowed, and a short exhale left him, like my answer was the sweetest of gifts. "Do you hurt?"

The question brought with it a new flash of memory: of shredded skin and exposed bone and *pain*, so much pain.

I sat up in a rush, head swimming with a nauseating dizziness. I flung back the covers to reveal my legs, bare and untouched beneath the short hem of a fresh nightgown. Pink scars swirled in a delicate pattern over my right leg, but otherwise, it was *just fine*.

I covered my face with my hands and let out another long, shaky sigh. I breathed. Breathed again. I remembered the well's magic healing me, but *this*? This was hard to wrap my head around. My leg had been ruined beyond repair.

"How does it feel?" Idris prompted.

I wiggled my toes, circled my ankle. "Like nothing."

He moved back to me, then, crowding the small bed with his huge frame. As he laid on his side beside me, the mattress dipped under his weight, tilting me against his chest like gravity.

I gave into its pull.

Nestling against his solid body, I snaked my arm around his waist, sliding my hand underneath his shirt to feel his warm solidity. He snaked his fingers into my hair, then ran them down my shoulder, over my hip, and around to the small of my back, pulling me closer. His movements were gentle, restrained, like he didn't want to break me. I squeezed him tighter, my limbs heavy, but also strong and needy for the delicious strength of his hold.

His chin grazed my cheek, and he pressed a kiss to my temple. I felt a bit of wetness cling to my hairline, and I pulled back to stare at his face. A tear slid over his cheekbone.

Here was a man who'd grown up in poverty, experienced the loss of his family one by one, who was huge and strong and incredibly brave, who fought terrifying abominations with a sword of fucking *flame*—and he was moved to tears of relief over *me*.

My heart pounded in my chest like it wanted to break free, to offer itself up to him just to take those tears away. I felt so full in that moment I thought my ribs might crack open.

Idris didn't wipe his face or turn away. He let me witness his emotion plainly. "I thought I'd lost you."

"But you didn't," I said, wiping his tears away with my fingertips. "I'm here because of you."

He leaned closer, the tip of his nose brushing the tip of mine. He breathed me in, then pressed a kiss to my lips, the touch so tender it felt breakable. I was done with feeling breakable, though. I deepened the kiss, fortifying myself with this moment. Idris acquiesced, cradling my face, opening his mouth to devour mine.

But new thoughts were rushing in from all sides. Questions that needed answering.

I pulled back. "Where are we?"

"We're outside the capital," Idris answered. "Oderin's sister's house. She's been tending to you."

I sat up again and considered the room. Idris did the same, adjusting so that his back rested against the headboard. When I looked at him again—his huge frame taking up so much space in my tiny sickbed—I remembered the last time I saw him propped up like this. Broad chest and hard abdominals. I flushed.

Seeming to note the direction of my thoughts, Idris smirked and pulled me to him, wrapping his arm around my shoulders. "Seems you're feeling better."

My attention found the dresser again, tinctures scattered atop it. "Wait—Oderin's sister Phina?" I asked. "That's who's been taking care of me?" *That's* why her strong jaw and coloring looked so familiar—she looked like a more feminine Oderin. At Idris's confused look, I elaborated. "Oderin told me about how you met. The horse thing."

Idris's smile widened for a flash, then he kissed me again, quick and chaste.

But other memories were beginning to seep in, cold as the draft wafting inside from the window. The rain poured harder, thundering on the roof.

It's for the best that we part ways, he'd told me in the dungeon.

And yet he'd followed me into the forest.

Found me.

Saved me.

"You're here," I noted.

"I'm here."

I touched the triangle of skin exposed by his shirt, then dipped my fingertips underneath, grazing the scar that crossed his right pectoral. The old injury had faded considerably, the scar tissue no longer so hard and gnarled. He caught my hand with his and kissed the center of my palm, then rested it back on his chest, over his heart.

I glanced up to find him studying me. "You came for me."

One corner of his mouth lifted, a mischievous grin taking shape. "I came for you."

Realizing the double-entendre, I smiled and shoved his chest—but our humor dissipated quickly.

"Are you...staying?" I asked, allowing the true implication—staying *with me?*—to go unsaid.

"I should've never left, Anya," he said quickly. "I was—" A sigh gusted out of him. "I thought I was doing the right thing, but I was wrong. I was afraid I'd endanger you even more than I already had. I was afraid that our tangled Fates would lead me to do something horrible. I was afraid I'd lose—" He broke off, voice catching, but he wasn't done. "I was afraid I'd lose you like I lost Grinnick. My fault. I thought you'd be better off without me."

"Clearly, I wasn't."

He tipped his head. "But you were," he insisted. "You took the risk. You did what few would *dare* do and braved the forest by yourself. You faced multiple foes and succeeded. You're *incredible.*"

"I would've died without you," I whispered.

He pulled me closer, hugging me against him. I could feel the tension rippling through him, the torment of his own dark memories. The worry that hadn't quite yet faded.

"How long have we been here?" I asked.

"Three days."

"Three—" I shook my head disbelievingly. "I've been asleep for three days?"

He nodded. "More, if you count the journey."

Though I'd noticed the weariness on his face when he'd walked in, I saw the depth of it now. A sleeplessness that seemed to have soaked into his marrow. "Have *you* slept?" I asked.

A doting expression—all up-tilted brows—spread across his forehead. "Fitfully," he answered, and the word warmed me to my core.

I slid my palm appreciatively over the expanse of his chest, then angled it up toward his throat, my thumb finding the deep hollow. His skin was smooth, tan, untouched by—

I jerked back. "Your Oath tattoo is gone."

"So is yours."

I swallowed, sensing the absence of the Oath of Proving I'd taken. But that was nothing compared to *Idris's* freedom. His neck didn't even bear the faded mark of retirement—his was completely gone. Like it never existed.

"You're no longer bound? *How?*"

He shrugged. "The Well," he said, as if the absence of his Oath was a simple thing, and not *everything*. "It healed my wounds, too. Even old ones."

I shook my head, struggling to wrap my head around what he was telling me. "Are you alright?"

He seemed surprised by the question. "Yes?"

"No, I mean..." I sat up taller, no longer leaning on him but regarding him fully. He hadn't *wanted* to give up his Oath, and yet the pool had taken it from him. "What about Grinnick? What about—"

"I'm glad it's gone," Idris said. "I planned to retire after I helped you anyway, but then I entered the water, and I felt it dissolving, and I was glad. I let it happen. I let it go."

"But—"

"You were right, Anya," he continued. "About Grinnick. About everything. I was hiding behind my Oath—not out of duty or true service of good, but self-punishment." He gripped the side of my neck, holding my gaze as he repeated firmly, "I'm glad it's gone."

"Your Fortune..." I trailed off. "It was the same as my Death, after all. My rebirth."

Idris nodded. "The end of one Fate and the start of another."

"How does that make sense, though? How is *that* your greatest Fortune?"

He tipped his head like he couldn't believe my question. "Don't you see, Anya? *You* are my Fortune. Searching for you. Helping you. Giving up my Oath for you. Loving y—" His eyes widened, like he hadn't meant to admit it now, like this. But then he smiled, settling into his truth. "*You* are my greatest Fate, and loving you is my greatest Fortune."

I stared at him, a torrent of emotion flooding my chest like a storm of liquid gold. I was overcome. I was speechless. I was...probably worrying him with my lack of response.

"You know I love you, too, right?" I managed. "And it's not just puppy love, it's *real*, it's—"

Idris interrupted me with a kiss—one meant to scorch. His mouth slid over mine, and I returned his vigor with my own, a blaze of joy streaking through me like a shooting star. I moaned softly into his mouth, clutched at his shirt, aching for his closeness—but my body was still weak and recovering. I could feel it in the way I lost steam, even now, my fervor cooling despite the curling need in my belly.

Idris seemed to sense it, too, his cascade of kisses softening until the moment faded altogether, and he simply held me against him, warm and safe and secure in his arms. For a while, we listened to the rain.

But there was still so much to know, to talk through.

"What of Halgren?"

Idris chuckled. "What about Halgren?"

"Does it still glow blue?"

"No," he said. "That was a magic bestowed upon the blade by my Oath. Without it, Halgren is just a sword. Does that disappoint you?"

"A little," I said, quirking a brow. "Can't say I didn't enjoy the sight of you wielding it." I held out my fist, miming a few sword slashes.

His chuckle morphed into a laugh, shaking us both.

"Without Halgren's flame, how did we escape the forest?"

His laughter died. "I carried you."

"Did you not encounter more foes?"

"We had unexpected help," he said, and for a moment I thought he wouldn't go on, but then he clarified: "Valiant Knights."

That shocked me. "Patrolling the forest?"

"Something like that."

I sensed there was more to that story, but we didn't have to unveil every secret now, in this bed. More answers would come in time.

"Oderin helped, too," Idris added.

"How did you get past him to begin with?"

"I bested him," Idris stated—not without a hint of pride. "Shackled him to a tree."

"I'm sure he loved that. Is he here?"

"He's out. He'll be back."

The more we spoke, the more I thought about everything I'd faced—everything I'd done. I wondered about the one-eyed man, the monsters, the other Orders, and their secrets. More topics to one day uncover with Idris—but not presently. Not when it was dawning on me that I'd faced all those horrors for a *reason*. For a place so dear to me that I'd do it all again in a heartbeat if it meant I could return...

"Can I...can I go home now?" I asked Idris.

He grinned. "Yes. But we have one more stop, first."

Right. Of course. My absolution wouldn't be complete without an audience with the Lord. A part of me feared he'd find another twisted way to keep me imprisoned, but Idris's assuredness eased my concerns.

I regarded him straight-on. I had one more question—and it was the most important one. "Will you...come to Waldron-on-Wend with me?"

"I will escort you, if you wish," Idris said, his tone reluctant.

Apparently, declarations of love weren't enough. He needed me to speak plainly—to ask for *exactly* what I wanted. I was happy to oblige.

"No," I said firmly. "I mean: will you *stay* in Waldron with me? Now that you aren't Oath-bound?"

His face remained stoic for a moment—then it quaked, like the first rumbling of an avalanche of devotion. He swiveled, cradling my cheeks with two big, beautiful hands. "If you'll have me," he said. "If you want me to stay with you, then I'll stay."

"Then you're staying," I confirmed, nodding my head. "You're escorting me to Waldron and you're staying and you're never leaving, because I love you, Idris, and the Fate I want is the Fate with you and me together."

"Good," he said breathlessly, "because that's the *only* Fate I want."

54

FREEDOM

IDRIS

"I admit I didn't expect you to return," the Lord said, leaning back in his throne and hooking one leg over the armrest.

"I aim to surprise," Anya said, showing no insult at the Lord's comment. She stood beside Idris wearing one of Phina's dresses, a plain blue one that was too long, but contrasted the warmth of her hair beautifully.

Minutes ago, Idris had entered the great hall feeling invincible—but seeing the Lord's shrewd expression had dimmed his optimism. The Lord was nothing if not selfish and unpredictable.

"Your Oath of Proving has vanished without record," the Lord continued. "You say that is the work of the Well?"

"So, too, does your Mighty Knight," Anya pointed out, inclining her head in Oderin's direction.

Idris's friend stood off to one side in full regalia, his expression flat. He'd been unwavering in his loyalty to Idris over the past week—even the gripes about Idris shackling him to a tree had been half-hearted in the aftermath of Anya's quest. Oderin had gone above and beyond to keep Anya safe, and Idris would forever be in his debt for that.

Oderin did not show his bias toward Idris now, though. Never before the Lord. He stared straight ahead, blank and indifferent.

Anya gestured at Hammond, who also stood nearby. "The historical records your Mirror Knight brought also state that Oaths—"

"I'm aware of the history of the Well and its effects on Oaths," Lord Haron said.

Then why did you ask her? Idris thought irritably.

"She entered the forest alone," Oderin cut in.

The Lord's beady eyes flicked to the Mighty Knight. "And she had no help on her path to the water?"

"She did not," Oderin replied truthfully, still not looking at Idris or Anya.

"What of my Valiant Knight?" Lord Haron asked Oderin. "What hand in this did he play?"

"No hand but duty," Oderin said. "He made a kill. Should be in the ledger."

"Did he make the kill in rescue?" the Lord pressed.

"Only in rescue of himself," Oderin said.

All true.

"And you wish to retire?" the Lord asked Idris. "After all this time?"

"I do."

The Lord's eyes narrowed on Idris. "I feel no loyalty from you anymore. Your Oath is already severed, your mark gone."

"It dissolved," Idris answered. "In the Well of Fate."

The Lord's eyes flicked to Oderin, who nodded.

The Lord lowered his leg and leaned forward, gripping the arms of his throne. "I am to believe that you both entered the forest separately, you both located the Well without the others' help, and you both dissolved your Oaths?"

"That is as it happened," Oderin said. "By my Mighty word, I swear it."

What Oderin didn't divulge: the fact that Idris carried Anya the last few feet to the water's edge. He hadn't witnessed that part, and Idris had told him only that Anya had found the pool on her own. It was the truth, if only the most favorable version. Oderin hadn't wanted to know more.

The Lord swiveled his cruel gaze back to Anya. "I am a man of my word," he said slowly, begrudgingly. "Therefore..." He paused, clearly enjoying making everyone wait. "You are absolved."

Anya's face lit up, and she squeezed her fists to her chest, jubilation making her bounce on the balls of her feet. Idris's heart felt just as joyous, but he held a firm expression, knowing that their victory would irritate the Lord if they flaunted it.

Indeed, the Lord held up a hand, limiting Anya's cheer. "You still know too much," he said to the both of them. "That in and of itself is no criminal offense, but without the binding of even retired Oaths, I am concerned. How can I trust that you won't spread knowledge to which you have no claim?"

"What knowledge?" Idris asked. He was already enjoying his Oathless existence, his ability to blatantly sidestep the Lord's questions with no recourse. No leash-yanking.

Oderin jumped in, just as Idris hoped he would. "The Well cleared their Fates, m'Lord," he said. "It's possible it cleared...other things, too."

It was not a lie, but the implication was far from accurate—that was the beauty of vague statements. Oderin was not inexperienced at playing his part, navigating his role. Though Idris didn't understand his friend's loyalty to the Lordship at times, he certainly respected Oderin's dedication to the *just* execution of his knighthood.

Lord Haron stroked his chin, considering the Mighty Knight's statement. His eyes narrowed on Idris and Anya, as if he could see inside their minds, find the lie. But after a few moments, he sat back, his concerns seemingly appeased—at least for now.

"Any hint of betrayal of knowledge, and I'll send knights to your door, Anya Alvara," the Lord said. "I know many who'd gladly bring harm to Idris and his associates."

An empty threat—but the Lord didn't know that. No one did.

Idris had been shocked to run into Heris, Mariana, and two other Valiant Knights inside the haunted wood. He'd been sopping wet, with Anya's unconscious body draped across his arms, not a half hour into his trek through the forest back to Oderin.

Puzzlingly, they had cleared the path of threats so Idris could carry her to safety. When asked why Heris would endeavor to kill Anya one moment and spare her the next, Heris had narrowed his cruel gaze on Mariana.

"Remember our mercy when the war comes," she had said.

A warning. A promise.

Idris didn't quite know what she meant, but paired with her hint about an uprising, he wasn't interested in learning more. When once such talk would've concerned Idris, he felt disconnected from politics and the factions of the Order of the Valiant now. He didn't much care about the Lord's Fate, nor the secret machinations of his former Order. Uprisings, secrets—Idris was henceforth uninvolved. The only future he cared about now was his shared future with Anya. For the first time in his life, Idris was eager to face what lay ahead. With Anya as his North Star, his Fortune, his Fate, he had no doubt that his future contained promise.

With his Oath dissolved, he planned to enjoy his freedom. It's what Grinnick would've wanted.

Even so, Lord Haron's certainty that many a Valiant Knight would be glad to hunt Idris down—to silence him—wasn't far *enough* from the truth for him to want to step out of line. Heris had, by Mariana's urging, begrudgingly shown him mercy this time—but he didn't trust the hidden intentions behind their help, nor would he rely upon it happening again. Idris would be honest with Anya about his past—his whole past—but there was no reason for them to extend that knowledge beyond the bounds of their relationship.

"There's one more thing I must see for myself," the Lord said, bringing Idris's attention back into the room. The Lord raised a hand, gesturing at an attendant.

From a set of double doors behind the throne, a series of Mirror Knights appeared. They carried the Mirrors of Fortune and Death into the hall, arranging them atop a pair of awaiting stands Idris hadn't noticed when he came in. Once the Mirrors were in place, the Guards fanned around them, standing at attention with hands on hilts.

Lord Haron opened his palm toward the Mirrors.

It took Idris a moment to remember this part of Anya's mission. The Lord wished for her to gaze into the Mirrors of Fortune and Death. And Idris, too, apparently.

Idris glanced back at Oderin. His friend's stoicism had fissured, revealing a flash of curiosity. Hammond, too, appeared quite interested. It seemed everyone wanted to know what the magical waters had done to his and Anya's Fates.

Idris grasped Anya's hand, holding firm as they walked together toward the Mirrors. Her palm was clammy, but she gripped him tightly, brave and self-assured as she approached her new visions. When they neared the Mirrors, they broke contact, and Anya stepped forward first.

In audience of the Lord, his ledgermasters and squires, Hammond and the other Mirror Knights, Oderin, and Idris, Anya positioned herself before the Mirror of Fortune. She waited two heartbeats, three. Finally, its silver-storm surface rippled like water—but rather than clearing into a specific vision as it normally would, the Mirror remained opaque as an overcast sky.

Anya glanced at Idris quizzically—then back to the Mirror. The surface of it stirred again, returning to its usual reflective appearance.

Her Fortune was…blank?

"Curious," the Lord said. "Try the next one."

Anya did as she was told, though her steps faltered as she faced the Mirror of Death. Idris's throat clenched around a ball of dread, fearing that the woman he loved would once again see *him* as her end. But the Mirror of Death did the same as the Mirror of Fortune: it showed nothing but a gray haze.

"Keep moving," the Lord prompted.

Idris stepped up to the Mirror of Fortune, remembering the vision he'd seen for so many years—one that had scared him. Made him doubt the type of man he was. He waited for what felt like an eternity before the Mirror of Fortune rippled, revealing the same sort of blankness Anya had seen.

He looked to her now, standing beyond the Mirrors. Idris walked toward her, then faced his Mirror of Death. What had once shown him countless deaths over the years was blank.

"Very curious," the Lord said. "You may go now."

The order snapped Idris out of the hesitant pause of his non-visions. There was no time to waste. He placed his fingertips on the center of Anya's back, guiding her quickly, eager to exit the chamber before the Lord could say anything more.

As they neared Oderin, Idris's friend turned, clearly intending to see them out—but the Lord called to the Mighty Knight. "Major Oderin, there are additional matters to discuss."

Oderin paused, sparing Idris one last glance. It was a look of kinship, a flash of kindness. Without the pull of his Order to Fenrir, Idris wasn't sure when he'd see his friend again—but he would. Oderin was too close a connection not to visit on occasion. The idea of traveling to Fenrir just for a drink with Oderin sounded quite pleasant, in fact. Better than any reason that had beckoned him here before.

Idris returned Oderin's quick grin, then guided Anya out of the hall. He kept his fingers on her spine as they hurried through the keep and out into the drizzly gray of morning.

"I thought the Well of Fate *changed* the future, not nullified it." Anya whispered as they walked across the courtyard. "What do you think it means?"

Idris didn't presume to understand why their Fates were blank instead of altered. Perhaps all that monster blood had warped the effects of the pool, just as their presence warped the Fates of anyone who neared them. He didn't know—and he didn't much care about the how or why. He only cared that Anya was here by his side.

"It means our Fate truly is what we make of it," he replied.

Anya smiled. "Then let's make it great."

55

HOMECOMING

ANYA

The air was cold, and the clouds were dark and heavy on the day we reached the juncture where the High Road branched off toward Waldron-on-Wend. The harsh wind smelled of snow, and ice crusted the thorny wild rose bushes that edged the road. Briar's breaths clouded around his wooly head, but his ears remained pricked forward, his steps even and assured.

"You're quiet," Idris murmured into my hair, his breath warming the shell of my ear.

For three weeks, we had ridden Briar in tandem, braved cold nights by snuggling close together under the shelter of our tiny tent, and made love under the stars and in the plush beds of welcoming small-town inns. Yet even now, his hot breath on my skin sent a thrill through me, awakening a pressure in my belly that never seemed to fully sleep. It seemed his hands couldn't bear to not touch me.

Without his Oath, Idris had lost some of his restraint—no less shy and somewhat taciturn in the presence of strangers, but when it was just us, he was open. He'd filled our travel days with flute-song and told me long-winded stories about his time in the Order of the Valiant with honest abandon. The change in him had been apparent, like a bulb opening to spring, and yet he was still the man I'd fallen for in the midst of my lowest lows—protective, humorous, kind.

The loss of his Oath had only increased the intensity of his qualities, like the pale shades of sunrise deepening into the richest chroma of dawn. I felt the warmth of it even now, with his body flush against mine. The absence of his breastplate—*Grinnick's* breastplate, strapped to the back of the saddle along with Halgren, his retired sword—only intensified the sensation of his closeness.

"I'm...nervous," I admitted, even as I tipped my head to one side, allowing him greater access to my neck.

"Are you not eager to return?" he asked, brushing my braided hair off my skin so he could speak against it. "After *weeks* of excitable stories about Waldron, are you suddenly reluctant to end our journey?"

I chuckled. "I admit I'll miss having you all to myself. I fear you'll be quite popular once folks realize how strong and capable you are."

"These hands are reserved for you and your needs first," Idris said, taking my thigh in a firm grip.

I hummed my appreciation for that statement—then sobered.

Since we'd left Fenrir, I'd been counting down the days until we reached Waldron-on-Wend. But now that we were mere minutes from home—cresting the final hill—my eagerness to see Hattie, Wicker, and my beloved neighbors was twinged with the faintest insecurity.

What if the town hadn't missed me? What if they'd only missed my usefulness? My excitement to return to everything I knew had waned with the coalescing knowledge that *everything I knew* wasn't the same anymore. *I* had changed. Would the new me fit with the life I'd come to cherish so deeply?

"You're afraid it won't be the same," Idris answered for me.

"I'm afraid I'll find that they've grown accustomed to my absence," I said. "What if I wasn't as important to the town as I thought? What if I didn't *belong* in the way I always believed?"

Snow began to drift down from above, swirling in the frigid breeze. Fat flakes collected in my hair, on my cloak, the pommel of the saddle, catching in Briar's mane.

"That's ridiculous, Dearest," Idris said, and I glanced back at him, seeing truth in those blue-green eyes.

He jerked his chin forward. "How could *you* not belong here?"

We'd reached the peak of the hill, and from its vantage—even with the gentle flurry swirling around us—we could see the town in full. Smoke rising from thatched-roof cottages. Sheep dotting the swell of the surrounding hillsides, their white fleece swiftly blending with the weather. Farmer Quinn's fence line.

The cobblestone curve of Swan's Row, nudged right up against the gray-blue slash of an ice-crusted river.

Waldron-on-Wend.

Idris clicked his tongue, urging Briar down the hill into town. As we descended, I caught sight of tents lining Stone Hill, and the bright flames of bonfires dotting the festival flats with flashes of orange and red.

A gasp escaped my lips.

"What now?" Idris asked.

"Astrophel," I said. "Today is the welcoming of winter. My...birthday."

"Your birthday," Idris repeated, realizing, "Your thirtieth."

How could I forget? This was the day my Fate became fixed. Arriving home *today* couldn't be more fortuitous.

"Fuck," Idris added, "I didn't get you a gift."

"Are you kidding?" I knocked my heels against Briar's side, encouraging our horse into a jog. "This is the best gift you could've given me. You got me home."

Snow blurred in my vision as Briar picked up speed. Idris sat steadily in the saddle behind me, his hips rocking against mine, one hand still gripping my thigh. The shepherd boy that Farmer Timmons stationed on the edge of the northwestern pasture—Dwin—poked his head out of the small shelter by the gate, taking note of our arrival. When I waved from the saddle, Dwin hopped the fence and took off over the bridge, racing ahead of us up Stone Hill.

By the time we'd reached the bridge ourselves, folks were collecting in the stone circle. Murmurs reached my ears, and I listened to the doubt and excitement that swept through the revelers as Briar climbed the rise. Evening was descending, brought on more quickly by the thick snow clouds—but the moment the raging bonfires came into view again—so close, now—I knew the long night would be filled with merriment. With joy. How could it not, when I was back in Waldron-on-Wend?

We were halfway up Stone Hill when I heard my name ripple through the throng of townsfolk. Then the cheers started. Shouts of glee, of welcome, of relief.

"Still afraid they didn't miss you?" Idris asked me.

The cheers intensified, folks jumping up and down, waving, crying out. Tears welled in my eyes and my muscles tensed with anticipation. I gripped Idris's hand, overcome.

A sharp cry pierced the air, and then I saw Hattie elbowing her way to the front of the crowd. She threw back the hood of her cloak, her blonde curls bouncing as she hurried closer. Seeing her flushed cheeks and freckled face broke all my remaining doubt and restraint. Without bothering to halt Briar, I dropped the reins, swung my leg over his neck, and slid onto the snow-dusted ground. Then I was running up the last little stretch of path.

"Anya!" Hattie called, her voice barely audible over the raucous, deafening cheering of the crowd at her back.

"Hattie!" I shouted back, running full speed through the field.

A dark shape broke free of the revelers, bounding past Hattie and straight toward me. I dropped to my knees and opened my arms, and then Wicker's gangly body slammed into me. He licked my face with hot wet kisses, whining and wiggling. I sunk my fingers into his wiry fur, hugging him close, tears slicking my cheeks.

Then Hattie was there, knocking me back with her own embrace. "You're here! You did it! What took you so long?"

"Lots to explain," I said, burying my face into the crook of her neck and shoulder, her cloak scratchy against my snow-chilled face. "But I did it. I'm here. I'm back." Then I was sobbing with joy, shuddering against my friend with one hand still gripping my old dog's fur.

The rest of the crowd was pressing in, now, familiar faces shouting joyful welcome.

"You brought a *man*," Hattie whispered into my ear as she released me. Her brow arched suggestively. "The man from your Mirror of Death?"

"Long story," I told her.

"I'll say." She pulled me to my feet. "Does it have a happy ending?"

I glanced back at Idris, who had just dismounted and was already fielding questions from Hugh and Vera. He made eye contact with me and smiled, amused, but warm and true.

When I looked back at Hattie, the suggestiveness in her expression was all the more plain. "Happy ending, indeed," she teased. "Death by orgasm, perhaps? By the Fates, look at him. He can't take his eyes off you." Her eyebrow arched impossibly higher. "Seems your Fate is fixed on *him*. Happy birthday, by the way."

"Just in time for Astrophel!" Martha said, sweeping me up into a big hug of her own.

"Martha, it's so good to see you," I said, rocking with her from side to side.

She pulled back and touched my cheek, affectionate as a mother. "We were worried *sick*," she said. "Are you well? Is it all resolved?"

"All resolved, yes."

With that out of the way, Martha leaned in. "You've missed quite a bit of town news. Illian is engaged to the jeweler's apprentice now!"

I glanced in Idris's direction. He was doing his best to make his way over, in spite of the town's curious attention.

"You hear that, Idris? Illian is engaged."

He smiled like this was the most welcome news of the evening. "It's about time."

Martha's mouth fell open in a look of shocked glee. "Seems you have some news of your own?" she prodded, eyeing Idris, but our conversation was cut short by a long line of others demanding hugs. Vera, Hugh, Farmer Quinn, Farmer Timmons, then Timmons' son, Francis, who appeared ever so slightly dismayed by Idris's presence.

By the time I made it to the tents, my muscles felt doughy from the constant kneading of my friends and neighbors. The festival was starting up again after the interruption of our arrival, music floating on the icy wind. Folks placed sausage rolls, mugs of cider, and snowflake candies into Idris and my hands, and encumbered, we walked with Hattie over to a table by one of the bonfires.

Hattie and I sat close, with Idris settling across from us and Wicker lying on my feet underneath the table. The snow was still falling in earnest, but nobody around us seemed to mind (though Wicker seemed happy to have found a bit of shelter).

"Where's Briar?" I asked suddenly, realizing the disappearance of our horse.

"Handed him off to…" Idris trailed off, glancing around. "Someone?"

I laughed, loving the look of him across from me, with the festival tents and lanterns spread out behind him. His cheeks were tinged gold in the light of the nearby bonfire. His eyes were boring into mine, dazzling even in the growing dark.

Hattie looped her arm through mine and rested her head on my shoulder. "I don't want to bring things down, Anya, but *Fates*, I was so afraid," she said breathlessly. "I felt so lost without you."

"I'm sure you were just fine without me," I said, leaning into her touch.

The smile hadn't faded from Idris's cheeks as he watched us. It remained even as he sipped his cider.

"Capable, sure," Hattie said, "but *'just fine,'* no. We all missed you sorely, but me most of all."

"Of course," I said, taking a hefty bite of my sausage roll.

"Of course," she emphasized.

A thousand questions spread between us, but there would be plenty of time to relay the long tale later. Right now, I needed a taste of normalcy.

"How's the Possum?" I asked.

"Prettier than ever," Hattie said. "While you were gone, I had a whole slew of repairs done. Hugh took care of the mold in the storeroom. Farmers Timmons and Quinn took care of the tree out back, going so far as to chop and stack it for firewood. Francis even swept your chimney, no strings attached."

"Seriously?" I asked, finding it hard to swallow another bite of sausage with the sudden lump in my throat. "You all pitched in for me?" An old panic rose, reminding me of my mother. "But how will I ever repay—"

"Anya, we love you," Hattie interrupted fiercely. "You've done so much for this town. It was high time they did something in return—and they were happy to. Excited, even, to get it all done in time for your return. Not because they felt indebted but because they care about you. I know your mother felt like love was a transaction, but…well, we all just want the best for you. That's it. You owe us nothing."

I swallowed the lump in my throat and squeezed her hand back, blinking the fresh tears from my eyes.

"Who's Francis?" Idris cut in.

"Her betrothed." Hattie waggled her eyebrows.

Idris looked to me, eyes wide.

"He's no one," I assured him.

"Just a chimney sweep," Hattie said with a wink.

I couldn't help but laugh, and Idris joined in reluctantly, still looking confused. I twisted my foot out from Wicker's weight and found Idris's leg under the table, nudging his knee with the toe of my boot. He caught my ankle—the one that had been injured—and, with a firm hand, slid his palm underneath the hem of my skirt and up my bare calf.

"Who's your betrothed?" Martha asked, sauntering over to our table and fixing her attention on Idris. Her cheeks were flushed, betraying her tipsiness. "Better be this tall glass of dark ale."

Idris released my leg, a mauve flush coloring his cheeks.

"Martha," I said. "The festival is exquisite. I'm sorry I missed the planning."

"Oh, not to worry, dear," she said. "You have many more years here to plan and organize, but for tonight, just enjoy yourself. You deserve it, after your long journey north."

Two months ago, before the Fate Ceremony, I would've been horrified to have given up my place among the planners of Astrophel. But tonight, as I looked around at the musicians and tents and fires, I decided Martha was right. I quite liked simply sitting here, enjoying the festivities.

"Oh, that reminds me," Martha added with a toss of her hands. She rummaged around in the front pocket of her apron and procured two baubles strung with colored yarn. One was a wooden horse painted in swirling gold. The other was a carved pine tree painted in many shades of green and brown.

She handed the horse to me and the tree to Idris. "Welcome to Waldron, Anya's betrothed," Martha said to Idris, then—before I could correct the misunderstanding—she danced away from our table and over to the nearby bonfire, around which folks were twirling to the rhythmic thump of drums and the accompanying lilt of a mandolin.

I glanced at Idris, wanting to apologize for Martha's teasing, but he was focused on the small tree she'd given him.

"It's a tradition in Waldron," I explained. "At Astrophel, we hang ornaments on our bedposts for the Fates. They're meant for good luck."

He looked up, appearing surprisingly moved by Martha's gesture. "I don't have a bedpost."

"You can borrow mine," I said, popping a snowflake candy in my mouth.

"Good luck, indeed," he murmured.

Hattie rested an elbow on the table, staring him down with a protective intensity I hadn't seen from her before. "So, tell me, Idris. Are you going to murder my friend?"

I choked on a sip of cider. "*Hattie.*"

"What? We all saw your Mirror. The rest of town might not remember his face, but I committed it to memory." She tapped her temple. It was uncharacteristically threatening.

"What happened to *death by orgasm*?" I whispered forcefully into her ear.

Now it was Idris's turn to choke on a sip of cider.

"It occurred to me that the handsome ones are usually the ones who get away with it," Hattie said.

I shoved her with my shoulder, knocking her off balance. "It's all been cleared up," I said. "I promise. I'll explain it all—but for tonight, just let me enjoy being home."

Hattie nodded, even as her eyes narrowed at Idris. "You promise not to harm her?"

Idris set down his own mug and met her stare with equal gravity. "I wouldn't dare."

56

A New Oath

"**M**artha was drunk," Anya said as she led Idris up the steps to the Possum and into the unlit common room.

Hattie was still out celebrating—as was everyone else. It was midnight, and Idris was loose-limbed from all the food, fermented cider, and the long journey here. The inn was quiet, peaceful, and all theirs—save for Wicker, of course, though he wasted no time trotting over to the unlit hearth, where a pile of blankets waited.

Idris could imagine himself coming home like this again and again. The woman ahead of him. The dog sighing by the fireplace. The glistening of bottles behind the bar. The worn floorboards underneath his feet. The pleasant scents of worn wood, washed linen, malted barley. He'd only been to the Pretty Possum Inn & Pub once, and yet it felt more like home than anywhere else.

He'd seen many different ends in his Mirror of Death, but one in particular had always stuck with him: his old body sitting by a hearth strangely similar to the one in the corner there, fading peacefully as he stared at the flames. The Well of Fate had given him a blank slate, and therefore Idris felt free to believe whatever vision he wanted.

This was what he wanted.

To bask in the glorious light of the woman before him and feel settled within the greater sense of belonging that a home—a *true* home—offered. Idris understood now why Anya spoke so highly of Waldron-on-Wend. It was exactly the sort of place he'd been craving since he was a boy. A community that was not bound by Oath or duty or even family, but by mutual desire, trust, and love. It was infinitely better than solitude.

"You can ignore her ramblings," Anya continued. "She means well, but she's also nosy, and somewhat obsessed with my *prospects*."

Idris thumbed the ornament in his pocket as he followed Anya deeper into the inn. Underneath the usual pub scents, the Pretty Possum smelled of roses and lemon and the ineffable warmth of its owner.

"I'm honored she considers me a prospect."

When they reached the bar, Anya turned, placing her palm on his chest. "I know Waldron"—she waved a hand—"all this—it's a big adjustment from living in the wilds on your own. We can take this as slowly as you want."

Idris stepped closer, invading her space, glad to finally have her alone again. He clutched her backside. "I have no intention of taking you slowly."

Before she had time to react, he hoisted her up, placing her on the counter. With their heights even, he stepped between her knees, barely having to bend down to glide his tongue along her sweet neck. He nosed under her jaw, smelling on her their travels: the sweat of exertion, snow-chilled wind, pine resin, Briar's fur, and *him*. Idris.

Fuck, he loved smelling himself on her skin.

"*Idris*." Anya enunciated his name like a swear—and though she was the one with hearing magic, the seductive lowness of her voice claimed something in him that he was happy to give to her.

He growled in her ear, a low rumble of need, making sure she knew exactly what her body did to him. She arched at the sound, clawing at his shoulders and back, pulling him closer.

"I'm *serious*," she said with a note of protest, but the way her body was squirming against him, he didn't think the conversation would go much further.

He could smell the erotic perfume of her arousal now, too—floral and beckoning—and he was eager to taste it.

"So am I," Idris said. "Martha's comments don't scare me."

Anya's lips parted, a tiny show of genuine gladness. If she enjoyed that small truth, maybe she'd relish his full honesty.

"Anya, for the longest time, my life was bound to monsters. Now, it's bound to a sweeter Fate." He squeezed her hips, willing her to understand, to listen carefully in spite of the desire building between them. "This is the last Oath I'll ever take, Dearest, so listen closely." A smile teased his lips as he stared into her fire-bright eyes. "I, Idris Togren, hereby take the Oath of the Order of Devotion, pledging my love and worship. You are my Fortune, and I will remain beside you until Death." Fearing that he sounded a little too intense for their first night in Waldron, Idris quickly added, "Or until you cast me away. Whatever happens sooner."

Anya's plush lips spread into the fullest, brightest smile he'd ever seen.

"Martha's comments don't scare me," he reiterated. "Do mine scare you?"

Anya shook her head, swiveling around to retrieve a piece of scrap paper and a nub of charcoal from behind the bar. Her tongue traced her upper lip as she scribbled something down.

"What are you writing?" With the way she was holding the paper in her cupped palm, Idris couldn't make out her script.

"I'm recording your name in my ledger—you know, to make it official."

Idris laughed. "How many others have sworn fealty?" he asked, playing along.

"How many do you think?"

He brushed an auburn strand of hair from her face. "How many men do I think would bind themselves to you by sacred Oath?" He stroked his chin, pretending to think. "*Legions.*"

Anya flushed, then showed him the scrap of paper with his name written on it in smudged charcoal. "Just you," she said, a corner of her mouth rising. "You're the only one worthy."

It was the most perfect thing she could've said to him.

For a moment, he was speechless—then he cupped her face and brought his mouth down on hers, claiming her with his tongue. She let out a soft little moan that he was immediately determined to draw out of her a second time—but her hands squeezing his biceps stopped him short.

"Did I ever tell you my Fortune?" Anya asked, her lips grazing his, her breath mingling with his own.

He pulled back, his forehead furrowing. "I don't think you did."

"It was water. At the time, I thought it stood for the Wend, but now…maybe it was the Well of Fate? I'm still not sure."

"Sounds strangely similar to mine," he observed.

"That's my point." She squeezed his arms a little tighter. "I think our Fortunes might've been the same."

His heart twisted at the memory of that day, the terror and desperation he'd felt as he lowered her into the water, and the overwhelming gratitude of holding her now. He grazed her cheek with the backs of his fingers—reverent.

"I think they're *still* the same," Anya went on. "I think my Fate has always been with you, even before I knew you. And now that our Fates are for us to decide, you are still the Fortune and Death I choose."

He took her jaw in his hand, guiding her face up to meet his mouth again, pouring all his devotion into the kiss. "Ask from me whatever you want," he said against her lips, "and I'll happily oblige."

Her pupils dilated, darkness swallowing up her pale brown irises. "Whatever I want?"

"Whatever you want."

"What a gentleman," Anya teased.

Moving swiftly, he gathered the layers of her dress up and ducked his head underneath. She squealed, laughing as he grazed his tongue up the length of her inner thigh. She hiked one leg over his shoulder, exposing all of herself to him under the cover of her dress. Before he reached all the way up, though, he paused to bury his face into the soft flesh of her leg—the one with the scars. The one that had almost caused him to lose her.

"Maybe I spoke too soon," Anya breathed, her voice muffled to his ears with so many layers of fabric over his head. "Maybe you aren't a gentleman at all."

"No," Idris whispered against her skin, kissing his way closer to her center. "I don't think I am."

Epilogue: When the War Comes

Anya

I awoke to a distant wail—one I knew, one I feared.

It wasn't the howl of a hound, nor the screech of an owl. It wasn't livestock or evening travelers or the foxes that lived along the forest's edge.

No—it was the whine of monsters.

Idris was already moving, pulling on pants, and lifting Halgren off its mount above our bed.

I lifted my magic to the other rooms of the Possum, hearing the soft snores of guests, as well as the shush of pages from Hattie reading. In two more days, my best friend was bound for the capital for a long-awaited apothecary apprenticeship; she'd been studying constantly since she got the letter of approval.

I extended my hearing further, into the peaceful stables where Briar and guests' horses were nibbling the remnants of their dinners with unbothered steadiness. Outside, the woods behind the Possum were silent, as if the nocturnal creatures there were listening, waiting, just as I was.

"Stay here," Idris whispered as he hurried for the door.

"Not on your life." I flung back the covers, shrugged into a heavy dressing gown, and patted Wicker's sleepy head on the way out.

Then I was rushing from our toasty room into the chilly hallway, following Idris barefoot down the stairs. The third step up from the bottom squeaked underneath my weight, and I made a mental note to have him help me fix it. These days, it was rare for me to repair anything on my own. With my plate full as ever at the Possum, Idris had gratefully stepped in as the town's handyman, and in the four months since my return, the town had already grown accustomed to sharing the load more fairly.

The downstairs was empty and cold; I'd extinguished the hearth hours ago.

Though Idris held the sword, I pushed past him toward the front door, yanking it open. This was still *my* establishment, after all. A harsh spring air gusted inside, ruffling my hair. A woman stood on the doorstep.

Her eyes were doe-like, but the rest of her was all sharp angles and lethal grace. She had a thin white scar through her upper lip. Wavy black hair. Tawny skin. Sharp cheekbones. A cocky, confident stance.

A Valiant Knight.

If there was any room for doubt in her physical countenance, the scratched-up breastplate, and the sword in her grip—unsheathed, dripping black blood onto my decking—confirmed it.

"Mariana," Idris said, wedging himself in front of me to face the newcomer. "What are you doing here?"

Mariana's gaze flicked to me.

"Speak," Idris insisted.

Mariana leveled her gaze on Idris again. "Is it true your Fate is untold?"

He stiffened. "My Fate is here."

"Not what I asked."

Idris inclined his head toward her sword. "Are there more nearby?"

It heartened me to hear his concern for Waldron. It was the same thing I was wondering.

"No," Mariana confirmed, and my shoulders relaxed an inch. "Now, my question."

"No offense, Mariana, but I am disinclined to let a knight such as yourself—"

I pushed Idris to the side. "I'm the proprietor here," I reminded them both, "and we're letting in all the cold. So, unless you plan on murdering us, maybe it's best you come inside?"

A wry smile pulled at Mariana's lips, but even with a touch of warmth in the expression, she appeared rather sinister. "Anya. You look better than the last time I saw you."

I angled my body to the side, beckoning her in. "I have no recollection of you, but I know who you are, Mariana."

"Should I be concerned?" she asked Idris.

"Yes," he and I responded.

"Leave the weapon outside," I added, "I don't need that sludge on my floor."

To my surprise, the Valiant Knight acquiesced, leaning her sword against the doorframe before entering. She did offer Idris a little snarl as she passed, and I had to admit I didn't despise her sass.

I circled round the bar and pulled a bottle off the shelf, pouring three glasses of amber. When Hattie appeared from upstairs, a dubious expression pulling at her sleepy features, I grabbed a fourth glass.

Idris took a seat beside Mariana at the bar, resting Halgren on the counter with a loud clatter. "Start talking."

"Not in mixed company," Mariana said, eyeing Hattie as she circled round the bar to stand beside me.

Hattie looked to me, her face morphing from confusion to question—as if she wasn't sure whether to be afraid of Mariana or curious. I offered her a quick little shrug, and—seemingly bolstered—Hattie swiveled round to face Mariana across the bar.

"You can't kick me out of my own home," she said.

"Want to bet?" Mariana said.

Hattie flushed—cowed but also indignant.

"Enough," Idris said at length. "Tell us what you want or go."

Mariana eyed Hattie again.

"I heard it," I cut in. "What you did just now."

"So did I," Hattie said, realization forming on her face. "Should I get the salve?"

"I'm uninjured," Mariana said, not without an edge of pride in her tone. "This isn't about that, although *that* is not...irrelevant to why I'm here."

She was speaking carefully in Hattie's presence. It reminded me of the way Idris had spoken when he was still Oath-bound. So much hidden behind vague words. I was glad to be past that with Idris, but Hattie was safer not knowing specifics.

"Your Fate is untold—yes or no?" Mariana insisted to Idris and me.

"Yes, yes," I said. "At least as of the last time we checked. What of it?"

"There are more like that—like you," Mariana said. "I'm here with a request."

"Who are you to request anything of us?" Idris asked, gripping his glass of liquor so hard I feared he'd shatter it.

I met his eyes, took a deep breath, willing him to do the same. He did.

"I'm just your brother's former lover," Mariana taunted.

When Idris had told me about the Valiant Knights who'd jumped him in an alley, only to later clear our path after the pool, he'd failed to mention *that* particular detail.

I reached for the glass in Idris's hands—about to lift it out of harm's way—but he took the hint. He tossed back the liquid, then set it aside.

"You're testing his patience," I said to Mariana—cooly. "And mine, for that matter. What's the request?"

Mariana threw back her own drink, finishing it in one gulp as Idris had. "Next time the Mirrors come to town, keep an eye out for other blank Fates. Don't trust anyone who doesn't show a future."

A strange look ghosted over Hattie's features, and she finished her drink as well. "Why not?" she asked, her tone overly casual. My friend had always had a clear vision in both Mirrors—but did she know someone who didn't?

"Thank you for the hospitality," Mariana said to me, then pushed away from the bar.

"Not looking for a bed?" I asked.

She shook her head, tension forming beside her doe-eyes. "My place is out there." She said it like she meant it, but I wasn't sure that in her heart she did. "Remember my mercy—"

"Yeah, yeah," Idris interrupted, showing her to the door.

Once the other knight was gone, Idris turned back toward Hattie and me, his face pale.

"What was that about?" I asked him, hoping his lack of Oath would allow him to explain what Mariana could not.

But my love merely shook his head. "I don't know. That's what concerns me."

From beside me, my best friend swallowed thickly. "I might have an idea."

To read a spicy bonus chapter with Anya and Idris, view the map of Fenrir, listen to the Mirrors of Fate playlist, and get notified about upcoming books and special editions, please join my newsletter:

nicolavictory.com/newsletter

Reviews mean a lot to independent authors like me—even one sentence can help new readers discover my books. I can't wait to hear what you thought of *Fate's Dangerous Fortune* in an online review!

Uncover the mystery of the monsters and the conspiracies among the Orders in book two of the Mirrors of Fate series, *Fate's Sweetest Curse,* Hattie and Noble's story of secret identity, alchemy, and forbidden love.

About the Author

Nicola Victory is the sword-wielding alter ego of an award-winning, bestselling, contemporary fiction writer. Nicola writes spicy romantasy books for adults about brave heroines and tortured heroes facing their fears for love.

When Nicola is not writing books, she enjoys reading, sipping coffee, and exploring the wilds of the Pacific Northwest. She spends her days with her very own romance hero and two cats named after celestial bodies.

Connect with Nicola on Instagram and TikTok @nicolavictorywrites or via her website: nicolavictory.com